LISA JACKSON

SEE HOW SHE DIES

ZEBRA BOOKS
Kensington Publishing Corp.
http://www.kensingtonbooks.com

ZEBRA BOOKS are published by

Kensington Publishing Corp.
119 West 40th Street
New York, NY 10018

All Kensington titles, imprints and distributed lines are available at special quantity discounts for bulk purchases for sales promotion, premiums, fund-raising, educational or institutional use.

Special book excerpts or customized printings can also be created to fit specific needs. For details, write or phone the office of the Kensington Special Sales Manager: Kensington Publishing Corp., 119 West 40th Street, New York, NY 10018. Attn. Special Sales Department. Phone: 1-800-221-2647.

First Printing: February 1994
Revised Edition Printing: August 2004

20   19   18   17   16   15   14   13   12   11

Printed in the United States of America

For the record I'd like to acknowledge and thank the following people for their help and encouragement: Nancy Bush, Anita Diamant, Sally Peters, John Scognamiglio and Larry Sparks.

PROLOGUE

1980

Needles of hot water pounded upon her bare back. Steam filled the large, tiled stall, fogging the glass doors. Kat Danvers stood beneath the spray, hoping the shower would clear her mind, help her shake the feelings of lethargy and dizziness brought on by too many drinks that had washed down a handful . . . was it two? . . . of her favorite pills.

The three V's.

Valium

Vicodin.

Vodka.

No wonder her mind was sludge, her vision blurry, her every movement seeming exaggerated. A bad taste crawled up her throat and she had the feeling she was slogging her way through quicksand. She let her breath out slowly. Wondered if she'd throw up.

Come on, snap out of it, Kat. Pull yourself together! Her conscience never seemed to miss an opportunity to nag.

She closed her eyes and leaned her arms against the slick tiles. The water was so hot it nearly scalded her. She needed to sober up, and fast. As quickly as she could, she twisted the faucet hard. Immediately the hot water turned to ice and she gasped, sucking air in through her teeth. Her mind cleared for an instant.

She felt it then, an odd sensation. As if something stirred

and she heard a faint, indistinguishable noise over the rush of cascading water. Her eyes flew open and she tried to peer through the misty glass. Did she see a shadow pass through the open doorway to the bedroom? Or was it her imagination? A trick of her tired, overdrugged mind and blurred vision? She needed her contacts or her thick glasses.

It was probably nothing.

And yet her skin crawled beneath the frigid spray; tiny goose bumps of fear pebbled her smooth, wet skin.

"It's all in your mind," she muttered, but turned off the water anyway and stood, shivering and dripping, while her ears strained to hear anything out of the ordinary.

There was nothing. Just the steady drip of water from the showerhead, the soft rumble of the heater, the strains of Christmas music drifting from hidden speakers—and farther away and muted, the quiet hum of traffic in the city. But nothing else. No sound of a shoe scuffing over the thick carpet of the presidential suite, no rattle of the room-service cart, no click of keys in the lock . . . nothing out of place.

Sluggishly, she clicked open the glass door and reached for her robe.

"Mama . . ."

A tiny voice. A girl's voice.

Kat's heart clutched. She froze.

No! It couldn't be. She wouldn't believe it. No toddler's voice had spoken. Her mind was playing tricks on her again . . . that was it. The drugs and booze had combined to—

"Mama?"

Oh God.

Kat's knees nearly buckled.

Frantically she stepped out of the shower and nearly fell on the slick marble as the notes of "Silent Night" filled the room. "Baby?" she whispered.

Barefoot, leaving a trail of water, she stumbled toward the door, somehow managing to force her unwieldy arms through the robe's sleeves. *Get a grip! You're hallucinating again and you know it.* There is no baby. Your daughter is *not* in any of the other rooms. *Grab hold of yourself!* Grasping onto the doorjamb, she peered into the bedroom. The king-sized bed was rumpled, a small impression visible on the comforter where she'd fallen asleep earlier. Her near-empty glass was sweating upon a bedside table near two empty bottles of pills.

The closet door was ajar, giving her a view of her clothes neatly lined up on hotel hangers.

"Mama?"

The sound was distinct. Clear.

Coming through the open French doors.

"Oh, sweetheart," Kat cried, her voice cracking as she turned quickly—too quickly—toward the living area and fell against the night table, scraping her arm and cheek. The antique lamp tumbled to the carpet, its bulb shattering.

Don't believe it, Kat! Don't think she's alive. Don't you dare trust your foolish heart.

But she couldn't stop that tiny sliver of hope from burrowing into her heart as she climbed to her feet again. The room spun. Using one hand, she braced herself on the wall and chairs as she staggered into the living area. She blinked hard. Tried vainly to focus. Nothing seemed disturbed. Nothing out of place. Flowers and a fruit basket sat upon a glass-topped table. Two Queen Anne chairs and a small love seat surrounded the antique fireplace where flames burned quietly.

No boogeyman lurked in the shadows.

Her daughter wasn't waiting for her.

Of course not. Her imagination and paranoia were working overtime again. She was falling apart. Unraveling. She caught a glimpse of herself in the mirror and cringed at the foggy image. Disheveled, wet hair, a gaunt body draped in a robe too large, no makeup on a face once beautiful and now ravaged by pain and guilt. Tears, unbidden, filled her eyes. She was losing her mind. Bit by bit.

Wiping her hand beneath her nose, she chided herself for

being a fool. She, a woman who had always known what she'd wanted and gone after it. She, who had used her beauty and brains to snag the wealthiest man in Portland. She, who so recently had everything any woman could ever want. And now she was reduced to shards of harsh memories, sleepless nights, and long hours trying to dull the pain with prescriptions and alcohol.

Cinching the robe around her thin body, she felt a draft . . . the tiniest breath of wind against the back of her neck. She looked over her shoulder. Saw the curtains near the balcony doors move. But she'd locked the French doors just before her shower . . . right? She'd taken her drink onto the small verandah and stood overlooking the city, contemplating suicide, and finally discarding taking her life as too dramatic, too frightening, too self-defeating.

So why was the door unlatched?

Hadn't she come back inside and turned the dead bolt behind her? Yes . . . that was right. After securing the lock, she'd taken one last swallow of her drink, then left the glass on the bedside table before stripping and heading unsteadily for the shower. That was right, wasn't it?

Or was she mixing things up?

Why couldn't she remember?

Why was everything so fuzzy?

Maybe she'd imagined locking the door.

Maybe she had heard someone prowling through these rooms while she'd stood under the shower's spray.

Her throat turned to dust.

Again she sensed a presence.

Something eerily out of place.

She started for the telephone.

"Mama."

A scared little voice.

Kat's heart nearly stopped. "London? Baby?" The sound was coming from the verandah, through the crack in the door.

This was insane. She should reach for the phone. Phone hotel security. Call the police.

Like you did before?

And have them all look at you like you're crazy?

Have them exchange glances as they noticed the vials on the nightstand?

Have them suggest you "talk" to someone?

Is that what you want to go through again?

No.

Heart thudding, she inched her way to the exterior doors where the curtains billowed slightly and the chill of December seeped inside. Through the sheers she saw a dark shadow. Small. Shivering.

London?

Precious, precious child!

Kat yanked open the door.

A blast of winter hit her hard.

A cacophony of street noise, traffic, music, voices rushed up nineteen floors.

The huddled little figure moved.

"Oh, honey—" Kat whispered, her throat suddenly tight.

The interior light snapped off.

The figure turned a face toward her, and even through the fog in her mind and the semidarkness of the city, she recognized the face—not of her missing daughter, but of a treacherous, wicked liar.

"You," she spat, trying to turn away. Blindly, she flailed, trying to escape.

Too late.

Strong fingers grabbed her shoulders and a fierce, intent weight shoved her closer to the short brick wall surrounding the verandah. Kat screamed. Her knees hit the century-old brickwork; she tried to grab something, anything, to no avail. The force of her body slammed against her backside—the sheer determination of her attacker propelled her forward, closer to the edge and the crumbling . . . "No! Oh, God, no!"

Kat cried, seeing a hand in her peripheral vision. Gloved fingers clutched a bit of brick. Kat cringed.

Bam!

Pain exploded behind her eyes. Blackness pulled her under. She started to sag, but was propped up, pushed forward, the railing hitting her in her middle and disintegrating with her weight.

And then suddenly she was falling, sailing through the cold night air . . .

PART ONE
1993

1

If only she could remember.

If only she knew the truth.

If only she were certain she wasn't on a fool's mission. She glanced up at the dark October sky and felt the gentle wash of Oregon mist against her face. Had she ever tilted her head back and let the moistness linger on her lips and cheeks? Had she stood on this very corner, across the street from the old Hotel Danvers, holding onto her mother's hand, waiting for the light to change?

Traffic rushed by, cars and buses spraying water as tires splashed through puddles. Deep in the folds of her coat she shivered, but not from the cool autumn air, or the breath of a breeze rolling off the dank Willamette River only a few blocks to the east. No, she shivered at the thought of what she was planning to do—her destiny, or so she'd been told. She knew she was in for the battle of her life.

But she was committed. She couldn't give up now. She'd traveled hundreds of miles, been through emotional hell and back, and spent days searching her soul during painstaking, laborious hours in libraries and newspaper offices throughout the Northwest, reading every chronicle, article, or editorial she could find on the Danvers family.

Now her plans were about to come to fruition. Or ruin. She stared up at the hotel, seven stories of Victorian architecture, which had once been one of the tallest buildings in the city and now was dwarfed by its concrete-and-steel counterparts, great skyscrapers that knifed upward, looming over the narrow city streets. "God help me," she whispered. As beautiful as it was, the edifice of the Hotel Danvers seemed sinister somehow, as if it knew secrets—dark secrets—that could change the course of her life forever.

Which was just plain silly.

Still, Adria felt a chill that had nothing to do with the wind whipping through Portland's narrow streets.

Without waiting for the light to change, she dashed across the street, the hood of her coat blowing off with a strong gust of wind. Daylight began to fade as the cloud-shrouded sun settled behind the westerly hills, hills still rich with green forests and dotted by expensive mansions.

Though the Hotel Danvers was closed to the public, as it had been for the past few months while it was being renovated and brought back to its turn-of-the-century grandeur, she walked through the lobby door that had been propped open for the workmen. The renovation was nearly complete. For the past two days she'd watched as delivery vans had brought tables, chairs, and other furniture to the service entrance. Today, linens, glassware, even some food had been delivered in anticipation of the grand opening, which was slated for the weekend.

The entire Danvers clan, Witt Danvers's first wife and his four surviving children, were rumored to be in town. Good.

A cold fist of apprehension tightened in her stomach. Ever since learning of the hotel's closure and reopening, she'd planned her introduction to the family, but first, to test the waters, she needed to speak with the man in charge of the hotel's face-life: Zachary Danvers, the rebel of the family and second son to Witt. According to every article she'd read, Zachary had never quite fit in. The Danvers family resemblance, so evident in his brothers and sisters, had skipped over him, and during his youth he'd had more than one brush with the law. Only the old man's money had kept Zachary out of serious trouble, and gossip had it that not only was he the least favorite of Witt's children but was also nearly cut out of the old man's will.

Yes, Zachary was the man she needed to see first. She'd studied his photographs so often, she knew she would recognize him. A little over six feet, with coal-black hair, olive skin, and deep-set gray eyes guarded by heavy brows, he was the one son of Witt Danvers who didn't resemble his father. Leaner than his brothers or the bear of a man who had sired him, his features were as chiseled as the cliffs overlooking the Pacific Ocean. He was a rugged man, rawhide-tough with a hard mouth that was rarely photographed in a smile. He bore a scar over his right ear that interrupted his hairline, and his broken nose was testament to his violent temper.

In the lobby two men were staggering under the weight of a long couch wrapped in plastic. She heard other workers talking in the background, saw hotel employees and workmen scurrying to and from the dining room and kitchen located opposite the front doors. The smells of cleaning solvent, turpentine, and varnish greeted her, and the whine of a skill saw screaming through the vestibule was muted by the rumble of industrial vacuums.

As the workmen shoved the couch near a huge fireplace, she paused in the lobby and eyed the hotel that had once been the most opulent in Portland, a place for dignitaries and town fathers to gather, where decisions were made and the shape of the future had been planned. She gazed upward to the intricate stained-glass windows that rose over the outer doors where they caught the last rays of daylight and cast a pool of amber, rose, and blue on the tile floor in front of the desk.

She swallowed against a lump that closed her throat; this hotel was her legacy. Her birthright. Her future.

Or was it?

There was only one way to find out. She headed for the wide, curved staircase that swept upward to the balcony.

"Hey, you! Lady, we're closed!" The voice, deep and male, was coming from a big, burly man poised on the top of a high scaffold positioned under the second-floor landing. He was fiddling with the chandelier situated over the lobby desk.

Ignoring him, she started up the carpeted steps.

"Hey, I'm talkin' to you!"

She hesitated, her hand trailing on the banister. This wasn't going to be easy, but the electrician was only a small stumbling block. The first of many. With a determined smile meant to disarm him, she turned and squared her shoulders. "Are you Zachary Danvers?" she asked, knowing full well he wasn't.

"No, but—"

"Are you related to the Danvers family?"

"What the hell?" Beneath the edge of his hard hat, he scowled at her. "No, of course not, but you can't go up there!"

"I have a meeting with Zachary Danvers," she insisted, her voice filled with chilly authority.

"A meeting?" the electrician repeated, obviously not believing her bluff.

She stared at the worker without giving an inch. "A meeting."

"That's news to me. I'm his foreman and he didn't mention anything about it." His scowl grew dark. Suspicious.

"Maybe he forgot," she said, as she forced a cold smile. "But I need to talk to him or a member of the Danvers family."

"He'll be back in a half-hour or so," the man said reluctantly.

"I'll wait for him. In the ballroom."

"Hey, I don't think—"

Without another glance in his direction, she hurried up the remaining stairs. Her boots were muffled on the thick carpet and her breath was shallow, a sign of her case of nerves.

"Shit," the man muttered under his breath, but stayed atop his perch and turned back to his work. "Damned women . . ."

Her heart was beating so fast she could hardly breathe, but at the top of the landing, she turned unerringly to the left and shouldered open the double doors. The room was dark. Her throat closed in on itself and with her fingers she fumbled for the light switch.

In a glorious blaze, the ballroom was suddenly lit by hundreds of miniature candles suspended in teardrop-shaped chandeliers. Her heart nearly stopped at the sight of the polished oak floor, the bank of tall, arched windows, the dizzying light from a million little bulbs that reflected in the cut crystal.

Her throat clogged and she blinked back tears. *This* was where it had all happened? Where the course of her young life had been thrown from its predestined path and into uncharted territory?

Why? She chewed on her lower lip. Oh, God, why couldn't she remember?

October rain slid down his hair and under the collar of his jacket. Dead leaves, already sodden, clung to the sidewalk and were beaten with the thick Oregon mist that seemed to rise from the wet streets and gather at the corners of the buildings. Cars, delivery vans, and trucks roared by, their headlights feeble against the watery illumination from the street lamps.

Zachary Danvers was pissed. This job had lasted too long, and wasted too much of his time. What little pride he had in the renovation was tarnished. Working here made him feel like a hypocrite, and he was thankful the project was just about over. Muttering oaths at himself, his brothers, and especially at his dead father, he pushed open the glass doors of the old hotel. He'd spent a year of his life here. A year. All because of a promise he'd made at his father's deathbed a couple of years ago. Because he'd been greedy.

His stomach soured at the thought. Maybe he was more like the old man than he wanted to admit.

The hotel manager, a newly hired nervous type with thinning hair and an Adam's apple that worked double time, was laying down the law with a new clerk behind a long mahogany desk, the pride of the lobby. Zachary had discovered the battered piece of dark wood in a century-old tavern located off Burnside in a decrepit building. The tavern had been scheduled to be razed, but Zach had decided to take the time to have the bar restored. Now the once-scarred mahogany gleamed under the lights.

All the fixtures in the hotel had been replaced with antiques or damned-close replicas, and now the hotel could boast an authentic 1890s charm with 1990s conveniences.

The advertising people had loved that turn of phrase.

Why'd he'd agreed to renovate the old hotel still eluded him, though he was beginning to suspect he had developed a latent sense of family pride. "Son of a bitch," he grumbled under his breath. He was tired of the city, the noise, the bad air, the lights, and most of all, his family, or what was left of it.

"Hey, Danvers!" his foreman Frank Gillette yelled from his position on the scaffold twenty feet above the lobby floor. He was tinkering with the wiring of a particularly bad-tempered chandelier. "Been waitin' for you. There's a woman here, in the ballroom. She's been here over an hour."

Zach's eyes narrowed a fraction. "What woman?"

"Didn't give her name. Claimed she had a meetin' with you."

"With me?"

"That's what she said." Frank started down the ladder. "She couldn't talk to me as I wasn't a—and I'm quotin' here—'member of the Danvers family.'"

Frank hopped to the floor and dusted his hands. He drew a wrinkled handkerchief from his back pocket and rubbed it under the brim of his hard hat.

From somewhere near the kitchen there was a crash and rattle of silverware that echoed through the hotel.

"Christ!" Frank's head snapped up, and he narrowed his eyes at the kitchen. "Damn that Casey."

"Is she a reporter?"

"The woman?" Frank fumbled in his pocket for his cigarettes. "Hell if I know. As I said, I'm not a Danvers, so she wouldn't talk to me. Not that I wouldn't mind spending a little time with her."

"Good-looking?"

Frank said, "Beyond a ten."

"Sure."

"Look, all I know is that short of bodily hauling her out of here, we got a problem. No one's supposed to be on the premises. If she slips and falls and breaks her neck and OSHA finds out—"

"You worry to much."

"You pay me to worry." Frank found his crumpled pack of Camels and shook out a cigarette.

"Just finish the job. I'll deal with the insurance people and the woman."

"Good." Smiling as he clicked his lighter, Frank inhaled deeply. "Now, let's see if this mother works. Hey, Roy, turn on the juice." Reaching around the desk, he flipped a switch and stared at the chandelier. Lights shaped like candles blazed for a second before flickering and dying. "Fuckin' wiring," Frank growled, his face turning red, his cigarette bobbing between his lips. "I told that half-wit Jerry to use . . . oh, hell!" Exasperated, he shot out a stream of smoke. "Roy, turn it off again!" he roared.

"I'll go talk to the mystery lady."

"Do that," Frank growled as he finished his smoke, then started back up the scaffolding. Zach didn't doubt that by the grand opening, everything would work perfectly. Frank would see to it, if he had to hold two wires together himself.

From the stairs, Zach glanced around the lobby and thought of his father. Witt Danvers. A royal pain in the ass. Right now, Witt would have been proud of the son he'd dis-

owned half a dozen times. Not that it mattered. Witt Danvers
was dead and cremated, his ashes spread across the rolling
forests of the Oregon hills two years ago. A just end to a timber baron who had spent all his years raping the land.

Through the leather of his jacket, Zach rubbed the scar in
his shoulder, the result of being the son of Witt Danvers. His
jaw tightened. It had taken him years to come to terms with
the old man, and now it was too late to make amends.

"Rest in peace, you miserable bastard," Zachary said, his
lips flattening as he opened the doors. His father had always
treated Zach differently from the rest of his children. Not that
he cared now. Zach had his own business, his own identity.
The noose of being the son of one of Portland's wealthiest
men didn't seem quite so tight.

He took two long strides into the ballroom, then stopped
dead in his tracks. The woman was there, dressed in a black
long coat and matching knee-length boots. She turned at the
sound of his entrance, and before she could say a word he
knew why she was waiting for him.

Glossy black curls swirled away from a flawless face.
Round blue eyes fringed by lacy black lashes stared straight
at him. Thin black brows arched inquisitively. He felt as if his
heart had stopped for a second as she smiled, showing off
beautiful teeth, finely carved cheekbones, and a strong,
slightly stubborn chin.

His breath seemed to stop somewhere in his lungs.

"You're Zachary," she said, as if she had every right to
stand in the middle of the ballroom—*as if she belonged.*

Zach's throat was suddenly dry and hot and forbidden
memories struggled to the surface of his mind. "Right."

"Danvers," she supplied, her voice low, her lips tightening
just a fraction. She smiled slightly, and with her hand extended, walked slowly toward him. "I've been wanting to
meet you for a long time," she said, forcing a smile. "My
name is—"

"London," he supplied as every muscle in his body grew taut with the pain of the past.

"You recognize me?" Hope lighted those blue eyes.

"There's a resemblance. I guessed."

"Oh." She hesitated, the wind suddenly out of her sails.

"But that's why you're here, isn't it?"

"Yes."

"You think you're my long-lost sister." He couldn't hide the cynicism in his words.

Those clear blue orbs clouded and her hand, the one she'd offered and he'd ignored, dropped to her side. "I think so, but I'm not sure. That's why I'm here." She seemed to find her confidence again. "For a long time my name's been Adria."

"You're not sure?" For a minute he could only stare into those wide blue eyes—eyes like another treacherous pair that had seemed to see right through him, but quickly his senses came back to him in a rush. Why did he think for even a second that this woman could be London? Hadn't he been close enough to elaborate frauds to smell one a mile away? So she looked like his stepmother. Big deal. "My sister's been dead for almost twenty years," he said in the flat tone he reserved for liars and cheats.

"Half-sister."

"Doesn't matter."

She glanced around the room. "I just wanted to see if I remembered this place—"

"London was only four."

"Almost five. And even four-year-olds have memories . . . maybe just impressions, but memories nonetheless . . ." She looked at one corner near a bank of windows. "The band was over there in that alcove, and there were plants . . . trees, I think." Her eyebrows bunched together as if she were trying to catch hold of a fleeting memory. "And there was a huge fountain and an ice sculpture—a . . . horse, no, not just a horse, a *running* horse, and—"

"You've done your research."

Her lips tightened. "You don't believe me."

"I think you'd better leave." Zachary cocked his head toward the door. "London's dead. She has been for over twenty years, so take whatever it is you're peddling and go back home, before I haul you out of here and drop you on the front steps with the rest of the garbage."

"How do you know London's dead?"

His throat closed and he remembered, with gut-wrenching clarity, the accusations, the fingers thrust in his direction, the suspicious looks cast his way. "I'm serious. You'd better leave."

"I'm serious, too, Zach." Ramming her hands into her pockets, she took one last look around the huge room, then faced him again. "You may as well know—I don't give up easily."

"You don't have a prayer."

"Who's in charge?"

"Doesn't matter." His voice was hard, his features drawn with brutal resolution. "You can talk to my brothers and sister, my mother, or the attorneys who are acting as the gods of finance in my father's estate, but no one's going to give you the time of day. You may as well save your breath and my time. Take my advice and go home."

"This could be my home."

"Bull."

"It's too bad Katherine isn't alive."

Zachary's blood ran cold at the mention of his beautiful and much-too-young stepmother. There was an unmistakable resemblance between the young woman standing so arrogantly before him and his father's second wife, Katherine—Kat—the woman who'd made his life a living hell for years. "Is it really too bad, or is it just convenient?" he asked, keeping his expression bland.

She blanched a bit.

"Get out."

"You're afraid of me."

"As I said, *Get out*."

She held his gaze for a heart-stopping second, then strode through the ballroom doors and down the stairs. Zachary moved to the windows and watched as she walked onto the street, her strides long and full of purpose, her head ducked against the thickening rain.

She'd be back. They always came back. Until the power and money of the Danvers family drove them away and they gave up their far-fetched dreams of stealing a little bit of the old man's money.

Good riddance, he thought, but, as she disappeared around the corner, he felt a premonition, like footsteps of the devil crawling up his spine, and he knew with absolute and bone-chilling certainty, that this one—this impostor posing as London Danvers—was somehow different from all the others.

PART TWO
1974

PART TWO
1974

2

"Happy birthday, darling," Katherine Danvers whispered into her husband's ear as they danced across the polished floor of the ballroom. From the alcove near the corner, a small dance band played "As Time Goes By" and the melody whispered through the crowd. "Surprised?" she asked, nuzzling him, her satin heels moving in perfect time to the music.

"Nothing you do surprises me." He chuckled low in his throat. Of course he'd known that she'd reserved the ballroom of his hotel under the fictitious name of some sorority. He hadn't spent sixty years learning to be the shrewdest businessman in Portland without picking up a few tricks along the way. He gave his wife a playful squeeze and felt her breasts, beneath her black silk dress, press closer to him. A few years before, he would have become aroused just by the scent of her perfume and the knowledge that beneath the gown she wore absolutely nothing—just the dress and a pair of stiletto heels.

She pouted prettily as the pianist played a solo. Her black hair gleamed under the muted lights from chandeliers suspended from the cove-shaped ceiling, and her eyes, a deep blue, glanced coyly at him through the sweep of thick, dark lashes.

There had been a time when he would have given away his fortune just for one night in her bed. She was sensual and smart and knew exactly how to please a man. He'd never asked her how she knew so much about the pleasures of love when he'd met her. He'd just been grateful that she'd taken him as her lover, bringing back the lust that he'd thought he'd lost somewhere near middle age.

A kitten who liked to be cuddled, Kat metamorphosed into a wildcat in bed and for a few years her raw sexual energy had been enough to satisfy him. He'd married her and remained faithful and managed to bed her every other day in the early years. But his desire had been short-lived, as it always was, and now he couldn't remember when he'd last made love to her. A hot fire crept up the back of his neck at the thought of his impotence. Even now, when her thighs were pressed intimately to his and her tongue touched a sensitive spot near the back of his ear, he felt nothing, no hint of wildfire in his blood, no welcome stiffness between his legs. Even a little harsh foreplay didn't bring him to an erection anymore. It was a miracle that they'd managed to conceive a child.

Suddenly angry, he swirled her roughly away from him, then jerked her back into his arms. She laughed, that throaty little laugh that bordered on nasty. He liked her laugh. He liked everything about her. He only wished that he could throw her on the dance floor and take her the way she wanted to be taken—like an animal, with four hundred horrified eyes watching as he proved that he was still a man and could satisfy his wife.

She'd tried all her tricks. Flimsy negligees. Peekaboo bras that outlined her nipples and long black garters that flicked at her shapely thighs. She'd coaxed him with her tongue and dirty words, slapped playfully at his butt and balls, but nothing she did aroused him anymore, and the thought that he couldn't manage an erection, might never have sex for the rest of his life, cut a hole in him that burned like dry ice and scared the living hell out of him.

The song ended and he pressed forward, bending her spine in a low dip, so that she had to cling to him, her eyes staring up into his, her black hair sweeping the floor that had been littered with pink rose petals. Her breasts, heaving with exertion, threatened to spill out of the deep cleavage of her dress.

In full view of the audience, he pressed a kiss to that glorious hollow between her breasts, as if he were so randy he couldn't stand it, then yanked her to her feet. Laughter and applause erupted around them.

"You old dog, you !" one man shouted, and Kat blushed as if she were an innocent virgin.

"Take her upstairs. What're you waiting for?" another middle-aged boy yelled. "Isn't it about time you two had a son?"

"Later." Witt winked at the crowd, content that they didn't know his secret and secure that Kat would never breath a word of his shame. A son. If this crowd of friends, relatives, and business acquaintances only knew.

There would be no more children. He'd sired three sons and a headstrong daughter from his first marriage to Eunice. With Katherine there would only be London, his four-year-old daughter and favorite child. He made no apologies for caring more about his little girl than he did all of his other children put together. The other kids—some of them adults now—had caused him so much heartache, and their mother . . . Christ, what had he ever seen in Eunice Prescott—a skinny woman with a sharp tongue who'd thought sex with him had been her duty—nothing more than a chore? He'd decided she was frigid, until . . . Hell, he didn't want to think about Eunice cheating on him behind his back—laughing at him.

Angered at the turn of his thoughts, Witt escorted his wife to the center of the room where, beneath the glimmering lights of the chandelier, an ice sculpture in the shape of a running horse was beginning to melt. Nearby a tiered fountain of champagne gurgled and splashed.

The band started playing "In the Mood," and a few brave couples strayed onto the dance floor. Witt snagged a glass

from a silver tray and drained the champagne in one long
swallow.

"Daddy!" He glanced up and found London, her black
curls dancing around her face, her chubby arms outstretched.
Dressed in a navy-blue dress with white lace collar and cuffs,
she ran up to him and threw herself into his waiting arms.

He hugged her tightly, the velvet of her dress crushed
against him, her legs, encased in white tights, clamped around
his waist. "How do you like the party, princess?"

Her crystal-blue eyes were round and wide, her cheeks
flushed with the excitement of the festivities. "It's loud."

He laughed. "That it is."

"And there's too much smoke!"

"Don't tell your mother. She planned this as a special surprise and we wouldn't want her to feel bad," Witt said,
grinning as he winked at his daughter.

She winked back, then snuggled her pert little nose into his
neck and he got a whiff of baby shampoo. She tugged at his
bow tie and he laughed again. Nothing could make him as
happy as this dynamic whirl of precociousness.

"Hey, that's *my* job," Kat said as she smiled and gently
nudged London's fingers from Witt's neck. Kissing her
daughter's crown, she said, "Leave Daddy's tie alone."

"How about a dance?" Witt asked his young daughter, and
those little lines between Kat's eyebrows, the ones that suggested silently that she disapproved, appeared. Witt didn't
care. He drained another glass of champagne and twirled a
laughing London onto the dance floor. The child, his princess,
squealed in delight.

"Sickening, isn't it?" Trisha observed from her position
near the band. She leaned against the glossy top of the concert grand and petulantly sipped from a fluted glass. She was
allowed, having just turned twenty-one.

Zachary lifted a shoulder. He was used to his old man's theatrics and he really didn't care what Witt did anymore. He and his father had never gotten along, and things had only become worse when Witt had divorced his first wife and eventually married a woman only seven years older than his oldest son, Jason, Zachary's brother. Truth be known, Zach didn't really want to be here, had only come because he was forced. He couldn't wait to escape the smoky, loud ballroom filled with boring old people—suck-ups, every last one of them.

"Dad can't keep his hands off Kat," Trisha said, her voice slurring a little. "It's obscene." She took another swallow. "The lecherous old fart."

"Careful, Trisha," Jason said as he joined his brother and sister. "Dad probably had this place bugged."

"Very funny," Trisha said, tossing her long auburn hair over one shoulder. But she didn't laugh. Her blue eyes were flat and bored and she continually scanned the crowd as if she were looking for something or someone.

Jason's eyes narrowed. "You know half the people here would like to see the old man fall."

"They're his friends," Trisha argued.

"And enemies." Jason rested a hip against the piano as the band took a break. He watched his father, still holding London, playing the crowd, moving from one knot of bejeweled guests to the other, never once setting London on her feet.

"Who gives a shit?" Zachary asked.

"Always the rebel." Jason smiled beneath his mustache, that know-it-all smile that bugged the hell out of Zach. Jason acted as if he knew everything. At twenty-three, Jason was already in law school and six years older than Zach, a point he never let his rebellious younger brother forget.

Zach tugged at the tight collar of his tuxedo shirt. He couldn't stomach Jason any more than he could his sister, Trisha. They both cared too much about the old man and his bank accounts.

Leaving Jason and Trisha to worry and fret over Witt's affection for London, Zach walked to the edge of the crowd.

He managed to grab a champagne glass from an unattended table, then sauntered over to the bank of tall, arched windows that overlooked the city and turned his back on the party. He felt a bit of satisfaction as he stared through the glass to the hot July night and swallowed champagne. Traffic flowed in a steady stream along the street. Taillights winked and blurred as cars and trucks labored through the city and over the yawning Willamette River, a sluggish black waterway that separated the west side of the city from the east. Steam rose from the city streets and the humidity level was high.

In the distance, beyond the expanse of city lights, a ridge of mountains, the Cascades, guarded the horizon. Thunderheads that had been gathering all day blocked out any view of the stars, and the quick, sizzling forks of lightning added unwanted tension to the brackish night. Zach finished his champagne and, hoping no one would notice, half buried his empty glass in the soil surrounding a potted tree.

He felt out of place, as he always had with his family. This black-tie affair thrown by Kat made him all the more aware that he was different from his brothers and sister. He didn't even look like the rest of the Danvers clan, all of whom were fair-skinned, blue-eyed, and were favored with varying hues of blond to dark brown hair.

He resembled his half-sister, London, more than anyone else in the family. Which didn't win him any points with Jason, Trisha, and Nelson, his younger brother, all of whom on one occasion or another professed to hate their half-sister.

With a snort, he considered London. He didn't care much about the kid one way or the other. Sure, she bothered him. Any four-year-old was a pain in the ass, but she wasn't as bad as the others made out. In fact, Zach found it amusing that she was already showing some of the traits Kat had perfected over the years. It wasn't London's fault the old man treated her like some kind of priceless jewel.

As if she'd read his mind, London pushed through the

crowd and grabbed hold of his leg. He turned to tell her to get lost, but by that time she'd discovered his glass pushed deep into the potting soil.

"Leave that alone!" he whispered in a harsh voice. She glanced up sharply, a naughty twinkle in her eyes. God, if he could just step out on the balcony and grab a smoke—another vice of which his father and stepmother disapproved, though Kat was never without her gold cigarette case and Witt enjoyed his share of cigars smuggled in from Havana.

She dropped the glass back into the dirt. "Hide me from Mommy!" With a wicked little giggle, she ducked behind his legs.

"Hey, don't get me involved in your stupid games."

"Shh. She's coming!" London hissed.

Great. Just what he needed.

"London?" Katherine's husky voice drifted over the slow strains of a ballad.

Behind him, London tried to smother a giggle.

"London, where are you? Come on now . . . it's time for bed. Oh, there you are!" Katherine sidestepped a group of men, her practiced smile well in place. Waving her fingers as she passed, she tracked down her wayward daughter with the precision of a bloodhound.

"No!" London cried as her mother approached.

"Come on, sweetheart, it's nearly ten."

"Don't care!"

"You'd better do what she says," Zachary offered, his gaze flicking slightly to his stepmother's. He knew what the old man saw in his young wife. Katherine Danvers was probably the sexiest woman Zachary had ever met. At seventeen he understood about unbridled sexual desire. Hot and thundering, it could roar through a man's body and turn his brain to mush.

"Come on." Katherine leaned down to pick up her daughter. The silk stretched across her shapely rump and her breasts seemed to bulge a bit, as if they might fall out of her plunging neckline.

"I'll get her into bed," another woman, London's nanny, Ginny Something-Or-Other, offered. She was a small, plain woman in sensible shoes and a drab olive-green suit. Next to Katherine she looked frumpy and old, a dowdy matron, though she was probably just over thirty, not much older than Kat.

"I don't want to go to bed," London insisted.

"She's being a brat." Katherine looked up and noticed one of the waiters motioning toward her. With a sigh, she turned back to her daughter. "Listen, honey, it's almost time to bring out the birthday cake. You can stay up and watch Daddy blow out his candles, then you have to go upstairs."

"Can I have some cake, too?"

The corners around Katherine's mouth tightened, though she said, "Of course, darling. But then you go with Ginny upstairs. We've got a special room for you, right by Daddy and Mommy's, and we'll be up later to tuck you in."

Mollified somewhat, London headed back to the party and Katherine straightened, smoothing her dress over her hips as Ginny followed her wayward charge.

Zach hoped that Katherine would hurry to the bandleader and order the musicians to strike up "Happy Birthday To You," but she inched her chin up a fraction and eyed her stepson. Zach was three inches taller than Kat. Nonetheless, she had a way of making him feel small. "Stay away from the booze." She plucked his empty champagne glass from the dirt and twirled the stem between her long, slim fingers. Even while reprimanding him, she was sexy as hell. As if she knew her power over him and any man who wasn't blind, she puckered her lips sweetly, then waggled the glass under his nose. "We wouldn't want anything to spoil this party for your daddy now, would we? If you were to get caught with one of these, there could be trouble."

"I won't get caught."

"Don't think you're so smart, Zach. I saw you swilling champagne, and I don't think I'm the only one who was looking in your direction. Anyone else could have seen you, including Jack Logan. You remember—he's with the police department. I think you two have met before."

Zach's teeth clamped together. Hot embarrassment climbed up the back of his neck. "As I said, I won't get caught."

"You'd better not, because, if you land your cute little butt in jail or end up in the juvenile hall again, Witt won't bail you out. So"—she smiled sweetly—"use your head."

As she sauntered away, mingling with one group of guests after another, Zachary seethed. His blood boiled through his veins and he fantasized about wrapping his fingers around her neck and shaking some sense into her, but he couldn't take his eyes off her ass and the way it shifted beneath the shimmering black silk of her dress. She moved slowly, as if each step were a deliberately sensual movement designed to make him squirm. The rose petals were crushed beneath her heels. Her smooth back, visible to the curve of her lower spine, was unblemished and supple, and he imagined it would arch perfectly beneath the right man.

He felt an erection beginning, and turned away from her image. Half the time he thought she put on a sexual show for him intentionally. Other times he told himself that it was his imagination, that he was finding sexual overtures in the most innocent of gestures.

To cool his blood he placed his head against the window. Steam fogged the inside of the glass. The room was so hot he felt that he was suffocating and his blood still pounded at his temples. At seventeen he was still a virgin, which wasn't a big deal, unless he had to spend any time alone with Kat, something he tried to avoid.

Stuffing one hand into his pocket to hide the swell in his pants, he walked to the nearest tray of filled glasses, grabbed one and downed it quickly, all the while staring at his stepmother. She didn't seem to see him. Buoyed by his newfound source of rebellion, he sauntered over to another unattended tray, snatched another glass, and downed the champagne in one gulp. A few drops drizzled along his chin but he didn't care.

The room began to get warmer still and he loosened his tie. A flush stole up his face and he felt a little light-headed. He was definitely getting a buzz. Well, good. He didn't want to be here anyway. Might as well enjoy himself.

Halfway through his next drink, he felt a smooth hand close over his arm. He jumped and champagne splashed down the front of his jacket and shirt. Kat's long fingers dug into the muscles beneath his sleeve. Her eyes were dark with rage, her full lips clenched in fury. "You just don't know when to give up, do you?"

He shook off her arm. "You can't tell me what to do."

"No?" She arched an eyebrow in a sexy gesture that scared him spitless. "Mmm. We'll see."

He finished his drink to spite her, but she didn't seem to mind. In fact, her face changed into a soft smile and her eyes caught the reflection of the chandelier, sparkling up at him. With an innocent grin, she linked her fingers through his. "Dance with me, Zach."

Zach, despite the friendly cobwebs in his mind, smelled trouble. "I . . . I don't dance."

"Sure you do. It's easy."

"But I can't—"

She leaned closer to him, put her lips against his ear. "People are staring. Come on."

His throat was suddenly desert-dry. "Katherine, I really don't want to—" But she was right. He felt the burning weight of the gazes of curious onlookers. He wanted to die. From the corner of his eye, he saw Jason staring at him, his expression unreadable. Trisha was downing champagne and God-only-knew what else. She smiled drunkenly at Zach's discomfiture. Witt, his father, was still dancing with little London and too busy to notice that Zach was trapped.

"Really, Katherine. I don't want to—"

"Oh, you want, Zach," she said, leaning to him, pressing

her hip against his groin. "I can tell. And I'll let your father know if you don't give me just one little dance."

Guiltily, Zach glanced at Witt but the old man seemed oblivious to the fact that his son, the one who always gave him so much trouble, was being led to the dance floor like a lamb to slaughter. He couldn't imagine dancing with Katherine, feeling her body pressed close to his. His blood was already roaring through his system. As they reached the dance floor, she turned, molding her torso to his, beginning to sway in rhythm to the music.

Her hips were pressed intimately to his and her breasts seemed crushed against his chest. "Now, isn't this better?" she murmured in a husky drawl and he closed his eyes, fighting the lust that burned through his body, feeling his stiffening erection even as he tried to deny it.

"Let me go," he begged.

"You don't want to go." She shifted slightly so that her lower abdomen was hugging his. God, she had to know that he was hard. "I can tell."

"Don't—"

Holy Christ, his right hand was on her bare back, feeling the silky texture of her skin, the sleek movement of her muscles. Was it his imagination or did she make some low sort of wanting sound deep in her throat?

"You lied," she whispered, her breath ruffling the hair covering the tops of his ears.

He was dying inside. So hard he ached, he couldn't think straight. A part of him warned him to back off, but the other part puffed up by male ego, champagne, and sexual desire, couldn't stop fantasizing. He wondered what she would do if he rubbed up against her, let his hand slip beneath the black fabric of her dress. What would happen if he slowly let his mouth and tongue wander down the delicate column of her throat?

As if she understood his need, she lolled her head to one

side, exposing more of her white skin, showing off just a little more of her gorgeous bosom.

"Mind if I cut in?" Witt's voice seemed to reverberate through the ballroom and Zachary started, dropping his hands guiltily. He tried to put some distance between his body and Kat's but she held him close.

Turning slumberous eyes toward her husband, her lips twisted into a wicked grin, she whispered, "Thought you'd never ask."

Witt's face was flushed. His eyes thinned on his rebellious son as Zachary took a step back and London, who was still clinging to her father, was plopped into Zach's empty arms. "Stay away from the champagne," Witt said. "It would be a hell of an embarrassment if Jack had to arrest you here. Now, give London a spin on the floor and ask one of the Kramer girls to dance—they've been watching you all night."

Gulping, Zachary wished he could knock the old man's lights out. When he glanced at Kat she was laughing, her eyes twinkling with naughty amusement. At his expense. His fingers clenched into fists and if it wasn't for the fact that he was holding London, he might have made an already ugly situation worse. It was as if his father and stepmother had conspired together to make him look a fool.

His shoulders tensed and heat surged up the back of his neck to spread through his face. Though several girls in expensive dresses were trying to capture his attention, Zach didn't even give them the time of day. He handed London to her nanny, and wished he could hit something . . . anything.

Ripping his tie from his neck, he wanted nothing more than to leave the goddamned hotel and cool off. Spoiling for a fight, he left the dance floor. How could he have been such a fool? How? Because of Kat. Damn the woman! His fists curled in angry impotence. He had to get out of here.

Jason, drink in hand, found Zach insolently leaning a shoulder against one of the pillars near the door as he plotted his escape. "Don't let her get to you," Jason advised.

"Who?"

"Kat." Sipping his drink—bourbon straight up—Jason smiled.

"What do you mean?" Zach asked, trying to sound nonchalant.

Jason snorted and cocked his head toward the dance floor. "I saw that little exhibition."

Mortified, Zach gritted his teeth.

"Christ, she can be a bitch." Jason raked an impatient hand through his thick, chestnut-colored hair. "I know what she's up to, saw her coming on to you. She damned near laid down and spread her legs right in the middle of the dance floor." He took a swallow of his drink and stared at Kat and Witt. "It's some sort of game with her."

A muscle worked in Zach's jaw. He felt the angry tic and couldn't control it.

"She did it on purpose, you know. Decided you needed putting in your place, which, I might add, she did."

"I hate her."

"Don't we all?" Jason replied, his eyes following his stepmother as she danced. "But she might just be the most incredibly sexy woman on this planet. I wonder what she's like in bed."

"I don't want to know." Zachary scowled and refused to look at the object of their discussion.

"Sure you do. Every man here would like a little piece of the Kat." He flung a brotherly arm over Zach's shoulders. "But she doesn't play her games with them. No way. For some reason she's picked you to toy with. If I didn't know better, I'd think she might have her sights set on you."

"Oh, Jesus! No way!" Zach said, though his heart skipped a beat.

"I'm not so sure. She sure hasn't come on to me like she just did with you and I've seen her, when she thinks no one's watching. The way she looks at you. Christ, it's hot."

"Stop it."

"But you can't mess with her. If Dad ever found out—"

"Cut it out, Jason," Zach said, suddenly anxious. First Kat and now his brother. "I'm not going to mess with her."

Jason lifted a shoulder. "Everyone's always said you were different—I guess Kat just wants to find out if it's true."

"God, Jason, listen to what you're saying! No, don't! It's sick."

"You know what you need to do?"

Zach didn't answer.

"Go out and get laid." Leaning closer to Zach, he pointed a finger at a swarm of teenaged girls, their makeup and hairstyles right out of *Seventeen* magazine. Compared to Katherine they seemed young and gawky and . . . desperate. "But not with Kat. Like I said, the old man would tan your hide if he found out. But Alicia Kramer is so hot for you she can barely stand it. I'll bet she's creaming all over herself just looking at you."

"Stop it!" Zach hissed, but Jason laughed, obviously pleased that he'd gotten such a violent reaction.

"I'm telling you, sliding into her would be like sticking it into hot pudding."

"For Christ's sake, cut it out!" Zach slid a glance in Alice's direction and caught her hopeful gaze. She was a petite girl with big boobs and a bad complexion she disguised with thick makeup. Her teeth were straight, compliments of the braces she'd worn for two years. She wasn't bad looking. She giggled and blushed when she caught Zach's eye. But Zach wasn't interested in the daughter of some big-shot banker. No way. Compared to Kat, Alicia seemed like a child.

"She's so horny she can barely keep her dress on. Look, I can tell you from my own experience that the Kramer girls are definitely hot-blooded. My guess is Alicia will give you a ride you'll remember for the rest of your life."

"No thanks," Zach replied.

"I'm telling you, little brother, it's time. I can hook you up with—"

"Forget it, Jason."

Jason grabbed his arm. "Really, Zach. I know how you feel, like a powder keg ready to explode, and believe me, you can only take it so long." His voice lowered a little. "There's a girl I know . . . well, a woman, really. She . . . well, she knows just what to do to make a man feel good. She's expecting me tonight."

"A hooker? Are you talking about a hooker?" Zach demanded, shocked, yet a little intrigued. Did Jason really know a prostitute? Holy shit!

Jason took his arm and steered him to a quiet corner of the room, far away from the guests and the linen-clad tables of food and drink. "Now, just listen. This girl, Sophia, she's . . . well, believe me, you'll like her. She's a good person."

Zach snorted. "Good people don't sell their bodies."

"She's not a streetwalker. In fact, she does this because she likes it. She's always ready."

"Oh, God—"

"She's pretty and clean and will only do what you want to do. You can fuck her brains out if you want to, or, if you'd rather just talk . . . she'll listen. Really. It's up to you." Jason's voice was filled with brotherly concern.

Zach knew he should walk away, but he couldn't. An honest-to-goodness hooker. Waiting for Jason? A hooker who would just listen?

"I know you and I don't always see eye-to-eye, but this time, for the love of Christ, listen to me. You need a woman. Bad. And it can't be Kat." Frowning slightly, he reached into his pocket, pulled out a room key, and pressed the cool metal into Zachary's sweating palm. "Three blocks down. The Orion Hotel. Sophia. Don't worry about money. It's all been arranged."

"I don't want—"

"Do yourself a favor. Forget about Kat. Get laid." With a friendly smile, Jason headed toward the bar, leaving Zach to clutch the damned hotel key in his clammy fingers. Swallowing hard, he opened his hand and stared down at the key to room 307, the key to his manhood, the key to his freedom from Kat.

Suddenly aware that any number of his father's guests could have overheard his conversation with Jason, Zach jammed his hands deep into his pockets and wondered how many of the other people at the party had witnessed his humiliation on the dance floor. How many eyes other than his brother's and his father's had seen Kat's lips brush against his ear, or watched as his sweaty fingers had itched to delve beneath the zipper of her dress to grasp one of those firm buttocks? Jesus, he had to quit thinking about her like this! The key felt heavy in his pocket.

The band broke into "For He's a Jolly Good Fellow." Though his mind was still on the mysterious Sophia, the hooker with a heart, Zach watched as a huge cake in the shape of a fir tree was wheeled into the room on an elaborate cart. Sixty candles arranged in a string, like holiday lights decorating a Christmas tree, had been placed upon the needles of green frosting. Tiny flames flickered and danced as Witt, with Katherine and London's help, blew out every last spark.

Laughter and applause erupted and Witt, like a bridegroom, cut a fat piece of cake and fed the gooey concoction to his wife. Everyone cheered and Zach thought he might get sick as Katherine returned the favor, then smiling up at her husband, licked her fingers slowly.

By the time London was hustled upstairs to one of the suites reserved for the Danvers family, the old man was starting to look a little tipsy. He hazarded a hard glance Zach's way, and even in the crowded room, Zach read the warning in his father's eyes. His heart sank. From years of experience Zach knew that Witt had not forgotten that his young wife had been flirting with his son. Nothing escaped the old man, and sooner or later, there would be hell to pay. Zach already bore several scars on his backside from the slap of his father's belt.

By this time tomorrow, he'd probably wear a few more—at least psychological scars. Witt Danvers was nothing if not brutal. He wouldn't spare Zach's feelings and would let his rebellious son know that he was no good, didn't live up to his expectations, would never amount to anything in life.

So who gave a shit what the old man thought?

The key pressed hard against his thigh.

Witt and Katherine began dancing again and his father's attention was diverted from his second son to his wife. Zach seized the opportunity for escape. Without a glance over his shoulder, he wended his way past loud groups of guests, slipped through ballroom doors to the landing where he stopped to catch his breath and fight the dizziness in his brain from too much champagne.

What was he doing? He couldn't just leave the party. The old man would come unhinged.

Good.

Maybe Witt Danvers might even worry a little.

Before he changed his mind, Zach steadied himself against the rail and hurried down the wide staircase.

"Hey, Zach. Where're ya goin'?" Nelson, his younger brother, demanded. At fourteen, Nelson, now hanging halfway over the rail, his shaggy blond hair flopping over his eyes, idolized his hellion of an older brother.

"Not now," Zach growled. He didn't need the kid's adoration any more than he needed Witt's disapproval.

"But—"

"Just keep quiet, Nelson. Okay?" Refusing to acknowledge Nelson as the kid ran down the stairs, Zach strode through the front lobby where club chairs, brass lamps, and glossy dark tables were positioned around a massive fireplace. Past the main desk and a forest of potted palms, he walked quickly, trying not to think about the ramifications of his actions when Witt discovered him missing.

Outside, the night was humid. The smell of the river drifted on air so still it seemed to cling to Zach's skin. He yanked off his jacket and began walking fast, heading north, trying to cool his blood and clear his head.

What he was contemplating was crazy, and yet, he'd consumed enough alcohol to feel bolder than usual. So what if the old man found out? What could he do? Kick Zach out of the Danvers family mansion, force him to live with his mother? That thought was a bitter pill to swallow.

Deep down, a part of him still cared for the woman who had borne him, but she didn't deserve that love, not after she'd abandoned them all and left them in the lonely house on the hill with Witt. Zach didn't know the full story, but the gist of it was that Witt had caught his wife in bed with his most hated rival, Anthony Polidori. She'd been carrying on with him for years and rather than expose herself, or her lover, to the media, she'd had no choice but to accept Witt's terms for the divorce: he'd get the kids and most of the wealth, she'd receive a stipend and be spared the ugly scandal of testifying in divorce court that she was an adulteress. Her social position had been left unscathed; her children's lives had not.

As much as Zach professed to despise the old man, he did have a grudging respect for Witt Danvers and the power he seemed to possess over the people of this city. As for his mother, Zach felt little but loathing for Eunice. She had shamed his father with an affair that had ripped out the old man's soul. It had been Eunice who had wounded Witt Danvers's pride so badly that eventually, though it was years later, Witt had fallen into the open arms of Katherine LaRouche. He'd met Katherine at the Empress Hotel in Victoria, British Columbia. They had married within the week. Witt had explained to his children that Katherine was from a wealthy Ontario family. Though she was thirty years younger than he, she would become his children's new mother.

The family had been in shock, the Danverses' lawyers nearly apoplectic, but the damage had already been done. Katherine LaRouche, whoever she was, had managed to become the bride of one of the wealthiest men in Portland. She'd seemed proper enough then, Zachary thought, remembering back, and the change in her attitude toward him had come subtly over the years. As he'd reached adolescence he'd felt her watching him more closely, caught her eyeing him whenever his shirt was off—either when he was swimming in the pool in his cutoff jeans or riding one of the horses bareback. As his muscles had developed, so had Katherine's interest in her stepson.

He'd told himself that he was imagining things, that it was only his newfound awareness of his own masculinity that had changed his perception, but now he wasn't so sure. And Jason had voiced the same suspicions.

Sighing through his nose, he shook his head to clear it. With one hand, he felt the key in his pocket and his stomach tightened into a hard ball of apprehension. What if he actually went into the Orion Hotel, took the elevator to the third floor, rapped hard on the door, and it was opened by a withered old woman without teeth? What if the damned door was opened by a man? A queer dressed up as a hooker? Oh, Jesus! What if this whole arrangement was a setup, the result of Jason's twisted sense of humor?

He gritted his teeth and glanced behind him as he reached the Orion. No one seemed to have followed him and no one other than Jason would guess that he was here. Somehow he found strength in his anonymity as he lingered on the steps of the high-rise that jutted upward, washed by floodlights, white concrete slicing into a sky as black as obsidian.

Hesitating a fraction of a second, Zachary locked his jaw, squared his shoulders, threw open the hotel's front door, and decided it was time he became a man.

3

The hotel corridor was empty, a long hallway of gold shag carpeting and metal doors painted to look like wood. The Orion had none of the charm of the Hotel Danvers, but Zach didn't care. Swallowing back the urge to turn tail and run, Zachary let the stairwell door bang shut behind him and walked, heart knocking, toward room 307. To Sophia. His destiny.

Before he lost his already-faltering courage, he rapped sharply on the door and waited.

"It's open," a cool, feminine voice called through the metal.

Oh, Christ! Zach's heart nearly stopped. He reached for the knob with clammy fingers and threw open the door.

The woman was lying with her back to him. Sprawled sensually across the bed, wearing only a black bra and a lacy black belt with long garters that dangled over a scanty pair of panties, she stretched. Zach could see the dimples above her smooth rump and long thighs and his mouth turned to sand. "You're late," she reprimanded gently.

Zach's diaphragm slammed up against his lungs and he could barely breathe. Heat radiated from his groin.

Turning slowly, allowing him a glimpse of full breasts crushed into a bra several sizes too small, she smiled up at him with a come-hither look that evaporated when her gaze met his face.

"Who're you?" she demanded. Her dark eyes shadowed with fear. "Get out!" She cast an anxious look around, as if searching for a weapon, or clothes to cover her body. "Get the fuck out!" She reached for a pink silk wrapper and started ramming her hands frantically down its sleeves.

"Jason sent me."

She froze. "Like hell," she muttered, her black eyes disbelieving. The robe still gaped enough so he had a view of the hollow between her breasts.

Zach's throat closed in on itself and he prayed to God that his voice didn't squeak. "He's still at Dad's party and—"

"Dad's?"

"I'm his brother, Zachary." He started to stick out his hand, knew it to be a mistake and wished he could just drop dead of a heart attack. She was a hooker, for God's sake, a professional, and he was a bumbling, tongue-tied, green, virgin! She could probably smell it.

Suspicion lingered on her features. "You don't look like him."

The bane of Zach's existence. "I know." Still he didn't move.

"Close the door."

Zach kicked it closed but didn't bother with the bolt.

Scooting closer to the headboard, trying to hold the robe closed over her skin, looking as if she might bolt for the door at any minute, she asked, "Why'd he send you?" She tossed a thick rope of coal-black hair off her face. "Jesus, you scared the living shit out of me."

"I didn't mean to."

"Well, come in," she ordered, obviously agitated.

Carefully, afraid she might jump up and run down the hall screaming rape, he walked across the orange carpet and eased himself onto the foot of the bed.

"Jason sent you?" she asked, reaching onto the nightstand for a crumpled pack of cigarettes propped against a half-finished drink. She shook out an unfiltered Pall Mall and her hands only trembled a little as she struck a match and lit up. "Why?"

"He, um, he had to stick around. Dad wanted him there."

She arched a fine black brow as she drew on her cigarette

again and finally lifted it from her lips. "But he didn't want you?" she asked skeptically.

"Jason's the oldest," Zach said, as if it explained everything, which it did. Jason had been groomed from the day he was born to be heir to the Danvers fortune. Nothing had changed just because Witt had sired a second son.

The hooker smiled. "So he's the favorite."

"London's the old man's favorite."

"Ahh. Jason's talked about her. The little kid. What is she, about three?'

"Almost five." Zach didn't see that London's age mattered at all, especially considering the situation. He was in a hotel room with a prostitute and they were discussing his baby sister! Well, hadn't Jason said she liked to talk? Somehow he'd expected the conversation to be a little more sensual.

Sophia set her cigarette in the ashtray on the bedstand, then picked up her drink. Swirling the melting ice cubes with one long finger, she stared at Zach, letting her eyes rove up his half-buttoned shirt to his windblown hair.

"Jason wants you to take his place?"

"That seemed to be the plan."

She took a swallow from her glass and the tip of her tongue rimmed her wet lips. "Are you a virgin, Zachary?"

The question hit him like a slap in the face. "Of course not."

"Mmm. Then you've had . . . a lot of women?" She sipped her drink, trying to smother a smile.

"My share," he said, realizing that they both knew he was lying. Hell, what did you say to a prostitute when she asked you things like that?

"You ever had a blow job?"

His head snapped up. Was she for real, or was she teasing him? He stared straight into her dark eyes and wondered if she was laughing at him. His gut tightened as she set the glass on the night table, allowing the robe to gape open and reveal her breasts. He couldn't help but stare.

He was already beginning to get hard, but he didn't try to

hide his erection. The robe fell off one of her shoulders and her skin looked soft and smooth, moving easily beneath the silky ebony strap of her bra.

"So what're we going to do about this?" she asked, as she settled back on the bed, the pink wrapper no longer clutched in her fingers, her navel and the top of lacy black underpants visible. When he didn't reply, she inched closer to him, first with her toe, then with the rest of her, sliding slowly down the bed, rumpling the coverlet with her rounded buttocks. Her eyes were hot, dark mirrors seeming to reflect the torment of his soul. She seemed to stare past all the lies he'd told her as she pulled herself up to her knees and moved her head close to his. She smelled of perfume and smoke and bourbon.

"So you won't tell me, eh? Well, just let me know when I do something you don't like, okay?"

She pressed her hot, wet tongue against the shell of his ear and he groaned. The swelling between his legs began to ache and as her tongue dipped into his ear, he wondered if he might embarrass them both by coming in his pants. "Come on, baby, what're you waiting for?" she whispered in a whiskey-smooth voice.

The invitation was impossible to resist.

He grabbed her and pressed his lips hard to her mouth, smearing lipstick in his anxiety, tossing her back on the bed so he could feel her under him.

"That's my boy," she growled as he shoved the robe off her and stared at her beautiful breasts. Round, dark nipples pointed upward through the sheer lace, inviting his hands and mouth and Zachary, finding her so willing, couldn't stop himself.

His thumb grazed a nipple and she arched, her butt coming off the bed, her naked abdomen slapping against the inseams of his pants. Her fingers found the buttons of his shirt and the wall of skin beneath. She lifted herself up and playfully nipped at his few chest hairs, causing him to lose himself in the wonder of her touch. Already dizzy from the champagne, Zachary felt the room spin as she touched him, her magic fingers caressing his bare skin, her tongue slick and hot as she slid down farther.

He groaned as she breathed across his groin and he closed his eyes in ecstasy. But as eagerly as she'd started, she stopped just as suddenly, jerking up her head.

Zach sensed trouble. He opened his eyes and found her staring at the door. He reached for his fly.

Bam! The door burst open. The knob banged against the wall. Sophia screamed, bucked beneath him, and tried to writhe off the bed. "No!" she squealed, trying to push him away.

Zach, still foggy, glanced toward the door. For a second he couldn't move, but Sophia, scrambling, managed to slide away from him.

Two men, one tall and dark, the other shorter, were silhouetted in the doorway, two dark, menacing figures.

"Get out of here," Zach commanded.

They didn't move.

"I said—"

"Shut up!" the big one cut in, stepping inside.

The short one slid a glance at Sophia, then kicked the door shut.

Zachary rolled off the bed and onto the balls of his feet. The smell of a fight hung heavy in the air; he stood between the men and the bed, torn between some silly chivalrous desire to protect the woman and the urge to run like hell out of the room. He stood his ground, staring down the men. "Call security," he ordered Sophia.

"Danvers?" The shorter one demanded.

"Yeah?" Zachary's guts shredded. These thugs knew his name? How? The hooker! This had to be some kind of setup.

He jumped toward the bedside table and phone. But he wasn't fast enough. The tall man kicked the phone out of Zach's hands.

"What the hell—"

Zach spun. Too late! The tall intruder grabbed Zachary's

arm and wrenched it painfully behind his back. Zach twisted
and writhed. Pain screamed up his arm.

"Cool it, you dumb fuck!"

Zach kicked, the heel of his boot connecting with the man's
shin.

Wind whistled between the attacker's teeth. "You son of a
bitch! You lousy little bastard!" The man yanked harder on
Zach's arm.

Agony ripped through his shoulder. Zach heard a sickening rip and his muscles turned to fire.

"Help me out, Rudy!" the tall man ordered.

From the corner of his eye, Zach noticed Sophia scoot
backward on the bed. Her face was white with fear as she
tried to grab the receiver that dangled from the phone.

"No way, sister," the shorter man—the one called Rudy
said, as he yanked the cord from the wall.

"Please—" she cried.

"Shut up!" the thug snarled.

Zach kicked his attacker again. "Let go of me!"

"No way, Danvers. You fucked up one time too many."
Again he wrenched Zach's arm.

Agony jarred through his body. Zach screamed.

"You tryin' to kill him, Joey?" Rudy barked.

"Maybe." Joey twisted Zach around and slammed his
face with his meaty fist. Bones shattered. Pain exploded
behind Zach's eyes. Blood spurted from his nose as his
knees buckled.

Rudy stared at Zach's pulpy face for a minute, then glanced
at his partner. "Oh, shit! Hey, man, I don't think this is the
right guy. This one, he don't look like—"

"You're making a mistake!" Sophia cried, clutching the
blankets around her, her lips trembling.

"I don't think so." The big one wasn't convinced. "Let's get
this over with, Rudy! Quit screwing around!"

Panicked, Zachary struggled, throwing himself toward the
door. From the corner of his eye, he saw Rudy reach into his

pocket. A flash of silver glinted in the lamplight. Zach's guts twisted with a new numbing fear. He heard a resounding click and he nearly wet his pants. A switchblade!

"Okay. Cut him," Joey said, his foul breath warm against Zach's head.

"No!" Zach fought even harder, hurling his weight sideways, throwing his attacker off balance.

"I said, cut him!" Joey yelled.

Rudy's switchblade sliced through the air.

Sophia screamed.

Zach flinched as he felt his scalp slitting open above his ear. White-hot, the pain nearly blinded him. "Stop!" Blood poured from the wound, over his eyes and face.

"This isn't the right guy," Rudy said, wiping the blood from his weapon on his pants. "I've seen Danvers—"

"Don't matter! 'Sides, he's claimin' to be him."

"Shit!"

Blindly, Zach kicked.

"Who cares who the fuck he is," Rudy finally agreed. The knife plunged into Zach's shoulder. Pain shrieked through his arm. He retched. His body sagged heavily. *They're going to kill me. I'm gonna die just like a lamb being slaughtered.* Zach tried to fight, but he could barely move.

"He said he's Jason Danvers, now let's just get it over with," Joey said.

Jason? They thought he was Jason? "Zachary." Zach spat words and blood from behind loose teeth. He tried to break free and his knees buckled. "I'm . . . I'm . . . Zachary Danvers."

"He's telling you the truth!" Tears rolled down Sophia's white face. "He's not Jason! For the love of God, just leave him alone!'

"Not Jason?" Rudy repeated. "I knew it!"

"Shit!" Joey let go of Zach and jerked the knife out of his shoulder. The wound burned like acid. Zach dropped to the floor, banged his head and couldn't move out of the sticky blood pooling beneath him.

"I told you he was the wrong guy. Shit, man, why don't you ever listen?" Rudy hissed. He pointed at the bed where Sophia was still huddled in fear. "You—get some clothes on and get out of here."

"But the boy—" Sophia whispered.

"He'll live," Rudy snarled, casting a dark look toward Zach before eyeing the hooker again. "Unless you want to explain what you're doing up here with the half-dead son of Witt Danvers, you'll move your sweet little ass out of here."

Don't leave, Zach tried to say, but the words wouldn't form over his thick tongue. He watched three sets of feet, her small, bare ones, the others in black work boots—moving in slow motion away from him. Footsteps scuffled on the shag carpet. Blood seeped from his body to the floor. He tried to lift his head.

"Bastard!" He saw the shoe, felt a hard kick in the groin and curled into a ball. Bile sprayed up the back of his throat. "Stay put, Danvers! You'll live longer."

A tide of black swirled around his eyes, though he willed himself to stay conscious. He saw the door to room 307 open, then close, and he gave in to the warm, dark void that swallowed him.

Katherine's feet ached, her head throbbed, and her eyes burned from cigarette smoke. The celebration had been a success and Witt, if he hadn't been surprised, had put on a good show of acting astounded at his wife's carefully planned party.

Seated on one of the chairs near the empty stage, she ignored the litter on the floor and took off one of her spiked heels to rub the bottom of her foot.

Soon dawn would be streaking the eastern sky, and still a few guests lingered, talking, laughing, refusing to call it a night.

"Come on upstairs," Kat suggested to her husband as she slipped her toes into her shoe again. "London will be up before we know it." She stood and stretched, aware that after hours on her feet, her hair tangled, her makeup all but gone, she was still beautiful and sexy. She caught more than one male gaze lingering on the swell of her bosom.

Witt, having consumed champagne for hours, yawned and wrapped an arm around her shoulders. He was heavy, this big bear of a man, and she staggered under the combination of his sagging weight and too many glasses of champagne.

Hours before, while she was getting ready for the party, she'd dressed with care and planned to seduce her husband, no matter how much work it was, but now she was tired, her feet ached, her head pounded, and she wasn't interested in anything but falling into the huge bed in their suite and sleeping for at least a million hours.

She helped Witt into the elevator. For a few hours the guests, dressed in their finest clothes and jewelry, had forgotten about anything other than celebrating Witt Danvers's sixty years.

With a groan, the elevator car moved upward, only to shudder to a stop on the seventh floor. "Come on, birthday boy," she said, still supporting him as they reached their suite with its panoramic view of the river. She didn't much care about the view as she unlocked the door, snapped on the lights, and helped him to the king-size bed that had already been turned down by the maid. Witt fell across the silk sheets like a heavy sack of potatoes.

"Come here," he said thickly, reaching for his wife as she pulled the draperies shut.

Katherine giggled. "Want me?"

"Always," he assured her. "I love you, Katherine. Thanks."

Tears stung the back of her eyes as the drapes snapped shut. She did care about him. "I love you, too, honey."

"I wish I could . . . I mean . . ."

"Shh. It doesn't matter," she said, and meant it at that moment. Sex was important, but it wasn't as valuable as love. Kat could find sex anywhere, but she'd learned long ago how stingy people were with love. Leaning over, she rumpled his hair playfully and placed a kiss on his cheek. "I'll be back in a minute. I just want to check on London."

"Me, too," he said, his foggy eyes clearing a bit as he thought of his little girl.

Kat sighed. As much as she adored London, a tiny part of her was jealous of the attention Witt lavished upon his youngest daughter—their only child. As Witt pushed himself upright in the bed, Kat cracked open the connecting door, allowing a thin shaft of light from their suite to pierce into the room occupied by London and her nanny.

At first she thought her tired eyes were playing tricks on her, that she'd drunk too much champagne and her cloudy mind wasn't focusing, but as she stepped into the smaller room, her heart began to hammer, thunder in her ears. She fumbled for the switch. Suddenly the room was flooded with light.

Both beds were empty; neither had been mussed. The sheets were turned down and two mints sat untouched on the pillows.

Katherine's throat constricted in a mind-numbing fear. "London?" she said weakly.

Sagging against the door frame, Kat glanced at the closet standing open, and noticed that there was nothing inside—no clothes, no bags, no shoes, as there had been earlier. There wasn't a trace of London or Ginny.

Dear God, please let this be a horrible mistake. She stepped into the room and felt a chill as cold as November. *Don't panic!* London was here. She had to be. But something was wrong and a black fear started crawling up her spine, clutching at her heart.

"Witt?" she called, surprised at the calm in her voice. After all, this was probably just a mistake. The nanny moved London to another room—to make sure that Witt and Katherine had the privacy they needed. "Witt!"

"Whaaaa?" Witt weaved to the doorway and propped a shoulder against the frame. "What's going on?" he asked thickly and Kat knew a moment of absolute desolation—as if her soul had been stripped from her.

"Call security! There's something wrong here—London and Ginny are gone. Probably in another room, but call the security guards and the manager just in case." Her mind, always so cool and dependable, was running away with her to horrible nightmares concerning her child, but she tried her best to stay calm and reasonable. There was just a mixup. That was all. No reason to become hysterical, not yet. Then why were her knees knocking? *Oh, God, please don't let anything happen to my baby!*

Witt strode into the room, knocked over the lamp and swore. Suddenly comprehending that his daughter was truly missing, he began tearing the dresser and bed apart, as if he could find his precious child or some evidence of her in the room.

"Leave it alone! For the police!" Kat threw herself at him. "Just call the damned security!"

"She's not gone," Witt said, suddenly stone-cold sober. "She can't be. She's in this hotel. In the wrong room." He opened the door and bellowed into the hallway, "Jason! Zach! For Christ's sake get in here!" Turning to Katherine, he said, "Well find her. And that damned nanny. And when I do, I swear I'll strangle Ginny Slade for this little prank!"

Witt's words were bold, but his face grew ashen and Katherine knew the cold, jabbing fear that she might never see her daughter alive again. Guilt and fear took hold of her. She loved London, she did. With all her heart. All the times she'd been jealous of her little girl because of the attention she received from her father flitted through her mind and she wondered, vaguely, if she were being punished. She didn't believe in God, but . . . Oh, please, please, let her be safe! She ran back to her room and with shaking fingers dialed the main desk. Before the clerk could answer, she said, "This is Katherine Danvers. Send up security. Room 714. And call the police. London's missing!"

4

Witt loosened the top two buttons of his collar and stared out the window to the city he'd loved, the town he'd trusted. The streetlights, skyscrapers, and traffic looked the same as they had on any predawn Sunday morning, but now the town seemed sinister and menacing. Portland, his home, had turned on him.

He saw his reflection in the plate glass, ghostly and faint over the eastern skyline. His face was ravaged and drawn, his eyes haunted, his shoulders slumped. He looked ninety rather than sixty.

Whoever had taken his baby would pay, but a dark fear tore at his mind. What if they were never found?

He wouldn't think such gloomy thoughts. Of course she'd be found. Of course she'd be fine. She was London Danvers, for Christ's sake. That part bothered him as much as the loss—that someone would dare defy him, someone who knew how to wound him until he was bled dry.

He reached for his wife's pack of Virginia Slims and lit up, hoping that sucking in smoke and inhaling nicotine would help. It didn't.

Turning back to the suite, he saw the faces of his family, tired and drawn, with dark circles and eyes dark with fear. Everyone was accounted for except London. And Zach.

A loud knock jarred through Witt's head. "Police, Danvers! What the hell's going on?"

Jason opened the door and admitted Jack Logan, who only a few hours before had been downstairs at the party. Jack, an honest cop before he'd met Witt, was now firmly trapped in Witt's gold-lined pockets. Four officers were with Detective Sergeant Logan.

"We got a call that London was kidnapped," Jack said, eyeing the group, taking a mental tally and coming up not one, but two Danverses short.

"Looks that way." He stubbed out the damned cigarette in a cut-glass tray, then showed the police London's room.

"Jesus, Mary, Joseph," Logan muttered under his breath. The room was photographed, dusted, and gone over with the proverbial fine-tooth comb; then Logan returned to Witt's suite, where he, along with another officer, Sergeant Trent, began his interrogations.

Questions were fired at each of the family members, sometimes together, sometimes individually. Logan trusted no one.

While the officers were still scribbling on their pads, Logan demanded a list of the people who had attended the party. He wanted names and phone numbers of the guests, the staff, as well as the band members, florists, and wait staff. Who were the delivery men? With what agency did Katherine book the entertainment? What about the baker and the ice sculptor? Were there any reporters or photographers present?

Who was Ginny Slade? Where did she come from? Did she have any family? What were her references?

What was her relationship with Zach?

"She has none!" Katherine said emphatically, her cool confidence shattered. Eyes rimmed with streaking mascara, she glared at the detective sergeant. "Zach isn't involved in—"

"He's missing, isn't he?" Logan countered, his lips thinning thoughtfully. "You call that a coincidence?"

"For Christ's sake, he's only seventeen. How could he be behind something like this? He was probably kidnapped as well," Witt interjected, and Logan sent him a harsh look that silently called him a fool.

"That boy's been in and out of trouble since he was twelve,

Witt. Face it. I've had to cover his ass more times than I can count."

"Nothing like this," Witt said quietly, though deep inside he felt a gut-wrenching fear that Logan was right. Zach had a chip on his shoulder the size of Nevada and he'd never gotten along with anyone in the family—even London, though the precocious child had hung on his every word. "You know who you've got to arrest, Logan. Polidori is behind this one."

"You don't know that."

"Like hell!" Witt growled, suddenly snapping. The tension in the room was getting to him and he felt as if his nerves were strung as tight as winch cables.

Logan, still staring at Witt as if he were a buffoon, ran a gnarled hand through his snow-white hair. Logan's face was lined and ruddy, weather-beaten by the winds that had blown incessantly down the Columbia River Gorge while he pounded a beat on the east side for ten years. Tiny lines webbed beneath the skin of his nose, adding a reddish tone created by a lifelong love affair with Irish whiskey. A no-nonsense man, Logan seldom threw any punches. It had taken years for Witt to get the goods on the man, make him bend the rules a bit, and take a simple bribe. Logan had fought him, but when push came to shove and Logan had needed help with his drug-dependent daughter, Risa, Witt had gotten the girl quietly into a private clinic and made sure that the story hadn't found its way to the news stations or been printed in any of the local papers.

Logan had been a trusted friend and ally ever since. But he still spoke his mind. "If you ask me, Zach knows what happened to your little girl, Witt." The detective glanced at Kat, who had turned a paler shade of white and looked as if she might faint. "Any reason why he'd want to harm her—?"

Katherine let out a whimper. "He's just a boy . . ."

"—or at least scare the bejesus out of the both of you?"

"No!" An uneasy feeling tightened in Witt's guts. He and Zach had never gotten along. They'd been oil and water for years, and the fact that Zach didn't seem to have one Danvers characteristic made Witt suspicious of the boy. There had always been rumors . . . ugly rumors suggesting that Zach wasn't his son. Then there was the problem with Kat . . . Witt had seen her dancing with her stepson, leading him on, whispering in his ear only to shut him down. Maybe out of vengeance . . . Hell, no! Zach was the only one of his older children who seemed to like London. And he was seventeen, for crying out loud. Seventeen!

"It's been known to happen," Logan was insisting. "One kid gets jealous of another—"

"No way. Zach's probably up to his butt in trouble, but he didn't take London."

"Think about it," Logan suggested, then started ordering some of his men to talk to everyone remotely associated with the Danvers family. Other officers were told to interrogate everyone staying at the hotel, then asked to check the records and contact guests who had stayed in the hotel for the last three months.

While each family member was interrogated a second and third time, the detective sergeant kept track of the investigation via walkie-talkie. His men were situated throughout the building and checking every available space in the hotel as well as working the grounds and spreading through the city, reporting anything remotely suspicious on the streets.

Informants were contacted, and anyone with an arrest record for kidnapping was in for a shock, though Logan suspected that this case was different. This wasn't the work of penny-ante crooks—this was different and deadly.

Logan was a practical man, a cop who had fought his way through the ranks to make detective sergeant. He hadn't earned his position because of his education or his sophistication; he'd built his reputation by the simple fact that he always got the job done. Over the course of his twenty-odd years with the force, he'd been called a mule, a terrier, and a self-centered bastard, but the bottom line was that he got results. Crusty and cantankerous, with four-letter words being the essence of his vocabulary, he'd devoted his life to cleaning up the filthy streets of Portland.

He called 'em as he saw 'em and in his book, Zachary Danvers was a bad seed. Maybe not even Witt's son. Rumor had it that Zach was sired by Anthony Polidori, and though Logan didn't give much credit to most of the gossip he heard, he did believe that where there was smoke there was fire. He'd caught more than one slippery criminal on the anonymous tip, the "gossip" of the streets. So maybe the grudge between Zach and Witt was stronger than the old man wanted to admit. Maybe Zach hated the man who had raised him. Considering the feud between the Polidori and Danvers families, anything was possible.

The sooner Zach was located, Logan was convinced, the sooner he'd find London, and when he did, his score with Witt Danvers would be even. Members of the family, swathed in hotel robes, hair mussed, smoking cigarettes, sat in the chairs and whispered quietly, hoping not to set off Katherine, who, arms wrapped around her middle, stared sightlessly out the window, a neglected Virginia Slim dangling from her fingers.

Trisha chewed at the corner of one fingernail. Jason paced from the window to a small table and back again. Nelson was wide-eyed and nervous, as if he was on speed, Witt thought with distaste. Everyone was there except London, her nanny Ginny, and Zach.

Witt stared at the bleary-eyed faces of his children and prayed to God that little London was safe, just misplaced. He hoped that the child, upon being hauled away from the party, had protested by "running away" to some hidden corner of the hotel and that Ginny, the idiot of a nanny, rather than lose face and admit that she'd lost his most precious possession, was tearing the hotel apart, searching for her missing charge. But he knew in his heart that he was wasting his time on empty hope. London was gone. Abducted and kidnapped and probably worse. His back teeth ground together in frustration as he wondered where she was—if she was still alive. He couldn't let his mind wander too far along that dark path, or he'd lose every bit of his sanity.

The police, except for Jack Logan, left the room.

Kat ran the fingers of one hand through her rumpled hair and glanced sightlessly at her husband. With effort she stubbed out her cigarette. "I think we should do something."

"Logan's got his men searching the building. He's going over the guest list. He'll question anyone who was in the hotel."

"That's not good enough!" she said with a deadly calm that belied her ravaged emotions. "My baby's gone, Witt. *Our* baby. Gone! Disappeared!" Blinking back tears, she walked to her purse, pulled out her gold cigarette case, and fumbled with the catch. She lit up again and wrapped one arm around herself, as if warding off a chill.

"What do you want me to do?" He felt so damned helpless and he hated the feeling. He was always in command, the man in charge . . .

"Use your influence, for God's sake. You're the richest man in this city, so you shouldn't sit around here waiting for the police to fumble all over themselves. Do *something,* Witt. I don't care who you have to bribe or threaten. Call in the god-damned FBI! Just find my daughter!" Her hands shook as she took another drag on her cigarette.

"They've already called the feds—in case she's been taken over state lines. And I'll do anything I can to find London, you know that. Believe me, I'm trying."

"Well, try harder!" She squashed out her half-smoked Virginia Slim in a glass tray. "She might be with Zach," she said, not for the first time, though at one point she'd defended the boy. She'd been the first to suggest that Zachary was involved, then changed her mind as if the thought were too distasteful. "Maybe Zach's got her somewhere and this is just a prank . . ." She must've noticed the skeptical expression on his face. "Well, he's involved, then. You know him, Witt, always in trouble . . . walking on the wrong side of the law . . . like his father."

Stung, Witt held his tongue. The crack about Zach's paternity struck home, but he didn't call her on it. He'd never believed, never let himself think for one minute, that Zach had been sired by Polidori. A bitter taste filled his mouth at the very thought. It was possible, but, no, he wouldn't believe that the boy he'd considered his second son for all these years wasn't his. But he wasn't going to argue the point with Kat. There was no reasoning with her now and he had to keep a clam head, no matter what else.

Nelson, his youngest son, looked scared. Witt had never much cared for the boy; at fourteen he was still a scrawny kid who seemed to take after him, but always reminded Witt of his first wife, Eunice. There was something about Nelson that was . . . odd. Unsettling. "Why didn't you tell me Zach didn't come upstairs?" he asked the boy, and Nelson swallowed hard, avoiding his father's eyes. "You were supposed to be sharing a room."

"Dunno."

"Where is he?"

"Dunno."

Witt let out a sigh and stared at Nelson with an intensity that had made loggers with inch-thick hides squirm. "You know where he is."

"No!"

"But you know something," Witt prodded, sensing that the boy was holding back. Hell, what a bunch of headstrong kids he was raising.

"I, uh, saw him leave the party," Nelson admitted sullenly, looking as if he thought he was Benedict Arnold, for Christ's sake!

Witt didn't move. "Leave? When?"

Katherine walked over to Nelson. "It must have been after Witt cut the cake, because I saw him earlier."

Nelson nodded mutely.

So Kat had kept her eye on Zach. "Was London with him?" Witt demanded, already knowing the answer.

Nelson shook his head furiously, his long blond hair brushing the back of his shoulders. "He left alone, didn't want to be bothered."

"Why didn't you tell us this earlier?" Katherine seemed tense enough to slap the boy.

"I didn't want to get him in trouble."

"London's missing!" she screamed. She was at the breaking point, nearly hysterical, not making a lot of sense. "I don't give a damn about your brother getting his ass in trouble again!"

Witt stepped between his son and young wife. "We don't know anything. Not yet. Let's not go jumping to conclusions."

"That kid's always had a mean streak," Katherine said. "I didn't want to believe it, but I wouldn't put it past him to—"

"Enough!" Witt turned his attention on his oldest son, who had watched the exchange with a hint of amusement on his lips. "You think this is funny?" he roared.

"No."

A muscle ticked in Witt's jaw. "You act as if you know where your brother is."

"Probably meeting a girl," Jason replied, then shrugged indifferently. "He's always horny. My guess is he's spending the night with someone he picked up."

Katherine looked stricken.

"Come on, Dad. Don't pretend you don't remember how it was when you were seventeen and horny as hell. Zach just wanted to get laid."

Witt could barely remember, but he didn't give a damn. Not now. Not when London was missing.

Sirens.

Somewhere in the distance sirens screamed through the night. Horns honked, people shouted, and the pounding in his head wouldn't fade. Slowly Zach opened an eye. The floor tilted and for a second he didn't know where he was. He tried to move and pain ricocheted down his arm. He was woozy and his head felt as if it weighed a ton.

Gritting his teeth, he got to his knees and saw the dark stain of blood—his blood—on the cheap carpet. The room swayed. He was dizzy, his mind a blur, until he saw his bloody reflection in the mirror over the bureau. The Orion Hotel. Room 307. Sophia. All at once he remembered everything—the pretty girl, the hoodlums barging in and nearly killing him.

Why?

Because the thugs had thought he was Jason.

That bastard. He'd been set up. By his own brother. Zach pulled himself upright and staggered into the bathroom. His head throbbed, his gut ached from being kicked and his shoulder felt as if it were aflame, but somehow he managed to twist on the faucets and splash some water onto what had once been his face. He looked like hell. His eyes were already beginning to blacken and swell shut, blood crusted in his nostrils and clotted over his lips. One cheekbone was crushed, and a clean slice ran from the top of his head and down to his cheek.

His monkey suit, the tuxedo Kat had bought for him, was torn and stained with blood.

Shame and rage grappled with each other as he glared at his reflection. Jason had lured him with a hooker—a lousy hooker—and then let Zach take the fall. Jesus, he could have been killed.

But he hadn't been. He was alive and though he'd probably have to be stitched up at a hospital, he'd survive long enough to beat the living shit out of his brother. With a white terry-cloth rag emblazoned with a black "O," he cleaned his face, wincing when the warm water touched the knife wound. He didn't dare mess with his shoulder, couldn't afford to have it start bleeding again. Besides, he had to leave quickly. No way did he want to try and explain what had gone on here or give the thugs another chance at him. He'd have to sneak back into the Hotel Danvers and up to his own room without being spotted by anyone.

That shouldn't be too hard. According to his watch, it was almost four-thirty, nearly dawn. Witt's party should have wound down to nothing. Anyone who was still awake would be too drunk to notice Zach slinking in.

And then he'd hunt down his older brother and beat the piss out of him. Jason had a lot to answer for.

He slipped out of the room unnoticed, took the stairs to the first floor, and while the desk clerk had his back turned, Zach crossed the lobby, hurried past the magazine stand where some old coot was hoping to sell the early edition of the newspaper, and was out the door.

A summer storm had hit. Warm rain lashed from the sky, puddling on the sidewalk and drizzling down the back of Zach's neck. Ducking his head against the wind, he started back toward the Hotel Danvers. He hunched his shoulders—his legs felt as if they were made of rubber.

As he rounded a corner, he noticed the police cars, six or seven of them, parked in front of the hotel like vultures hovering over a dying sheep. Blue and red lights flashed against the side of the building and a dozen uniformed officers milled around the grounds.

Zach stopped dead in his tracks.

His anger turned to fear as he realized what had happened. Joey and his pal had probably left Zach and attacked his older brother right in his father's hotel! Jason was dead! Oh, God! Without realizing what he was doing, Zach started running, forcing his heavy legs forward, unaware of the sight he made, unafraid of the police with their riot sticks and guns. His footsteps pounded on the wet cement and he dashed across the cross streets, ignoring the early morning traffic, mindless of the brakes squealing and the horns honking as he flew toward the hotel.

Jason. Oh, God—

"Hey, you!" a loud male voice yelled.

Zach didn't pay any attention. He sidestepped between two parked cars.

"Kid, I'm talkin' to you. Stop!"

Zach was barely aware of anything except the fear that gripped him and a burning sensation in his shoulder.

"Police! Freeze!"

He skidded to a stop as the words sank in and whirled on the two officers who approached him. They emerged from one of the cars, their weapons drawn, no-nonsense written all over their features.

"Hands in the air! Do it!" Zach slowly raised his one arm. The other hung limply at his side. "Shiiiit, look at him, will ya, Bill?" the one with the loud voice said. "Looks like our boy here got himself into a fight. What happened to you? Haven't seen a little girl, have you?"

"What?" Zach figured they must be talking about Sophia, but he kept his mouth shut. Something wasn't right and he didn't trust the cops.

The stocky officer—Bill—smiled without a trace of humor in his suspicious eyes. "Don't you know who this is, Steve? It's the Danvers kid. The one who's supposed to be missing."

"Zachary?"

"Yeah, so what?" Zach snarled.

The policemen exchanged glances and Zach's blood ran cold as ice. The tall one, Steve, said, "So where's the girl?"

PART THREE
1993

5

The memory of her fight with her mother was vivid. It had started as an argument about a boy Adria had been seeing on the sly and accelerated quickly to a full-blown battle.

"The Lord thy God is a vengeful God, Adria—"

"He's not my God," Adria, then eighteen, had said. "He's your God, Mom. Yours. But he's not mine!"

The slap had been one of the few blows Sharon Nash had ever inflicted upon her adopted daughter and it had stung deeper than Adria's skin; the pain had reached the thick hide that covered her soul.

"Don't you ever, *ever* talk like that again." Sharon's breath, bitter from the coffee and tinged with the underlying odor of gin, had drifted over Adria's face. "Now, go wash up, and you forget about ever seein' that boy again. He's trash, y'hear. Trash. Just like his ma. Bad blood flows through his veins, girl."

"And what kind of blood flows through mine?" Adria had demanded.

"We don't know—you don't need to."

"Of course I do!"

"The Lord works in mysterious ways—he brought you to us for a reason. You're not to question His wisdom, y'hear?"

Adria had turned on her heel and fled to her little bedroom tucked under the eaves of the second story.

Years ago. But it seemed like yesterday and the argument seemed to ring through the tiny motel room near the airport.

She'd remembered the fight because of Zachary Danvers, another rogue, another man she should avoid. Though she'd only talked with him for a few minutes, she'd read all about him and his family, *her* family, and she hadn't been disappointed.

He was the black sheep of the family—kicked out of the house and cut out of his father's will more often than not. He did things his own way, didn't give a hang that he was born rich, and he was cursed with an irreverent spirit that just might want to help her find the truth.

Or maybe not. In the year before his father's death, Zach and Witt had seemed to bury the hatchet. Nonetheless, she knew instinctively that he would be her only ally in the family; the others appeared to be ready to pick at the old man's bones and take his fortune.

Maybe Zachary was like the rest.

If so, her battle would be harder than she'd thought.

She stared at her reflection in the mirror over the sink in the bathroom and bit her lip. Was she on a fool's mission? How could she ever hope to battle the powerful Danvers family? And why was Zachary Danvers—her half-brother, for crying out loud—so attractive?

Adria had always been drawn to the kind of men her mother despised—the rebels and misfits and loners whom Sharon Nash found repulsive. The Zach Danvers of the world.

Yet Zach was the one member of the Danvers family she instinctively turned to, the only one of her siblings she felt she could trust. *Trust!* She snorted a laugh at her own foolishness. Zachary Danvers was about as trustworthy as a hungry rattler with a trapped mouse. She walked into the bedroom and found a copy of the videotape that had led her to Portland and tucked it into her bag. As she snapped the purse closed, she wondered why she never seemed to learn that very important lesson about men.

Just because Zach might be her half-brother didn't mean he was safe. He was a predatory man, a man who would take any challenge, a man with a wild streak that he hadn't yet tamed, a man who wouldn't care one bit if she were his half-sister. There was an animal side of him—pure male and extremely lethal—that defied the bounds of kinship. He was sexy and rough and seemed about as stable as a blasting cap.

No wonder she was attracted to him. It had been the flaw in her character to be attracted to rough-and-tumble, irreverent boys and men all her life.

"You're an idiot," she told her reflection as she stood barefoot on the tan carpet that had worn thin near the door.

So if she couldn't trust Zachary, who in the family could she trust? No one. Just as they couldn't trust her.

Half dressed in her lacy slip, she walked back into the tiny bathroom where her dress hung on a hook in the door. She'd found the dress in a boutique that handled "previously worn" items. A white, silky confection with a designer label, the gown fit her perfectly. She'd never owned such a creation before, never spent so much money on one dress—and a used one at that!

Her adoptive mother had been a frugal, God-fearing woman who didn't believe in women wearing ornaments of any kind—no jewelry save a gold wedding band or a gold cross suspended from a necklace and clothes that were practical, shoes that were sensible and sturdy.

Not so her father. Unlike his wife, Victor had been a dreamer, always expecting a larger crop than the land would yield, always certain that the next year, life would become easier.

And she'd believed him. When she'd discovered his secret, that he thought her to be London Danvers, she'd grabbed that gold-plated carrot he'd swung before her nose and held on with a death grip.

She'd done her research, read every clipping on the Danvers family and the kidnapping, searched through all the old papers in her father's desk, called her deceased Uncle Ezra's secretary, searching, digging through every scrap of information, praying she'd find some irrefutable evidence that either proved or disproved that she was the little lost princess. Ezra Nash, a lawyer known to bend the law, had handled the adoption. Either he hadn't bothered with records, or they'd long-since been destroyed, or there was a secret surrounding her birth that he'd wanted to keep hidden.

She'd fought the anticipation that had raced through her bloodstream when she'd learned that she might be London Danvers, that she might finally discover her true identity. She told herself the chances that she was the missing heiress were a billion to one, but in the end, she'd followed her heart—her father's dream—and driven her beat-up Chevy steadily westward to Portland, London's hometown. She'd nearly convinced herself that she was London Danvers, believed that she would finally find her family, and after the initial shock had worn off, they would welcome her with open arms. Now, as she tilted her head and screwed on the back of her zirconium earrings, she bit her lower lip. The teardrop earrings sparkled in the light, as if they were diamonds, but they were fakes, made to look like expensive jewels when they were really cheap and common.

Like you.

No! She wouldn't believe the speculation she'd heard all her life from the people in the small town where she'd grown up. Wouldn't!

She ran a brush through her hair and started working with the long, black curls. Wild, "witchy hair," her adoptive mother had often called the long, riotous waves that Adria didn't bother taming, and she was right.

She planned to crash the party celebrating the grand opening of the Hotel Danvers. It was time to face the family. She'd tried to call Zachary Danvers after their first meeting in the ballroom, but hadn't been able to get past the hotel reception desk and though she'd left messages, Zachary hadn't seen fit to call her back. She hadn't bothered trying to reach anyone else in the family. She knew too much about them to try and trust any of them. Zachary was the one with the least to lose, the only one of Witt's children to make something of himself on his own; the others—Jason, Trisha, and Nelson—had, from what she'd read, been content to stay in Witt's shadow, doing his bidding, waiting, like vultures, for him to die.

But Zach was different and had been from the beginning when there had been speculation about his paternity. He'd been in trouble with the law and he and the old man had been rumored to be at each other's throats. When Zach was still in school, there had been a major blowup and rift, though she never found out why, and Zach had been thrown out of the house and disowned. Only recently, before Witt's death, had he been back with the family.

Adria figured that someone who had been on the outside so long would be her most likely ally. So far, she'd been wrong. So tonight, she'd make public her claims and if nothing else, get the Danvers family's attention.

She was a fraud.

Zach could smell a fake a mile away, and this woman, this black-haired woman with the mysterious blue eyes and hint of irreverence in her smile when she claimed to be London, was as phony as the proverbial three-dollar bill.

But he couldn't get her out of his mind. He'd tried, but she kept swimming to the surface of his consciousness, toying with his thoughts.

Already in a foul mood because of the grand opening, he poured himself a drink from the bar in the suite he'd called home for the past few months, the very same set of rooms he was to have slept in on the night London had been kidnapped. The suite on the seventh floor looked different now, as the decor reflected the turn of the century rather than the 1970s, but it was still eerie remembering that night. Witt had raged, Kat had wept, and the rest of the children . . .

the survivors . . . had cast suspicious glances at one another and the police.

He ran a finger along the smooth surface of the window, then pocketed his hotel-room key. He didn't have time to reminisce and he resented Adria for bringing back the pain of his checkered past.

Right now, Zach just wanted out. He'd held up his part of the bargain, which was to renovate the hotel, and now he wanted his due—the price he'd extracted from the old man before Witt had died.

It had been a painful scene. His father had tried to break the ice and admit that he'd been wrong about his faithless wife, but the words had gotten all tangled up and once again they'd ended up arguing. Zach had nearly walked out, but Witt had enticed him back.

"The ranch is yours, if you want it, boy," Witt had declared.

Zach's hand rested on the doorknob of the den. "The ranch?"

"When I die."

"Forget it."

"You want it, don't you?"

Zach had turned and skewered his father with a stare intended to cut through steel.

"You always take what you want, if I remember right."

"I'm outta here."

"Wait," the old man had pleaded. "The ranch is worth several million."

"I don't give a shit about the money."

"Oh, right. My *noble* son." Witt was standing near the window, one hand in his pocket, the other wrapped around a short glass of Irish whiskey. "But you still want it. What for?" His white eyebrows had raised a bit. "Nostalgia, perhaps?"

The jab cut deep, but Zach didn't so much as flinch. "It doesn't matter."

Witt snorted. "It's yours."

Zach wasn't easily suckered by the old man. He was smart enough to know the ranch had a price—a high one. "What do I have to do?"

"Nothing all that hard. Restore the old hotel."

"Do what?"

"Don't act like I've asked you to fly, damn it. You have your own construction crew in Bend. Move them over here or hire new people. Money's no object. I just want the hotel to look as good as it did when it was built."

"You're out of your mind. It would cost a fortune to—"

"Indulge me. It's all I'm asking," Witt said, his voice low. "You love the ranch, I'm fond of the hotel. The logging operations, the investments, they don't mean much, not to me. But that hotel has class. It was the best of its kind in its day. I'd like to see that again."

"Hire someone else."

Witt's eyes narrowed on his son and he swallowed the last of his whiskey. "I want you to do it, boy. And I want you to do it for me."

"Go to hell."

"Already been there. Seems as if you had something to do with that."

Zach's throat tightened. He'd never seen eye-to-eye with the old man, but knew an olive branch when it was thrust under his nose. And this particular branch was attached by a silver chain to the deed to the ranch.

"Don't let your pride stand in the way of what you want."

"It won't," he lied.

Witt extended his big hand. "What d'ya say?"

Zach hesitated just a fraction of a second. "It's a deal," he'd finally said and the two men had clasped hands.

Zach had started to work on the hotel and Witt had changed his will. The project to reclaim the Hotel Danvers and refurbish the old building to its earlier grandeur had lasted over two years, and Witt had died long before it was finished, never realizing his dream. Zach had been able to spend most of his time at the ranch, until a year ago. Then the job had become so involved that he'd been forced to move to Portland to ensure that all the finishing touches were just right.

Now, he tightened the knot of his tie around his throat. He had to get through the grand opening, check a few last bugs, and then get the hell out of Dodge.

What about Adria?

Christ, why couldn't he stop thinking about her? It seemed that she was always there, close to the surface of his thoughts, just as Kat had been. A curse, that's what it was. For, like it or not, she did resemble his deceased stepmother. That black hair, her clear blue eyes, her pointy chin and high cheekbones, replicas of Katherine LaRouche Danvers. Adria wasn't quite as small as his stepmother had been, but she was every bit as beautiful and had the same special grace that he hadn't seen in a woman since Kat.

His gut twisted as he remembered his ill-fated, one-night affair with his stepmother. The passion, the danger, the thrill that he'd never found with another woman. At the memory of his stepmother, a forbidden heat curled through his blood. She'd seduced him, taken his virginity, showed him a glimpse of heaven, then heaved him through the gates of a hell that was to be the remainder of his life. Not that he would've changed a thing.

So why did his one meeting with Adria Nash conjure up such vivid memories of what he'd tried to hide for so long?

He hadn't seen Adria since she'd appeared in the ballroom, all starry-eyed as she'd tried to convince him that she was his long-lost half-sister, but he knew she'd turn up again. Like the proverbial bad penny. They always did. She'd tried phoning him and he hadn't bothered returning her calls. He wouldn't give her the satisfaction or the false hope. She wasn't the first impostor trying to claim to be darling little London and she sure as hell wouldn't be the last.

Sticking two fingers under the stiff collar of his tuxedo, he growled at his reflection and wondered why he bothered with the stupid monkey suit at all. Formality. And he hated it. Just as he hated the party he was about to attend.

He glanced at his duffel bag. Packed and ready to go. He'd be out of here by noon tomorrow.

"Good riddance," he muttered as he locked the door behind him and strode along the corridor to the elevators. He hadn't told the rest of the family about Adria's visit. No reason. They'd all just wind themselves in tighter knots than they had tied themselves into already. The old man's estate hadn't been settled yet and if the principal heirs got wind of the fact that another London impersonator had shown up . . . One side of his mouth lifted at the thought. He ran his thumbnail along the edge of the brass rail in the elevator car and considered dropping the bomb, then discarded the idea. He was well past toying with his siblings just to get a reaction.

The car stopped on the second floor and Zachary stared into the open doors of the ballroom. Guests, like flocking birds, had already collected. A sense of déjà vu crept over him as he heard the rustle of silk, the clink of crystal, and the murmur of soft laughter. There hadn't been an event in this room for almost twenty years; the last party had been Witt's sixtieth birthday.

Beneath his tuxedo jacket and shirt, his shoulder muscles bunched, as if he expected trouble. From the corner, a pianist in long tails was playing on a concert grand that gleamed like polished ebony. Zachary recognized the tune, the theme from a recent movie, but he didn't pay much attention.

Champagne flowed from a fountain that gurgled to a pool at the base of an ice sculpture of a rearing horse, the symbol for the Hotel Danvers. Pink roses floated in crystal vases and petals were strewn across linen table clothes. A fist knotted in Zach's stomach. This was too much as it had been on that fateful night when London disappeared.

He'd let Trisha handle the arrangements for the event, barely listening as she'd rattled off the guest list, the menu, the musicians, the artists, or anything else to do with the damned celebration. He'd told her to do what she wanted; he'd done his part in fixing up the old hotel and he'd stick around for the party, but that was it. He had no interest in the grand opening itself.

Now he wondered if he'd let loose a demon. This celebration was certain to evoke memories of the surprise party Kat had thrown for Witt on his sixtieth birthday. The twinkling white lights in the trees, the polished dance floor, the prestigious guest list, even the champagne, served in long throated glasses, were reminiscent of the fated celebration.

He swept past a table laden with hors d'oeuvres. Making a beeline toward the bar, he ignored his brother, who was waving for him to join a group of his friends. The men with him looked a lot like Jason. Neatly trimmed hair, impeccable and expensive tuxedos, polished shoes, bodies built at exclusive athletic clubs. Zachary was willing to bet they were all junior partners in some stuffy law firm in the city. Who needed them?

Insolently, Zach leaned an elbow on the bar. The bartender, barely twenty-one and sporting a thin mustache, trimmed beard, and gold earring, smiled. "What'll it be?"

"A beer."

"Pardon?"

"Henry's. Coors. Miller. On tap or in a bottle, I don't care. Anything you've got."

The bartender offered a patronizing smile. "I'm sorry, sir, we don't have—"

"Get some," Zachary growled, and the bartender, though perturbed, spoke quickly to a passing waiter, who scurried off in the direction of the service elevators.

"Hey, Zach, great job. The place looks fabulous," a female voice enthused from somewhere behind him. Zach didn't bother to respond.

Another woman—someone from the press, he thought—caught hold of his arm. "Just a few questions, Mr. Danvers, about the hotel—"

"I think my sister sent out a press release."

"I know, but I have some questions."

Zach was barely civil. "Speak to Trisha. Trisha McKittrick. She's the interior decorator."

"But you were the general contractor."

"She handled all the interior design." Turning on his heel, Zach left the woman with her questions and glanced pointedly at his watch. Jason was going to make some sort of speech and be congratulated by the mayor, the governor, and someone from the historical society. Zach would stick around, get his face photographed a couple of times, then make good his escape.

Still waiting for his beer, Zach paced to the windows, frowning, wishing the evening were over. He shouldn't have agreed to stay. Damn, he was getting soft. There was a time when he would've told Jason explicitly what he could do to himself if his brother had asked that Zach be a part of this farce. As it was, probably because of some sort of egotistical pride in what he'd accomplished here at the hotel, Zach had reluctantly agreed. *You're as bad as the rest of them, Danvers, always hoping for a little glory.*

"Mr. Danvers?"

Zach blinked and found the waiter carrying a silver platter with a long-necked bottle of Henry Weinhard's Private Reserve and a frosted glass. With a crooked smile, Zach grabbed the beer. "Don't need that." He pointed to the glass as he twisted off the cap and dropped it onto the tray. "But I will want more than just this one."

"At the bar, sir. When you're ready."

"Thanks." Zach took a long tug on his bottle and felt better. He glanced out the window and saw the stream of glossy white limousines waiting to pull up to the striped awning and deposit their guests, the elite of Portland, to the front doors. Men in dark tuxedos, women in jewels, furs, and silk emerged from their modern-day royal coaches and dashed into the hotel.

It was a joke.

He itched for a smoke and told himself to forget it. He'd given up that particular vice nearly five years ago. Leaning a shoulder against the windowpanes, he glared out at the night. Then he saw her. Like a ghost from his past, Adria Nash appeared on the opposite street corner. His insides twisted as he watched her weave through the clogged traffic, dashing among cabs, limos, and cars idling near the front door of the hotel. Wrapped in the same black coat she'd worn before, she sidestepped puddles and swept past the doorman.

So she'd had the guts to show up here.

With a final swallow, he finished his drink, left the empty bottle on the corner of the table, and moved quickly through the crowd. Several people tried to stop him; women offered him encouraging smiles and men looked up as he passed. He was probably the subject of more than one conversation, but he didn't really care that he was labeled the black sheep of the family or that people thought he'd reconciled with the old man just before Witt had died to get himself back in the will.

As he dashed through the double doors, he saw her, smiling at the hotel manager, assuring him she had an invitation.

"You said your name was Nash—?" the manager asked with a friendly smile as he scanned his list.

"Actually, it's Danvers."

The manager's smile didn't waver. "Danvers? Then you're related."

"Yes—"

"It's all right, Rich. She's with me." Zachary grabbed hold of Adria's chilled fingers but didn't bother to smile.

She looked at him with those clear blue eyes that seemed to cut straight to his soul. "Thanks, Zach," she said, as if she'd known him all her life.

The tightening in his chest warned him that he was making a colossal mistake—he could feel it in his bones—but he helped her leave her coat with an attendant guarding the closet and walked with her into the ballroom. He felt almost as much a traitor as he had on the night he'd slept with his stepmother; that same sense of doom, of stepping onto a path that had no beginning or end, was with him, and yet he let her link her arm through his.

More than one head turned in her direction. She was as beautiful as the woman whom she claimed was her mother. Her black hair gleamed, as it brushed against the bare skin of her back. Her dress, white and shimmery, fell off one shoulder, draped across her breasts, nipped in at her waist and flared again over her hips to sweep the floor.

"What're you doing here?" he demanded when they were out of earshot of most of the guests.

"If you would have called me back I would have explained."

"Sure." He didn't believe her.

"I belong here."

"Like hell!"

She smiled tightly. "Why'd you come to my rescue?"

"I didn't."

"Sure you did. Otherwise old Richard would have tossed me out on my ear." A waiter stopped to offer them each a drink and Adria took a fluted glass from the silver tray. Zach shook his head and the waiter disappeared through the crowd. "Face it, Zach, you saved me."

"I just avoided a scene."

Her smile was bewitching. "That's what you thought I'd do—create a scene?"

"I know it."

"You don't know anything about me."

"Except that you're a gold-digging fraud."

"You don't believe that."

"Sure I do."

"Then why not let me make my 'scene' and let me hang myself." She sipped from her drink, somehow managing a smile for the eyes of the curious.

"Bad publicity."

"Since when do you care?"

"This family has had enough scandals," he said.

"And I thought you didn't care about the family name." Her eyebrows arched in a sensual manner that caused a tightening in his groin.

"I don't." He watched her closely. She wasn't as confident as she pretended to be. There were questions in her eyes, but also a challenging light that dared him to defy her. As beautiful as Kat, with full lips and high cheekbones and eyebrows that arched over those mysterious blue eyes, she was sensual and earthy. Yet there was an innocence about her that had never been a part of Katherine LaRouche Danvers. Even at her most vulnerable, Kat had seemed to play a part, and that role was always sexy and manipulative.

"You can prove you're London?" he asked, deciding to get to the point.

"Can and will."

"Impossible."

She lifted a bare shoulder and sipped slowly from her glass as the pianist found the notes of an old Beatles tune and managed to strip the melody of any hint of nostalgia. Laughter drifted to the ceiling where the chandeliers sparkled with a million tiny lights—just as they had nearly twenty years before.

Zach ignored the sense of déjà vu that threatened to swallow him whole.

"I think you should introduce me to the rest of the family."

"Is that why you came here tonight?"

She smiled slowly and Zach's heart nearly stopped. "I came back to see you, Zach."

Just like Kat. His chest squeezed tight, but he wouldn't be fooled. "I doubt it. Don't try and pander to my male ego, all right? It won't work."

Smiling as if she knew he was joking, she said, "You're the

only one I could approach, the only family member who might believe me, give me a chance."

"You've got that wrong, *sister.* I don't believe you at all. I don't care who you are or what your game is, but I don't believe that you're London. Now, you can sell your story to the press if you want to, and you can tell it to the rest of my family, but even if you turned out to be the Queen of England, I won't give a damn."

"You're a liar, Zachary," she said in a tone that chilled him a little because she was at an advantage. Obviously she'd done her homework and she knew a helluva lot more about him that he did about her.

"Fine. Meet the rest of the clan. They're charming." He grabbed her by the arm and pulled her through the knots of guests, raising eyebrows and causing whispers to follow in their wake.

Much as it bothered her, Adria let Zach propel her through the crowd. She knew that showing up tonight would be the best way to capture every member of the Danvers family's attention. She held out a slim hope that she'd find an ally within the family, someone who would be honest with her. She'd thought that person might be Zachary because of everything she'd read about him; how, soon after his sister's kidnapping, he'd been disinherited. How he was always at odds with his father. How he'd struck out on his own and made a small fortune out of a bankrupt construction company that he'd managed to turn around. There was a time when he'd been thrown out of the family, but somehow he'd weaseled his way back in. Street-smart with a ruthless edge, Zach always seemed to land on his feet.

She recognized Jason from the photographs she'd studied. He was tall and raw-boned with red-brown hair flecked with gray. His expression was serious. Caught in conversation with a reed-thin woman about half his age, he glanced up at the commotion, took one look at Adria and hesitated for just a second, his eyes narrowing as if to focus. The skin beneath his tan paled and he swallowed with sudden difficulty before he recovered to look the part of a poised, successful attorney.

Adria wasn't surprised by his reaction. She knew of her uncanny resemblance to the woman who was supposed to have been her mother; saw in the fear flashing through Jason's blue eyes that he recognized it, too.

"I think you might want to meet someone," Zach said, as they approached.

"Excuse me a minute," Jason whispered to his thin blond friend. The girl's gaze slid to Adria and small wrinkles appeared between her perfectly arched brows. "I'll be just a little while, I promise, Kim."

With a thrust of her lower lip, Kim didn't move, obviously ready to meet Adria's challenge.

Zach's fingers clenched around Adria's arm, as if he expected her to bolt. "This is Adria Nash—my brother, Jason."

"Have we met?" Jason asked.

"In another lifetime," Zach intervened. "Adria thinks she's London."

Kim's mouth rounded a little, but Jason managed to smile. "Another London. How perfect, considering the circumstances." His voice was as cold as his eyes. "Let me guess—you showed up tonight to make a big splash, be sure that the reporters and photographers saw you?" He took a swallow from his glass and observed her over the rim. "Am I right?"

"Actually, she showed up last week," Zach said as he released her arm.

Jason turned on his brother. "And you didn't say anything?"

"I thought she might go away."

"Just go away." Under his breath Jason muttered something about thickheaded fools. A ruddy stain began to crawl up the back of his neck as he pinned Adria under a harsh, uncompromising glare. "How'd you get in here?"

"I said she was with me," Zach intervened.

Jason's lips flattened over his perfect teeth. "You let her in and you don't know what she plans to do? Or are you in on it, too? Is that it?"

Zach didn't bother to answer, just lifted a shoulder.

"You just like to see the rest of the family squirm, don't you?"

"She's a fake," Zach said flatly. "Let her do what she wants."

"Not here. Not now." Jason lowered his voice, suddenly aware of more than a few curious glances cast in his direction. "Don't you know what the law firm for the estate will do if—" His blue eyes suddenly sharpened on Adria and it was all she could do to keep from shrinking away from that hate-filled glare. "Take her upstairs. To your suite—no, better yet, to my house. You've got a key."

"No one's *taking* me anywhere," she said.

"You started this," Zach reminded her.

"Which means we'll do things my way," she countered, knowing she had to appear strong—any sign of weakness in front of the Danvers clan would be suicide.

One side of Zach's mouth lifted in a crooked, amused grin. "Maybe you are London after all. She was a stubborn thing, too."

"Just get her out of here. I'll meet you at the house."

"What about Nicole?" Zach asked and watched his brother's mouth tighten at the mention of his wife. Theirs was a rocky marriage at best.

"She's out of town. Visiting relatives in Santa Fe."

Zach didn't ask any questions. Why Jason's wife was away on one of the most important nights of her husband's life didn't concern him.

"I'm not going anywhere," Adria stated. "And don't talk about me as if I'm not here. As far as I'm concerned, I have as much right to be here as the rest of you."

"She has a point."

"Get her out of here, Zach."

"As I said, Jason, I'm not budging," Adria insisted, un-moved by the older Danvers brother's anger. She hadn't grown up on the Montana range without learning a thing or two about arrogant, self-important men. She could be just as headstrong as any man when it came to something she be-lieved in and she was certain . . . well, nearly . . . that she was London Danvers.

Adria noticed the glint in Zach's eyes and she realized that he was enjoying watching his brother lose his cool. Jason, the attorney. Jason who had married well. Jason who seemed to be the one in charge of the family fortune.

"This is not the time or the place—"

"Then name them," she said firmly and caught a move-ment from the corner of her eye. Kim, the waif-thin blonde, inched closer, listening to every word.

"What?"

"The time and place, name them." Adria wasn't backing down, not after she'd come this far, swallowed all her doubts, and found her nerve.

"My God!" another male voice whispered behind her and Adria turned to find a man, tall, blond, and lanky, with star-tling blue eyes that widened when he caught sight of her face. "She looks just like—"

"We know, Nelson," Jason said, obviously irritated.

"Nelson, this is Adria Nash," Zachary drawled as if enjoy-ing his family's discomfiture. "She's here claiming to be London."

Nelson looked quickly from his oldest brother to Zach. "But she couldn't be. Not really. Everyone knows that Lon-don was killed . . ."

"Everyone assumed," Adria cut in.

Jason's temper snapped. He glared at Zach. "You got her in here, you get her out."

"Maybe I'm not ready to go."

"If you want anyone in this family to listen to your story

with an open mind, you'll haul your sweet ass out of here," Jason ordered.

"I'll take care of her." Zach's hands were coiling around her arm again but she jerked away from him.

"I don't need anyone to take care of me," she said, suddenly defiant.

"Then why are you here?" Jason asked. "If not for a piece of the pie, for someone to take care of you, why didn't you stay wherever it is you came from?"

"Because I need to know."

"So this isn't about money?"

She didn't answer and Jason smiled without a trace of warmth. His companion, the woman he'd called Kim, watched her with interested eyes.

"It's always about money, Adria," Jason said as the pianist took a break and the music suddenly stopped. "No reason to lie about it."

Before she could respond, Zach had grabbed her and this time he didn't let go. No amount of wriggling could pull her arm free and rather than make a scene, she allowed herself to be shepherded from the familiar ballroom. She knew she'd been here years before; everything was nearly the same. The lights, the music, no . . . there had been a band instead of a solitary pianist and the champagne glasses had been a different shape. And there were other changes as well: there had been a huge green cake ablaze with sixty candles and the ice sculpture had been of a running horse rather than a rearing stallion. And the rose petals had been cast upon the floor, creating a fragrant pink carpet.

Surely she was remembering Witt's sixtieth birthday, her last night with her parents—or was she only dreaming, caught in the fantasy that was London Danvers? In the past few months she'd read every newspaper article, studied every photograph, read every word she could find about the Danvers family. She recognized her half-brothers from the pictures she'd seen of them and would have recognized her parents, had they still lived.

Witt had never given up believing that his favorite daughter would return to reclaim her heritage and he'd left a million-dollar reward for anyone who could find her; he'd also provided for London in his will, and his estate was rumored to be valued at well over a hundred million.

The money wasn't important, she told herself as Zachary retrieved her coat, but she was determined to find out the truth, and damn the consequences.

Gold digger! Bitch! Fraud!

Watching from the shadows of a tiny alley, Katherine LaRouche Danvers's killer stared after the car that sped away. Rain drizzled relentlessly from the sky, gurgling in the gutters, dripping from the eaves, doing nothing to soothe the white-hot rage that was being experienced by Katherine's killer.

Hadn't Katherine's death been enough?

Why would this spawn of the she-devil show up now?

If Adria Nash did prove to be the bitch's daughter, then everything would be ruined, the Danvers fortune splintered . . . but, of course, she was a fraud. She had to be.

The fists of Katherine's killer were clenched so hard they ached. Near the curb there was the scratch of tiny claws, barely discernible over the gurgle of water in the gutters and downspouts. Glancing down, the killer spied a wet, half-crippled rat, long tail dragging behind, slide toward a crevice in the sidewalk. Tiny eyes caught in the reflection from the street lamps and blood dripped from a wound near one motionless back leg.

"Go away," the killer hissed, rattled for a second before thoughts of Adria Nash and her outrageous claim returned.

Calm down. Collect yourself. You can handle this. Haven't

you always? The family owes you a big debt and they don't even know it.

"She's not London."

Probably not. Most likely not. But you can't take a chance. You've worked too hard to let it fall apart now. You have to stop her.

"She's *not* London."

Perhaps so, but she's the right age, isn't she? And she's the spitting image of Kat. You saw the features of her face; she has the same bone structure, identical cheekbones and eyes. And her hair. Could it be more like Kat's? She's a dead ringer.

Rage curled white-hot at the thought of Katherine. Beautiful. Sexy. Sleek. No wonder she'd turned so many heads. Women had found her strangely fascinating; men had felt the eroticism that was so innately a part of her.

A bad taste crawled up the throat of Katherine's killer.

It couldn't happen.

The Danvers fortune couldn't be destroyed.

A pitiful squeak caught the killer's attention.

The rat again!

It was too large or wounded to squeeze through the crack in the curb. The frightened rodent was eyed as it hobbled quickly back and forth, searching anxiously for a way out of the alley. Its pinkish nose quivering in the darkness, tiny teeth ready to be bared if it were to be cornered, the rat scurried to the relative safety behind a parked van. With a new deadly calm, the killer moved closer to the drenched beast and it, sensing fear, panicked and slithered into the gutter, searching frantically for a way to escape.

"You can't get away," the killer whispered, but wasn't thinking of this near-dead rat, but about the beautiful woman who had just slipped away into the night.

But she would be back.

It was inevitable.

And one way or another, this new London, whether a fraud

or the real thing, would have to be destroyed. If she wouldn't leave on her own, then she would simply have to die.

So Adria Nash looked like Katherine Danvers?

Enough that she could be considered a *dead* ringer?

The trapped rat was eyed again.

Exactly.

6

"What makes you think you're London?" Zachary shifted down for a light that reflected red on the rain-washed streets The engine of his Jeep idled and the wipers slapped drops of water from the windshield.

"I have proof." Well, that was a little bit of a lie, but not a big one.

"Proof," he repeated, easing up on the clutch as the light changed. He punched the throttle and the Jeep started climbing through the steep, twisting streets of the west hills. As she gazed out the window, staring past the thick branches of fir and maple, Adria saw the city lights winking far below. "What kind of proof?"

"A tape."

"Of what?"

"My father."

"Your father—meaning Witt?" He took a curve a little too fast and the Jeep's tires skidded before holding firm.

"My adoptive father. Victor Nash. We lived in Montana."

"Oh," he said derisively, "that clears that up."

"You don't have to be sarcastic."

He slid her a glance that silently called her a fool as they crested a hill and he turned sharply into a drive complete with electronic gates that whirred open when he pressed a numerical code into a key pad.

He parked near the garage of a rambling Tudor home. Three stories of stone and brick with dark cross beams and a gabled roof, the house seemed to grow from the very ground on which it had been built. Exterior lamps, hidden in dripping azaleas, rhododendrons, and ferns, lined the drive and washed the stone-and-mortar walls with soft light. Ivy clung tenaciously to one of several chimneys and tall fir trees rose above a stone fence that guarded the grounds.

"Come on," Zach instructed, leaning across her to open the door of the Jeep. He climbed out and led the way up a brick path and through a breezeway to the back door. "Bring back any memories?" he asked as he flipped on the lights of a huge kitchen.

She shook her head and he lifted a brow, as if surprised that she would admit that she couldn't remember. "This is it—home sweet home."

Swallowing hard, she looked around, hoping for a trace of re-membrance, but the gleaming tile floor meant nothing to her—the glass doors of the cabinets, the hallways that angled in different directions, the plush Oriental carpets, nothing sparked any old, long-dead memories. "We can wait in the den," Zachary said, watching her reaction. "Jason will be here soon."

Adria's stomach knotted at the thought of squaring off with the Danvers family, but she hid her uneasiness. The den, located in a back corner of the house, smelled of tobacco and smoke. Coals glowed from a stone fireplace and Zach tossed a piece of mossy oak onto the embers before straightening and dusting his hands. He shed his jacket and dropped it over the back of a leather chair. "What about this, hmm? Dad's private room. You—well, London—used to play in here while Dad worked at the desk." His eyes were challenging, his chin thrust forward.

"I—I don't think so," she admitted, trailing fingers on the timeworn desk.

"Gee, isn't that a surprise," he mocked. "The first of many, no doubt." He propped a foot on the edge of the raised hearth. "Now, you want to get this over with and tell me your little story or wait for the rest of the clan?"

"Is there a reason you need to be so offensive?"

"This is just the start. Believe me, I'm the prince of the family."

"That's not what I read," she said, holding her ground. "Rebel son, black sheep, no-good, juvenile delinquent." He wasn't pulling any punches, so neither would she.

"That's right, the best of the lot," he admitted with a grin that lifted one side of his mouth. "Now, what's it going to be, Miss Nash?"

"I don't see any reason to repeat myself. We can wait for the rest of the family."

"Your choice." His gray eyes were glacial, as warm as an arctic sky as he gave her a cursory glance, then walked to the bar. "Drink?'

"I don't think it would be such a good idea."

"Might take the edge off." He found a bottle of Scotch and poured a stiff shot into a short crystal glass. "Believe me, you'll need it before they're done with you."

"It you're trying to scare me, it's a waste of time."

He shook his head as he raised the glass to his lips. "Just warning you."

"Thanks, but I think I can handle whatever it is they have to say."

"You'll be the first."

"Good."

Shrugging, he drained the drink and set the empty glass on the bar. "Have a seat." Waving to a couch, he pulled off his tie, unbuttoned the top button of his shirt, and rolled up his sleeves. Dark hair dusted his forearms, and despite the season, his skin was tanned. "Just for the sake of argument," he said, "how much would it take to have you close your mouth and go home?"

"Pardon?"

He rested his hands on the bar and pinned her with an uncompromising glare. "I don't believe in bullshit, okay? It's a waste of time. So let's cut right to the chase. You plan on making a big stink, start talking to the press and lawyers and claim that you're London, right?" He poured another drink, but let it sit untouched on the bar.

"I am London. At least I think I am. And so far, I'd like to keep lawyers out of it."

"Of course you're London," he said, his voice dripping with sarcasm.

"You don't need to patronize me."

"All right. Then we're back to square one. How much money would it cost to change your mind and decide that you are, after all, just Adria Nash?"

"I am Adria."

"So you want it both ways."

"For now."

"Until we accept you as London." The fire popped loudly.

"I didn't expect you to believe me," she said, refusing to leap at his bait. Her stomach was jumping. Sweat collected at the base of her neck and dampened her palms, but she told herself to remain outwardly calm. *Don't let him get to you. That's exactly what he wants.* "I wouldn't have come all this way if I didn't think I was—I am—your sister."

"Half-sister," he said with a smile that didn't touch his eyes. "Get it right. If you're gonna do this thing, Adria, get all the facts and do it right."

Rankled, she said, "I have the facts and I know all about your family."

"So you decided to take advantage of your resemblance to my stepmother."

"Maybe you should just see the tape."

"The tape?" he challenged.

"Yes, the videotape that brought me here." The tape that had been the catalyst but certainly not the proof—not all of it. Suddenly it seemed frail, as fragile as her father's dreams and beliefs that she was some sort of modern-day princess. "I found it after my father died. He left it for me."

"Can't wait," he muttered sarcastically. Glancing at her for a moment, he poured a second glass. "But we'll wait to start the show." He set her drink on the corner of a glass-topped coffee table, then snatched his off the bar and claimed his position at the window. He stood like a sentry, staring through the rain-drizzled glass.

Standing, she said, "If you don't mind, I'd like to use the powder room."

"Powder room?" he said with a snort. "Kind of a fancy term for a farm girl from Montana."

She stared at her hands for a second, then lifted her eyes to meet his. "You love this, don't you?"

"I don't *love* anything." His gaze raked down the length of her body.

"Oh, but you enjoy baiting me. You get a perverse pleasure in taunting me, trying to trip me up."

"You started this." His lip curled slightly. "Find the 'powder room' yourself. See if you can conjure it up from all those hidden memories."

Silently counting to ten, she grabbed her bag and hurried out of the room. The hallway was unfamiliar, but she turned to the right, rounded a corner, and stopped dead in her tracks when she saw what could only be described as a shrine to the family of Witt Danvers. Pictures, plaques, and trophies resting in a glass case cut into the wall were displayed prominently.

She swallowed with difficulty when she spied a large portrait of the three of them: Witt, Katherine, and London. Could this be . . . ? Adria's heart caught and she touched the glass, her finger displacing a tiny sheen of dust. Seated in a wicker chair, Katherine was dressed in a wine-colored dress with a scooped neck and long sleeves. Diamonds encircled her throat and winked from her fingers. She held a grinning London, who appeared near the age of three. London's wild hair fell in ringlets and she wore a pink velvet dress with a lacy collar and cuffs on the short, puffed sleeves. Witt stood behind them both, one hand placed possessively over his wife's shoulder. He was smiling at the camera and his eyes seemed to twinkle mischievously.

"Dad," she mouthed, though the word wouldn't come. Could

this have been her family? Her natural family. Her chest seemed to cave in on itself. "Oh, God." Tears stung the back of her eyes and she felt her teeth sink into her lower lip. After all the years of not knowing, could she be looking at her family? Her throat grew hot and she blinked as she traced the line of Katherine's jaw, so like her own, with a finger and then looked into the child's smiling face. True, there was a resemblance, though Victor and Sharon Nash had taken very few pictures when she was young.

Were you my mother? she silently asked the woman in the portrait and again she lifted her finger to the glass.

"Touching, wouldn't you say?"

Startled, she jumped backward. She hadn't heard Zach approach, didn't realize he was standing behind her, one shoulder propped on the opposite wall, watching her reaction. Her heart drummed wildly in her chest. "I—I didn't hear you."

He lifted his shoulder. "What do you think of the family memorial?" Sipping his drink slowly, he gazed at the wall of pictures. "The Danvers family et al. Kind of reminds you of Ozzie and Harriet, doesn't it?"

Adria stared at the case. There were diplomas and football trophies, an art school award for Trisha, an "outstanding student" certificate for Nelson, a swimming medal with Jason's name engraved on it, and a key to the city issued to Witt Danvers. Surrounding the case were the pictures: shots of Witt with dignitaries, Witt with one or more of his children, Witt as a young man with his father, Jason in a football uniform, Nelson in cap and gown, Jason's wedding, even Trisha dressed in a long formal with a scrawny, longhaired beau.

But there wasn't one snapshot, not one, single, faded black-and-white Polaroid of Zachary. She couldn't believe what her eyes told her and she searched again.

"I didn't win too many popularity contests," he explained, as if reading her mind. "The old man wasn't into mounting mug shots."

"I—uh—I didn't expect to see this." She motioned toward the wall.

"Who would?"

He gazed at the framed portrait of Witt and his second wife and daughter and Zach's eyes seemed to lock with those of Katherine. A muscle worked in his jaw and Adria felt as if she were suddenly intruding, that this place was somehow sacred and intimate and she was, indeed, the interloper. The air seemed suddenly hard to breathe as Zach stared at Katherine.

"I couldn't find—"

He snapped out of his reverie and the darkness in his eyes disappeared. "Around the corner. Second door on the left."

She didn't wait for other directions but hurried down the hall. Her steps were quick, as if she were running from something, something so private and dark that she felt a cold jab of dread.

In the bathroom she splashed cold water over her face. *Don't let them get to you,* she told herself as she saw her pale reflection in the mirror. *Don't let him get to you.* But she couldn't shake the sensation that something menacing and evil existed here in this expensive home.

When she returned to the den, he was back at the window, staring out at the gloomy night.

Reminding herself that she needed at least one ally in a family that was certain to try and discredit her, she picked up the drink he'd left for her and took a sip that burned all the way down her throat. "Do you know why I came to you first?" she asked, hoping to break down the barriers that he'd erected around himself.

He didn't answer, just glared out at the night as if the blackness was hostile.

"I thought you might understand."

"I don't understand anything fake."

She plunged on. "You know what it's like being on the outside."

His shoulder muscles bunched and he took another swallow of his Scotch. "Don't let a few pictures on the wall make you think that you and I have anything in common. So I was on the outside."

"But you wanted back in."

His back stiffened. "Get this straight, *sister,* I never wanted in. It was the old man's idea."

"Was it?" she asked, then decided that she wouldn't learn anything if she didn't push a little bit. "What did you do to him to have him disown you?'

"Why did it have to be something *I* did? Why not him?" He slid her a cold glance that cut to her bone, then looked back through the window.

"I'm just guessing," she admitted, but her hands were shaking a little and she gripped the glass more tightly. Just being around him was unnerving; sitting calmly under his harsh stare was nearly impossible.

"Then figure it out yourself."

"What happened, Zach?"

He turned on her then and his eyes, once so cold, had shifted subtly and she felt as if the temperature in the room had suddenly elevated. From the fire, the flames reflected on the hard contours of his face, the flickering shadows making the angles and planes appear harsher, rougher, but she felt another sensation as well, one that started deep within her and caused her heart to pound, a sensation she didn't want to analyze too closely. She licked her lips.

"It's really none of your business."

Despite the knots in her stomach, she said, "I tried to find out what happened between you and Witt, but couldn't dig up anything substantial. I thought it was because you were considered a suspect in the kidnapping, that somehow what had happened to you that night was confirmation that you were involved."

He snorted. "That was probably part of it."

"And the other?"

Zach's jaw tightened and for a second she thought he might confide in her. Instead he turned back to the window and continued to glower. "Doesn't matter."

"Of course it does—"

"Leave it alone, Adria." She heard the warning in his voice and decided it was better to back off. For now. But she was determined to find out Zach's secret. More than ever, she wanted to find out what made Witt's rebellious son tick. Maybe there was some truth to the rumors that he wasn't really Witt's boy, that his father was Anthony Polidori. And maybe there was more. The way he had stared at Katherine's portrait had been chilling. There were far more secrets in this house than she'd guessed. She took another drink and slowly settled back into the cushions of the couch to wait.

Jason Danvers threw caution to the wind as he put his Jaguar through its paces. Speeding up the narrow, rain-slickened streets of the west hills, he tried to think rationally. He'd left the celebration early, after giving his well-rehearsed speech and spending enough time to dance with the mayor, a woman recently elected and surprisingly popular. He'd made small talk, accepted congratulations from the president of the historical society for refurbishing the old building, smiled at the appropriate times, and even managed a clever quote or two for the reporters of the *Oregonian* and *Willamette Week*. Finally, after two hours, he managed to stuff Kim into a cab and leave the celebration behind.

He felt sweat beading along his collar line and remembered Adria's beautiful face, so much like Kat's. Could she be the real thing—after all these years? Jason's biggest fear—his worst nightmare—was that someone impersonating his long-lost sister would turn up and look so much like her that people might believe she was truly London. For nearly twenty years he'd sweated it out, suspecting that someday the impostor would waltz into Danvers Manor, calmly say she was the little lost princess, make a statement to the press, and start a legal battle over the fortune that would be tied up in court for decades.

Jason had thought his father, while alive, would be foolish

enough to believe any beautiful, black-haired, blue-eyed woman who would smile at him and call him "Daddy." But Witt had proved to be made of tougher stuff than Jason had given him credit for.

Soon after London's disappearance, when the police, the FBI, and even Witt's private eye, Phelps, had given up hope of ever locating the little girl again, Witt had determined he had to find her himself.

He'd bought some airtime on television and offered a million-dollar reward, no questions asked, if anyone could lead him to his little girl.

The television appeal had created chaos. Thousands of phone calls and letters had poured in not only from this country but from as far away as Japan, Germany, and India. All of the would-be heiresses had been fakes, of course, screened by Witt's team of specialists and defrauded quickly, but the search had cost millions of dollars, only to turn up fruitless.

Now, this new interloper was here and her resemblance to Kat was so damned creepy. It scared the shit out of him.

What if she's really London?

That thought settled like lead in his gut, but he knew, damn it, he *knew* she had to be a phony.

The beams of headlights splashed against the window and Zachary felt a sense of relief knowing that his brother had finally arrived. Good. Jason could deal with Adria and Zach could get the hell out of town. He didn't want or need to be so close to a woman who reminded him of Kat. "Looks like we've got company."

"About time." She was seated in a corner of the couch, her shoes kicked off, her knees drawn up beneath the silky folds of her gown.

As if she belonged. As if she were really a Danvers. As if she were London. Shit. He watched his brother's car screech to a stop near the garage. "He's not gonna be happy."

"Neither are you."

Zach caught the irony in her voice and felt the corners of his lips curve upward. She was something. Trouble was, he didn't know what. But she'd rattled Jason and that, in and of itself, was a trait Zach respected.

The Jaguar's powerful engine shut down and a door slammed.

"Still time to back out of this."

"No way."

Jason, like many lawyers, was one of the most consummate actors Zachary had ever met. Always aware of presence, drama, and effect, Jason never appeared surprised, unless it was to his advantage. Except tonight, when he'd been forced to face his deepest nightmare—that London, his half-sister, was back and ready to claim her portion of the estate, which just happened to be the lion's share.

Jason's expression was grim as he strode into the room, but he seemed composed. Not a hair out of place, his tuxedo as crisp as when he'd taken it from his garment bag, he'd managed to regain control of his emotions. With a smile as cool as November, he walked to the bar and poured himself a drink.

"Let's just get down to it, shall we?" he said as he recapped a bottle of expensive Scotch.

Zach rested a hip against the fireplace.

"What is it you want, Miss Nash?" Jason asked.

She was ready for him. "Recognition."

"That you're London?"

"Yes."

Jason's smile was so cold, Zachary felt a moment's concern for Adria. "You know we don't believe you."

"I expected it, yes."

"And you know that there have been hundreds of young women who have claimed to be our half-sister."

She didn't bother answering, but her eyes never left Jason's face.

"She says she has proof," Zach interjected, uncomfortable with Jason's arrogant attitude.

"Proof?" Jason's eyebrows raised and a muscle tightened in his jaw.

"I have a tape."

"A tape of—?"

"It's from my adoptive father. It explains what happened."

Jason looked at his brother. "You've seen it?"

"Not yet."

"Well, what're we waiting for? I assume you have it with you, Miss Nash."

"In my purse." She reached for the purse near her feet.

Zach stuffed his hands in his pockets. "Don't you think we should wait until Nelson and Trisha are here?"

"Why?"

"We're all involved, Jason," Zach said as Adria handed Jason the tape.

Opening the plastic cover, Jason asked, "Is this the only copy?"

Adria slanted him a glance that told him to quit acting as if she didn't have a brain in her head. "Of course not."

"Didn't think so." Jason stared at the videocassette, flipped it over, and slipped it onto the corner of the desk. "Everything on this tape can be verified, right? If there's any question of legality, there would be documents to back it up."

"Such as?"

"Adoption papers, that sort of thing."

"The papers were destroyed."

Jason's lips twitched. "Destroyed?"

"By a fire."

"Convenient."

"I don't think so."

For a reason he couldn't explain, Zach stepped in. "There must be copies filed with the start."

Adria shook her head. "I think the adoption was illegal."

Jason's mouth swept into a grin. "This just gets better and better."

Zach felt his stomach curl at the way Jason stepped closer to Adria—moving in for the kill. "Back off," he warned his brother.

"Oh, no, she started this." Jason was suddenly enjoying the evening.

But Adria didn't back down. "Look," she said, getting to her feet and staring the brothers down. "I know you're going to do everything you can to disprove me. I expect you to put me through hell. I did a lot of soul-searching before I came here, because, to put it frankly, I'm not sure I'm London Danvers."

Jason looked smug, as if he thought she was already hedging her bets. "You've changed your mind."

"No," she said emphatically and stepped toward him. "I just want you to know where I stand. My father thought I was London."

"Your father?"

"Victor Nash. He died last year. I didn't find out the truth until I discovered the tape."

"That makes things easy, doesn't it?" Jason asked. "Your father—and I presume your mother, as well—aren't around to be questioned. But, happily for you, he leaves you a mystery tape telling you that you're going to inherit millions. Have I got it right so far?"

"Dad thought I should know," she said, a slight defensive edge to her voice.

"So he gave you some sort of deathbed swan song about you being the lost princess of the Danvers kingdom, is that it?"

She pinned him with eyes that darkened with the pain of her past. "That's it."

"And you must believe it or you wouldn't be here."

"Of course. But I'm not sure."

"How much would it cost to convince you that you're no blood relation?"

"As I said before, it's not a matter of money. If I find out I'm not London, I'll leave."

"And you won't go running to the press?"

Suddenly she crossed the short distance between Jason and the couch so quickly, Zach's breath caught. Without the added inches of her heels, she was a full head shorter than Jason, yet she craned her neck upward and glared at him. Two spots of color stained her cheeks. "You may find this impossible to believe," she said in a voice so low it was nearly inaudible over the hiss of the fire, "but I don't really care about money. I've seen what it's done to your family as well as a few others, but it is important to me to find out the truth." Her lips flattened in distaste and her eyes narrowed just a fraction. "Be honest, Jason—wouldn't you like to know if I'm really London?"

"I already know," Zach said.

Jason glanced at his brother.

"She's a fake." Zach finished his drink.

So like Zach to make a snap judgment, Jason thought. He was so damned cocksure. To Zach, everything was black or white, right or wrong, good or bad. Once again, Jason's hot-headed brother wasn't reading the situation the way it was. The reason this woman worried Jason wasn't because of her incredible resemblance to Kat. Hell, any decent plastic surgeon could alter her face, her black hair could come out of a bottle, and she could be wearing sky-blue contact lenses for all he knew. Her looks weren't the real problem, though they did worry him more than a little, but it was her attitude that bothered him. Adria was the first person to claim she wasn't sure of her birthright. Whereas every other imposter, the pretenders to the Danvers crown, were sure of themselves and threatening lawsuits, adverse publicity and stories in newspapers coast to coast. Adria was different . . . chillingly so.

"Sit down, Miss Nash," he suggested in a voice that most witnesses in a court of law obeyed instantly.

Unmoving, she stood her ground and from the corner of his eye, Jason saw Zachary's mouth twitch in amusement. He was enjoying this, because he didn't have much of a stake in the inheritance. The old man had written him out of his will once and then, as he'd aged Witt had mellowed, tried to patch things up with Zach and offered him the ranch, the only asset that Zach cared about.

Zachary had been reluctant, but finally capitulated. The old man and his rebellious middle son had struck a deal of sorts, something no one ever brought into conversation. There were no signed papers and yet somehow Zach had ended up doing Witt's bidding and refurbishing the Hotel Danvers. In return, Zach would inherit the ranch in Bend—acres and acres of rich farmland, a drop in the bucket as far as the family fortune was concerned, but worth something nonetheless. The fact that Zach wanted it gave Jason a bargaining point with his headstrong younger brother. Jason suspected that deep down, Zach was just as greedy as the rest of the clan.

If London suddenly were to appear, Zach's share of the estate wouldn't alter too much. He had no percentage of the assets, just the damned ranch, which would shrink by a few hundred acres if he had to pay off London for her share. But Jason, Trisha, and Nelson would suffer seriously because Witt, damn him, had talked his lawyers into leaving fifty percent of his holdings, including the value of the ranch, to his youngest daughter. Fifty goddamned percent. There was no provision for the fact that she couldn't be found. Only after fifty years—*fifty years*—would the assets revert back to the rest of the estate. By that time, Jason would have one foot planted firmly in the grave.

Hell, what a mess!

Fortunately, most people didn't know the terms of the will, or there would be London Danvers after London Danvers crawling out of the woodwork trying to get their hands on the fortune.

And this one was glaring defiantly up at him, and looking so much like Kat that he felt the same hot urges he had when he was in his early twenties and his stepmother had been the most gorgeous and sexy woman on this earth. He'd had dreams about her, fantasized about making love to her, but she'd had the hots for Zachary, who had only been a boy at the time.

Zach, for God's sake!

Zach's attitude reeked of insolence and he had no respect for the good things in life, yet women seemed to flock to him. Kat had been the first in a long succession of women who would have given their eye teeth, or their diamond earrings, just to get him into their beds. The fact that Zach had always appeared uninterested had seemed to drive them into wild and hot pursuit.

Jason didn't understand it, never would. All he knew was that Zach had always been more trouble than he was worth.

"Look," Adria was saying, her chin lifted several notches. "Why don't you just play the tape?"

"I will," Jason assured her as he glanced at his watch. "But we can wait a few more minutes, until Nelson and Trisha get here."

"So it's a family party after all," Zach said, cynicism edging his words. "Should be a barrel of laughs."

"I tell you, Trisha, it was downright eerie," Nelson said as he braked in front of the garage. Zach's old Jeep and Jason's Jag were already parked in the drive. "I mean, I felt like I'd traveled back in time about twenty years. She looks just like Kat."

Trisha wasn't impressed. She'd been through this routine too many times before. Nelson was quick to jump off the deep end. "So what does she want?"

"No one knows. Money, I imagine."

"Where does she come from?"

"I'm telling you no one knows a damned thing about her."

"Don't you think it would have been smarter to check her out before we confront her?"

"Jason didn't want her to cause a scene at the party. Too many reporters were there."

"So he hustled her out here. Great." Trisha climbed out of

Nelson's Cadillac and slammed the door shut. She didn't have time for these kinds of games. There had always been women who claimed they were London Danvers, and there always would be. Why was this one any different? Either intimidate the bitch into leaving the family alone, or buy her off. The imposters could usually be purchased cheaply. Offer them a check for twenty-five or thirty thousand and a promise not to prosecute them for fraud, and they were only too happy to do anything anyone asked. They all signed sworn statements that they would never pretend to be London Danvers or bother the family again and in some cases, Trisha suspected, they'd slept with Jason. He seemed to get off on bedding any woman who remotely resembled Kat. Some sort of weird Oedipal thing. Trisha didn't care, just as long as the women took off. Paying off the little fakes saved a whole lot of time and lawyers' fees and everyone was happy. So why not do the same with this one?

Nelson was babbling. "Right now we can't afford any adverse publicity. My job—"

"Isn't worth diddly squat. You work for the public defender's office," she reminded him. "If you didn't get checks from the trust fund, you'd be scrounging every month to pay the rent."

Nelson's eyes thinned on his sister. "You know why I work where I do. It's a stepping-stone, Trisha."

"Politics," she said with a sneer. "You're as bad as Dad was. Delusions of grandeur."

"Politics is power, Trisha, and we both know how you feel about powerful men."

"Kind of the same way you do," she cooed, though she felt like slapping him. He'd hit a raw nerve, but then Nelson had the uncanny ability to find a person's weak spot and expose it. Sometimes Trisha wondered if there were any secrets in the family that Nelson didn't know and wouldn't use for his own personal gain. Well, he had a few skeletons in his closet as well.

As they walked through the front door, she checked her watch. It was after midnight and she was tired. The hotel opening had been a success and she would much rather have bathed in the accolades of the guests than return here, to the house where she'd been raised, a house filled with ghosts and bad blood, treachery and lies. There had been little laughter echoing through the hallways of the Danvers Manor. In truth, she remembered nothing but the continual arguments and explosive outbursts as Witt Danvers tried to force his five bullheaded children into becoming exactly what he wanted them to be.

Trisha reached into her purse and found her cigarette case. Pausing in the foyer, she lit up. She needed something stronger. A drink or a hit of cocaine would help, but she settled for nicotine and ambled farther down the hall, trying not to remember the emotional fights, the hate that had filled this house when her father had found out that she'd been seeing Mario Polidori.

"You did this to spite me!" Witt had screamed, his face flushed scarlet, the veins in his temples throbbing.

"No, Daddy, I love him—"

"Love?" Witt had cried, his blue eyes electrified with disgust. *"Love?"*

"I want to marry him."

"For the love of Jesus! You're not going to marry him. Don't you know what the Polidoris are? What they've done to this family?"

"I love him," she said firmly, tears standing in her eyes.

"Then you're a fool, Trisha, and of all the things I've ever thought about you, I've never thought you were stupid."

She began to shake inside, but she squared her shoulders. "You hate Mario because of Mom. Because she slept with Anthony—"

The slap sent her reeling backward and she fell against the wall of Witt's den, her head bouncing off the corner of the mantel. "Don't you ever speak of that woman again, do you hear me? She left me as well as every one of you kids so she could carry on her affair with Polidori. So don't you be lecturing me about how you're in love with that bastard's son!"

"You don't understand—"

"No, Trisha, *you* don't understand! You're never to see him again! Got it?"

Cowering against the wall, faced with her father's horrid rage, she refused to agree. She loved Mario. She did. Her fists had curled into tight balls and tears rained from her eyes and it became blindingly clear that her father was an ogre, an ugly, ruthless monster who cared about only one thing: his precious daughter, London. Trisha rubbed the welt on the side of her cheek and bit her lip to keep from crying. At that moment she hated Witt Danvers and she'd do anything she could to hurt him!

Now, years later, she still felt the shame. Her father had been a bastard while alive and he was still controlling his children from the grave, putting reins on his money, making them jump through hoops. Angrily, she walked down the hall. Her father had never loved her, not at all. He'd only loved his youngest daughter and now she, or more probably some imposter, was back, trying to get her greedy little fingers into the old man's fortune. Well, Trisha was bound and determined to fight the gold digger tooth and nail. London had escaped when the rest of them had been forced to suffer and face their father day after day, to cower and shudder and kiss the old man's ass so he wouldn't cut them out of his will.

Except for Zach. He'd managed to tell his father to go to hell and then slip back into Witt's good graces. Much as she hated to admit it, Trisha admired her brother for his grit.

As for Adria Nash, even if she could prove that she was London, Trisha silently vowed she'd never get a penny of the Danvers fortune. She hadn't paid her dues, hadn't lived with the heartless tyrant who was Witt Danvers. London didn't deserve half the old man's estate and besides, this woman was probably just another fortune hunter.

"What're you thinking about?" Nelson asked, his eyebrows pulled together anxiously as he glanced at his sister.

"Nothing."

He didn't believe her. "Just be on your best behavior, Trisha, and hear what she has to say. Brace yourself. She looks like our dear departed stepmother did twenty years ago."

They entered the den and Trisha nearly missed a step as her gaze fastened on the woman—a beautiful woman. The resemblance was uncanny, and although this girl didn't have the innate feline sensuality of the woman she claimed was her mother, she was nearly a dead ringer for Kat.

Someone, Nelson probably, thrust a drink in Trisha's hand and she took a sip. Zach made introductions, but Trisha didn't pay much attention; she was too wrapped up in memories of her stepmother. Her throat tightened. God, could it be? Was this woman really her half-sister? She took another calming drink and stubbed out her cigarette. Jason was talking . . .

". . . so we waited for you two before we looked it over. Adria assures us this is the proof we'll need." He slapped a black video into the VCR and turned on the power and Trisha pulled her attention away from the woman with the uncanny resemblance to Kat and watched the screen.

Zachary took his position at the window. The room was tense, but he found a grain of amusement in the tight smiles of his brothers and sister. Adria had gotten to them. All of them. They were worried. For the first time in nearly twenty years.

He heard a voice and turned his attention to the television screen where an emaciated, bald man was lying on a hospital bed and speaking with obvious difficulty.

"I suppose I should have told you this before, but for reasons I'll get to later, selfish reasons, Adria, I kept the story of your birth a secret. When you asked me about it, I swear to God, I didn't know the truth and later . . . well, I couldn't bear to tell you.

"Your mother and I, rest her soul, always wanted children, but, as you know, Sharon couldn't conceive. This was a constant torment to her and she somehow thought that God was punishing her, though why, I'll never understand. So when we found you . . . when you were handed to us, it was the blessing she'd been praying for.

"We adopted you through my brother, Ezra. You probably don't remember him much as he died in '77. But he was the one who brought you to us. He was a lawyer, practicing out of Bozeman. He knew that your mother and I were desperate for children. Already in our fifties and with debts that were burying us and the farm, we were considered too old and too poor to adopt through the usual legal means."

The man paused, took a sip of water from a glass on a nearby table, then cleared his throat and looked at the camera again.

"Ezra told me that one of our distant cousin's daughters had herself in a fix. The girl, Virginia Watson, was divorced and penniless and had a five-year-old daughter whom she couldn't care for decently. All she wanted was to see that Adria, her girl, was placed with a loving family. Ezra was a bachelor. He didn't want a child but he knew that Sharon and I would do anything for a baby.

"And we did. The adoption was secret and the papers . . . well, there weren't many, let me tell you. We didn't want the state involved, you see. So, anyway, Virginia came with you and dropped you off and from that day forward we thought of you as our own."

He paused, the next words difficult. "I suspected everything wasn't on the up and up, but I didn't care. Your mom, she was happy for the first time in years, and I had no idea who you really were. I told myself someone didn't want you and we did and that was that.

"Only years later, after Sharon had passed on, did I start to figure it out. I swear, until that time, I didn't have a clue that you could be someone's missing daughter. Hell, Adria, truth to tell, even if I had known, I'm not sure I could've given you up. But the long and the short of it is that I was cleaning some old newspapers out of the barn and I saw one with the story of the Danvers girl being kidnapped. The police were searching for her nursemaid, a woman by the name of Ginny Slade. That didn't mean anything to me, either, but about two weeks later I sat down in my chair by the fire to read a little from the Bible and the page opened up to the family tree and right there I see the name, big as life: Virginia Watson Slade. According to the tree, at one time Ginny Watson was married to Bobby Slade from Memphis."

He licked his lips nervously. "I'm not a stupid person and even I can put two and two together and come up with four. It looked like you could be the missing Danvers girl, but I wanted to be sure so I tried to contact Virginia, but no one had heard of her for years. From the time she dropped you off at the house, she seemed to have disappeared. No phone calls, no letters, no address. Her parents didn't know if she was dead or alive and had no idea where Bobby Slade was. It was almost as if she'd fallen off the face of the earth and I hate to admit it, but I was relieved. I didn't want to lose you." Victor blinked rapidly and took another sip of water.

The man sounded and looked sincere, as if he were really a dying father, but Zach wasn't going to let this dog-and-pony show get to him. In his mind Adria was a fake.

"I know this sounds callous," Victor said in a hoarse whisper, "but I couldn't stand the thought of losing you, Adria. You were all I had in the world. As for the Danvers family, I figured the damage was already done. I couldn't undo the kidnapping. And I had to consider the adoption. At the time we'd taken you in, we knew that all the proper papers weren't filed, that the adoption wasn't by the book. Hell, it was probably illegal. I was afraid that somehow I'd be implicated in the crime, even though I had no idea where you'd come from. So, I've decided to die with this secret intact and leave this video in the safe by my bed. If anyone questions the tape's authenticity, so be it. Saul Anders lent me his equipment, set up the tripod and saw to it that I had some privacy. He has no idea what's on this tape and has sworn to me that he wouldn't view it."

The old eyes turned glassy for a second. "Okay, kiddo, that's all I know. I hope it helps. I guess maybe I just loved you too much to tell you the truth. I'll miss you, baby . . ." He forced a smile and the tape went blank.

Nelson whistled low under his breath.

Jason scowled into his empty glass.

Trisha clapped her hands as if she were at a theater production. "Well, if that wasn't an all-time low in the history of videotaping! Did you really think we'd believe that schmaltzy story?"

"I don't know," Adria said huskily and her eyes shone a little brighter than they had before. "But it's the truth."

Zach told himself that this was all part of an elaborate con, that the man in the video was probably an actor, or her father trying to run a scam on the wealthy Danvers family.

"The truth. Sure it is," Trisha said, unable or unwilling to hide her sarcasm.

Jason pressed the "eject" button and pulled the video cartridge from the machine. "This is your 'proof'?" he asked.

"Yes."

"All of it?"

Adria nodded and the quiet rage drawing Jason's features into a knot of anxiety seemed to fade. "Well, Miss Nash, it's not much is it?"

"What it is, Jason, is a start," she replied, standing and slipping into her shoes. "You don't have to believe me. God knows I didn't expect you to, but take this as a warning. I'm going to find out who I really am. If I'm not London Danvers, trust me, I'll walk. But if I am," she said, her small chin thrust in determination, "I'll fight you and every lawyer you sic on me to prove it." She grabbed her purse and slung her coat over her arm. "It's late and I know you have a lot to discuss, so I'll just call a cab and—"

"I'll drive you," Zachary said, unwilling to let her leave just yet, though why, he couldn't say. He was better off without her, but there was a part of him that was intrigued by her story. Who was she really?

"Don't bother."

"I want to."

"It's not necessary."

"Sure it is." He caught a speculative glance from Trisha and a harder-edged, more pointed glare from Jason. "Danvers hospitality," he drawled.

"Look, Zach, don't do me any favors, okay?" She started out of the room and he caught her by the elbow.

"I thought you said you needed a friend." His fingers clamped over her arm and she felt his breath, warm and smelling faintly of Scotch, brushing the nape of her neck.

She reminded herself that this was the man like her, the man who had no past if the family portraits could be believed. "Maybe I changed my mind," she said, and her voice sounded ragged.

"Wouldn't be wise, lady. Looks like you need all the friends you can get."

Hesitating a heartbeat, she glanced over his shoulder to the rest of the Danvers family. *Her* family. Or was it? In a show of independence, she yanked back her arm and stepped away from him. "Thanks, anyway."

Obviously, Zach wasn't about to let her make a fool of him. He followed her out of the den and through the kitchen where she reached for the phone and he deftly plucked the receiver out of her fingers. "I'd think you'd jump at the chance to be alone with me."

"Don't flatter yourself."

His lips twisted into a self-deprecating grin. "No, I mean, to get more information on the family. That is what you want, isn't it?"

A little wrinkle of contention formed between her eyebrows. "Whose side are you on?"

"No sides," he said, opening the back door. The night seeped into the room. "I only look out for myself." A solitary man. A man who needed no one. Or so he wanted her to believe.

"Humble of you."

"I didn't think you were looking for humility—just the truth."

"I am."

His expression was hard and unyielding. "Then you may as well know that I really don't give a damn about the family or the money."

"But you do care about the ranch," she said, slipping her coat over her shoulders.

His eyes flashed in the darkness. "My weakness."

They stepped into the breezeway and the cold midnight wind whistling through the fir trees lining the drive. She was struck by the width of his shoulders, the angle of his jaw. Raw-boned and sexy. "Do you have many—weaknesses, that is?"

"Not anymore." He opened the door to his Jeep. "I gave up on my family when I was seventeen, I quit trusting women when I was twenty-eight, and I'd give up drinking, too, but I think a man should have at least one vice."

"At least."

"At least I'm not a pathological liar." He slid behind the steering wheel and his features seemed more rugged and dangerous in the encroaching darkness.

"So why would you want anything to do with me?"

He switched on the ignition and flipped on the headlights.

"Let's get one thing straight, okay? I don't *want* anything from you." Pumping the accelerator, he jammed the Jeep into reverse. "But I have a feeling you're going to shake things up a little, Miss Nash."

"That doesn't worry you?"

"Nope." He cranked on the wheel and the Jeep turned easily on the slick asphalt. His eyes were dark as obsidian. "Because I still believe you're a fake. A good one, maybe, but still just a cheap fake."

7

What the hell was he going to do with her? He drove through the gates and shot a quick glance in her direction. She was huddled against the door, staring through the windshield, and her profile was so like Kat's it caused his gut to clench into a painful fist. If she wasn't London Danvers, she was one helluva look-alike, a dead ringer for London's mother. The curve of her jaw, the thick black hair, even the way she slid a glance through the fringe of curling lashes, half seductive, half innocent. So much like Kat.

He clutched the wheel in a viselike grip, his knuckles showing white. He didn't need to be reminded of his self-destructive, sexy stepmother. It had taken years to purge Kat from his system. Then, just when he'd convinced himself he was over her, she'd taken an overdose of pills and all the demons of his guilt had awakened and screamed through his mind.

Now, this woman, this mirror-image of Kat, had appeared like a ghost and had come back to haunt him. He should run like hell. But he couldn't and there was a magnetism about Adria that pulled at him and seeped under his skin, burning like dry ice promising heat but searing with a frigid intensity that scarred deep. Just like Kat.

"Tell me about my mother," she said, as if reading his thoughts.

"If she *was* your mother." Zach flipped on the wipers.

Adria ignored the jab. "What was she like?"

Squinting into the darkness, Zach asked, "What do you want to know about her?"

"Why she committed suicide."

A tic developed under his eye. "No one knows if she tried to kill herself or she just took a few too many pills and fell."

"What do you think about it?"

"I don't. Won't do any good. Won't bring her back." His jaw was hard as granite.

"Would you want that? Her alive?"

He flicked her a disdainful glance. "Let's get something straight, okay? I didn't like Kat. In my book, she was a manipulative bitch." He slowed for a corner and added, "But I didn't wish her dead."

She'd obviously hit a nerve, but she didn't believe he was being completely honest with her. Too much tension coiled in his muscles, too much anger grooved in the lines of his face. There was more he wasn't telling her. "What about the rest of your family—how did they feel?"

He snorted. "You'll have to ask them." The Jeep reached the bottom of the hill and Zach merged into the traffic heading east. "Where are you staying?"

She was ready with her lie. "The Benson."

He lifted an interested brow and Adria knew why. The Benson, like the Hotel Danvers, was one of Portland's oldest and most prestigious hotels. Its lobby was reminiscent of an English club with warm wood walls, a huge fireplace, and sweeping stairs to an upper floor. Visiting dignitaries, ambassadors, Hollywood stars, and politicians stayed at the Benson as well as the Hotel Danvers. The price of a room wasn't cheap.

Yet, she needed some privacy, a little space away from the watchful eyes of the Danvers family, so she lied. What did it matter if she was really spending her time in a fleabag on Eighty-second? None of the Danvers clan needed to know anything more about her. At least, not yet. Until she was ready. She wasn't going to fabricate her life. She would tell them all the truth when she deemed it necessary, but right now she was tired, the fight was out of her, and she wasn't ready for round two of the battle.

"Where do you live—when you're not staying at the Benson?"

Fair enough question. A smile touched her lips. His cynical humor touched her. "Montana—I already told you—I grew up in a small town near the Bitterroots called Belamy."

"Never heard of it."

"Not many people have."

"Lived there all your life?"

She eyed him carefully. "For as long as I can remember."

"With your folks?"

"Yes." His questions put her on edge. He was looking for lies. She stuck close to the truth. Though she'd never been really close to her mother, Victor had been kind and loving to her and she was beginning to suspect that he was a far more patient parent than Witt Danvers had ever thought of being.

"Did your mother think you were London as well?"

Adria shook her head. "I don't think so."

Accelerating through a yellow light, he asked, "Don't you remember the first time you met your folks? If you were London, you would have been around five. As you pointed out, even five-year-olds have memories."

She watched as the skyscrapers fingered upward into the night-black sky. "I don't have memories, not real ones. Just images."

"Images? Of what?"

He nosed the Jeep into a side street, near the Benson. "Of the party. It was loud and exciting and . . ."

"You read about it."

"I remember Witt. With his silvery hair, he reminded me of a polar bear . . . so huge . . ."

"Again the newspapers." He pulled into the lane reserved for guests of the Benson and she turned her startling blue eyes at him. "You're right, of course," she said, reaching for the door handle, "but there's something that doesn't quite fit. In all the faded images that I have stored in my mind, there's one that's so clear, it's frightening."

"What's that?" he scoffed, though he felt as if a vise had clamped over his chest and his heart began to thud.

She stared at him. "I remember you, Zach."

"I doubt it." The clamp twisted tighter.

"As clearly as if it were yesterday, I remember a sullen, dark-haired boy whom I adored." She pushed open the door and stepped onto the curb. Zach reached for her, but she was gone. Like a faint puff of white smoke, she disappeared into the hotel.

He considered chasing her down—calling after her and making her explain herself. What did she remember about him? But he didn't move. The last throwaway line was obviously planned, a comment intended to get under his skin.

A horn blasted behind him and he stepped on the gas, but he didn't leave her words behind; they hung on the air and followed him all the way back to the Hotel Danvers where, to avoid any guests still lingering in the bar after the party had wound down, he took the service elevator to the seventh floor and walked into his room. The red message light on his phone was flashing. He wasn't surprised to learn Jason had called.

"Great." Zachary looked at his bags. They were packed and ready to go but he knew with sudden clarity that he wasn't going anywhere. At least, not tonight. Kicking off his shoes, he sat on the edge of the bed and dialed. Jason picked it up on the second ring.

"About time. Where were you?"

"I dropped her off at the Benson."

"That's where she's staying?" Jason sounded suspicious.

"A nice touch, don't you think? Claims she's the long-lost Danvers heir and stays at the competition."

Jason's voice was muffled but Zach heard him ordering Nelson to call the Benson on the other line, talk to Bob Everhart, who had once worked for Witt, and find out Adria's room number. His voice was stronger when he turned back to Zach. "You should have hung around after you dropped her off at the hotel."

"Why?"

"Why? To follow her, of course."

"Of course," Zach mouthed. "Why didn't I think of it?"

"She represents a threat, Zach."

"I don't think so." Flopping back on the bed, he wondered why he was even bothering with the conversation. "Look, it's late, I'm taking off—"

"Now? You're leaving *now?*"

"Soon."

"When we're in the middle of a fucking family crisis?"

"I don't give a shit."

"Sure you do," Jason said, and Zach stared up at the ceiling.

He was lying a little. He did care. About the ranch. And he was curious about Adria. Just what was her game?

Jason wasn't giving up. "You think your ranch is protected, right? Because it was a specific bequest? Well, things change if this woman proves she's London. A lot of the extra acres were bought after the will was originally signed and all those wouldn't be considered part of the ranch, per see. And if everyone else has to cough up to make sure she gets her fifty percent, you will, too."

Zach frowned into the receiver. "You've been busy."

"Now, listen. Adria seems to trust you. She came to you first. Get close to her. Find out what makes her tick—What?" His voice faded as he turned his head and the words were muffled, but Zach heard them all. "I knew it! Okay, so start calling cab companies . . . I don't know. Just do it. The police do it all the time—right, call Logan—he's still on our payroll and he has connections even though he's retired. Oh, for Christ's sake, don't give me that conflict-of-interest crap." There was further argument and Zach was about to hang up, but Jason turned back to the receiver. "Big fucking surprise.

No Adria Nash or London Danvers, or London Nash or Adria Danvers at the Benson. She probably just ducked into the ladies' room and, satisfied that you were gone, took a cab to God-only-knows-where."

"She'll show up. Her kind always does."

"You're forgetting something, Zach. She's different. She's not here claiming she's London, screaming that she's our darling long-lost sister; no, she's got a different story and one the press would love. 'Is she or isn't she?' And she looks so much like Kat, there's bound to be speculation. We've got to keep her mouth closed."

"How?"

"First, you've got to follow her—"

"You've got to be kidding!"

"I'm not."

Zach's jaw was so tight it ached. He didn't like being manipulated, and for as long as he could remember, someone in his family—Witt, or Kat, or Jason—was trying to pull his strings.

"My guess is that she's working with an accomplice."

"Come on—"

"Why not? We're talking a lot of money here. *A lot.* People would do just about anything to get their hands on it—even impersonate a dead girl. Think about it, Zach—our biggest worry has been that someone would show up now, after Witt and Kat are both dead, claiming to be an heir, and there's no way to take DNA tests or anything of the sort."

"I'm not worried about it."

"You should be—whether you like it or not, you're a member of this family and . . . hang on a minute." His voice was muffled for a second, then clear again. "Look, Logan's checking with the cab companies. I'll call you when we hear something."

"Don't bother." Zach slammed the phone back in its cradle. He was tired of Portland, tired of his family, tired of all the mess. He stripped out of his tuxedo—a rental—stuffed it back in its bag, and left it hanging in the closet. By the time he'd changed into jeans and a sweater, the phone was ringing insistently. He wanted to ignore it, but snapped up the receiver again. He didn't have to guess who was calling.

"She's at the Riverview Inn on Eighty-second, somewhere near Flavel," Jason said, pleased with himself. "Seems our little gold digger isn't so well off, is she?"

"It doesn't matter."

"Of course it does. She can't afford the best lawyers if she can't even pay for a decent room. Why don't you go out there, Zach, check out what the situation is? If she's working alone, take her to the ranch with you."

"No way."

"She'd be safe there. Isolated."

"The lady won't want to come."

"Convince her."

"How? Tell her that maybe she'll get a piece of the estate? Forget it."

"Come on, Zach. Do it. Who knows? She might even be London."

"Not in a million years," he said and ignored the funny feeling in his stomach when he remembered her clear blue eyes and her low, seductive voice. *I remember you, Zach. As clearly as if it were yesterday, I remember a sullen, dark-haired boy whom I adored.* His palms began to sweat around the receiver.

"I hope you're right, but I sure would like to find out."

"Drive over there yourself."

"As I said, she trusts you."

"She doesn't even know me." He tapped a foot in frustration and thought of Adria. She was beautiful and seductive and he was attracted to her. That fascination, in and of itself, was dangerous. He didn't want or need a woman in his life, especially one who had her eye on the family fortune. He'd already learned that lesson.

"This'll blow over soon. But we need to get a handle on

her. All you have to do is convince her to come to the ranch with you for a couple of days."

"No way."

"Well, at least go talk to her. Ask her to stay at the Hotel Danvers, compliments of the family."

Zach barked out a laugh. "As if she'd believe you. She went to a lot of trouble to hide herself. I don't think she'll want to stay in a hotel where she could be watched day and night."

"My guess is she'll like the higher-rent district. She's after money, remember, and it must gall her to stay in some dump of a motel."

"Maybe she likes her privacy."

"Then she should never have started this, because before it's over she won't know what the word means." He paused for a second and Zachary imagined Jason running a nervous hand around his neck. "Hell, Zach, we have to keep our eye on her."

"Then invite her to stay at the damned hotel."

"She trusts you."

Zach snorted. "If she's smart, she won't trust anyone in the family." He thought about the way she'd gazed at the picture of Witt and Katherine and London. As if she really cared. She either believed her far-fetched story herself or was the best damned actress he'd ever met.

"Talk to her," Jason insisted.

"Oh, hell." He hung up, not agreeing and not disagreeing. Grabbing his bag, he mentally kicked himself all the way to the parking garage. Adria Nash was trouble. Big-time trouble. Trouble he didn't need or want.

"Shit!" He threw his single piece of luggage into the back of the Jeep and drove away from the hotel, heading east, through the drizzle and across the murky Willamette River and along the grid of streets on the east side. Traffic was light and he pushed the speed limit, suddenly anxious to find her. He was as bad as the rest of the family. He'd never heard of the Riverview Inn, but found it easily, a low-rent cinder block building painted stark white. The flickering lighted sign advertised free cable television. All the units were connected in a "U" shape. The panoramic view from the windows of the units was a pockmarked asphalt lot and an all-night bar across the street. Riverview stretched the imagination. No river. No view. But cheap daily rates.

Zach studied the cars in the lot and spied a battered Chevy Nova with Montana plates parked in front of unit eight. "So you are here," he said, backing the Jeep into an unmarked spot near a solitary oak tree. He turned off the ignition and stared at the bank of rooms facing each other.

The manager's unit was dark and he hoped no one peeked out the window and wondered what he was doing. He slid lower in the seat, glanced at his watch and frowned. It was nearly four in the morning and traffic still whizzed by, throwing up rainwater and creating a low, constant hum. He wondered if Adria was an early riser and told himself he'd soon find out.

Jason ran a nervous hand around the back of his neck. He had to think. He was the brains of the family, the only person who knew how to run his father's vast holdings. Trisha dabbled with her art and decorating, Nelson practiced some archaic form of law as a public defender, Zach had earned his trade as a builder and now owned a construction firm in Bend while he managed the ranch in central Oregon, but Jason was the one who held the whole fraying fabric of the family business together.

He stripped off his tuxedo, threw it over the back of a chair for the maid to deal with in the morning, and frowned when he looked at his bed. Ever since Adria Nash had crashed the grand opening of the hotel, Jason's plans for the night had been thrown into a tailspin. Right now, if things had progressed as he'd hoped, he would be in bed with Kim, rolling in the sheets, arms and legs entwined, mouths pressed to body parts, groans and moans of pleasure filling the room. Instead he was standing here half dressed, wishing he had another drink and worried that somehow a woman—a cunning and gorgeous woman he'd never seen before tonight—might find a way to steal the family's fortune.

After Zach and Adria had left, he'd been forced to deal with his neurotic younger brother and sister, both of whom, in Jason's opinion, needed to spend a few more hours a week on psychiatrists' couches.

Zach was a pain, but at least he didn't have any hangups, not like Trisha and Nelson. Trisha, though she'd been through a dozen lovers and one marriage, had never been happy and Jason suspected that she'd never really gotten over Mario Polidori. As for Nelson, different demons attacked that boy. Working for the public defender's office was bad enough, but there was more about the youngest Danvers son to worry Jason. Nelson had a high set of moral standards, which he expounded for endless hours, and yet, there was a darker side to Nelson, a secretive side that only surfaced when he was angry or worried.

He poured himself another drink and kicked off his Jockey shorts, so that he was completely naked. From his bedroom he stood at the sliding glass door, backlit by the light from the hall, as he stared over the tops of trees and across the lights of the city. He was a man of action, a man who made quick decisions and lived with them, a person who got things done.

Without a qualm he reached for the phone and dialed a number he'd memorized and used years before. An answering machine clicked on and Jason sighed. His message was brief. "Yeah, it's me. Danvers. It's time to call in all my markers and you owe me one. A big one. I've got a job for you. I'll call back tomorrow."

His conscience twinged a bit, but he took a long swallow and felt the familiar warmth of Scotch as it burned down his throat, curled in his stomach, and warmed his bloodstream.

A few hours of rest and he'd be ready to face anything. And that included exposing Adria Nash as a fraud.

* * *

Adria's head was pounding as she turned out the light. The room smelled musty and stale with the lingering odors of old cigarettes and years of filth. But the motel was cheap and anonymous. At least for now.

She fell back on the bed and closed her eyes. Images of Zachary went through her mind. She couldn't be distracted by him. She had to stay focused. She'd spent too much time on her mission. In the past few years she'd written letters, met with lawyers, people from government agencies, and kept a diary, trying vainly to find Virginia Watson. Only now, after her father's death, did she have an inkling as to who she was.

And she was going to go through hell and back trying to find out if, as her father insisted, she was really London Danvers.

Zach glanced at his watch. Not long until daylight. Staring through the windshield to the motel where Adria Nash was sleeping, he wondered if she might just be his long-lost half-sister.

Impossible.

Crazy.

But she looked so damned much like Kat.

His gut tightened when he considered his hot-blooded step-mother and all the pain she'd brought his family. He didn't want to think about her and what had happened after London's abduction, didn't want to consider his part in tarnishing the Danvers name. He slid lower on his back as rain began to drizzle down the windshield in earnest.

He remember standing, bleeding in the rain, the night London had been abducted. He'd run into the policemen who had pointed their weapons at him and demanded answers . . .

PART FOUR

1974

8

"I asked you a question, Danvers," Steve, the taller cop barked. "What happened to the girl?"

"What girl?"

"Your sister."

Trisha? London? "What about my sister?" he asked. "Where's Jason?"

The stocky one took hold of his arm and Zach nearly fell into the street. "Jesus, get your hands off me!" He sucked in his breath through loose teeth.

"Look at this, Bill." The officer opened the front of Zach's jacket, shoving aside the expensive lapel with his riot stick, showing off the sticky purple stains of blood. "You okay, kid?"

"Let's get him up to his old man. There was a paramedic in the hotel—with the mother. And the old man's called his personal physician. Come on, son, through the back door. We don't want the press to get a picture of you looking like this, do we?"

"What happened to Trisha?" Zach asked, dazed. The two thugs, Joey and Rudy, they'd found his sister. She'd been drunk and . . . Oh, God. Rage burned through his blood.

"Maybe you can tell us," Bill said as he hauled Zach in the direction of the service entrance. "My guess is you've got one helluva story."

"I don't give a good goddamn what time it is," Witt yelled, his patience worn thin. London was missing. His precious little girl—gone without a trace! His heart had nearly stopped at the news and he'd been foggy, but after six cups of coffee he was clearheaded and he knew who the bastard was behind the kidnapping. "I want you to send a car over to Polidori's house. You wake up that goddamned son of a bitch and find out what he knows about this!" Witt yelled at Logan.

"Back off, Witt. We'll question Mr. Polidori, after the search of the hotel is complete."

"You bet your ass you will," Witt said, reaching for the humidor of cigars he kept on the desk of his office on the main floor of the hotel. Katherine was sleeping, thanks to Dr. McHenry and several sleeping pills. Witt lit up and stalked around his massive desk. "You've checked all the rooms?"

"Twice," Logan snapped. He had no patience for Witt's inference that he and his men weren't capable of doing their jobs.

"And the service elevator—"

"And the boiler room, the linen closets, the conference rooms, the rest rooms, even the air shafts, elevator shafts, maintenance rooms, and freezers. We also checked out the parking lot, restaurant, bellboy's closet, wine cellar, and every nook and cranny this old hotel has. It's been renovated half a dozen times and my men have gone over every set of blueprints hoping to find some secret room that everyone here's forgotten about. Take my word for it, Witt, she's not on the premises."

"Then what're you waiting for?"

"I still haven't heard from the men outside. We're covering a ten-square-block area, talking to people on the street, checking other buildings nearby, and literally beating the bushes. We've got people at the airport, the train station, and the bus station."

"You're wasting your time," Witt growled impatiently. "Polidori's—" He glanced up and saw two officers and Zach, bloodied and beaten, stumble into the office. Witt's guts twisted. The boy's face was the color of chalk and a nasty cut had ripped his skin open near his ear. He was still bleeding and his nose was a pulpy mass. On his feet in an instant, Witt rounded the desk. "Get the doctor," he ordered a policeman, then faced his son. "What happened?"

Zach glanced suspiciously to the police. He ran his tongue over dry, swollen lips. "What's going on?" he asked, squinting against the light. "Did something happen to Trisha?"

"Hell, no! What're you talking about?"

"They said, the police, that she was missing—"

Witt's guts twisted. "They were talking about London."

"London? But she's only a kid—" Zach swallowed hard.

"You weren't with her?"

Zach, stricken, shook his head.

"Christ." His entire world was collapsing and he knew where to put the blame.

"What happened to her?" Zach asked.

"She's missing," Witt said.

"Missing? But she was at the party. I saw her. You saw her."

"It happened later. Ginny's gone, too. That's all we know." Through his silent fear, Witt forced himself to turn his attention to the boy who was nearly beaten beyond recognition. "Are you all right?"

Zach gritted his teeth. "I'll live."

"So how'd this happen?" Witt demanded, then picked up the phone and dialed three digits. "Is McHenry still there? I sent a man for him. Well, just tell him to come down here, on the double. Yeah, my office. What? Oh, it's Zach. He's back and he's been roughed up. Looks serious." He slammed down the receiver and motioned two police officers off a green leather couch. "Come on, you'd better lie down. Looks like you've lost a lot of blood."

"I'm okay."

Witt felt his temper snap. "Just do it, okay? For once in your life, Zach, don't fight me. Lie on the couch and let McHenry examine you, for crying out loud!"

Zach looked like he was about to snarl back a hot retort,

but instead he sat on the couch as Dr. McHenry walked through the door. A spry man nearing seventy, he'd been Witt's physician for years and the best doctor money could buy. McHenry knew his stuff, but he could be trusted to keep his mouth shut, which made him invaluable.

"I'd hate to see the other guy," the doctor quipped, as he helped peel off Zach's shirt. Witt's stomach turned over at the sight of the ugly wound, red and angry, that sliced down Zach's skin.

"Okay, Zach, start talking," Witt said, sitting on the corner of his desk. He reached for a fresh cigar while the old one smoldered in his overflowing ashtray. Zach, sullen and wincing as the doctor attended his wounds, didn't say a word. As usual. "Look, Zach, I don't care what you think of me. Hell, nothing matters but London's safety, so you'd better tell me what happened to you tonight. Your sister's life could depend on it."

Zach sent him a look of pure hatred, but Witt didn't care. He turned his gaze to Jack Logan and stared straight into the detective's eyes. "And nothing that we hear in this room goes any further, right?"

Logan nodded curtly, and satisfied, Witt settled back in his chair. "We're listening, Zach."

Zach closed his eyes, hoping the room would stop swimming. He wanted to lie, but didn't and told his story, with only two slight changes. He didn't admit that his stepmother had turned him on during their dance at the party and he kept Jason's name out of the mess. He didn't rat on his brother and claimed to have made the arrangements with Sophia himself. Why, he wasn't sure. Maybe he wanted to deal with Jason himself. Or maybe he held some latent brotherly affection for the older brother who had been a thorn in his side for as long as he could remember. Or maybe he was just scared shitless.

Doc McHenry didn't say a word as he worked over Zach. He grunted to himself as he applied ointment and something that burned like hell, then began stitching his shoulder back together and tended to the gash above his ear. Once satisfied with his stitches, he worked on Zach's face. "You're nose is broken again, kid, but it'll give you character in your old age," the doctor said, cleaning off the dried blood. Each time he touched Zach's nose, Zach nearly passed out all over again. "This is something for the pain." He found a hypodermic needle in his black bag, rolled down the waistband of Zach's pants, and punched the needle into Zach's butt. "And another tetanus booster."

Zach refused to be mortified that McHenry had shown his ass to his father and several of Logan's men. He didn't give a damn what the old man or the doctor did to him. It wasn't any worse than dealing with the cops.

Finally Detective Sergeant Jack Logan had his turn. Zach felt the skepticism in Logan's eyes as he asked questions, noticed the way two officers shared a dubious look when he told them about the prostitute. No matter what he said, he knew they thought he was lying.

Even though Logan went through all the motions, recording the conversation while the officers took a few notes, Zach read the disbelief in the old policeman's eyes.

"These men who attacked you," Logan finally said as McHenry packed up his doctor's bag. "Rudy and Joey?"

"That's what they called each other."

"You ever seen them before?"

"Never."

"He's got to go to the hospital," the doctor interrupted.

Logan didn't miss a beat. "Look, Doc, we're trying to find Witt's little girl. I shouldn't have to tell you that time is critical. We just need Zach to come down to the station and look at a few pictures, that's all."

"I'd advise against it."

Witt's frown deepened. "Zach?"

His mouth tasted foul, his head thundered, and his shoulder throbbed like holy hell, but he nodded to his father. "I'll go."

There was nothing further McHenry could do. He pulled

Witt aside, warned him about something, but Zach couldn't make out what. They rode in a squad car to the police station and, seated in a small room with flickering fluorescent lighting and the thin smell of stale cigarettes and old coffee, Zach flipped through pages of mug shots and stared at black-and-white pictures through a haze of pain.

"What about this one?" an officer would ask and Zach would focus, only to shake his head. There were more people in the room than had been in the hotel. As the hours passed, officers would come and go, glancing at him as they strapped on weapons, took statements, or told dirty jokes.

"Him. What about him?"

The questions didn't stop and Zach stared at photograph after photograph—grainy black-and-whites of men he'd never seen. He thumbed the pages, shook his head, and thumbed some more. His father was in the room, pacing, looking as if he wished he could tear someone, anyone, limb from limb.

The pictures started to look alike and swim before his eyes. His back ached and he felt as if he hadn't slept for a hundred years. One officer sat on the corner of the table, watching his reactions, while another went out for coffee.

Zach slumped in his chair and craved a cigarette. The coffee didn't help.

"That's it. Nothing," a burly officer said over a yawn as another, a slim woman who had just come on duty, started gathering the books.

"I guess Rudy and Joey weren't processed here," Officer Ralph O'Donnelly said as he squashed out the butt of his cigarette in his empty coffee cup.

"Rudy?" The woman glanced from Logan to Witt.

"Yeah, the kid, here, heard their names." Officer O'Donnelly stood and stretched. His back popped loudly.

"Why didn't you say so?" she asked, searching through the books again and flipping one open. She shoved the open pages under Zach's nose. "Look again."

Every eye in the room was on Zach, as aching, he ran his

finger under the pictures and forced his eyes to each face. They blurred for a second, but he kept looking and he felt the air in the room charge. "I don't think—"

"Look again! Imagine your man clean-shaven or with different-colored hair or whatever," Logan muttered angrily. "Let's get an artist in here."

Zach gritted his teeth, eyeing the mug shots, knowing that there wasn't a clue on the page, when he stopped at a shot on the bottom row. The hair was different, longer now, and a beard and mustache in the photo covered what appeared to be a pock-marked jaw, but the eyes, the malicious eyes, were the same.

His throat barely worked as he laid a finger on the incriminating shot. "I think—"

"Rudolpho Gianotti," the woman officer said with a satisfied grin. Zach got the impression she liked beating the men at their own game. "A speed-head who hangs out with Joseph Siri."

"Hell," Witt ground out. He strode across the room and glared at the mug shots. Red in the face, he trembled. "I bet they're connected with Polidori."

"Bingo," the woman said. "The vice squad is checking them out—drugs and prostitution, maybe even some penny-ante gambling."

"I told you!" Witt growled, kicking at the leg of the table. "When I get my hands on Polidori, there's gonna be hell to pay. Let's go!"

"Whoa!" the woman officer said. "We're not talking about the old man. These guys"—she tapped a short-clipped nail on Rudy Gianotti's mug shot—"are involved with the kid. Mario."

Witt's eyes darkened to the color of midnight. He hated the son as much as the old man. "Bring him in, Jack. Let's talk to him."

"We will," Logan assured him, "but first, let's find Gianotti and Siri. See what they have to say, what they know. Then we'll round up Mario Polidori."

"And his old man."

"Maybe."

Witt's face twisted in ugly rage. "He's behind it, Jack. I told you that from the beginning. He took my little girl and God only knows what's happened to her."

"Don't worry, Wit, we'll find her." Logan's voice lowered and Zach didn't really care what was said. The room was spinning, his head reeled, and his bones seemed to melt. He blinked to stay awake, but blackness enveloped him. With a moan, he slid from the chair and lost consciousness.

Two days later, Zach woke up in a hospital room, his shoulder on fire, his mouth tasting like puke. He couldn't breathe right because something—cotton wadding, he guessed—was rammed up his nostrils. Bandages swathed his head and held his shoulder together and everything reeked of antiseptic.

"You look awful."

He turned quickly at the sound of Jason's voice. Pain seared down his arm. Memories—Sophia, the thugs, the switchblade, and London—ran through his mind. "You bastard," he said, his tongue thick. "You set me up." He tried to rise up, yanking hard on the IV taped to the back of his hand.

"You've got it all wrong, Zach, I'm sorry. I had no idea that—"

"Liar!"

Jason squeezed his eyes shut for a second time. "It's true, I knew I was in a little trouble with Sophia's pimp."

"A little trouble—those guys wanted to cut off my balls!" So angry he could barely talk, Zach silently swore at himself for being such a fool, falling into Jason's lust-filled trap. "You make me sick!"

"I didn't know they were going to be there."

"Like hell!" Zach turned away and stared out the window. He could see the sky and the wake of a jet as it streamed across the blue vastness. Jaw clenched so tight it ached, he refused to look at his brother. The pillowcase felt rough against the wounds on his face and his head pounded. God, he hated hospitals. Almost as much as he hated Jason right now.

"Dad thinks Polidori's behind London's kidnapping."

Zach didn't respond. The feud between the Polidoris and the Danverses had existed for generations. Anything that went wrong in Witt's life was quickly laid at the feet of Anthony Polidori, deserved or not.

"We haven't heard anything new. Not even the FBI has an answer. No one's asked for ransom and Jack Logan's afraid that London may have been taken by some terrorist group."

"Logan's a prick."

"But he has a point." Jason walked around the end of the bed, forcing himself squarely in the middle of Zach's line of vision. "Look, I know this all looks bad, Zach, and I feel . . ." His face screwed up as he searched for the right word. Shaking his head, he said, ". . . Well, I feel responsible, I guess."

"You should."

"But I really didn't think they'd come after you."

"You knew they'd be there."

"No way, man! I swear. I only knew that Sophia was waiting for me. I had no idea that her pimp would be pissed off enough to send some goons with switchblades." He tugged anxiously at the corner of his mustache. "You gotta believe me, Zach—if I'd had a clue, I wouldn't have sent you to the Orion."

Zach let out a sound of disgust.

Jason sighed loudly. "I don't blame you for not believing me, 'cause the truth of the matter is, I'd already decided not to meet with Sophia. I would have avoided the place like the plague, but I didn't think you'd get cut. I thought you'd get laid, that's all. I swear it. You gotta believe me."

Zach didn't. He'd been a fool to trust Jason the first time and he wouldn't make that mistake again. He shifted his gaze to the metal bureau near the bed.

"If I could change things, man, I would." Jason thrust one hand into his pocket and rested the other on the bureau. "You may as well know, things are bad at home. Dad's on the warpath against Polidori. Kat's usually either drunk or on sleeping pills and Valium. And Trisha. Well, she's a basket case, but what else is new?"

Jason moved into Zach's limited field of vision but Zach wouldn't give him the satisfaction of looking up at his eyes.

"As for Nelson, you're a hero in his eyes."

Zach gritted his teeth.

"Yep," Jason said, grabbing the jacket he'd draped over the back of the one chair in the room, "Nelson thinks that anyone who makes it with a whore, then gets cut by a switchblade, is some kind of hero."

"Zach?" Her voice was familiar and brought back warm memories from a long, long time ago. In his mind he heard childish laughter and smelled the scents of cinnamon and hot chocolate and the jasmine of her perfume. Somewhere, maybe on the back porch, a dog barked. But it had been so long ago . . .

"I came as soon as I heard."

Groggily, Zach opened an eye. The lamps had been dimmed. Only the night-light illuminated the hospital room, though from the window, the reflection from the security lights guarding the parking lot splashed against the wall. He squinted and saw a movement before he made out the features of a tall, big-boned woman in an expensive blouse and skirt. His mother, Eunice Patricia Prescott Danvers Smythe. She stood on the far side of the rails of his hospital bed. A dozen emotions riffled through him, none of which he wanted to examine too closely, and his head throbbed. "Wha—what're you doing here?"

Her eyes were sad, filled with a lifetime of grief for the mistakes of her youth.

"Nelson called . . . explained what happened and I took the first flight out of San Francisco." She reached across the rails and folded her long, cool fingers over his hand. Her grip was strong, the lines around her face desperate. "I'm so sorry this happened, Zach. Are you all right?"

He'd never been all right. They both knew it. "What do you care?" he said, drawing his hand away and forcing his thick tongue to form words.

She winced, but didn't move. "I do care, Zach. I care lots. More than anyone you'll ever meet."

He snorted.

"You don't believe that I love you," she said, her voice losing all inflection. "You never did."

He closed his eyes again and wished he had the strength to cover his ears so he wouldn't have to hear her lies. If she'd loved him, really loved him, she wouldn't have left him with Witt.

He didn't reply, just pretended, as he had for years, that she didn't exist. It was easier that way. Her rejection didn't hurt anymore. He'd had a long time to recover and heal. She could say what she wanted, Witt had bought her off, paid her enough money so that she gave up her children.

"I thought you and I shared something special," she said on a tremulous sigh. He felt, rather than saw, her move to the window. How long had it been since he'd trusted her? Eight years? Nine? Maybe never. "I hate to admit it, Lord knows a mother shouldn't, but you've always been my favorite. Of all my children, you were the one closest to my heart."

"Don't lie to me, Mom. We both know you've never had a heart."

Her intake of breath was swift. "Zachary, don't you ever—" As quickly as her anger had come, it disappeared. "I suppose I deserved that."

What a bunch of crap! Why didn't she just shut up? Yet he couldn't stop listening.

"I would never have left you, but . . . well, your father made sure I couldn't get near you kids. You probably don't believe this, but it was a horrible price to pay. I've regretted it . . ."

He closed his eyes. He wouldn't trust her. She'd carried on her affair with Polidori for years, knowing the inevitable consequences. In Zach's mind, she'd turned her back on her children, on her husband, on her life, for a fling with a man who used her just to get even with Witt. Zach didn't believe for a minute that there had ever been any love between Anthony Polidori and his mother. No, what they'd shared was sex, pure and simple, and that thought turned his stomach. Polidori had chosen Eunice to best his opponent and Eunice had slept with her husband's sworn enemy for a quick thrill in a life devoid of any kind of excitement. She'd had the affair to prove that she was still attractive to a man and to show her neglectful husband that she could still make her own decisions.

Zach had heard her rationalizations and deep in his heart he knew that she and Witt had never been happy. The house had always been tense while they were married, no safe refuge. He wondered how she'd become involved with Polidori, where she'd met him, who had taken the first step . . . but those were things children weren't supposed to know and he figured he was better off left to his imagination.

"You judge me too quickly, Zach," she said, her voice barely a whisper. "You don't know what it's like to be lonely and ignored, to have your life sorted out and planned for you, to have to pretend to be happy when you're not, to smile when you feel like crying your eyes out."

He cracked a lid and saw that she'd rested her forehead on the window, her chin nearly touching her neck, her breath fogging the glass. She looked weary and he wondered if that aura of exhaustion was from her stormy marriage to Witt or her guilt over choosing her lover over her children, or because of her new marriage to one of the most well-recognized heart specialists in the country.

She glanced over, as if sensing that he was staring at her. "Don't hate me, Zach," she said, blinking and dabbing the tips of her fingers at the corners of her eyes. "Don't hate me for loving you."

"You don't know what love is."

"Oh, yes, I do. I know love and the pain it causes. Unfortunately, so will you. No one, not even you, will get through life without it." She wrapped her arms around her middle section and rocked back on her heels. "You want to hate me, Zach, because it's easy. I hurt you because I cheated on your father."

"I don't want to hear this."

"Well, I had to, do you understand? Witt was so . . . inconsiderate and he had other women, plenty of them before . . . Anyway, I met Anthony at a fund-raiser, he was charming and attentive and even though I knew I shouldn't . . . well, that's what started it," she admitted. "So now you know. I suppose you still want to strike back at me. That's understandable."

"I don't really give a shit."

"Sure you do. Does it make any difference if I tell you I'm sorry?"

He didn't bother responding.

"I'd do anything for you, Zach." She sounded so sincere that he was tempted to trust her, but only for a second.

"What about sticking around? Was that too much to ask?"

"You don't understand."

"I don't want to." His head was beginning to throb again.

She opened her mouth, then snapped it shut. When she spoke again, her tone was icy. "You know where to reach me, Zach. You can pretend all you want, but I know that life with your father isn't easy for you. If you want to come to San Francisco and live with Lyle and me for a while, I'd—"

"No, thanks." He didn't need this. If Eunice had some latent maternal feelings, fine, but he didn't want to hear about them. As far as he was concerned, she came up to see him only because her guilt was gnawing away at her again, the same as it did during each Christmas and some birthdays. She was a part-time mother at best and content to be no better.

"You might change your mind." She was gathering up her purse and a navy jacket that she slung over one arm.

"I won't."

"Whatever you say, Zach, but I only came here because I love you."

She walked out of the room, the scent of the same expensive perfume that he remembered from his earliest days trailing after her.

Pain and loneliness engulfed him but he fought it. He didn't belong with anyone. His father didn't trust him, his mother—despite her protests—didn't love him, and he felt little kinship with his brothers and sisters. He thought of his stepmother in indecent terms and he didn't have many friends—didn't want them. And now London was missing. He was surprised how much it bothered him, thinking that she was small and scared and alone. He blinked rapidly and refused to cry. Not for his mother. Not for London. Not for himself. He'd shed enough tears when Eunice had walked out all those years ago; he wouldn't be foolish enough to do it again.

He decided it was time to move on. As soon as he was well enough, he'd sell his car and . . . God, quit dreaming. He couldn't leave. Not yet. Not until this thing with London was straightened out; otherwise he'd look guilty as hell and half the cops in the state would be after him. But maybe, hopefully, by the time he was released, London would be found and home safely. Then no one would notice if he left.

He'd have to be patient, which wasn't going to be easy. Patience had never been his long suit. But right now, he was stuck. There was just no damned way out.

9

Jack Logan didn't like the Polidoris. Especially Anthony. Never had, never would.

He snapped in the cigarette lighter of his pride and joy, a 1969 Ford Galaxy two-door. Cherry red with an ivory top and horsepower that wouldn't quit, the car was a gift from Witt Danvers—an expensive gift. Logan didn't want to think of it as a bribe. Frowning as he caught a glimpse of his weathered face in the rearview mirror, he tried not to dwell on the fact that he, who was basically an honest cop, had been bought by Witt Danvers. Idling at a light near Seventeenth, he slid out a Marlboro from the pack he kept on the dash and stuck it between his lips. Truth to tell, he didn't like Danvers much more than he did Polidori. The lighter clicked and he lit up as the light changed.

Logan didn't trust people with money, especially rich people with political ambitions; at the top of his list of most untrustworthy were Anthony Polidori and Witt Danvers. Polidori was making noise about running for the state senate, and the Catholic and Italian voters were on his side; Witt had his eye on becoming mayor or governor, Logan suspected, and the WASPs in Portland would vote for him. Logan's stomach turned at the thought. If things worked the way Witt hoped they would, Witt Danvers would end up as Logan's boss. Hell, what a mess!

He wheeled the Ford through a yellow light on McLoughlin Boulevard and headed south, out of the city, toward

Milwaukie, where an entire enclave of Italian truck farmers thrived for the better part of a century. The Polidoris had been vegetable vendors once, but they'd saved their money, invested in cheap land, sold their produce to the finest restaurants in Portland, and quietly amassed a fortune—not as large as the Danvers wealth, but substantial just the same.

Yep, Logan thought, drawing in a lungful of smoke, he'd love to see Anthony Polidori go down for the Danvers kidnapping. It would be fun to see that little creep squirm in the interrogation room. But it wasn't going to happen. He knew it, Polidori knew it, and Witt Danvers, whether the stubborn old man wanted to admit it or not, knew it, too.

He flipped the ash from his cigarette out the window and stepped on the gas pedal. Ignoring the speed limits, he wheeled through the crooked streets of Milwaukie to the fir-lined drive leading to Waverley Country Club, where mansions and landscaped grounds surrounded the most elite country club in the city. Acres of lush greens and fairways were part of the exclusive club that sprawled along the eastern banks of the Willamette River.

Frowning slightly, Logan turned unerringly into the drive and waited at the gate for a security guard to determine if he should pass. Logan didn't have time for any bullshit. He flipped open his wallet, showing his badge—which was a waste of time, as the guard knew who he was anyway—then stubbed out his cigarette in the tray.

With a whine of electrical gears, the gate slowly opened. Logan pushed on the throttle and the Galaxy rolled past rose gardens and fountains to the rambling manor.

Anthony Polidori met him at the front door. A short man with a widening girth, thin mustache, dark eyes that flashed when he was angry, and teeth rimmed in gold, he motioned Logan into a vestibule the size of which would hold all of Logan's little bungalow in Sellwood.

"Don't bother explaining why you're here," Polidori said, ushering him through double doors of polished dark wood. "I know it's about the Danvers girl again." With a wave toward a tucked leather chair, he strode to the bar, splashed three fingers of Irish whiskey into each of two cut-crystal glasses, and handed a drink to Logan.

The smoky scent of the whiskey tickled Logan's nostrils, but he left the glass on the corner of Polidori's massive desk. He longed for the drink, but managed to hide it. "Your name keeps coming up."

"So I've been told." Polidori didn't bother sitting, just stood near the leaded glass windows and stared at the view of the river. "Your men have been here daily. You know I'm a patient man, but even I consider this a waste of my time and the taxpayers' money. There's nothing more I can tell them or you. Call them off, Logan. Tell them to go after the real criminals."

Logan didn't bother replying. Let the jerk talk. He was on a roll.

"I'm surprised you showed up in person."

"I wasn't satisfied with Taylor's report. It, uh, seemed incomplete."

Polidori sighed. "Look, Logan, I had nothing to do with that little girl's disappearance."

"Cut the crap," Logan said in a voice so low, he didn't recognize it as his own.

Polidori's dark eyes flashed. "You don't believe me, either."

"Let's just get down to it. Two of your goons attacked Zachary Danvers, messed him up bad enough to send him to the hospital, and, at about the same time little London Danvers and her nanny disappeared. Coincidence?"

"Do I need to call my lawyer?"

"You tell me."

"I had nothing to do with either incident," Polidori insisted, then strode to the bar and poured himself another drink. "Nothing."

Logan didn't believe a word of it. "Maybe you'd like to know why we're riding you so hard. I've got a pretty long memory and I remember you making some pretty rash statements when your old man died."

"That was years ago."

Without blinking, Logan stared him down. "You made no bones about the fact that you blamed Julius Danvers, Witt's father, for that accident at the restaurant."

Anthony's face flushed.

"You swore vengeance on the whole Danvers clan."

The corners of Polidori's mouth tightened but his eyes shone with a hate so pure it chilled Logan's leather-tough soul. "That was years ago. Julius Danvers—"

"Is dead."

"—was a murdering bastard. He killed my father, Logan. You and I and all of Portland know it. He hired one of his thugs to pour some kerosene in the hotel and the whole damned thing went up in flames." His nostrils flared as he leaned closer to the detective. "That inferno killed seven people. The only reason more didn't lose their lives is because the hotel was closed that weekend. Someone who knew my father would be there gambled. And won."

"Or your old man set it himself to collect the insurance." Logan loved playing devil's advocate.

Polidori's jaw clenched. "He was killed, Logan. He was knocked over the head and left in his office in the hotel while kerosene was poured all around and over his body and then someone just struck a match and dropped it. I'll never know if my father died unconscious or if he was awake, screaming and writhing, feeling the agony of hot flames eating away his flesh. There isn't a day that goes by that I don't wonder." He sipped his drink and caught Logan's gaze in the mirror over the bar. "Stephano was a decent man. A faithful husband. A good father. And he was turned into a human torch by Julius Danvers. Witt knew all about it."

"Conjecture."

Polidori's smile turned deadly. "How much is he paying

you to keep you in his corner, Jack? Whatever it is, it isn't enough."

A muscle ticked in Logan's jaw. He thought about reaching for his drink, but settled back in the chair, hoping to appear unruffled. "Let's get back to Witt's little girl. Where is she?"

"I don't know. As I said before, there's nothing I can tell you."

"You didn't decide to finally extract your revenge by stealing the kid?"

"Get serious." Polidori snorted, but his knuckles whitened as he gripped his glass.

"What better way to make Witt twist in the wind than by stealing his daughter? You couldn't do anything that would hurt him more."

"Trust me, I didn't do it. Now, if you're going to continue to badger me, I'm calling my lawyer." He walked to his desk and reached for the phone.

"I don't believe you." Logan's voice was flat and he stared at Polidori so hard he noticed the tiny beads of sweat collecting at the old man's graying sideburns. He was guilty as hell. But of what?

"Doesn't matter what you believe, Jack. It's what you can prove. Now, either you're here for a social visit and if you are, mind your manners and drink the whiskey I so graciously offered you. If you're here on police business, you'd better charge me with something or get the hell out of my house."

Jack didn't budge. Now he was getting somewhere. Polidori had lost his cool. "Joey Siri and Rudy Gianotti worked for you."

"Not recently."

"Then they worked for your boy."

Polidori's calm face flushed red and he leaned across the desk. "Leave Mario out of this," he ordered, his lips barely moving beneath his neatly trimmed mustache.

"He could be in it up to his eyeballs," Logan replied. "Rumor has it he was involved with the Danvers girl—the older one—a few years back. She was underage at the time—sixteen, if memory serves—when the romance went sour."

Polidori's nostrils flared. "My boy was in Hawaii when the little girl turned up missing."

"Convenient."

"He knows nothing about the kidnapping."

"Everyone in town knows about it, Tony. It's been in all the papers, even hit national television. I'll even bet it made it into the news on Waikiki." He pinned Polidori with one of his hard-ass, bad-cop stares. "The way I see it, someone just wanted to fuck Witt Danvers. So I've been checking into things, digging up people who have a grudge against the guy, and guess whose name keeps showing up at the top of the list?"

"I don't need to listen to this." Polidori reached for the phone.

"Is Mario around? I'd like to talk to him." Logan finally felt that he had the upper hand. He reached for his drink. So he was on duty. What the hell.

"You have nothing to say to Mario."

"I can talk to him here," Logan said, rimming his glass with his finger. "Or I can cuff him and haul him down to the station." He frowned thoughtfully, as if considering. "Still a lot of reporters hanging around there. Hungry guys. Looking for a story. But it's your choice."

"You're a pig, Logan."

"And you're a liar." He leveled his gaze at the shorter man in the expensive suit. "So what else is new?"

Polidori dropped the receiver and straightened his jacket. Logan could almost see the wheels turning in his mind. God, it felt good to make the bastard sweat a little.

"If Mario cooperates here, I probably won't have to run him in. If not—" Logan lifted his huge shoulders and watched Polidori over the rim of his glass. The whiskey was expensive. Smooth and warm, it burned a familiar and welcome path to his stomach. "—Well, it wouldn't look too good in the society papers if all that old trash about your son was brought up again." He smiled into his glass. "Scandals have a way of raising their ugly heads time and time again. People in this town have long memories."

Polidori's eyes narrowed just a fraction. "You'll keep this quiet?"

"I might be a pig, but I don't lie."

With a snort of disbelief, Polidori dropped into an oxblood chair, pressed a buzzer hidden in the drawer of his desk, and a guard appeared. After a rapid-fire exchange of Italian in which Mario's name was repeated several times, the guard slipped away. Logan sipped his drink. Within minutes, Mario appeared in the doorway.

About twenty-six, he was taller than his father by a full head and his eyes were a lighter shade of brown. Curly dark hair, easy smile—the playboy son of the rich father. When he wasn't racing cars, or sailing the Caribbean, Mario ran the family restaurant downtown. And he was edgy. A restless energy kept him moving. Drugs? Adrenaline? Or plain old, kick-you-in-the-gut fear?

Anthony motioned toward Logan's chair. "You know Detective Sergeant Logan."

"We've met," Mario said, his gaze flicking toward Logan for only a second. Logan didn't bother to get up.

"He thinks you might know something about the Danvers kidnapping."

"In your dreams, Jack," Mario said, resting a jean-encased hip against the edge of the desk. His foot never stopped bouncing nervously. "I was in Hawaii."

"You know Joey Siri and Rudy Gianotti."

"They used to work for me."

"Doing what?"

"Whatever I asked," Mario said with a charming smile of even white teeth. "Mainly odd jobs down at the restaurant. I fired Rudy six months ago—he was into drugs, uppers and downers. Caught him dealing and cut him loose. Joey had a fit, claimed he wouldn't stick around if I let Rudy go. So I fired him, too." He shoved away from the desk, moved to the window. Avoided the policeman's gaze.

"That was it? You've never seen them again?" Logan finished his drink.

Mario lifted a shoulder. "I've seen them around. Some of the guys who work for me know 'em, but Rudy and Joey stay clear and I like it that way."

"You know Zach Danvers claimed they attacked him?"

Mario's shoulders bunched. "Zach Danvers lies."

"Not this time." Logan pretended interest in his empty glass. "Rumor had it that you and Trisha Danvers were . . . well, involved."

Almost imperceptibly, the corners around the younger Polidori's mouth tightened. "I know her."

"The way I heard it, you knocked her up."

"What's your point, Logan?" Mario's eyes snapped with an inner fury as dark as hell. Despite all his wealth, the boy carried one helluva chip on his muscular shoulders.

"Somehow Danvers put a stop to it. Wouldn't let his daughter be seen with a Polidori. Made sure she never had the kid." Logan set his empty glass on the desk.

"Is that so?"

"I don't know all the details, but I'm looking into them. My guess is you've got plenty of motive to get back at Witt Danvers."

"Lots of people in this town would like to see Danvers go down," Anthony said from his position behind the desk.

Logan lifted a bushy eyebrow. "Some more than others."

"I was in Hawaii. On business. At the time of the attack on Zach Danvers. I was—"

"I know, sipping Mai Tais on the beach in Waikiki." Logan set his glass on the desk. "But somehow Joey and Rudy messed up Zach Danvers and at the same time his kid sister and nanny were abducted."

"My money's still on Zachary." Mario's smile had turned cold. He shifted on the desk. "It's no secret that Zach hates

Witt. If you ask me, he staged the whole thing about the attack against him to get back at his father. If you want to find out what happened to London, talk to Zach."

"You think Dad would go to this much trouble if anyone else had been abducted?" Trisha demanded, her blue eyes cloudy with anger. "No way. He's in a state because it's London!"

Zach didn't want to hear it. Stretched out on a chaise near the pool, he closed his eyes behind the lenses of his sunglasses and wished Trisha would just go away. No such luck. She set up her easel in the shade from the old-growth fir trees that towered along the brick wall rimming the grounds. Sunlight dappled the grass and reflected off the water as Trisha adjusted a three-legged stool, trying to catch the right light.

The day was sweltering. Heat rose in waves that shimmered off the concrete near the pool house. Zach's head throbbed and his shoulder ached. He was recovering, but slowly. He grabbed his can of Coke and smiled to himself because he'd had the foresight to pour "the real thing" out of the can and fill it with Colt 45 malt liquor from a bottle he'd taken from the refrigerator. He'd probably get caught, but he really didn't care. He took a long swallow of the ale and felt it cool against the back of his throat. In a few minutes, he'd relax. In the meantime he'd ignore his sister.

"Dad's fit to be tied because the police and the FBI can't find out who's behind it," she said, smudging her charcoal drawing with the tip of her finger. "He wants to blame the Polidoris just because those two guys who attacked you worked for them once."

Why was she bothering him? Zach had only been home from the hospital for four days and this was the first time he'd ventured out of his room. He'd decided to rest by the pool because the four walls were closing in on him and he was going out of his mind staring at posters of Jimi Hendrix and Ali McGraw.

"Mom called the other day to see how you were doing . . . but you were sleeping or something."

He didn't want to think about his mother. Eunice. Some mother she'd turned out to be. *A mother shouldn't admit this, Zach, but you've always been my favorite.* Her words still echoed in his mind. His chest was suddenly tight and he had trouble saying, "She stopped by the hospital."

"And you wouldn't talk to her."

"Nothin' to say."

"Christ, Zach, you can be such a prick," Trisha said, frowning at the image on her easel.

"Family trait."

"Be serious."

"I am." If she only knew. He reached onto the table and flipped on his transistor radio, hoping that music, hard rock, would drive her away. The radio crackled with static before he found a station blasting an old Rolling Stones hit. The throbbing beat of "Satisfaction" echoed over the aquamarine water.

"I can't get no . . . no, no, no, no . . ."

"I can't hear myself think with that blaring at me!"

He didn't respond. He didn't give a damn if she was stone deaf, he just hoped she'd quit yammering at him. He needed to be left alone. And he didn't want to think about his mother. Or London. Or anything. He took another gulp of the brew. Most of the time he felt that everyone, including Trisha, was pumping him for information about the kidnapping, as if they could make him slip up and admit that he'd taken the kid. But why? And how? And where?

He didn't trust anyone named Danvers. Maybe there was some truth about Polidori blood running through his veins, he thought with a sarcastic grimace. Wouldn't that be something—if he really turned out to be Anthony Polidori's son after all these years? It would explain a helluva lot—why he was Eunice's favorite, for crying out loud. But he didn't like the idea. Not a bit. It was true that Witt was a class A-1 bastard, no doubt about it, but Polidori was no better. For years the police had tried to connect him to organized crime.

"Turn that thing off!" Trisha screamed.

Zach ignored her request. "They have any luck trying to track down Ginny Slade's relatives?" he asked. Jason had told him how they'd torn the nanny's room apart. She seemed to be the key in the kidnapping. Her references had proved false and her family had all but disappeared.

"Not that I know." Trisha angled her head, wrinkling her nose as she eyed her work. "But no one thinks she was in on it, otherwise she would have demanded money. And her checking account hasn't been touched. Still has a couple of hundred dollars in it. She's got savings, too, over at First National, I think. Nearly a thousand dollars. Still there."

"How do you know so much?"

Trisha glanced at him a second. "I listen. At keyholes and open doors and air shafts."

For the first time, Zach was interested in what his sister had learned. For years he'd thought Trisha totally self-absorbed. He assumed that she didn't care about anything other than herself, her manicure, and her latest boyfriend or a new mind-expanding high. Though lately, come to think of it, she hadn't gone out much. After the fiasco with Mario Polidori . . . Zach squinted at his sister. She was pretty, he supposed, with her thick reddish-brown hair and blue eyes. She wore too much makeup and her clothes too tight, but there was something about her that was appealing. For the most part, though, she was a pain in the ass.

At twenty, she was still taking art classes, had moved out of the house three or four times and had always returned with a broken heart, busted for drugs, or flat broke. Sometimes all three. The drug busts—mainly marijuana and once in a while a little hash—were handled discreetly and without arrest by good ol' Detective Jack of the Portland police, and Witt had always covered her bad checks and escalating credit card balances. The broken hearts weren't so easily mended. Trisha

had a long track record of picking losers. Including Mario
Polidori.

No matter what the circumstances of her latest source of
rebellion, Trisha always returned—tail between her legs, fingers stretched toward Daddy's wallet. Zach figured it was
because the world, with its demand of rent and electricity payments, was too difficult for his sister. She was better off
having Daddy pay the bills.

He leaned back in the chaise and regarded her. Already, she
had a pinched set to her mouth that reminded him of his
mother. In the past few years, ever since the Polidori mess, Trisha had changed. Zach didn't know exactly what had
happened between Mario and her, but he'd heard arguments
that had reverberated through the timbers of the old house
and Zach had guessed that Mario Polidori had used his sister
to get back at Witt. Trisha had been an innocent, but more
than willing, accomplice in the war of hate that had existed
between the families for nearly a century. The feud didn't
seem to be stopping anytime soon. Not that Zach cared.

"You know, Zach," Trisha said, spinning her easel around
so he could see her work, a caricature of him as a laid-up, unshaven, generally slovenly teenager lying on a chaise lounge
and swilling Coke. A blaring radio and can of Colt 45 were
propped on a nearby table. "You'd better be careful."

"Very funny," he remarked, pointing at her picture.

"I'm not the only one who can see through you, you know."
She stuffed her charcoal back in its box. "Kat and Dad,
they're on to you. There's a lot of talk about boarding school
or sending you off to the ranch to and I quote, 'work his butt
off and keep him out of trouble.' "

"No way," he responded. He gazed up at the thin clouds
moving in from the west.

"Any way you look at it, boarding school or shoveling shit
at the Lazy M beats MacLaren," she said, mentioning the
Oregon school for underage male criminals.

"Is that where they think I'll end up?"

"I don't know what they think, but it's my guess, Zach. You haven't exactly been easy to live with since you got out of the hospital and that stunt with the reporters—"

He grinned, rubbing the swollen knuckles of his fist with his other hand.

"—you're not winning friends."

"The guy deserved it." Zach could still hear questions, see the cameras pointed at him as he'd tried to get out of Witt's Lincoln and away from the reporter who had appeared from behind the hedge.

"Can you explain why you were attacked on the night your half-sister—"

He'd reacted and his fist had slammed into the guy's jaw with a bone-jarring crunch. Blood had spurted. Pain had ricocheted up Zach's arm and the man had fallen, groaning to the ground. There was already talk of a lawsuit.

Now, as if reading her brother's thoughts, Trisha sighed and gathered up her easel.

"You think I kidnapped London?" he asked, telling himself he didn't care one way or the other.

Shaking hear head and staring pointedly at the scar that still edged his face, she said, "I don't know what you did that night, but you're not telling the truth . . . not all of it, and you're going to end up taking the blame for this one unless you come clean."

The muscles in the back of his neck tightened because he'd thought the same thing. "Since when are you the goddess of virtue?" He took another gulp of beer, drained the Coke can and crumpled it in his fist.

Trisha pinned him with eyes that had seen too much pain for so short a life. "You don't know anything about me, Zach. You've never even tried to get to know me, have you? Look, I was just trying to do you a favor, but forget it." She headed back to the house. "I made a mistake. It's your funeral."

* * *

Katherine's eyelids stuck together. Her mouth tasted like she'd been licking an ashtray and her head pounded above her temples. She forced one eye open and sunlight streaming through a partially open window, nearly blinded her. Groaning, she rolled over and wondered about the sadness that was a horrible weight on her heart.

She was in her own bedroom and . . . Oh, God . . . the reality came crashing back to her fragile brain. London was gone, abducted nearly two—or was it three?—weeks before. Desperation, like the horrid beast it was, clawed at her from the inside. She needed a cigarette. With numb fingers she reached to the bed table and found an empty pack of Virginia Slims, which she flung onto the floor. Tears flooded her eyes. She couldn't take this, day after day. The bumbling policemen, the useless FBI, and the media. Damn the media. The few reporters who had gotten past the guards had asked questions that made her heart bleed and the fire in their eyes, all looking for a story, and insensitive to her pain . . . No wonder Zach had punched out a reporter and broken a photographer's camera as he'd returned to the house from the hospital.

She stood on unsteady legs, then drew the drapes open a little farther. Two squad cars and a plain, stripped-down Chevrolet were scattered on the circular drive. Farther away, past the sloping front lawns and tended rose gardens, she caught a glimpse of the front gates where the vultures gathered. Two or three cars were parked in the shade of an ancient oak that spread its branches over the brick wall which kept the scavengers at bay.

"I hope you all rot in hell," she muttered, letting the drapes fall back into place.

What time was it? Bleary eyes focused on the clock. Two in the afternoon. She'd slept seventeen hours, drugged by Doc McHenry's sleeping pills and God-only-knew what else. Somehow, some way, she'd have to pull herself together. With or without London.

That thought caused her knees to buckle and she grasped

the edge of the bureau to steady herself. She'd find her baby. She had to. She couldn't trust the federal government or the police, and Witt, well, he hadn't been much help. The fact that he would no longer sleep with her, insisting that she needed her rest, bothered her. She knew the real reason. He was afraid that she would require more than a pat on the head, that she might need a kiss, a hug, even her husband to make love to her to comfort her.

God, she needed a cigarette.

Running her tongue over filmy teeth, she forced herself into the bathroom, where she stripped off the nightgown that she'd worn for days and turned on the shower. Before stepping under the hot spray, she got a glimpse of her reflection and cringed. No makeup, hair lank, her once-curvy body beginning to look gaunt from lack of food. Hazily she remembered Maria, the cook, coming into her room, trying to force soup of some kind down her throat.

In all her life, Katherine had never once let herself go; she believed that her greatest commodity was her body and she spent hours in the gym, with a masseuse, at the hairdresser, having her nails manicured. Her clothes were always flattering—a little sexy, but classy and pressed.

But now she looked like hell.

She stepped into the warm spray and let the hot water run over her hair and skin. Closing her eyes against the dark depression that settled over her whenever she thought of London, she leaned against the slick tiles. She couldn't let this get her down because she was London's only chance. If she gave up on her daughter, everyone else would as well.

Sobs burned deep in her throat and, telling herself that she could allow herself the freedom to cry, to grieve a little by herself, she let the tears drizzle down her cheeks, their salty tracks mingling with the rivulets from the shower as the steam billowed around her.

As long as she was alone, she could wail and scream and

gnash her teeth in frustration, but when she was with the others, then she had to pretend to be strong.

An hour later she'd made it downstairs. Her hair was washed, blown dry and brushed until it shined, her teeth were polished, her makeup impeccable, her shorts and top a blue that matched her eyes. She grabbed some orange juice from the refrigerator, ignored Maria's pleas that she eat breakfast, and found out that Witt and the police were holed up in the den with strict orders not to be disturbed. Fine. Turning her back to Maria, she splashed a couple of shots of vodka into her juice, swallowed two double-strength Excedrin, reached for a new pack of cigarettes, and tucked the *Wall Street Journal* under her arm.

She was ready, or so she thought, but the intensity of the daylight made her reach for the sunglasses she kept in a drawer near the French doors. Outside, there wasn't a breath of breeze and the sun beat mercilessly against the cement and brick that skirted the pool.

She heard a noise, glanced up, and realized, as she passed by the ferns and rhododendrons flanking the path, that Zachary was swimming laps. He knifed through the water like an athlete and his wounds, still visible against his tanned skin, had healed enough to allow him easy, even strokes.

A knot of something akin to desire unwound in Katherine's stomach. Of all of Witt's children, Zachary held the most appeal. He didn't look like the rest of the Danvers brood—his skin was a darker shade, he was more muscular in build, and his eyes were a stormy gray rather than the clear blue that seemed to be a Danvers trademark.

His nose wasn't straight and arrogant like Witt's, but Katherine had decided that was because it had been broken at least three times—once recently on that horrid night when London was abducted, once during a motorcycle accident, and another time during a fistfight in junior high. The kid had been twice Zach's size but had left with two black eyes and a swollen cock when Zach's pointed boot had connected with the kid's groin. Zach had gotten the worst of it; not only had his nose been broken but his ribs as well, and the boy's father, a lawyer, had threatened to sue. Fortunately, Witt had bought him off—which was exactly what the lawyer-father had hoped for.

Irreverent and sexy as hell, Zach was attractive on more than one level. Katherine dropped onto a chaise lounge, propped up her feet, and watched her stepson glide through the water. Sleek, sinewy muscles, damp and gleaming in the sunlight, moved effortlessly. She wondered if his skin was tanned everywhere or if, beneath the ragged cutoffs, his buttocks were a lighter shade.

Since she'd taken her marriage vows, Katherine had never been unfaithful to Witt. Even in the past few years when he'd all but stopped trying to make love to her, she'd ignored the desire that curled restlessly through her blood when she saw a particularly interesting male. She'd had opportunities, plenty of them over the years—some suggested by Witt's closest friends—but she'd laughed off the passes as if they were bad jokes and never given in to the lust that had some nights nearly driven her mad.

But she was tempted by Zachary. No doubt about it. She wasn't alone. He could protest it as loudly as he wanted, but he was attracted to her. The last time they'd been together, when her temper had gotten the better of her and she'd forced him to dance with her at Witt's party, she'd felt the hardness between his legs, saw the stain of embarrassment on his cheeks, knew that he'd responded to her.

Stop it! He's Witt son, for crying out loud! Your stepson! With shaking fingers she peeled the cellophane from her pack of cigarettes, shook out a Virginia Slim, and lit up. He didn't look her way, didn't acknowledge that she was near the pool, just kept swimming as if he would never stop.

Blowing smoke to the sky, she tried to turn her thoughts away from her secret attraction to Zach. However, if she wasn't considering his seduction, her mind turned back to

London and the deep depression that enveloped her whenever she thought of her little girl. Where was she? Still alive? Huddled and scared? Or dead already, brutally murdered? Oh, God, she couldn't think about that. She wouldn't! "London," she whispered, her eyes filling with sudden tears again.

She took a long sip from the cool orange juice and hoped the vodka would calm her nerves. If only someone would hold her, place strong arms around her, whisper in her ear that everything would be all right . . . that London was safe and would be returning home. The inside of her chest seemed to cave in on itself.

She needed someone. Anyone. Zach.

Gritting her teeth against the mind-paralyzing fear that had been her constant companion for weeks, she snapped the paper open and pretended interest in the bond market when all the while she watched Zach over the top of the newspaper. Her eyes were hidden by her sunglasses and she was certain that Zach didn't know that as she stared at him, she was beginning to plan his seduction.

Zach's lungs burned and his shoulder was beginning to ache. He'd been in the pool fifteen minutes, hoping Kat would finish her drink and leave, but he'd had no such luck. It looked as if she'd parked herself indefinitely. He was relieved she'd finally emerged. It was weird for her to be locked in her room, hardly venturing out.

But then, these days, everything at the house was weird. The cops and FBI, the reporters clustered around the gates, Witt's quiet rage and Kat's isolation. Jason had moved back to the house and paced like a caged animal; Nelson, after following him around for a few days, had holed up in his room.

Zach didn't trust anyone and thought people were always staring at him, as if he had any idea what had happened to London and the damned nanny.

Surfacing, he tossed the water from his hair and took in a

huge gulp of air. He hoisted himself out of the pool and stood dripping because his towel was at the other end, near Kat, and ever since the party he'd wanted to avoid her. He was uncomfortable around her, partly because being near her reminded him of his fear for London, but partly because he was embarrassed about what had happened on the dance floor that night. He was even more humiliated because Kat knew that he'd gone to a hooker. A whore. Like he had to pay for it!

He'd had plenty of chances with girls his age, but he hadn't been interested in some giggling ninny who would let him touch her tits in exchange for his class ring or some such garbage. Girls were always looking to fall in love and he wasn't interested. He didn't believe in love and knew he never would love anyone. His parents and his siblings had convinced him that love was a foolish notion. It just plain didn't exist.

The cement was hot against the bottoms of his feet as he jogged the length of the pool and snatched up his towel. He was still sore and knew with his bruises and scar, he looked like hell.

Kat glanced up and offered him a blinding smile that caused his diaphragm to slam into his lungs. "You're feeling better," he said weakly, knowing she expected conversation.

"Yeah."

She lifted her sunglasses to squint up at him. God, she was beautiful. Her lips were a slick, glossy pink and her cheekbones were carved gently. Standing above her, he could see down the column of her throat and lower still to the deep cleft between her breasts. Her tan line, faded somewhat, was still visible and if she moved just the right way, he was certain he'd catch a glimpse of her nipples. "No permanent damage?" she asked, as if she really cared.

"Looks that way." He swiped the towel over his face and through his hair, trying to ignore the raw sensuality that seemed to radiate from her. Hell, why was she looking at him like that?

"That's good. I was worried about you." She stretched and

the motion seemed somehow feline in the hot sun. A hot summer breeze kissed the back of his neck.

"Were you?" He didn't believe her and he was suddenly wary.

She swallowed and licked her lips. Somewhere in the house a door slammed. "Yes . . . there's so much that's happened, some of it so awful." Tears moistened her eyes and for the life of him he felt sorry for her. "Anyway, I know I've treated you badly—that display at the hotel was uncalled for. I was drunk and angry and . . . oh, God, Zach . . . I'm making a mess of this, but I just wanted you to know that I'm sorry."

"Forget it," he said, feeling his face turning a darker shade of red.

"I will. If you'll forgive me."

Jesus, what was going on here? He cleared his throat and glanced at the shadows shifting beneath the trees. "Sure."

"Thanks." Again the smile, though this time there were teardrops drizzling down her cheeks and he realized how devastated she was about the loss of her child.

He felt awkward and stupid for even thinking about her in any way sexual. She was grieving, for Christ's sake. Nervously, he knotted the towel in his hands. "I . . . uh, look, don't worry about London. She'll turn up."

"You think so?" She sounded so hopeful.

Did he do that—give her a sense of false hope about a poor little girl who might already be dead? He felt absolutely wretched. "I dunno, but . . . everybody's looking for her . . ." It sounded lame, even to his own ears, and he noticed the ghost of pain crossing her eyes. Hell, he was just no good at this!

She reached up and grabbed his hand with hers. Heat swirled up his arm. "I hope so, Zach," she whispered, blinking hard as her fingers tightened over his. A jolt of electricity kicked his heart into high gear. She looked so young suddenly, so vulnerable and small. He had to remind himself that this was Kat. "God, I hope so." She used his arm as a brace and climbed to her feet, her body only inches from his. He barely noticed the lingering pain from his beating.

To his utter amazement, she stood on her tiptoes and brushed a chaste kiss over his cheek. "Thanks for understanding, Zach. I needed a friend." He turned his face, staring into her eyes, feeling her moist, smoky breath against his skin, half expecting her to kiss him again, but she smiled sadly and let go of his arm, then picked up her things and walked back to the house.

He was left standing by the pool, dripping, and wondering what the hell had just gone on.

Pain, as hot as if it erupted straight from the bowels of hell, shot through Witt's chest. For a second he couldn't breathe. It was as if someone had locked their fingers over his throat and was strangling him. Where were the pills? He yanked open the desk drawer and saw the vial in the pencil rack. Agony tore at his heart as he managed to retrieve the nitroglycerin pills and shove one under his tongue. He was nearly gasping now and waiting, his elbows propped on the leather desk pad, his head resting in his palms. Sweat broke out over his forehead and the damned intercom began to buzz impatiently. He didn't answer and knew that Shirley, his secretary of more than twenty years, would get the message.

The buzzer stopped and five minutes later, he was collected again—the angina had passed and he straightened his tie. No one save McHenry knew about his condition and he planned on keeping his secret to himself. Witt hated weakness and this heart condition was just that . . . a sign that he wasn't as strong as he once had been.

He reached for his humidor, opened the lid, and the heavy scent of Havana tobacco wafted to his nostrils. He grabbed a cigar, wedged it between his teeth, but didn't light up. Not now. Not after the angina attack.

He pushed the intercom button, learned that Roger Phelps

was waiting in the reception area of the offices of Danvers International, and growled at Shirley to show him in. Disgusted, he didn't bother lighting up though he longed for a few relaxing lungfuls of smoke.

Within minutes Phelps was seated on the opposite side of Witt's desk. He looked like Joe Average. Tan slacks, brown jacket, off-white shirt, and nondescript, department-store tie. His face wasn't noteworthy, just even features with the beginnings of jowls that matched the paunch developing at his belt line. Witt was more than a little disappointed in the man who had supposedly been an agent with the CIA before dropping out of the government to do independent work.

"What can I do for you, Mr. Danvers?" Phelps said in a nasal voice. He hiked up his pants a bit and Witt noticed that his shoes—cheap loafers, from the looks of them—were scuffed.

"You must've guessed why I wanted you. My daughter, London, was kidnapped. The police and FBI are incompetent jerks. Don't have a clue where my daughter is and it's been damned close to a month."

Phelps didn't comment.

"You come highly recommended."

A lift of a shoulder.

Witt was growing irritated. "Tell me why I should pay you when the government and the police seem to be baffled?"

Phelps's expression changed slightly and Witt was reminded of a wolf with his nose to the wind, scenting a wounded doe. "Simple. You want her found."

"And you can do that?" Witt settled back in his chair. Maybe there were more layers to Phelps than met the eye.

"If I don't, you owe me nothing besides my retainer."

"Of ten thousand dollars."

"Cheap, isn't it?" He set his untouched coffee on the edge of Witt's desk. "All I ask is that your family comes clean with me. No secrets. No lies. No skeletons tucked into closets."

"Fair enough. You can question everyone here while we're

still in Portland, but you may as well know that I'm moving them—even the older kids—to the ranch near Bend. I'm not going to chance losing another one. Zachary—" He scowled when he thought of his middle son. Always the rebel. Always cocksure. Always in trouble. "—he's going first, but he doesn't know it yet. The rest of the family will follow in a couple of weeks. So you'd better start with him."

"He's the one with the phony story about the hooker."

Witt's back went up. "The story was true. The police talked to the girl . . . Sophia something or other."

"Costanzo. I already spoke with her."

Witt moved the unsmoked cigar from one side of his mouth to the other. "What'd she say?"

"Same thing she said to the police. Not much. Gives your kid his alibi, but I have the feeling she's lying."

"A feeling?" Witt was skeptical.

"Believe me, she's not telling everything she knows." He smiled grimly. "But that won't be a problem. I'll handle her. And as for Zach, I'll talk to him, see what he says—maybe he'll slip up. I'll catch everyone else before you send them packing." He pulled out a notepad from the inner pocket of his jacket, scribbled quickly, then frowned slightly, wrinkles lining his brow. "What about your wife? Can I reach her here or is she going to the ranch with your kids?"

Witt hesitated just a second. He'd been wrestling with this decision, but he couldn't put it off any longer. She needed to get away. "Katherine will be at the ranch." Why sending her to central Oregon was a relief to him, he didn't understand, but he hoped the change of scenery would do her some good.

Phelps cocked his head at an angle. "And you?"

"I've got a business to run, Phelps." Already the man was getting on his nerves. "You can reach me here."

"Good." Phelps folded his hands over his thickening girth. "There's only one thing I want from you, Danvers, and that's honesty, from you and your family."

"You've got it," Witt agreed, anxious for the interview to

be over. This blend-into-the-woodwork guy was giving him a case of the creeps, but Witt needed him. He needed someone to help him find London. The police were beginning to look like a bunch of bumbling idiots and the FBI wasn't any better. A darkness settled into his soul and he wondered if he was being punished. He didn't much believe in God, though he attended church, but he'd committed more than his share of sins.

"But maybe you don't really get it," Phelps said, cutting into his thoughts. He leaned forward and pinned Witt with eyes that had suddenly come alive. "If I find out that a member of your family is behind this, then I expect to be paid anyway."

"You will be," Witt agreed, though his collar seemed to tighten around his throat like one of those chains you slip around the neck of a guard dog.

Phelps managed a phony grin and Witt felt as if he'd pulled on that invisible chain. "Good. Just so we understand each other."

10

A dry wind blew across the stubble of the fields, bringing dust and chaff and the thin smell of diesel from the tractor rumbling along the hillside beyond a ragged copse of pine trees. Digging in the heels of his boots, Zach stretched the barbed wire between the posts, his muscles straining with the effort. Sweat stained the red bandanna he'd rolled and tied around his head. The sun was relentless, but Zach didn't care.

"Hang in there," Manny, the ranch foreman called. "Hold tight and I'll tie 'er off."

For the first time in weeks, Zach felt free. His wounds had nearly healed and he loved the ranch, three thousand acres northwest of Bend in central Oregon. Sheltered by the eastern foothills of the Cascade Mountains, the Danvers spread stretched as far as the eye could see. Unlike the brick-walled fortress of the Danvers home in the west hills of Portland, the Lazy M was wild and open and touched the vagabond spirit of Zach's soul.

He'd been sent here just after being interrogated by Roger Phelps, some sort of private eye his father had hired. The detective was patient, talking slowly, luring Zach into saying things he hadn't intended. Zach had left the interview feeling as if Phelps considered him a prime suspect in London's kidnapping. He'd thought about telling the truth, but couldn't see what good it would have done to rat on Jason about the whore. Who cared? One incident wasn't related to the other.

Zach had his own moral code, loose though it may be. One thing he never did was snitch.

After the interview with Phelps, he'd been shipped out here. Witt had figured that long hours working on the ranch, bucking hay, stretching fence line, herding cattle, and wearing himself out in the saddle would be good for him, better than the dreaded boarding school that had been a constant threat ever since London had disappeared. Witt had told his son that he thought the endless hours of work would keep him out of trouble, and Zach hadn't argued. He'd wanted out of the house, away from the suspicious glances thrown in his direction by everyone in the family, far from the distraction of his stepmother and nowhere near the cops. Jack Logan, like Roger Phelps, seemed to think he was guilty of all kinds of crimes.

If they only knew. ✒

Sure, he'd had his trouble with the law. He'd been caught as a minor in possession of alcohol more times than he'd like to admit, and he'd stolen the hearse from the local funeral home and gone joyriding, leaving the funeral director and a grieving family fit to be tied. Witt had been forced to do some fast talking on that one so that Zach, though underage, hadn't been charged with grand theft auto. He'd been expelled from school for blowing up the faculty room john and he'd been in his share of fights and motorcycle accidents—some before he'd gotten his license.

Hell on wheels, Jack Logan had called him on more than one occasion.

Jason had stood up for his younger brother. "It's just a phase, a kid sort of thing," he'd told their father. "He's rebelling a little, that's all. No big deal. Let him do his thing."

Kat had seemed amused. "I bet you did your own bit of hell-raising in your time, Witt," she'd said when Witt, in a fury over the hearse incident, looked as if he'd wanted to strangle the boy he'd raised as his second son.

Nelson, each time Zach was returned home in the middle

of the night, handcuffed and bleeding from some fight, had wanted all the intimate details and followed Zach around for days after, telling Zach how he hoped his brother had "kicked ass."

Only Trisha had said nothing, smiling as if she were glad Zach was taking the heat instead of her.

Yeah, he'd been trouble for his folks and he didn't really give a shit. That bothered Witt the worst, that Zach had no direction, no drive. At least Trisha had her art and Jason was going to be the best damned lawyer in the entire Northwest, but Zach had no ambition, no focus, didn't seem interested in the hotel business, or the timber business, or anything remotely connected with Danvers International.

But Zach did love the ranch.

And he had nothing to do with the kidnapping. Why didn't anyone believe him?

Sure, London had been a pain and Witt had spoiled her rotten, but, truth to tell, Zach had liked the little kid who could get away with anything just by smiling impishly up at her father while her blue eyes twinkled as if with a private secret. Anyone who could manipulate the old man was someone Zach respected. Even if she was only a precocious four-year-old.

He was sorry she was gone and had to keep his mind from wandering too far toward the murky thoughts of what had become of her. He, for one, had written her off as dead. Or else whoever kidnapped her wasn't going to let her go—not after so long.

"Okay, that should do it!" Manny tested his post, and, satisfied that this section of fence would stand, gave Zach the high sign. "It's Friday. Let's call it a day."

Zach checked his watch. Five-fifteen. Since he'd been at the ranch, a little over a week now, Manny hadn't let him off work until eight at night. The routine had been the same. Dog tired, Zach had returned to the house each night, washed, eaten, and fallen asleep before nine, so that he would be ready for a new day starting at five the next morning.

He stripped off his bandanna, wiped the sweat and grime from his face, and walked to the shady banks of the creek where he'd left his horse after lunch. He could've ridden in the dusty cab of the truck, or even sat on the flatbed as it bounced along the rutted dirt roads of the ranch, but he preferred the horses and this one, Cyclone, was his favorite. A headstrong sorrel colt with four white stockings who was known to kick and bite, Cyclone was the fastest horse on the ranch.

"Come on, boy," he said, hoisting the blanket and saddle onto the colt's back. "It's time."

Ears back, the horse shifted and kicked but Zach was quick enough to dodge the blow and tighten the cinch. "You're a mean son of a bitch, aren't you?" He swung into the saddle and yanked on the reins. "Well, that's all right by me, 'cause I am, too. Hiya!" Heels pressed into the colt's sides, he leaned forward in the saddle and Cyclone took off. Wind streamed through Zach's hair and brought tears to his eyes. Spindly jack pine and red-barked ponderosa pine trees flashed by in a blur and once again Zach felt wild and free—as if he could do anything he damned well pleased.

He didn't miss his siblings. Jason would sell his soul to the devil for a small amount of cash, while Trisha was rebelling in the best way she knew how—by getting involved with Mario Polidori, son of Witt's old nemesis, yet again. Obviously she didn't subscribe to the "once burned, twice shy," theory. There were whispers that she was into drugs, though Zach had seen no evidence of it. As for Nelson—the kid was a pain—plain and simple. Ever since the kidnapping, Nelson had puppy-dogged after Zach, wanting to hear over and over again about the hooker and the thugs with the knife—like Zach was some kind of war hero. It bothered Zach because Nelson was a little on the soft side, his adoration a little too intense.

But London, she was another matter. He closed his mind to all thoughts of her, preferring to be numb rather than think about the horrors his little half-sister might have endured. "Come on," he yelled at the colt.

Zach kicked the sorrel and the horse responded without a second's hesitation, gathering speed like a comet streaking across the sky, approaching the ravine where the creek slashed through the field. Massive muscles bunched, then lengthened, and horse and rider were soaring across the rock-strewn chasm where only a thin stream of water trickled.

The colt landed with a thud on the pebble-strewn bank and, with renewed energy upon sight of the stables, ran flat out across the yellow stubble of the pasture. Grasshoppers and pheasants, wings flapping in a frenzy, were flushed from the straw.

Zach leaned low over the sorrel's neck and urged the horse ever faster. Cyclone took the bit between his teeth, his legs flashing over the cracked earth. Wind screamed past his ears and sweat darkened the horse's coat. Laughing for the first time in weeks, Zach yelled, "Move, you miserable hunk of horseflesh."

Only when they were near the paddock did Zach pull back on the reins, wrestling control from the headstrong beast. "Slow down," he growled, standing in the stirrups. By the time they entered the paddock, the colt had switched from a gallop to a trot and finally into a reluctant walk. Cyclone tossed his head, his bridle jangling as he fought the demanding demon on his back.

"You did good," Zach said. Cyclone was blowing hard and Zach kept him moving, walking slowly, until the colt's breathing was normal again. "That's better."

Zach didn't see Trisha watching him, didn't notice her lurking in the shadows of the scrub pine until he'd reined up at the fence and she climbed onto the top rail. With a sinking sensation, he knew he'd have to deal with his family again and suddenly his wings seemed clipped. All the old anger and resentiment welled up in him and the ranch that had moments before appeared so vast quickly became confining and small.

"This place is a prison!" Trisha said as she pushed aside a long-needled branch encroaching over the fence.

"What're you doing here?" But he knew. They were all here. For good.

"Family vacation," she said with more than a trace of sarcasm. Her nose wrinkled when she saw the horseflies gathering near the colt's rump. The smells of manure mixed with urine, sweat, and dust apparently offended her. "Believe me, I tried to talk Dad out of it, but you know how he is when he makes a decision."

"Humph." Zach swung down from the horse's back.

"In a way, I understand. Dad's tired of everyone just sitting around and waiting for the phone to ring at the house in town—even the police and the feds. Doing nothing!"

Zach remembered.

"Dad said we were all getting on his nerves—now, there's something new," she added sarcastically.

Zach didn't respond.

"Anyway, I think he was worried about another kidnapping."

"No way." Zach hauled the saddle off the horse and hung it over the top rail of the fence. "Aren't you the one who pointed out that he wouldn't care if one of us was abducted? Just London."

Trisha pouted.

"You know, if I turned up missing, I think he might buy a bottle of expensive champagne and have himself a celebration."

"He's not that bad," she said without much conviction, then catching Zach's steady gaze, sighed. "Okay, so he is that bad. Anyway, it doesn't matter why he sent us here—the fact of the matter is that we're all stuck in this godforsaken place."

"Is that so?"

"Including Kat."

Zach's stomach dropped a little, but he managed to keep his face from registering the slightest trace of emotion. "She'll hate it here," he said flatly.

"Already does." Plucking a few needles from the branch near her head, she sighed and twirled the sprig between her fingers. "You should have heard their fight. It reminded me of Mom and Dad before they split up. Kat put up a battle, I'll give her that, but despite her excruciatingly loud protests against being shipped out of Portland, she wound up here, with the rest of us, and that really pissed her off. She wanted to stay close to the investigation and I thought she might grab Dad's .22 and put a bullet through him before she'd leave town. But, of course, Dad got his way." Trisha's eyes clouded and Zach knew she wasn't thinking about Kat any longer.

"He always gets his way."

Trisha glanced up at her brother. "I think Dad had an ulterior motive for shipping her off."

Zach lifted a disinterested eyebrow.

"Kat'll freak, 'cause I think the investigation's winding down. The cops are out of leads and the FBI isn't doing any better. All a bunch of fools with their thumbs rammed up their asses."

"What about Phelps?"

"The private investigator? He's a joke. Have you ever seen anyone so . . . ordinary in your life?" Dropping the pine needles, she dusted her hands and glared up at Zachary as if the situation were all his fault. "It's all a front, anyway. Dad wants to believe that the Polidoris are behind the kidnapping."

"Are they?"

"They're not stupid, Zach. Anthony has to know that he'd be at the top of the suspect list."

Zach wasn't convinced, but he didn't bother to comment. Let Trisha believe what she wanted.

"It's all such a pain. Ever since London disappeared no one can go anywhere without some damned bodyguard prowling around behind."

Zach tied the reins to the second rail of the fence. He wasn't in the mood to listen to his sister's whining. Trisha was just ticked off because she couldn't sneak around meeting Mario Polidori. Both families disapproved of the romance between Mario and Trisha. The only subject the Polidoris and Danverses had agreed upon in the last hundred years was to forbid Mario and Trisha from seeing each other. They were adults, she'd argued, and Witt had told her that she'd better start acting like one and move out, but as far as he was concerned, while she lived under his roof, she'd abide by his rules.

Trisha had other plans. She seemed to think she was some modern-day Juliet and Mario was her Romeo. The thought made Zach sick and he spat on the dusty ground. She should have learned her lesson about Mario Polidori. With a grunt, he grabbed the saddle and slung it over his shoulder to carry it into the stable.

Following him inside, Trisha said, "I thought you and I could work a deal."

Zach sent her a look telling her silently to get lost. He didn't need Trisha's kind of trouble. He had enough of his own. Though he'd gotten a slight reprieve, the old man was still making noise about boarding school and Zach was considering walking through the Danvers gates and never looking over his shoulder.

"C'mon, Zach. I need your help."

Zach swung the saddle over a sawhorse, then dropped the blanket over the top rail of a stall. Dust and horsehair rose in a cloud that clogged the air.

Trisha coughed and Zach swallowed a smile. Served her right. She'd never shown any interest in the horses—she was only here because she wanted something. And badly.

"Okay," she said. "Here's the deal—I need to find a way to sneak out of here. At night."

"Why?"

"It's personal."

"To meet Mario, right?"

"The less you know the better."

"No."

"What?" Her face crumpled into a look of wounded pride. "I stood up for you—"

"How?" he demanded.

"I told Kat that you wouldn't hurt a hair on London's head."

"Thanks for the vote of confidence," he muttered as he yanked the bandanna from his pocket and wiped the sweat from his neck.

"That's more than anyone else did for you, and Kat's still not convinced that you weren't involved somehow. If you were any older everyone would think you were behind it, but since you're only seventeen—"

"Why would I kidnap London?"

"For money," Trisha said slowly and Zach couldn't help his reaction. His head snapped up and his eyes narrowed on his sister.

"Then wouldn't I demand ransom?"

"It's only been a little while."

"So how would I do it? How would I grab Ginny and London and stow them away God-only-knows where while I got myself cut for an alibi. It doesn't make sense, Trisha, and everyone knows it. They're just pointing at me because I was gone that night and there's no one else to blame."

"Tell that to Jack Logan."

"Logan's a jackass. Oh shit, who cares?" Zach stormed outside and unknotted the reins. Cyclone sidestepped and tossed his head as Zach led him into a stall. Muscles knotted in quiet rage, Zach filled a bucket with water and let the colt drink before rubbing him down. "You're way off base, Trisha," he finally said.

Trisha dusted off the burlap and sat gingerly on a sack of oats. Leaning forward, propping her elbows on her knees, she cradled her chin. Her gaze narrowed through the dusty window and she chewed on her lower lip. "Okay, okay, maybe you really shouldn't be the number-one suspect."

"Thanks."

"So who do you think took her?"

"I don't even want to think about it." And that was the truth.

"Well, someone had to."

"Okay, Ginny, then."

"Yeah, but who was she working for?"

"Don't know. Hell, do we have to do this—dredge it all up again?" Zach hated to admit it, but he missed the little kid. True, she'd bugged the hell out of him and tagged after him. More often than not he'd told her gruffly to "get lost," but he worried about her and had trouble sleeping at night just wondering what had happened and if she were all right.

Trisha plucked a piece of straw from the manger. "One word from me and you'd be shit out of luck."

"How's that?" With the currycomb, Zach worked on a knot in the colt's mane.

"I could say that Mario told me you were involved in the kidnapping."

Zach tensed. Where was this going? Slowly, he resumed brushing the horse. "It would be a lie."

"Everyone would believe it. You know, there are still a few rumors floating around about you."

"Can it, Trisha." He'd heard all the gossip and didn't want to be reminded that when he'd been conceived his mother was having an affair with Polidori. His teeth ground together but he just kept working, ignoring Trisha's innuendoes and veiled threats. Christ, what did she want from him?

"It's just that I hate it here, Zach. This is . . . nowhere. I want to go back to Portland."

"You just got here."

"Doesn't matter."

"You want to be close to Mario."

"So what?"

Zach slid her a look that called her stupid. "Get smart, Trisha. It's never gonna work between you and Polidori. Dad'll never approve."

"Since when do you care?"

"I don't. I'm just giving you some free advice."

"Save it."

"Fine." He opened the door at the back of the stable, then let the colt trot outside. With a snort and toss of his head, the horse ran free, bucking and kicking up his heels before lying in the thick dust and rolling. Clouds of dry earth roiled to the sky and the colt grunted in pleasure. Soon all Zach could see of the animal were four white-stockinged legs thrashing madly.

Trisha made a face. "You're not going to help me?"

Zach shook his head. "No way."

She arched a delicate brow and set an expression somewhere between a sneer and smile on her pouty lips. "You'll be sorry."

"Tell me something I don't know." Irritated, he strode out of the stable and wished that the rest of his family would just leave him alone.

It was hours later when Kat found him. The sun had set and Jason had taken Trisha and Nelson into town. Zach, avoiding his family as much as he could, had stolen two beers from the refrigerator and had climbed onto the roof of the tack shed that butted up to the stables. The dark sky was alive with shooting stars and Zach sat alone, his back propped against the rough outer wall of the second story of the stables, his legs stretched out on the sloping cedar shingles. Through the tar paper and split shakes, he heard the muffled sounds of horses, snorting, rustling in the straw, letting out an occasional whinny.

The moon was small, just a sliver, but gave off enough light so he could see the stands of trees flanking the rambling ranch house and outbuildings. The house was lit like a Christmas tree, patches of warm light glowing through the windows. Kat was still awake, prowling the rooms. He caught glimpses of her now and again, moving restlessly from one window to the next, and he decided he wouldn't slip through the French doors to his room until all the lights had been turned down and he knew that she was asleep. So far, he'd avoided her, but he wouldn't be able to sidestep her forever.

He opened a can of Coors and beer foamed over the side. He took a gulp, catching most of the overflow when he heard the old dog let out a quiet bark, then the unmistakable sounds of footsteps walking unerringly to the stable. His heart nearly stopped. Seconds later the rungs of the ladder to the hayloft clicked as someone climbed to the top. Now what?

He smelled the scent of her perfume before he saw her in the open window of the hayloft, her face white, her black hair the color of midnight. His chest felt as if it were suddenly constricted with iron bands.

"Manny said you might be here," she said as casually as if she'd spent all her life creeping around barns and climbing into haymows.

His gut tightened as she slid through the window and stepped onto the roof. Balancing herself with a hand on the roof of the stable, she walked the short distance to his side and slid onto her rear.

The scent of her perfume was stronger as it drifted to his nostrils, and her arm was so close to his that he could feel the heat of her body. He remembered how she'd felt in his arms, supple and pliable and willing . . . Oh, God . . . "What do you want?"

"Company." She offered him a smile. "I thought we were friends."

Off in the distance a coyote howled.

"I don't know if that's possible."

"We could try to be. Especially if you offered me a beer."

Throat so dry it felt like sand, he handed the second can to her, and she, with a smile that flashed in the dark night, popped the tab and giggled when the foam erupted and spilled across her fingers. She lapped it up with her tongue and Zach tried not to notice how sexy she looked with the white flecks on her lips.

"It's beautiful tonight," she said, staring up at the heavens and sighing loudly. "If you like this kind of thing."

"You don't?"

"I'm a city girl." She drank from the beer, then drew her legs up and wrapped her arms over her bare knees. Her shorts barely covered her butt, but Zach tried to keep his eyes and mind on anything but how damnably sensual she was. "Grew up in Ottawa."

He didn't reply, couldn't.

They sat in silence for what seemed forever. Zach's heart was drumming so loudly, he wondered if she heard it, and though he pretended disinterested insolence, he suspected she saw right through him.

"I didn't want to come here," she admitted. "I don't like being this far away if there's any news about London . . ." Her throat caught on her daughter's name, but she didn't break down. Instead she sighed and ran her fingers through the thick black curls that framed her perfect face. "You don't like me much, do you, Zach?" she asked suddenly.

"You're . . . my stepmother."

"As in *wicked* stepmother?"

He lifted a shoulder and took the last gulp of his beer. His fingers were still around the empty can when she turned her eyes up to him and they sparked with an inner light. Zach could barely breathe as she, staring at him boldly, placed her hands on his shoulders and brushed her lips across his.

"Jesus, Katherine—" he breathed, his heart knocking crazily. "Don't!"

"Shh." She placed those supple lips against his again, just for a second—a second he was certain would change the course of his life forever. Her mouth was teasing and warm, filled with promise.

Zach groaned low in his throat. "Don't do this, Kat."

"You want it, too," she murmured in a sigh as soft as the summer night.

He told himself that he couldn't kiss her or touch her or even think about her, and yet he was too weak to tear away from her embrace. Her lips fastened over his and her breasts, beneath the fragile barrier of her T-shirt, brushed across his bare chest.

A thousand reasons to stop screamed through his head but when her tongue skimmed his lips, then pressed urgently, demanding entrance, he gave up and he kissed her back, closing his mind to the warnings.

Her tongue was wet and slick and wonderful. It touched the roof his mouth, flicked against his lips and teeth, and promised untold delights.

Heat swirled through his blood and his cock was so hard it strained against the zipper of his cutoffs. *Don't do this! Don't!* an inner voice cried, but instead of protesting, he reached up and his fingers wound in her thick hair. She slid down him and kissed his naked chest, her tongue licking its way against his skin.

A shudder that felt like fire ripped though him. He dropped his beer and the empty can rolled noisily down the roof. His body convulsed and hot desire pumped through him. Grabbing her with strength born of desperation, he kissed her hard on the lips and all he could think about was kissing her and touching her and riding her all night.

She's your father's wife, Danvers! his mind yelled, and for once he listened to it. He found the strength to push her away. "This isn't gonna work," he said, breathing hard, wishing he could call back the words. He was so hard he was sure he would explode. His fingers clamped around her shoulders, keeping her at arm's length.

Katherine chuckled deep in her throat and the sound seemed to echo off the distant hills. "What is this, Zach?"

"Wrong. That's what it is!" He dropped his arms, scooted farther away from her, and ran sweaty, trembling fingers through his long hair.

She pouted a little in the darkness. "Since when did you care about right and wrong?"

"Don't play with me, Kat," he warned and was surprised at the conviction in his voice.

"I just felt we had an understanding." With a lift of her shoulder, she tucked her feet under her and stared down at him. "I don't get it Zach. I thought—no, I knew—you wanted this."

"I don't."

She snorted. "As a matter of fact, I was certain this is what you needed."

"I don't need you, Katherine," he said, wishing he could put more distance between her sensual body and his own. "I don't need anybody."

"Oh, baby, that's where you're wrong." To his mortification, she slid closer and patted his head as if he were a naughty little boy finally forgiven. Zach jerked away from her touch as if she repulsed him.

"Leave me alone, Kat," he muttered between his teeth. His groin still ached and he was on fire inside, but he stared off into the distance, refusing to look at her. He focused instead on the ridge of dark mountains that loomed on the horizon and heard her sigh before she climbed to her feet, walked the short distance along the roof, slipped through the window, and disappeared into the hayloft.

When she was gone he flopped back on the weathered cedar shakes, angrily gazed up at the stars, and wondered why he was such a fool. He could have had her; she was there for the taking and he, because of some latent sense of nobility, had shrugged off her advances. He could still smell her perfume mingled with the lingering smoke from her cigarettes and he remembered her touch—that warm, bone-melting touch.

Jesus, you're an idiot!

For the next few days, Zach managed to keep his distance. Up hours before Katherine ever thought about rising, he worked long hours in the fields and returned at sundown. Kat, invariably, was locked in her room, the television blasting. He never ran into her. As for his siblings, they all bothered him. Jason kept crowding him, offering to take him into Bend to meet women, but Zach declined and Jason went off prowling on his own. Trisha was pining for Mario and probably plotting her escape from the family compound. Sometimes she reeked of marijuana smoke and her eyes were often glassy. Zach had less trouble dealing with her stoned than when she was straight and plotting ways to escape. As for Nelson, the kid was still in the throes of hero worship, tagging after Zach as he went about his chores, trying to find ways to talk about his night with the prostitute. It didn't seem to matter how many ways Zach explained that nothing really had happened except that he'd managed to get a few new scars; Nelson was still enthralled, certain that Zach had really "scored" with the whore but was protecting her honor, or some such crap.

The kid was sick, Zach thought as he stepped out of the shower and threw on a pair of cutoffs. Nelson's fascination with all things sexual seemed bent. He wanted to know all about bondage and S&M and all that shit that Zach didn't really know about and didn't want to know. Men and women in leather and chains—like some kinky group of Hell's Angels or something. It kind of made his skin crawl.

Pushing all thoughts of Nelson aside, Zach found leftovers in the kitchen, and since the maid had already retired for the night, he heated up the pork chops in the microwave, snatched himself a beer out of the fridge, and took his meal onto the back porch where the old collie was curled near the swing.

Shep perked up at the smell of the meat and whined as Zach sat down and started in on the chops.

"Don't give me that," he said to the dog. "You're too fat as it is." Shep thumped his tail on the floorboards. Somewhere in the distance an owl hooted softly and the sounds of bats' wings disturbed the silence. The air smelled of horses, dust, and sagebrush. Zach thought he could find peace out here in the middle of nowhere. If it weren't for his family.

Zach finished his dinner, tossed the bones to the dog, and wiped his fingers on the frayed edges of his cutoff Levi's. He finished his Budweiser in two swallows, then walked back to the kitchen for another. Downing the second can quickly, he began to feel a slight buzz as he crushed the aluminum in his fist. He made his way back to his room, where he flipped on his stereo and flopped onto this bed. The song was an old one by the Doors.

". . . Come on baby, light my fire . . ."

Like Kat. Boy, could she light dangerous fires. Zach closed his eyes and let the music surround him.

". . . Try and set the night on *fire!*"

The French doors were cracked and the hint of a breeze stirred the curtains. His eyes opened and he stared up at the ceiling. He was hard, as hard as he'd been when Kat had kissed him on the roof of the tack room. Just thinking about being with her had given him wet dreams for three nights running. The ache in his loins was so bad that he'd even considered driving into Bend with his brother and looking for some woman who would ease his pain, but the memory of his last visit to a whore had kept him at the ranch. He didn't need any more trouble but, Lord, did he need some release. The pressure. Pounding, pounding . . .

Deep down, in the darkest oblivion of his soul, he knew that he didn't want just any woman, that though he would go through the motions with any willing female, he was certain that anyone but Kat wouldn't do and Kat, his *stepmother,* was the worst choice of all. He rolled over to his side and considered jacking off. It sure as hell wouldn't be the first time, but it left him so . . . empty or lonely or feeling stupid. *Face it, Danvers, you want her. All you have to do is walk down the hall, turn the corner, and tap on her bedroom door and the sweetest bit of pussy this side of the Rockies will be waiting to give you any fantasy you can dream up!*

His throat was so dry he couldn't draw up any spit and he squeezed his eyes shut, resigned to his fate as he reached for the fly of his pants.

He heard the creak of the door, felt the wind turn, and his heart jolted. His eyes flew open. At first he thought she was a vision, the beautiful woman on the other side of the glass. Moonlight spangled Kat's black hair silver and her silk pajama top shimmered. His heart began to pump so loudly that he was certain she could hear it.

The doors opened further and dry leaves blew into the room. The wind tossed her hair away from her face and as she entered the room, he saw the tears glistening in her eyes. Her lips trembled and her nose ran.

"What—what are you—?"

"Just hold me, Zach," she whispered in a voice strangled by grief.

"What is it?"

Walking numbly to the edge of his bed, she sniffed loudly, then stood in front of him, as if hesitating.

He drew himself into a sitting position. "You shouldn't be here, Kat—"

"I know, but . . . Oh, God . . ." She rolled her eyes toward the ceiling and tears trickled down her cheeks. Between the broken sobs she said, "Witt just called and the police have run out of leads . . . the investigation is still open but they all think, the police and the FBI, that London . . . that London is dead." The last word was barely a squeak and Zach couldn't help himself. He stood and took her into his arms, trying to comfort her as sob after heart-wrenching sob shook her body.

"Oh, God. Oh, God." Burying his face in the crook of her

neck, holding her close, he willed himself to think of her not as a woman, but as a person to whom fate had handed a crushing blow. She clung to him and cried like a child, her tears raining down his chest. He told her it would be all right, that of course London was alive, that someday they would all see her again, but even as he said the words, he believed them to be lies.

When at last the racking sobs quieted, he lifted his head. "You should go back to the room, take some sleeping pills—"

"I can't. I don't want to be alone. Please, Zach, don't make me go. Let me stay with you. Just hold me. Please." Her words held the echo of doom, but he couldn't deny her and when she turned her face up to his, he kissed her trembling lips, knowing that he was about to cross a threshold from which there was no return. Life would never be the same. The truth would be blurred with lies, but he kissed her and she responded, her body quivering in fear and desire.

His brain thundered and his blood turned to liquid heat as she let her fingers slide down his scarred back, along the slope of his spine and lower still to his buttocks. He felt his already stiff cock rise to the occasion, knew there was no turning back as she tugged and the buttons holding his cut-offs together popped in a ripple and her hands were upon him. Warm and soft, her fingers brought a magic that he never dreamed existed.

They tumbled on the bed together, lips searching, tongues eager and before he could consider all the consequences of his actions, Zachary stripped her of her nightshirt, ripping the buttons from their holes as the seams of the soft fabric gave way. Then he gazed at her breasts, felt the gentle pressure of her fingers on his spine, and watched as she licked her lips. He could barely breathe when she ran her tongue across his nipples and anxiously parted her legs, lifting her hips to rub her dewy nest of curls to his crotch.

He thought he might come all over her. "Kat—"

"Just do it, Zach. Please." Her fingers dug deep into his muscles.

Closing his eyes, he entered into that moist, dark warmth. A primal cry rumbled from his throat and he couldn't stop himself. In three long strokes it was over; Zachary came fast and hot and fell against her, realizing dimly that he'd just doomed himself to a living hell. No son dared lose his virginity to his father's wife and expect to survive.

But he didn't care. He wrapped himself in her warmth and kissed her again, more sure of himself. He'd take it slower with her this time, learn from her and be the best damned lover she ever had.

Zach couldn't remember when he'd slept so soundly. He moved slightly and felt another body, warm and soft and naked. With a smile, he remembered the night of lovemaking and he rolled over to find Kat, her eyes half open, staring at him. Dawn was breaking over the horizon and soon the ranch hands would be up; she had to leave.

"I wondered how it would be with you," she said as she slid a finger along the scar that was still visible near his hairline. Though she smiled, a sadness lingered in her eyes.

"How was it?" He nuzzled her cheek. Though it was dangerous to be with her, he couldn't give up. He'd made love to her three times last night, and he'd woken up with a hard-on. Maybe there was still enough time for a quick . . .

"It was the best, Zach," she said, though her face remained troubled and he knew she was lying.

He touched her hair, brushing soft curls off her face and wished he could stop the agony that pinched the corners of her mouth. As if reading his thoughts, she began to weep; tears suddenly starred her lashes and he pulled her closer to him, holding her naked body next to his. "Don't worry."

"I can't help it, I—"

"Shh. We'll find London." He felt suddenly strong, as if he could change the world. "I'll find her."

"Oh, Zach, what can you do—"

"You'd be surprised." His hands found her breasts and he toyed with a nipple that stiffened expectantly under the gentle teasing of his fingers. "Let me show you—"

She broke off suddenly, her eyes wide. "Do you hear anything?"

"No—"

"I do." She scrambled away from him. "I hear something—"

Zach listened and groaned at the sound of an engine whining as some kind of vehicle—most likely a truck—approached.

"Probably Pete coming early. He does that sometimes," Zach said, already aroused again. God, he couldn't get enough of her. He let one hand rest on the curve of her waist.

"You sure?" she asked.

"Mmm." He listened again and felt his heart knock a bit. The engine wasn't the deep rumble of a truck, but the smooth purr of an expensive car's engine as it sped down the lane. An expensive car like a Lincoln Continental. "Oh, God."

Gravel crunched and brakes squealed.

"Witt," Katherine mouthed.

"No—" But even as he denied it, he heard the car door open and brisk footsteps sound on the path. Footsteps he'd recognize anywhere. Authoritative footsteps belonging to his father. Footsteps of doom. "Damn it, Kat! You've got to get out of here."

But it was too late. The front door opened and the footsteps continued the short distance to the master bedroom. Kat froze at the muted rap of fingers against wood.

"Oh, God," she whispered. "Oh, God, oh, God."

"Leave. Through here." He was pushing her now, toward the open French doors. She rolled out of bed, grabbed her torn nightshirt and was stepping outside when Witt's voice reverberated through the rooms. "Katherine? Are you here?" There was a worried edge to his voice.

"Go!" Zach reached for his cutoffs as he heard the first door in the hallway open, then close. Only a few more seconds.

The door to his room opened just as Kat disappeared through the doors.

His father looked gigantic. Zach didn't bother feigning sleep and Witt didn't say a word, just looked at the rumpled sheets and sniffed at the lingering odor of Katherine's perfume. His mouth flattened to a white line of fury and an ugly tic developed under his eye. "Get out," he said under his breath. Zach rolled off the bed as his father's fist collided with his face. Pain exploded in his jaw. "You no-good bastard!"

"Witt!" Kat stood in the doorway, her fingers curling over the brass door handle. "Don't. It . . . was my fault."

"Your fault? You forced him to screw you?" He slammed Zach against the wall. Zach's head smacked against the plaster and pieces of stucco crumbled to the floor. Pain ripped all the way down his spine. "You fucking son of a bitch!" Witt snarled, shaking the life from him as the mirror over the bureau rattled. "I always suspected you were no son of mine and now I'm sure of it. Get out before I kill you!"

Zach staggered toward the door. His eyes barely focused and he felt something sticky and wet running down the back of his head.

"You can't do this!" Katherine cried and Zach heard a slap that made his stomach turn over. He turned and saw the welt forming on Katherine's cheek and Witt's stunned expression, as if he couldn't believe that he'd struck her.

"Don't you ever touch me again!" she said, backing outside.

"I'm sorry. Christ, Katherine, I swear, I'd never do anything to hurt you—"

He took one step toward her but she kept backing up. "Stay away from me, Witt. I mean it," she said, before turning and running into the grayish dawn. Witt's great shoulders slumped and he sagged against the wall. He turned damning eyes up at his son. "Now look what you've done, Zach," he said, barely able to breathe. With an expression straight from hell, he loosened his tie then reached for his belt buckle. Zach remembered the times he'd been whipped by a thin leather strap. Not again. He wouldn't suffer like he had when he was eight, leaning over the bed and biting his lower lip until it bled to keep from crying out as his father flayed him with the stinging leather. No way.

"Leave now and don't ever . . ." Witt, suddenly ashen, reached into his pocket, fumbled for a vial of pills and popped the top. He stuck one of the tablets under his tongue. "Don't ever come back here."

"I won't," Zach promised, jaw clenched in determination. Injustice burned through his veins and he held his father with his remorseless stare. "You'll never see me again."

Witt's blue eyes were cold, his fury evident in the white lines of strain near his mouth. "That's the way I want it, boy." He took one menacing step toward his son. "However, if I find out that you had anything to do with your sister's kidnapping, I swear I'll personally hunt you down like the lying dog you are and rip you apart with my bare hands."

Zach stumbled back toward the door. His head throbbed, his jaw ached, and he glared at the man he'd called father all his life. He had to leave. Now. Run as far and fast as he could. And if he never saw Witt Danvers alive again, it would be much too soon.

PART FIVE
1993

11

Adria woke up to the squeal of hydraulic brakes and the thrum of a huge engine as a truck idled in the parking lot. With a groan she rolled out of the bed and surveyed her shabby surroundings. It certainly wasn't the Ritz, or the Benson, or the Hotel Danvers, for that matter. But it would have to do.

The pipes were rusty, the drain of the tub stained, but she closed her eyes to the flaws of the Riverview and quickly showered under tepid water. She towel-dried her hair, tamed it by snapping a rubber band around a ponytail, and ignored her makeup bag. She didn't need to look glamorous when she planned to spend the day in the library, the offices of the *Oregonian,* the historical society, and the Portland Police Bureau if need be. But as she glanced in the mirror, she remembered the family portrait and her heart began to thud. All night long she'd tossed and turned, thinking of the portrait and of Zach as he'd stared so intensely at Katherine, as if he wanted her approval.

"Dysfunctional," she told herself. "The whole family. And you want to be a part of it. Stupid, stupid girl."

With an eye on the silk dress in its plastic casing, she yanked on a sweatshirt, a pair of worn jeans, and slipped into ancient Reebok running shoes. She grabbed an oversized purse that doubled as a briefcase and was out the door.

Reading an old city map, she drove to the drive-in window

of a McDonald's and while waiting for her coffee, reacquainted herself with Portland.

Basically the city was divided by the river, and the east side spread away from the banks of the Willamette in a careful grid that was infrequently interspersed with winding streets or slashed by a freeway. The west side, however, was more difficult. Though the streets ran north-south and east-west, they were older, more narrow, and tended to follow the contour of the Willamette River, or meander through the hills that rose steeply from the water's shore.

She paid for the coffee, took a sip, and drove steadily westward, through the low-rising office buildings and shops toward the river and the twin spires of the Convention Center. As she drove she wondered what her half-brothers and -sister were doing.

At that thought, she glanced in the rearview mirror. Worried blue eyes stared back at her. Was she really London Danvers, or was this all a fierce joke that her father had played on her? Well, it was too late to start second-guessing herself. For now, she was London Danvers and Jason, Nelson, Trisha, and even Zachary were not only her enemies, but her closest blood kin.

She studied the traffic behind her and had the crazy notion that she was being followed. But no car seemed to be tailing her, at least none that she could identify. She stepped on the accelerator. Tires singing on the metal grid, her Nova sped across the Hawthorne Bridge. Unfortunately, she had to drive downtown again, close to the Hotel Danvers, to the building only three blocks down the street from where the offices of Danvers International were housed.

She parked her car in a corner lot, finished the coffee, and grabbed her bag. Though the sun was making a valiant effort to warm the wet streets, the wind was cold as it blew down the Columbia River Gorge, rolled across the Willamette, and whistled through the narrow streets of the city.

She hurried up the steps to the library doors and felt a chill against the back of her neck, as if someone were watching her. "You're just being paranoid," she told herself, but couldn't shake the feeling.

"Something happened last night at the grand opening." Eunice Danvers Smythe had the uncanny ability to read Nelson like a book. He was edgy and restless and chewed at the corner of his thumbnail. Dressed in a sloppy T-shirt and jeans that had seen better days, he hadn't shaved or bothered to comb his unruly blond hair and his lips were pinched. "Something went wrong," she guessed again, shooing her Persian cat off one of the chairs.

"You could say that." Nelson was slouched in a chair across the table from her in the morning room of her home in Lake Oswego. He'd called from his condo and been on her doorstep in less than the fifteen minutes it took to make the drive within the speed limit.

"What is it?"

"Another imposter." Nelson ignored the newspaper sitting next to his plate.

"London?"

"So she claims."

Sighing, Eunice sipped from her coffee cup and stared past Nelson and through the bay window over his shoulder. The lake, reflecting the clouds that had moved quickly in from the west, was a desolate, steely gray. A rough winter wind caused a few whitecaps to surface. On the opposite shore, like bony fingers, empty boat slips jutted into the cold water.

"She's a fake," Eunice surmised.

"Of course she's a fake, but she's trouble just the same. When the press gets wind of this, the shit's really going to hit the fan. It'll start all over again . . . the speculation and dredging up of the kidnapping. Reporters, photographers . . . just like before." He plowed both hands through his thick blond hair.

"It's always going to be a problem," Eunice said with a lit-

tle smile that she reserved for her children. "But it's something you have to deal with. And it might help you. If you're
really interested in running for mayor someday—"

"Governor."

"Governor." She clucked her tongue and shook her head.
"My, my, but aren't we ambitious." She didn't mean to sound
scathing, just concerned.

His eyes crinkled a bit at the corners, but he wasn't laughing. "I suppose *we* are. We'd both go through hell and back to
get what we wanted, wouldn't we?"

She ignored that little dig. "You could use the adverse publicity to your advantage, if you're smart."

"How?"

"Welcome her with open arms," she said, and Nelson
stared at her as if she'd suddenly lost her mind. "I'm serious,
Nelson, think about it. You, defender of the downtrodden,
you, seeker of truth, you, the one-day politician—listen to her
story, try to help her and then . . . well, when she's proved a
fraud . . . you don't even denounce her, not really, just explain
to the press that she was an opportunist."

"You're not serious."

"Something to think about." She added cream to her coffee—not too much, as she prided herself on working out and
keeping her body in shape, then watched the clouds swirl to
the surface. "Come on now," she encouraged, blowing across
her cup before she took a sip. "Tell me about her."

Cradling the warm porcelain between her fingers, Eunice
waited. Nelson would tell her everything. He always did. It
was his way of trying to be special to her. After the divorce
from Witt, all the children suffered and she felt an incredible
sense of guilt for their pain. She'd never wanted to hurt the
children—they were her most precious possessions. Never
would she intentionally wound any of them. It had been Witt
she had hoped to cripple, but he seemed to have survived the
divorce, even thrived as a businessman, and had taken that

slut of a young girl for his second wife. Suddenly her special blend of French roast seemed to curdle in her stomach.

Nelson scraped his chair back and stood near the windows. Throwing out a hip, he gazed through the glass. Though he'd called her, begged to come by and unburden himself, she sensed that he regretted his decision to open up to her. He'd always been volatile—not so openly hostile as Zach had been—but energized by a pent-up anger just under the surface, a blasting cap primed to explode. She wondered if he even had a clue about how he'd been conceived, but held her tongue.

Nelson was the child who should never have been born. She and Witt were estranged when she'd gotten pregnant. Witt had finally found out about her affair with Anthony Polidori and all hell had broken loose.

"You stupid, stupid bitch!" Witt had roared when he'd discovered the truth. He'd sensed that Anthony had been in his house, his room, his bed, though Anthony had slipped away minutes before.

Witt had slapped her so hard her head had snapped back on her neck and she'd stumbled to fall back on her bed. He was on her in an instant, pinning her to the mattress with his enormous bulk. "How could you?" he'd yelled, straddling her and crushing her face between his meaty hands. She was a big woman, a strong woman, but no match for him. "You lying, cheating bitch, how could you?"

She was crying, tears streaming down her cheeks and through his fingers, and she knew that he might kill her. His palms squashed her cheeks and she stared up at eyes bright with rage and hatred. Saliva collected in the corners of his mouth and his lips were pulled into a snarl of malice.

"I . . . It just happened," she'd choked out.

"Like hell! You're my *wife*, Eunice, my *wife!* The wife of Witt Danvers. Do you know what that means?" He gave her head a little shake and she mewled a protest. She could barely breathe. "You may not like me—"

"I detest you!" she spat.

"So you go crawling to Polidori. Taking off your panties and spreading your legs and screwing his brains out. Why? To get back at me?"

"Yes!" she screamed, not daring to utter that she loved Anthony as she'd never loved Witt and the hands around her face pushed harder. Pain jolted through her brain.

"You're unbelievable."

"At least he's a man, Witt! He knows how to satisfy a woman!"

He roared back and this time the hand that came down against her cheek landed so hard she heard bones crack. A moan escaped her throat.

"A man, eh?" Witt thundered. "I'll show you a man."

She'd shivered as he'd held her down with one hand and undid his belt with the other. He'd never beaten her before, but now she was certain he was going to flay her until her skin was raw. Swallowing all of her pride, she whispered, "Don't, Witt . . . please . . ."

"You deserve it."

"No." She got one hand free and held it up to protect her face. "Don't—"

He hesitated, his shirt undone, his breathing hard and fast. "You're a whore, Eunice."

"No—"

"And you deserve to be treated like one."

Still straddling her, he took her hand and guided it to his fly. "Undo it."

"No, I—" She withdrew her hand and then held back a little scream as she saw his muscles flex beneath his shirt. He slid his leather belt out of the loops and for a second she saw the flash of a silver buckle—a running horse with sharp little hooves, made of metal that could cut and scar. Oh, God. Pain jolted through her body. She bit her lip to keep from crying out.

"Take the zipper down."

"Witt, no—"

"Just do it, Eunice. You're still my wife."

"Please, Witt, don't make me do this," she whispered and watched as his nostrils flared and his eyes bulged. How had they ever come to this? How had she ever thought she loved him.

"Now!"

Her hands were shaking and she felt revulsion when she noticed the bulge beneath his fly. He was enjoying torturing her and had become hard, after months of impotence, months of silent fury. He'd blame the business, then her, and now he was wreaking his vengeance.

The zipper slid down with a sickening hiss.

"You know what to do. Do for me what you do for Polidori. Show me what it takes to make that filthy bastard come."

"Witt, no, I don't want—" He grabbed her by her hair and his eyes glowed with evil rancor. Thick fingers knotted in her French braid as it fell loose.

"We're going to do what I want, Eunice. You're going to make me feel good, Eunice, no matter what it takes, no matter how it hurts." The fingers pulled hard on her hair. "And when I'm finished with you, you'll never run back to that bastard again!"

Sick to her stomach, she had closed her eyes and given herself up to her husband and all his perversity.

"Mom?" Nelson's voice broke into her painful reverie.

Startled, she cleared her throat and quickly reached for her napkin to dab at her eyes.

Nelson was staring at her. Her baby. The last of her children. The boy conceived during that night of hell. Never once had there been any question of Nelson's paternity. Even now, staring at her, his carved features set with worry, he was the spitting image of his father as a young man, a man Eunice had thought she'd loved, a man she could barely remember. Witt Danvers with all his energy, his ambitions, his vision for Portland had seemed the perfect match. Though she wasn't a dainty woman, he hadn't minded, probably because she was from the "right" family, had a small fortune of her own, and he felt that she would help and support him.

"It will be ours one day," he'd said, smiling from a penthouse apartment and looking down at the city. "Every block will have a building with the Danvers name!" She'd believed in him then, trusted him. Until the other women. And the fact that after two children his sex drive at home had dwindled.

Anthony had been the balm for her ego and she'd stupidly fallen in love with him.

"Are you all right?" Nelson asked, snapping her back to the present. His handsome face was etched in concern, his blond brows beetling to form one line. So like Witt. Poor child. Despite the rough, humiliating way Nelson had been conceived, Eunice had loved him, as she'd loved all her children.

"I'm fine," she lied, forcing a smile. As she stared up at her son now, she thought all the agony and humiliation had been worth it. Clearing her throat, she took her boy's hand. "Now, tell me what you know about this girl—the one who claims she's London."

"There's not much to say. No one knows anything, except what we heard last night."

Eunice stirred her coffee as Nelson unburdened himself and she heard the sketchy details of the woman pretending to be London Danvers. Nelson was worried, but that was nothing new; he'd been born worried. As a child he'd had a wild imagination, dreamed of fantasy worlds, and as an adult he was always trying to prove himself—as if he silently knew that he hadn't been wanted, that he'd been created during an act of violence. His job with the public defender's office was just to show the populace that although he had been born with a silver spoon wedged firmly between his Danvers gums, he still cared about the little people.

She would help him, of course—as she would help all her children. To make up for the years when she hadn't been there, when she'd been banished to the role of unfit mother and Jezebel. Witt's power and money had seen that she had been forced to watch from the outside as he molded her children into little carbon copies of himself.

Of course, it hadn't worked. Her offspring were too strong-willed on one hand, and too weak on the other. Jason was the most like Witt in personality and he, too, seemed to care little about anything other than the Danvers name, the Danvers money, and the Danvers corporation. Trisha would never really be her own woman. Witt had taken care of that a long time ago. Zach . . . She smiled as she thought of her second son. He was special. He'd been a thorn in Witt's side from the minute he was born and Eunice had reveled in her son's rebellious nature. Nelson was more of a conformist, but he'd only gone along with Witt for his own purposes.

The divorce had been ugly, most of it replayed in the newspapers. Eunice was portrayed as a bored, rich woman who had partaken of numerous affairs, including sleeping with her husband's sworn enemy. She hadn't had the energy or the resources to fight Witt's power, so she'd agreed to a nice little settlement and left her children with their beast of a father. Even now, as she thought about how Witt had manipulated her into losing her darlings, her teeth clenched in silent rage. She should have known better than to have pushed him so far; she should have sacrificed herself and lived with his mood swings and impotence and rage, so that she would never be separated from the children, but she'd been cowardly and accepted his token alimony—blood money—and left.

Her life had never been complete. Even when she'd remarried, she'd been restless and there hadn't been a night she hadn't gone to bed feeling guilty as sin and lonely for the chubby little arms and adoring eyes of her babies.

As for her affair with Polidori, it had cooled and cracked as quickly as hot glass dipped in ice water once Witt got wind of the situation. She often wondered if Anthony had used her. If he'd seduced her for the express purpose of tormenting

Witt. She blinked rapidly and once again fought the threat of hot tears.

"You're sure you're all right?" Nelson said, touching her lightly on the shoulder.

"Right as rain," she replied, refusing to break down. "Now, come on. Surely we can find out more about this imposter who's posing as London."

Adria zipped her huge purse shut, then closed her eyes and rotated her head, straightening the kink that had tightened between her shoulder blades. She'd learned a lot about the history of the Danvers family. They were powerful and influential and had been for over a hundred years. Some of the scandals had been reported to the press, others had only been hinted at, but she felt as if she'd made progress. She had names and dates and more information than she'd ever found in Montana.

She'd started her search in 1974 at the time of the kidnapping and worked backward and forward, learning as much as she could. She wasn't finished; the Danvers name littered the newspapers before and since the kidnapping, but she needed a break. Gathering her papers, she left her table by the window on the second floor.

Outside, the sun had won the weather battle. Beams reflected off the puddles on the sidewalk and the breeze had died. A few clouds drifted over the sky, but the day, for winter in the Pacific Northwest, was mild. She decided to walk south to the Galleria, an old department store that had been converted to several stories of shops.

She found a café on the first floor.

She'd just picked up the menu when she spied Zachary and her breath caught at the base of her throat. Without a word or an invitation, Zachary picked up the chair opposite hers, turned it around, set it back down, and straddled it.

In the few hours they'd been apart, she'd forgotten how imposing he was. Dressed down in faded Levi's, flannel shirt, and jacket, he was formidable nonetheless. He hadn't bothered to shave and his features bordered on harsh. He seemed distinctly displeased as he folded his arms over the back of the chair and glared at her.

"You lied to me."

"Did I?" she asked as she ignored the sexy slope of his jaw.

"Big time. You didn't stay at the Benson."

"Is that a crime?"

"I really don't give a damn where you stay, but the rest of the family seems to think it's important."

"Then I must worry them."

"Appears so," he drawled, his gray eyes cloudy.

"What about you? If you don't 'give a damn,' then why are you here?"

"I got elected."

She wasn't buying it. She didn't think that Zachary was the kind of man who let anyone talk him into doing something he opposed.

"How did you find me?"

"It wasn't hard."

She had to hold onto her temper. "You followed me."

He shrugged and the tense little smile that touched the corners of his mouth infuriated her.

"How?"

"Doesn't matter. I'm here to extend you an invitation."

She eyed him suspiciously, but a waitress, dressed in a white blouse, black skirt, and bow tie, appeared to take their order and the conversation lagged for a few minutes.

"You weren't invited here," she told him once the waitress turned her attention to the next table.

"Just like you weren't invited last night."

"Why are you following me?"

"You make some members of the family nervous."

"You—do I make you nervous?"

He hesitated and stared at her with such scrutiny that she

wanted to squirm out of his range of vision. Cold, assessing gray eyes searched her face. "You bother me," he admitted, tilting his head back, "but you don't worry me."

"You still don't believe me."

"You don't believe it yourself, not really."

There was just no winning this argument. Zach Danvers was obviously like a terrier with a bone and he believed what was convenient. Fine, she told herself, let him think what he wants, but the cynical disbelief in his eyes made her uncomfortable. She took a sip from her water glass and decided she should try to make some peace with this man. He was her only link to the family.

"You said something about an invitation," Adria reminded him as she buttered a slice of sourdough bread.

"The family thinks it would be a good idea if you would stay in the Hotel Danvers."

She should have expected as much, but she hadn't. "So it's easier for them to spy on me."

"Probably."

"Well, you can tell *the family* to go to hell."

One side of his mouth lifted. "Already have."

"Look, Zach. I don't like being manipulated, I hate being followed, and I detest the feeling that Big Brother is watching me." She broke off a piece of bread and chewed it.

"You came looking for us, remember?"

That much was true. With a sigh, she blew her bangs out of her eyes. She shouldn't have let her temper get the better of her. She was tired from too little sleep on a sagging mattress, grumpy from lack of food, and her nerves were strung tight as piano wires at the thought of facing the Danvers family, *her* family, again.

"I just want you to help me find the truth."

"I know the truth," he said.

"If you're so sure, why are you following me?"

Zach studied her another long minute. "I think you're

going to stir up a hornet's nest the likes of which you've never seen before and I think you'll regret it."

"My mistake to make."

"I'm just warning you."

"About what?" She leaned her elbows on the table and pushed her face closer to his. "I've had months to think this through, Zachary. I had doubts, of course I did, but I can't spend the rest of my life wondering who I am."

"What if you find out you're not London?"

Her smile was slow and sexy and caused Zach's diaphragm to cram hard against his lungs. "I believe in crossing bridges when I come to them."

The waitress brought their orders and Adria dived into her soup with a vengeance.

"Jason thought you might be more comfortable at a suite in the hotel." Zach took a bite of his sandwich.

"Concerned for my health and safety, is he?" she mocked.

Zach lifted a shoulder.

"Tell him 'thanks but no thanks.' The cost's a little too high."

"The room is gratis."

"I wasn't talking about money." Her eyes met his for an instant and again Zach felt an unwanted tug on his gut. She was getting to him, with her clear blue eyes, sexy smile, and quick wit. He didn't say another word until they were finished with their meal and he insisted on paying. She argued, of course, but he wouldn't take no for an answer and in the end, she gave up, deciding that she'd forgo the small battles for the larger ones to come, or so she'd said.

The streets were crawling with people by the time they started walking back to the library. Cars, trucks, bicycles, and pedestrians clogged the alleys and sidewalks. Adria yanked the rubber band holding her hair away from her face and shook the loose curls free. Zach's mouth went dry as the wild blue-black strands shimmered in the sunlight. She looked so damned much like Kat it was eerie.

"So what was it that caused the rift between you and your father?" she asked as she shifted her shoulder bag from one arm to the other.

"I was a pain in the neck."

She let out a little laugh. "That, I believe."

"Always getting into trouble with the law."

"Oh."

"Witt didn't approve. He wanted all of us to graduate at the top of our class from an Ivy League school . . . or if we couldn't get in, then Reed College would do since it's kind of a family tradition . . . afterward we were to finish law school and join a prestigious firm."

"You're a lawyer?" She knew better, of course, but wanted to see his response.

"Not hardly," he said with a distasteful snort.

"But you just said—"

"I didn't really count, though, remember?" His face was set in a hard expression she was beginning to recognize, though he didn't look contrite, nor did he seem to want to elicit her sympathy. His eyes were hard, his chin thrust forward as if he were about to prove his worth.

But to whom?

"Just what is it you do, when you're not renovating hotels?"

"Come on, Adria, don't play stupid. It doesn't wash. You already know that I'm a builder. I spent a lot of years remodeling houses, then ended up fixing the ranch. I guess I just stayed on."

"The family's ranch?"

He shot her a look. "Yep."

"You run it, now?"

"You already know this."

"What about building?"

"Still have a construction company. In Bend."

"A jack-of-all-trades?"

"I do what I have to." They reached the park surrounding

the library. Cocking his head toward the building, he asked, "So did you dig up all the dirt on the family?"

"Not yet, but I will."

"And then you'll know if you're really London."

"I hope so."

His lips compressed. "I can save you a whole lot of time and money and effort—you're not."

A breeze feathered through her hair. "How can you be so sure?"

"Practice," he said.

She lifted a finely arched brow in a gesture that mimicked his stepmother's so perfectly that his stomach squeezed. "So are you going to follow me around for the rest of my life?"

"I'm just waiting for an answer."

"An answer?" she asked, squinting a little as the sun was behind his shoulder.

"That's right. What's it going to be, Adria?" he asked, unable to camouflage the contempt in his voice. "Are you content to stay in that dump on Eighty-second or are you going to gamble and move into a higher-rent district and take the all-expenses-paid suite at the Hotel Danvers?"

This one is different.

No one could dispute that she looked so much like Kat. The eyes, the hair, the cheekbones, the smile . . . Damn it all to hell! Why now? *Why?*

A fist pounded the steering wheel and the car shimmied and shivered along the familiar, rain-slickened streets of the West Hills. Heart hammering, the driver grasped the steering wheel in a death grip, straightening the wheels while disturbing images of Katherine LaRouche Danvers came to mind.

So supple.

So sexy.

So assured of her sexuality—that with a come-hither smile

or naughty laugh she could cause any man, *any* man, to do her bidding.

And she'd been right.

Bile rose in the driver's throat with the erotic pictures that Kat could evoke.

But it had all changed in the end.

A smile toyed at the edge of the driver's mouth as the car approached a traffic light.

The images of a healthy, sleek woman changed to the pathetic creature Kat had become. A skinny, scared, naked woman who had lost most of her beauty and perhaps part of her mind. How easy it had been to push her off the balcony.

This one would be more difficult.

Adria Nash was young. Vibrant. Strong. Not broken because of the loss of a child. Not dependent upon pills to get through the day. Not depressed and frail.

And yet she had to be destroyed.

At the traffic light, the car idled and Katherine's killer checked the glove box. A tiny light illuminated the knife, its blade gleaming through the plastic bag.

Sharp.

Deadly.

Ready.

For anyone who pretended to be London Danvers, including Adria Nash.

She was an enemy.

And all enemies had to die.

12

He wasn't cut out to be a detective. Zach shoved his hands deep into his pockets and watched Adria run up the steps to the library. Though she hadn't agreed to take the family's offer of a free room at the hotel, Zach figured it was only a matter of time before she caved in and gladly accepted the first of what would be a string of gifts—bribes, really—to get rid of her. He'd thought, well, at least he'd hoped that she was smarter and had more integrity than that.

Of course she hadn't. She was a gold digger, for Christ's sake—a gold digger who looked a helluva lot like his dead stepmother.

Clouds were beginning to gather again when he jogged back to the street where he'd left his Jeep. He had more important things to do than chase after Adria Nash and yet a part of him was reluctant to leave her. She was an interesting creature—sly and beautiful, shrewd and fascinating. He wondered just how much like Kat she was. For an instant he imagined what she would feel like writhing beneath him in bed.

"Stop it!" He was as bad as the rest of the family. Slamming the door on those dangerous thoughts, he drove toward the river, pulled into the parking garage under the hotel and told himself that he'd stay a couple more days. That was all. Just until things with Adria were settled. It shouldn't take long. A little game of cat and mouse, money offered and declined until the family reached a number she liked or until someone dug up the dirt on her and threatened to expose her for a fraud.

Either way, the end result would be the same. She'd be gone. He sat in the Jeep for a minute and listened to the engine tick as it cooled. Sightlessly he stared into the middle distance but was unaware of other cars or people emerging from the elevator. Adria was getting to him and he didn't like a woman—any woman—starting to turn his thinking around.

Snapping back to the present, he hoisted his bag from the back of the Jeep, then walked to the service elevator and rode to the main lobby. Three clerks in green jackets were working at computer terminals at the front desk and bellboys ducked in and out of the front door. Several people loitered in the lobby and one woman was angrily arguing with a clerk about the telephone charges on her bill. Though the Hotel Danvers had passed final inspection and was up and running, there were a few bugs left to iron out. Cable television trouble on the upper three floors, plumbing leaks in the basement, faulty locks on the doors on the sixth floor, a chlorine problem with the pool, and a touchy stove in the kitchen were just a few of the minor headaches that his crew was fine-tuning.

He found Frank Gillette in the kitchen, with one of the ovens pulled away from the wall. He frowned and checked the wiring. Glancing up, he spied Zach. "Whatever we paid for this, it was too damned much."

"You ordered it."

"So I made a mistake," Frank grumbled. "Give me a minute—" He twisted to look over his shoulder. "Okay, Casey, let's give this bitch some juice!"

Within seconds there was a whir and more lights in the kitchen blinked on. Frank stood and, with Zach's help, shouldered the oven back into place. "It's a heavy bastard," he said. "Fire it up!" he told the cook, who was a thin Chinese man with a small goatee. With a skeptical glance at Frank, the cook did as he was told. The lights on the face of the oven winked on and when the cook switched on the gas, after a series of clicks and a whoosh, blue flames eagerly licked upward. "How about that! Looks like it's fixed," Frank said. "Sometimes I amaze even myself."

"Why don't you tell me everything else that's gone wrong." Zach said.

"Got a few hours?"

"All the time in the world," Zach said as they walked out of the kitchen, along a short hallway that opened to a small office located behind the lobby desk. "Good," Frank said. "Let's start with the security system—"

Oswald Sweeny prided himself on being everything Jason Danvers was not—well, almost everything. Short, with a thickening waist, and dark eyes that could see nearly a hundred-and-eighty degrees without moving, Oswald had spent a decade with army intelligence before being dishonorably discharged over a small matter of beating up an enlisted man who'd made the mistake of trying to pick him up. Oswald had knocked out his two front teeth and the kid had taken offense. He'd had enough balls to file charges against Oswald. In the end, they were both kicked out of the service.

Which was fine with Oswald. Just as it was fine that he wasn't a stuffed shirt like Danvers. They were as opposite as two men could be.

Jason was rich, Oswald was always sweating out his next paycheck. Jason was educated, Oswald thought academics were for idiots. Jason was married and kept a mistress. Oswald took his pleasure in thirty-dollar streetwalkers and never asked their names.

His only vices were unfiltered cigarettes, cheap women, and fast horses. Sometimes, unfortunately, the women were faster than the nags he picked.

Despite their differences, however, Oswald and Jason had a common trait: they both were willing to do whatever it took to get what they wanted.

Right now, Jason wanted the dirt on some woman named Adria Nash, a woman who claimed she was London Danvers, and Jason was willing to spare no expense. It seemed that this woman was the spittin' image of his stepmother—a beautiful woman who managed to kill herself with booze and pills. Few people understood the reason Katherine LaRouche Danvers took a flyer. Sweeny was one of the privileged who thought he knew that particular piece of information. He should write a book. He could make a fucking fortune in a "tell-all" about the Danvers family.

"I don't care what it takes," Jason said as he paced restlessly on the cracked linoleum in Oswald's hole-in-the-wall office. The single room contained a few army-surplus file cabinets, an answering machine hooked up to a phone he never picked up, a desk in which every drawer stuck, and two chairs.

Oswald didn't trust anyone; he did his own books and typed his own letters. He paid his rent month to month for the little cubicle overlooking Stark Street—in case he had to blow town quick. No need to be tied into a yearly lease. Oswald needed to keep mobile and though this old concrete building didn't have an uptown address, it served his needs just fine. He kept his money in a safe-deposit box and figured he had nearly fifty thousand tucked away. Not a fortune, but a nice little nest egg. He squashed out the stub of his cigarette in an overflowing ashtray.

"Find out everything you can about her, and here"—Jason snapped open his leather briefcase and withdrew a video-tape—"this is a copy of her 'proof,' which is some guy who's supposed to be her father making a tear-jerking confession that he thinks she could be Witt Danvers's long-lost daughter. It's schmaltzy enough to turn your stomach."

"You think she's in this alone?"

"Hell, I don't know." Jason slid the tape across the desk. "All I know is she's trouble. If she runs to the press with this, it could hang up probate another couple of years."

"You give a copy to the police?"

Jason frowned. "Not yet. Too many leaks in the department."

So Danvers was trying to avoid the press. Oswald fingered the black plastic case holding the videotape. "Couldn't you get Watson to handle this?" Oswald needled and was rewarded with a look that would melt steel. Bob Watson was the private investigator sometimes used by Danvers International. Bob wore three-piece suits and eighty-dollar ties and had more secretaries and flunkies than Kellogg's had cornflakes.

"You know why I want you."

Oswald knew, all right. He was willing to push the limits of the law, go a little further than anyone else, including Watson. Oswald Sweeny was only called in when Jason was desperate and needed more than a simple surveillance job.

"I want you to follow Ms. Nash. Find out if she's working alone or if she has any accomplices. Also, dig up everything you can about her. She says she's from some hick town in Montana—Belamy, I believe—and that uncle of hers, Ezra, practiced law in Bozeman. See what you can find on him and everyone else in the family."

"How much do you want?" Sweeny asked, resisting the urge to rub his hands together in anticipation of his payment.

"Everything. All the dirt on this woman, enough so we can discredit her and force her out of town. Everyone has a secret or a weakness. Just find out what hers is. I'll handle the rest."

Sweeny couldn't help but smile as he flipped the cassette over and studied it. He enjoyed seeing Danvers sweat, and right now Jason Danvers seemed more desperate than ever. Good news for Oswald Sweeny. "Any chance there's some truth to this?" He tapped the case with a nicotine-stained finger.

"Of course not. But she worries me. She's working this differently from anyone else." With a scathing look at the cracked seat, Jason settled into the single worn chair for visitors and clients. "Instead of making harsh demands, threatening to go to the police and the press, she's playing it cool. Too cool." He tented his hands and stared at Sweeny, but the detective guessed his mind was miles away. With Adria Nash.

"She still wants to score. She's just in it for more bucks," Oswald said.

Jason seemed to snap back to the present. His lips pinched together. "It's up to you to prove it. Unfortunately, this may take some time."

Sweeny grinned, showing off a gap between his front teeth. "You're in luck. I got nothing pressing." He grabbed a legal pad from under the desk and a pencil that had been chewed repeatedly, then plopped a recorder onto the desk, as a backup. "Let's go over it. From the top. Your old man, he hired a PI when London was kidnapped."

"Phelps—but he came up with nothing. He was supposed to be the best and he couldn't find anything. You can talk to him if you want, but he's retired. Lives with his daughter up in Tacoma."

"I'll talk to him and put a tail on Ms. Nash," Oswald said. Though he didn't like the idea of having someone else following her, he couldn't be two places at once and he felt he should shag out to Montana, find out what he could about her while she was away from her hometown. He had a couple of men he could trust to stick to her like glue and report back to him.

"I just don't want any fuckups."

"There won't be." Sweeny smelled money and he wasn't about to let it slip between his fingers.

As Jason gave him the particulars, Sweeny scribbled the information and decided if nothing else, this Adria Nash had balls. Hard to find on a woman.

Two hours later, Jason stood, brushed a little lint off the sleeve of his jacket, and left Sweeny with a retainer of ten thousand dollars. Oswald stuffed the check into his shirt pocket and moved to the window, tipping the blinds. He watched Jason, bareheaded in the rain, slide into the expensive interior of his Jaguar before firing the engine and nosing the sleek car into traffic.

Bastard. Filthy-rich bastard.

Noticing the dead insects and cobwebs on the window

ledge, he frowned and let the blind snap back to cover the brittle little carcasses. Yes, this place was a dump, but it suited him just fine. He reached into a lower drawer of his desk, pulled out a bottle of Jack Daniel's, and screwed off the cap. Wiping the greasy cuff of his jacket over the top of the bottle, he grunted, then took a slug. The whiskey hit the back of his throat and seared all the way to his belly.

He loved it when Jason Danvers came crawling to him. It wasn't just the money, but the satisfaction of having that rich, arrogant son of a bitch begging for his services. He'd seen the disdain in Jason's eyes as his gaze traveled over the bleak furnishings, the unswept floors, the full ashtrays, and the grimy window. Oswald remembered the flare of Jason's aristocratic nose at the smells of sweat and stale cigarette smoke.

Chuckling to himself, Oswald slid a Camel from the pack he kept on the desk and lit up. Still holding the cigarette in the corner of his mouth, he took another tug on the bottle. Yep, things were definitely looking up.

Zach hung up the phone in his suite and swore under his breath. Despite assurances from Manny the ranch foreman that everything was running smoothly and that his presence wasn't needed, Zach felt restless and short-tempered. All because of that damned woman.

He'd tried to reach Jason and tell him to do his own leg-work, but he'd been informed by a secretary with no inflection that Mr. Danvers was in a meeting and would be unavailable all day. She assured Zach that Mr. Danvers would get back to him.

The phone rang and he snatched up the receiver.

Adria's voice drifted like smoke over the wires. "You said you wanted an answer."

"Right."

"I've decided to accept the Danvers hospitality."

His hand clenched tighter over the receiver and he felt a shot of disappointment, though he'd known this was the way things would turn out. She'd take the handouts, one by one, until she had what she wanted, or a neat little compromise thereof.

Zach checked his watch. "Meet me here at six."

She hung up and Zach told himself it didn't matter what she did. So she was taking a room in the hotel. Why not? He wondered what she'd discovered in the library, checking old newspaper clippings and magazine articles about the family. While Witt was alive, he'd managed to keep most of the Danvers secrets locked tightly away from the press. After the old man's death, Jason had taken over that responsibility. But Adria would dig deep—she wouldn't be content to just scratch the surface; she was too thorough.

So how had she been fooled into thinking she was London? Or was that all an act? There was a chance, and a damned good one, that she was lying through her beautiful teeth.

They must really be worried, Adria thought as Zach unlocked the door to the suite on the top floor of the hotel. With a sitting room complete with a fireplace, two bedrooms, two baths, Jacuzzi, French doors opening onto a flagstone veranda, and a view of the city that stretched for miles, the suite was spacious and decorated in hues of soft peach and ivory. The furniture looked to be antique, though Adria guessed the highboy, Queen Anne canopied bed, tea table, and Chippendale side chairs were all modern imitations, not authentic pieces. The carpet was plush, the bar stocked with the best labels, and a vase filled with pink roses rested on a glass-topped coffee table.

"Is this a bribe?" she asked as Zach hung her garment bag in one of the closets.

He lifted a shoulder. "Call it anything you want."

She'd only agreed to stay in the hotel as a gesture of good faith. Though she suspected that the family just wanted to watch her closely, she decided to accept their offer. "Any strings attached?" she asked.

"Not to me." His eyes narrowed on her. "You'll have to ask Jason what he expects of you."

"If he thinks he can buy me off—"

"He does." Zach cast her a look that silently called her naive. "But it's just his nature. Don't take it personally. And don't be fooled. This little bit of generosity isn't because the family has all of a sudden decided to welcome you with open arms."

"I know that."

"Good."

She tossed her jacket onto the back of a chair. "You don't much like your family, do you?"

He snorted and didn't bother hiding his sarcasm. "What's not to like?" Reaching into his pocket, he withdrew the hotel key and flipped it through the air. "You're now a guest of the Danvers family. I'm not really sure what, exactly, that entails, but I'm sure my brother will let you know."

He started for the twin doors of the suite, but she laid a hand on the crook of his arm. "Look . . . is there a reason we have to be at each other's throats?"

He turned and stared into eyes as blue as a summer's day. Glancing at the throat in question, he felt his gut tighten and sultry memories clouded his mind. He'd too often been mesmerized by Kat's treacherous and seductive eyes. Just as he could be with this woman. "You want to be what . . . well, I mean besides brother and sister, you want to be friends?" he asked, unable to hide the cynicism in his words.

"Why not?" she asked. Her smile was sincere and cracked open a dark corner of his heart, a corner he preferred to keep locked. "I don't know a lot of people in town."

He waited, his face a mask, not daring to move a muscle but singularly aware of the smooth hand upon his forearm. "Christ."

"I thought maybe you'd let me buy you dinner."

"Why?"

"Because it would be easier on both of us if we weren't always looking to kill each other."

"You think that's possible?"

"Sure it is," she said and her breath seemed to catch for a second. "Trust me."

. He knew he should just walk away. Yank the door open and slip through. Instead he stared at that vulnerable face and wondered how anyone who looked so guileless could be considered dangerous.

"This isn't a good idea," he said and saw the edge of her teeth dig into the soft flesh of her lower lip. Desire curled in his guts. It was suddenly hard to breathe and between his legs he felt the stirrings of an erection.

"What are you afraid of?"

He could barely speak. The room seemed suddenly hot. He had to get away. "It's not a matter of fear."

"Then what?"

He hoped to sound callous. "I don't think I should be consorting with the enemy."

Her laughter was low, like the seductive roll of an ocean tide. It thundered through his ears. "Didn't your brother send you out to spy on me? Didn't you camp out by my motel, then follow me to the library? Sorry if it wasn't all that interesting, not the usual cloak-and-dagger stuff. Anyway, you're in this as deep as I am, Zach, and you can protest as loud as you like, but deep down, you want to know as much as I do whether I'm your sister or not."

"Half-sister," he clarified.

"Right." She removed her hand and tossed her thick, wild hair off her shoulders. "Half-sister. Give me a minute to change."

He should tell her no and get out. Now. But he didn't. Instead, his gaze skated down her worn sweatshirt and jeans. "You look fine."

"I look like I just stepped off the farm in Belamy, Montana. I'll only be a minute."

She didn't wait for him to answer and hurried through the door to the master bedroom. She wondered if he'd second-guess himself and leave, but, by the time she'd slipped into a white cowl-necked sweater and black jeans, slid a tube of lipstick over her lips and tugged a brush through her hair, he was where she'd left him, in the sitting room, one shoulder resting against the window casing, a drink in one hand as he stared out the window. His hip was thrown out and she noticed the way his jeans had faded across the buttocks and the movement of muscular thighs beneath the timeworn denim.

He caught sight of her reflection in the mirror, turned, and didn't move. His lips thinned at the sight of her, as if he were suddenly angry and his gaze raked her down and up again.

"Ready?"

He tossed back his drink. "As ready as I'll ever be."

All the way to the lower level he was broodingly silent and his eyes had darkened with accusations she didn't begin to understand. The elevator car seemed close, the air thick with the scents of whiskey and leather, and though he'd made a point of standing as far from her as the small car allowed, she could feel the heat radiating from his body.

His boots rang on the concrete floor of the parking garage and Adria half ran to keep up with him, stepping around puddles of condensation that splattered the ground from the low-hanging pipes webbing across the ceiling.

"Where do you want to go?" he asked as he unlocked the passenger door of his Jeep.

"You're the native," she said as she climbed into the seat.

"Well, hell, I thought you were, too." He slammed her door shut and strode to the driver's side of the Cherokee.

"I just meant—"

"I know what you meant, lady." He climbed in, jammed the key into the ignition, threw the rig into reverse, then shoved it into first. Within seconds the Jeep had emerged from beneath the hotel and joined the traffic of the clogged Portland streets. A light mist was falling, catching in the headlights and adding a silvery sheen to the streets.

"I thought we were going to be civil to each other."

He slid her a noncommittal glance.

"Why do you hate me?"

His lips compressed as he headed east across the river.

"Zach?"

"I don't hate you. I don't even know you."

"You act as if I'm poison."

His jaw clenched visibly as he stopped for a light. "Maybe you are."

"Why won't you give me a chance?"

He practically stood on the brakes as the light changed at a crosswalk and an elderly couple crossed the street. Zach's fingers drummed impatiently against the steering wheel and the instant the light changed, he tromped on the accelerator. "I'm not giving you a chance, because I don't buy your story, Adria."

"Why not have an open mind?"

"What good would it do?"

"Nothing. For you, I suppose." She crossed her arms over her chest and glared out the windshield. There was no use trying to force him to believe in her when she didn't really believe in herself. But she'd hoped that he would become her ally. She looked at him from the corner of her eye and felt an impending sense of doom. Of course he couldn't be her friend. If he weren't her half-brother, she would find him attractive. Long and lean, rugged and cynical, quick to anger but with a killer smile that could warm even the most frigid heart. Intense. Cocky. Irreverent. Just plain bad news.

He caught her looking at him. Shifting down, he shot her another murderous glance. "You look a helluva lot like Kat, I'll give you that."

"Is that a crime?"

"It should be," he growled.

"Kat . . .is that what you called Katherine?"

"Behind her back."

She leaned against the door and rubbed the kinks from her neck. "What did you call her to her face?"

He snorted. "Mommy dearest."

"What?"

"That was a joke, Adria." Zach's expression hardened. "To be honest, I tried to avoid her."

"Why?" She watched as his fingers curled around the steering wheel in a death grip.

"She was trouble," he said as he flipped on the radio and soft jazz filled the interior. So he didn't want to talk about Katherine. Adria wasn't surprised. Throughout her research, she'd learned very little of the woman she suspected had borne her. It seemed as if Katherine had been content to let her husband bask in the spotlight; she'd always hidden in the wings, hauntingly beautiful and supportive. Adria wondered if Katherine truly avoided the limelight or if her powerful husband had found ways to keep his family, including his beautiful wife, in the shadows.

Adria didn't know much about London's mother; the information had been spotty, but she'd thought Katherine and Witt had met in Canada. After a whirlwind romance, they'd been married, to the shock and horror of Witt's entire family. That was to be expected, Adria supposed. After all, rumor had it that Witt's divorce from his first wife, Eunice, had been messy and harsh. Accusations had been hurled and in the end, Witt, ever powerful, had ended up with his kids. No wonder Katherine wasn't greeted with open arms.

But Adria couldn't help making comparisons between herself and the second Mrs. Witt Danvers. As Katherine had been an outsider to the family twenty-odd years before, Adria was the outsider now. For the first time Adria felt a kinship with the woman who was supposed to be her mother, and yet she also suspected that Zach wasn't being completely honest with her. There was something he was hiding, something dark and mysterious about Katherine. He didn't admit it, but obviously, whenever the subject of Katherine LaRouche Danvers was broached, he grew silent and brooding.

As he drove, the skyscrapers gave way to shorter complexes, the city lights became less frequent, the traffic thinned, and eventually the offices gave way to homes lining the streets. Adria wondered about his childhood. Witt Danvers had been a powerful, dominating man. His first wife was weak, and his second . . . how little she knew of the woman who had become Zachary's stepmother.

"What kind of trouble was Katherine?" she asked, when Zach didn't elaborate.

"The worst." Deep lines bracketed his mouth. An unspoken emotion—guilt—surfaced, then disappeared.

"Meaning—"

"Meaning that she came on like gangbusters. If she saw something she wanted, she'd use every means possible to get it. She never stopped until she got it."

"What did she want?"

Hesitating, he stared through the windshield and he seemed lost in a whirlpool of murky memories. His mouth compressed into a hard, unyielding line; the cords in his neck seemed more pronounced, as if he were angry and waging an inner battle with himself. Seconds passed without an answer as the Jeep sped out of the city and through rolling pasture land surrounded by black, looming hills. He braked for a corner as the mist thickened into rain.

"What did Katherine want?" she repeated as the road angled upward through the hills.

Again, he slid her an insolent glance. The tires whined on the wet streets. "Everything."

Adria felt that he was talking in circles and yet at least he was speaking. After hours in the library, reading dry accounts of the Danvers family, she finally had someone who was willing—albeit reluctantly—to give her information. She cautioned herself to tread softly.

The road had narrowed into two twisting lanes winding through the foothills. Adria barely noticed—she was too intent on finding out about the woman whom she thought was her mother. "Did she get it? Everything?"

He snorted in disgust. "Don't you know?" he asked sarcastically.

"No, I—"

"After all those hours in the library, digging through the dirt. Kat's dead, Adria. She killed herself. Jumped off a damned balcony."

Stunned, she could barely speak. The temperature in the Jeep seemed to drop ten degrees and she shivered. "I thought it was an accident," she whispered. "The accounts I read said she inadvertently overdosed on sleeping pills—and stumbled . . ."

"It wasn't an accident," Zach said as he yanked on the steering wheel and turned into the gravel parking lot of some kind of tavern or inn. "Kat took her life. She opened up a bottle of sleeping pills and downed them all with half a bottle of eighty-proof whiskey, then took a walk on a balcony and took a flying leap."

"You don't know—"

He slammed on the brakes, cut the engine, and grabbed her with both hands. His fingers dug into her shoulders as he gave her a little shake. "She committed suicide, Adria. It was whitewashed in the papers, but Katherine Danvers was a victim of her own fantasies, her own dreams."

His eyes had narrowed at the memory, his nostrils flared in the close interior of the cab. Raindrops beat against the roof of the car and music, floating out of the door of the inn whenever a customer entered or left, drifted through the closed windows of the Jeep. Adria licked her lips and stared up at him, this man who could be her half-brother.

His breath was warm against her face, his hands strong and forceful, his eyes as dark as the night. Adria's throat caught and she couldn't look away. Spellbound, she held his gaze and knew in an instant that he was going to kiss her. Her heart squeezed. Unwanted desire—wicked and wanton—crept stealthily through her blood.

"Damn you," he whispered hoarsely, his face so close to

hers she could see smoky desire in his eyes. "You look so much like her!"

"Zachary—"

"Go home, Adria," he said, letting go of her so suddenly she nearly fell against him. His expression turned harsh. "Go home, before you get hurt."

13

"Who's going to hurt me?" she demanded, pushing away from him and creating as much distance as possible in the Jeep. Her heart was pounding so loudly she could barely breathe. She'd thought he would kiss her, knew it was on his mind, and he'd run scared. She *couldn't* get involved with him. The windows of the rig had fogged, seeming to cut off the rest of the world, and as she stared at him, she felt as if they were the only two people on earth.

"You're going to hurt yourself."

"How?"

His eyes glittered in the darkness. "You're playing with fire."

"And you're talking in circles."

"Am I?" He reached for her again and this time when he drew her close she could feel the heat of his body, found her own heart beating with desire. His breath was warm and ragged, his eyes defiant. "Why are you doing this?" he asked before he lowered his head and his lips crashed over hers in a kiss that was almost brutal and his fingers wound in the thick strands of her hair. Anger and passion sizzled through her blood. She tried not to respond, to push him away, but her hands were useless against his broad chest and he ground his mouth over hers in a way that was wickedly possessive and seared her to her very soul. His tongue prodded insistently at her teeth, gaining entrance to and plundering the dark recess of her mouth.

A low moan escaped her and she wanted to die from embarrassment, yet she kissed him back. Her pulse throbbed and for the first time in years a hot, yawning desire uncoiled deep within her. She couldn't think, couldn't move, couldn't deny. She wound her arms around his neck, feeling him yank her closer, knowing that her breasts, already full, were crushed against his leather jacket.

As suddenly as he'd taken her into his arms, he released her. "Jesus H. Christ," he swore, breathing hard. Closing his eyes, he let his head drop back against the seat cushions and gritted his teeth, as if suddenly struck by the magnitude of what he'd done. It seemed as if he were mentally willing his desire away. "Damn it, Kat, what is it you want from me?"

"I—I'm not Kat," she whispered, horrified.

A deep stain crawled up his neck as he realized his mistake. "And you're not London. Look, we can't do this."

"I don't want to—" The glare he sent her cut her to the bone.

"And don't give me any crap about wanting to be friends. I think I just proved we're way past that."

She swallowed with difficulty. Desire pulsed through her veins. "Zachary, I can't—this isn't—"

"What isn't?" His eyes flew open and he searched her face as if he intended to kiss her until she finally shut up. For several heartbeats she felt his indecision. "Hell," he ground out before reaching for her again and roughly folding her into his arms. He kissed her without restraint, his lips anxious and hungry, his body hard and straining against hers as he forced her back against the seat, his weight pinning her. Again, his tongue delved deep and she felt the hardness between his legs. She should stop him, but she couldn't. Delicious little flames of desire lapped at her, caused her lungs to constrict. He kissed her lips, her face, her eyes, his hands restless, but not moving from her back. When he finally lifted his head, he glared down at her and there was hatred in his eyes—intense, self-loathing hatred. "Don't tell me you can't," he said through clenched teeth. "You can and would. But I won't give you the satisfaction! You're as bad as she was." He struggled to a sitting position and reached for the door handle.

"As . . . who?" she asked, but knew that he was talking about Kat.

"She came on to anything in pants."

"No—"

"You didn't know her."

"But I didn't mean—"

"Neither did I."

"I'm sorry."

"Sorry?" He raked stiff fingers through his hair. "Sorry?" His smile was cold in the darkness. "Don't play the innocent with me, Adria."

She itched to slap him, to deny what had so obviously been the truth, but curled her hands into tight little fists. "I didn't . . ." If only she could lie and tell him that she didn't feel any attraction to him, but she held her tongue. Her heart was still racing, her hands shaking.

The look he sent her seared her to the most forbidden recesses of her mind, and she knew then that what they felt for each other—this pure animal lust—was part of her destiny. A horrid attraction that she would have to fight. Her throat went dry and she wanted to deny the desire that pumped through her veins.

"I just wondered how much you were like Kat," he said, his gaze raking over her uncombed hair, mussed sweater, and swollen lips. "How far you'd go."

She didn't believe him and her anger sparked. "So you expect me to believe that you kissed me out of curiosity?"

He shrugged. "I don't give a shit what you believe."

"Don't lie, Zach. I didn't. You kissed me because you wanted to. Hide it any way you like, but you felt what I did."

"Christ, now you even sound like her!"

A sickening thought rolled through her mind as she pictured Zach, not quite eighteen, and Katherine, her mother, locked in a compromising embrace, bodies shining with sweat and hard with desire. Oh, God. Was it possible? Had they been lovers? "What are you trying to say?" she whispered as the horrid thought congealed in her mind. "That she came on to you—that she was your—"

"She was nothing to me!" He sliced her a glance that cut her to the quick.

"I don't believe—"

"Believe what you want, Adria. As I said before, it's no skin off my nose how you want to delude yourself." He opened the door of the Jeep and cool air swept inside. She scrambled out and half ran to keep up with his long, furious strides. Rain peppered the ground and washed down her neck but she didn't care.

"Wait—" Her fingers grabbed for the crook of his arm, but he tossed her hand aside and whirled upon her. His face was twisted into a mask of rage and he seemed larger than ever in the darkness. Rain caught in his black hair before trickling down the contours of his face and disappearing beneath his collar.

His lips flattened and the neon lights from the restaurant reflected red and blue in his eyes. "I don't know what you want from me, Adria, but you'd better be careful. You might just get it!"

He turned and walked up two long, low steps to the porch of the log cabin.

Adria had no choice but to follow him. Slowly counting to ten, she followed his path, shouldered open the door, walked through a pine-paneled vestibule, and found him standing at the bar, one boot resting on a tarnished brass rail, his elbows propped on the battle-scarred surface of glossy cherry wood.

"I already ordered for you," he said as the bartender, a slim woman with kinky blond hair and red lipstick, slid two frosted glasses of beer to him, then deftly snatched up the bills he'd left on the counter. His eyes met Adria's in the mirror over the bar and his gaze had become cloudy again.

"Come on. Let's grab a table." He cocked his head to an empty booth.

Adria tried to put a lid on her simmering temper. Though she was boiling inside, she slid onto the cushions and accepted the beer—his notion of a peace offering.

Zach gulped half his beer in one swallow. "Anything else you'd like to know about the Danvers family?" he asked with a scornful lift of his eyebrow.

"Whatever you want to tell me."

"That's the problem. I don't want to tell you anything. I think it would be better if you just packed it all in and drove off to Bozeman—"

"Belamy."

"Whatever."

"Now you're sounding like the rest of your family."

"God forbid," he muttered and drained his glass. He signaled for another drink, which a waitress, a heavier version of the blond bartender, brought over along with menus.

She winked at Zachary as if they were longtime friends, then smiled at Adria. "Refill?"

"Not right now."

"I'll give you a few minutes to decide." She moved to a nearby table and Adria kept her voice low.

"You know," she said, not really believing her own words, "despite what you said earlier, we could be friends if we tried."

He made a sound of disgust. "Friends." His lips curved into a smile without any warmth. "Is that how you treat all your 'friends'?"

"Don't do this—"

"*You* don't do it! We can never, *never* be friends—I thought I already made that clear," he growled, leaning over the table and grabbing her shoulders.

She threw off his hands and glared furiously at him. "Why are you trying so hard to hate me?"

He hesitated, then sighed and looked away. "Maybe it's just

easier that way." Dropping back onto his bench, he studied the head of his beer and his jaw clenched. "For both of us."

"You're afraid I might end up with the Danvers fortune," she said, realizing he was more like his family than he wanted to admit.

He snorted and rolled his glass between his fingers. "I don't care if you end up with the whole damned lot of the inheritance—the logging company, the sawmills, the hotel, the house in Tahoe, even the ranch. If you did, I'd say good riddance. I'm not afraid of you."

"I don't believe you."

"Your prerogative," he said with a shrug.

"You can be a real bastard, Danvers. You know that, don't you?"

One side of his mouth lifted insolently. "I work at it."

"A true Danvers."

His smile faded. "Let's order."

They didn't say another word to each other and Adria watched while the waitress flirted outrageously with Zachary as she spouted off the specials of the day. In the end, they both ordered steak sandwiches.

Some country song about lost love and broken hearts was overshadowed by the clink of glasses, rap of pool balls, and murmur of differing conversations. More tavern than restaurant, the old log cabin seemed home to a dozen or so blue-collar types. Hard hats had been exchanged for baseball caps and cowboy hats, but it seemed as if the men sitting on stools in the bar were at home. It reminded Adria of Belamy.

"Why'd you bring me here?" she asked as the waitress slid their drinks onto the table.

"It was your idea, remember."

"But out here—in the middle of nowhere?"

"You'd rather go to some restaurant downtown?"

"Not really." She took a sip from her beer.

"Thought you wanted to know the real me." His eyes glinted sensually. "Now you do."

"I don't think so. I think you're hiding something, Zach. Trying to scare me off." She stared him down. "It won't work." Leaning back against the tufted plastic upholstery, she said, "You were raised in Portland."

"I try to forget about that."

"Why?"

He hesitated and gazed at a point over her shoulder where, she suspected, he saw his own youth. "I was always in trouble. Gave the old man nothing but grief."

"And you're still cultivating that bad-ass attitude, aren't you?"

He relaxed against the back of the booth and took a long drink from his glass. "Maybe."

"No maybes about it."

Lifting a shoulder, he said, "So what've you found out about my illustrious family?"

"Not enough."

He pinned her with a look and she thought twice about answering. Finally, as the meals were delivered, she said, "Okay. The library was pretty much a bust. Sure, the microfilm from the newspapers had information on the kidnapping and on the family, but there wasn't much . . . much substance to it all."

"So you came up empty."

"Almost. But I'm not done digging." She started in on her salad and Zach muttered something about mule-headed women under his breath. She let the comment slide.

"Where are you going to look next?"

She smiled and took a sip from her glass, her eyes meeting his over the rim. "Lots of places. I'm going to talk to reporters and the police. Believe me, I've only just begun."

"You're going to wind up empty-handed."

"Is that right? Why?"

"You've got one helluva hole in your father's story. It's about as big as all of Montana."

"I'm all ears," she invited, anxious to hear what he thought. Somehow it was important, as if his opinion would help.

He picked up half of his sandwich. "If everything you say is true—why did Ginny Slade take London in the first place?"

"Who knows?"

"No one, I guess," he said thoughtfully. "But it wasn't because she wanted a child or she wouldn't have left you with the Nashes."

"I know, but—"

"And it wasn't for the money because she left some cash in her bank accounts in Portland and never demanded ransom."

"Maybe she was paid off."

"My father offered a million dollars, no questions asked, for the return of his daughter. In 1974 that was a helluva lot of money."

"It's a helluva lot of money today."

"But Ginny didn't claim it."

"She could've been worried about prosecution. Your father—our father—wasn't known to be as good as his word. He had a reputation for retribution."

"The plain truth of the matter is you might not be London."

"There is still one motive left," she said as she finished her beer and set the empty glass on the table.

"Which is?"

"Revenge. Witt had made more than his share of enemies, Zach. He'd walked all over people, didn't care who he stepped on to get what he wanted. Seems to me there were plenty of people who would have loved to see him hurt. I just have to figure out who it is. I was hoping you would help me."

"Why would I bother?" he asked.

"Because London was your half-sister and a lot of people in town thought you were somehow behind her disappearance."

"I was a kid at the time."

"A kid who was always in trouble. A kid who had more than his share of run-ins with the law, a kid who suffered big-time at Witt Danvers's hand, and a kid who was involved in some kind of mugging that night."

"I didn't have anything to do with what happened to London," he growled, the skin over his cheekbones stretching tight.

"Okay, Danvers, now's your chance to prove it. All you have to do is help me find out who I really am. If I'm London, then your name is in the clear—the little girl didn't really die, she was raised in Montana."

"And if you're not?"

"You're no worse off than you were before. At least your family and the people who care will know that you tried to find out the truth."

"Except—" he said, nudging his plate aside.

"Except?"

"Except I don't give a shit what the 'people who care' think." He settled back in his chair and regarded her with eyes suddenly smoky with desire. "Your offer's not good enough, Adria." His gaze drilled into hers. "I'm not interested."

Oswald Sweeny shivered in the breeze that roared off the mountains and cut through his coat. He drew one last warm lungful of smoke from his Camel and ground the butt into the gravel lot surrounding the rooming house. In his opinion, Belamy, Montana, was about as far from civilization as he ever wanted to be. He locked the car door and shuffled up the steps to the wide front porch.

Inside, heat and the smell of something cooking—soup or stew, maybe—enveloped him.

He heard the landlady rattling around in the kitchen, but didn't bother with any chitchat just now. He hurried upstairs, snapped on the light, and yanked off his jacket. He hadn't found more than he'd expected in Belamy, Montana, and that bothered him because he was already tired of this little town and its straight-arrow, salt-of-the-earth citizens.

He'd suspected Adria Nash was broke, and it looked like she was drowning in red ink—hospital debts, a large mortgage on the farm she owned, college loans, doctor bills. He had to do a little more checking to find out just how desperate she was for money—Danvers money.

For the last twenty-four hours he'd trudged around this podunk town and nearly frozen his butt clean off trying to pick apart Adria's story. There were discrepancies, but not many, and the part about her growing up as the adopted daughter of Victor and Sharon Nash was absolutely true.

But there was more dirt yet to dig. He'd seen it in a few of the good citizens' eyes when he started asking questions about the Nash family in general and Adria in particular. Sweeny was certain she was hiding something—he just didn't know what.

The pieces as he'd put them together from the few people in Belamy who were willing to talk to him linked into a straightforward picture. Sharon Nash had once been a pretty girl who had married Victor, a decent farmer a few years older than she. All she'd wanted in life was to be a wife and mother, but her dreams had been stolen away when she wasn't able to get pregnant and medical research in the fifties and sixties was more interested in preventing births than helping sterile couples conceive. She'd gone from doctor to doctor, becoming more desperate as the years passed. When medical technology had swung around and fertility pills were available, she was too old. Fertility pills didn't work. She reluctantly accepted the fact that she was barren and she convinced herself that God, in keeping her from having children, was punishing her for not believing more strongly in Him.

The farming years had been lean and no adoption agency would offer the land-poor couple a child they couldn't afford. A private adoption, because of the cost, was out of the question. It seemed as if Sharon was destined to be childless.

As the years passed, Sharon threw all her energy into the church. Though her husband rarely attended services, Sharon never missed a Sunday or a weekly prayer meeting. As everyone here on earth—her husband, the doctors and the lawyers—had failed her, she decided to trust in God completely and became nearly fanatic in serving Him.

Suddenly her prayers were answered, though not through the church, but through Victor's brother's law firm. A little girl—a relative, most people thought—had become available and, if Sharon and Victor asked few questions, the adoption could be handled. Sharon didn't need to have any answers. There were no questions. In her mind this girl was sent from heaven. Victor was more hesitant, as he and his wife were getting up in years, but as much to help out the struggling mother of the girl—a shirttail relative, Sweeny had gleaned—as to keep his wife happy, Victor agreed. In the end, Adria became the apple of her father's eye.

Sweeny pulled a small flask from his jacket pocket and took a warming swallow. Everything he'd found out so far was all just town gossip and speculation, the idle talk of neighbors and friends. There were no public records of the adoption and Ezra Nash, the lawyer who had handled the case, was dead, the paperwork in his office in Bozeman destroyed in a fire. It was frustrating as hell. All the information fit neatly into Adria's story and matched the testimony of the pathetic man in the video, but Sweeny could smell a rat. Something didn't quite mesh.

And it had to do with money. Money she didn't have.

Ms. Nash could have all the good intentions in the world, but Sweeny was certain that she was after the Danvers family fortune. Somehow she'd managed to put herself through college and graduated at the top of her class with a double major in architecture and business, but she'd only worked for a construction company after graduation.

Tomorrow he'd ask for a simple credit report that would confirm the town gossip, then he'd request some information from the Department of Motor Vehicles that would give him some personal insight into the woman, help him find out what it was that made her tick.

He took another swallow from his flask and, without removing his shoes, dropped onto the bed. For the next couple of days he was stuck in Belamy, which was little more than a stoplight stuck in the middle of no-goddamned-where. The sooner he was out of here, the better.

His only lead was Ginny Slade, aka Virginia Watson Slade, and he'd have to track her down, but it wouldn't be easy. It would take time and money. Lots and lots of Danvers money.

Adria rubbed the knots from the back of her neck as she peeled off her clothes. She tossed her sweater onto the bed, then stepped out of her slacks. Finger-combing the tangles from her hair, she walked to the bathroom with its cool marble floor, gold-colored fixtures, and expansive mirrors. Plush robes emblazoned with "Hotel Danvers" in gold script hung on hooks near a shower big enough for two. She twisted on the faucets to the Jacuzzi and added bath oil from the tiny bottles the maid had left earlier.

"A far cry from the Riverview Inn," she muttered as she unhooked her bra and stepped out of her panties. Within seconds she was immersed in the warm water, letting pulsating jets ease her tired muscles. With a sigh she closed her eyes and tried not to think of Zachary Danvers and the unwanted emotions he evoked in her.

He was too sexy and raw for his own damned good—or hers. She remembered him staring at the portrait of Katherine, his stepmother, in the hallway of the Danvers mansion. There had been secrets in his eyes, and what else—longing? Guilt?

"You're making too much of it," she told herself as lavender-scented bubbles surrounded her and the Jacuzzi rumbled, churning the warm water. How long had it been since she'd indulged in a bubble bath? Ten years? Twenty? It wasn't the kind of luxury Sharon Nash believed in, not even for a child. How different her life would have been had she been raised as a Danvers, in the kind of opulence most people could only dream of, but the family seemed to take for granted. The family. Her family? God, that wasn't a pleasant thought.

She'd already decided Jason was a snake, Trisha not much better, a bitter woman with her share of secrets. Zach was surly at his worst and sarcastically seductive at his best, and Nelson was unreadable, a man who seemed torn. But then, those had only been her first impressions.

"Probably only gonna get worse," she told herself and smiled until she considered Zach again. He'd made the mistake of calling her "Kat." Or had it been on purpose, some kind of test?

She lathered her arms and decided against that particular theory. Zach had slipped. Kat's name had fallen from his tongue in a heated moment when they'd been kissing and touching . . . and . . .

Oh, God, had he done the same with Katherine? His stepmother? She wondered about Zach and Kat's relationship. Something wasn't right about it. Not at all. Her mind began to wander down a hot, dark path as she remembered his expression as he'd studied Kat's portrait. Had it been yearning? Forbidden desire?

"This is getting you nowhere," she warned herself as she turned off the jets and the room grew quiet. She tried to clear her mind, to stop her thoughts from reverting to Zach. She couldn't get involved with him. It was suicide to think otherwise. Everyone in the family distrusted her. Even Zachary. She had to remember that. They would do anything to dispute her story, to prove her a fake.

She leaned back again, closing her eyes and letting the warm water lap around her. She just needed some time to relax. Unwind . . .

She drifted, dozing, daydreaming of Zachary Danvers and what it would be like to be his lover, to feel his strong arms upon her, to touch the naked muscles of his back, to kiss him with a wild abandon without any thought to the consequences, without any concern about her identity, to just love him sensually and totally and feel him straining above her, his body gleaming, his eyes dark with smoky passion and . . .

Click!

Her eyes flew open and she realized she'd been dreaming, asleep long enough for the water to grow tepid. She strained to listen. She'd heard something—the door?

"Hello?" she said, reaching for a towel and standing. Her skin prickled with goose bumps and the air seemed chilled, colder than it should be. "Is anyone there?"

No answer.

And yet she sensed that someone had been close by.

Heart thudding, she threw on one of the robes and slipped quietly into the bedroom. Nothing looked disturbed—her clothes were where she'd tossed them, her shoes near the closet. The French doors leading to the living area were ajar, but she hadn't closed them. She walked into the sitting room where the furniture was arranged just as it had been when she'd walked in less than an hour earlier.

The door was shut, but she hadn't thrown the dead bolt.

What does it matter?

Whoever was in here—if someone had intruded—would be connected to the family. Your family. All part of the Danvers clan. With access to a key.

"Stupid, stupid girl," she muttered, and hooked the privacy chain that she'd forgotten.

But why would anyone risk coming into her room?

Is it really yours? How do you know it's not set up with spy cameras? How do you know that someone isn't looking at you right now, didn't have a view of you lounging naked in the bathtub?

"Stop it," she whispered under her breath. This was paranoia talking, nothing more.

Still, she eyed the ceiling and walls, checking for tiny cameras, her skin crawling at the thought of unseen eyes observing her. She'd been a fool to accept a room here—the old hotel had been so recently remodeled that it could be equipped with all sorts of spy devices. After all, *she* didn't choose this room; it was chosen for her. By a member of the family.

"Have a little trust," she advised herself, but looked at the carpet, searching for footprints or tracks that someone else had been in the room. She couldn't discern anything and after searching through the closet and finding nothing disturbed, she donned a pair of pajamas and slipped between the covers of the king-sized bed.

Nothing was wrong.

Nothing.

Her imagination was just running away with her, that was all. But deep in her heart, she didn't believe it. Not for a second.

Zachary slung his bag over his shoulder. It was time to leave this town. Being in the same hotel with Adria, on the same damned floor, no less, was asking for trouble, big-time.

It had been two nights since he'd last seen her and he'd been unable to close her out of his mind. He had plenty to keep him busy, still working out the kinks of this damned hotel, but he'd been tense, his muscles tightening when he thought he caught a glimpse of her or heard her voice. He was, slowly but surely, losing it. He'd never considered himself a fool, nor had he ever had any kind of death wish. He'd always thought clearly and known what he wanted.

Until he'd met Adria.

Whenever he was around her, his senses were on overload and his normally clear mind became muddied. She was beautiful, damned beautiful, and she looked so much like Kat he felt an icy drizzle of dèjá vu whenever he looked at her. Yet, mingled with that cold drip of memory was a flame of desire, melting away his inhibitions, heating his blood and causing him to lose sight of reality.

Which was what?

That she was really his half-sister?

Or that she was a beautiful treacherous woman whose greed had blinded her to the truth? Had she used her uncanny resemblance to Kat for her personal gain, or did she really believe that she was London?

Christ, what a mess! He hitched his bag up a notch and headed for the elevator. This time he was leaving, if only for a little while. He welcomed the three-hour drive over the mountains, was anxious to get back to the ranch. He needed time and space alone. Away from the enigma that was Adria Nash. Jason wouldn't like it, but it didn't really matter.

In the parking lot, he threw his bag into the backseat and drove to Jason's house in the west hills. His older brother had requested that he show up for a family meeting and Zach had decided he'd make an appearance, then drop the bomb that he was taking off. If only for a few days. He just needed a little time and space to get his head on straight again.

The garage doors were open and Jason's Jag was parked near his wife Nicole's white Mercedes. In the third bay, a vintage Rolls-Royce gleamed glossy black under the lights. One of the men who did yard work and basic mechanics for the family was running a soft white rag along a sleek, spotless fender.

Toys. Jason loved toys. From racehorses to classic cars, to rich wives and sexy young mistresses, Jason had always loved toys.

Zach eyed the house where he'd grown up, tamped down any unwanted memories, rapped on the door with his knuckles, and waited. Within seconds Nicole opened the door and smiled wanly at her brother-in-law. A waif-thin woman with tanned skin and white-blond hair, she stepped out of the way. "Zachary."

"Is Jason here?"

"In the basement."

"Good. I'll see myself down," he added, when she seemed intent on leading him down the stairs he'd played on as a kid.

He and Nelson had slid down the staircase in cardboard

boxes, raced each other up and down the steep steps, and been hauled downstairs whenever Witt wanted to discipline them. Witt, one hand on the back of Zach's collar, the other clenched firmly around his belt, had dragged his second son down the stairs more times than Zach wanted to remember. Witt had seemed determined to break Zach's spirit, and despite Eunice's pleading to "go easy on the boy, Witt, he's just a child," Zach had felt the razor-sharp sting of Witt's leather belt against the skin on his back time after time.

"Shit," he muttered as the memories and pain thundered through his brain. The beatings had been brutal, but had never broken Zach's spirit. Clenching his teeth until his jaw ached, he shoved those hideous memories to the dark corners of his brain as he rounded the corner of the staircase.

He found his older brother, shirtsleeves rolled over his forearms, throwing darts at a target mounted on the wall near the mirrored bar. A pool table dominated the room and a flagstone fireplace climbed up one wall. Through steamy French doors, a sauna and Jacuzzi waited, and on every wall hung trophies—the heads of bear, antelope, tiger, and bison, contributions from his grandfather, Julius Danvers, who'd prided himself on being a big-game hunter. A polar bear, claws extended, stood in one corner, and a zebra hide was stretched beside that of a kangaroo. Glassy eyes and snarling teeth greeted all who entered.

"What did you find out?" Jason didn't even look his way, just threw another dart toward the bull's-eye.

"From Adria? Not much." Zach grabbed the cue ball and rolled it in his hands. His conversations with Adria had been minimal, but he did know a few facts. However, he wasn't particularly interested in sharing them with Jason. "She grew up a poor farm girl in Montana. Her mother was kind of a religious nut and her father put up with it but wasn't a fanatic." He leaned a hip against the table. "She's bound and determined to see this through no matter what the outcome."

"So it's her personal quest."

Zach frowned and stared at the fire. "I think she's just trying to find the truth."

Jason glanced at him, then threw a dart, hitting the target dead-on. "Sounds like you're weakening where our new little-lost-sister is concerned."

"I still think she's a fake."

"Of course she is." He threw another dart and just missed the red bull's-eye. "We'll watch her and she'll trip up."

"I'm going back to the ranch."

"Not now."

"Tonight."

A tic developed beneath Jason's eye. "Can't it wait? Manny seems to be more than capable—"

"I'll be back in a couple of days. I just need to do a few things. Check what's going on at the ranch and in the office."

Jason looked about to argue, but held his tongue at the sound of footsteps on the stairs. Trisha didn't bother saying a word to either of her brothers, just ambled over to the bar and poured herself a straight shot of tequila. "Where's Nelson?" she asked as she hoisted a hip onto the stool and sipped her drink.

"He'll be here."

"I heard Mother was invited, too."

"Hell," Zach muttered, placing the cue ball back on the table.

"She was included in the will," Jason said.

"Part of her deal with Dad when they divorced."

"Nonetheless, she counts."

"Christ."

Trisha motioned to the bar. "Maybe you need a drink, Zach?"

"Not tonight."

She glanced at Jason. "And the girl's coming, too?"

Zach's neck muscles bunched. "Adria? You invited her here?"

Jason checked his watch. "She should be arriving any

minute. Didn't want to leave her out, you know. I thought maybe we could hammer out a deal and send her packing back to the farm."

"I don't think so." Zach was irritated. He didn't want to see Adria again, didn't want to smell her perfume or get lost in her eyes.

"Look, even if she is a fraud, she looks too much like Kat to let it pass. The press will go crazy. There will be pictures in the paper—old photos of Kat put up against new ones of Adria. Comparisons are going to be made whether we like it or not and unfortunately, we all have to admit that the girl does look a lot like our late stepmother."

"I'm not admitting anything." Trisha tossed back her drink and poured herself another. "I don't want to hear this."

"The newspapers and television reports are just the beginning. Then she'll get herself a lawyer, a good lawyer who wants some notoriety, someone who's willing to take a risk just to score big and get his face in the papers. A lot of attorneys are more interested in fame than money."

Trisha snorted.

"Well, nearly as interested."

"So, what do you plan to do?" Zach asked, his gut twisting a little. Talking about Adria behind her back, plotting against her, bothered him more than it should have. Maybe Trisha was right, maybe he needed a beer.

Jason's lips curved into a smooth smile. "What's the saying from *The Godfather*—I'm going to 'make her an offer she can't refuse'?"

"There is none."

"I think a hundred grand will do it."

Trisha's mouth fell open. "You'd give her that much?"

"Not to begin with, of course. We'll start low and try to intimidate her, but a hundred thousand isn't much when you think of the cost of attorneys if we have to go to court. And think of all the time the estate will be tangled up in probate. It's bad enough as it is—an estate this size takes forever."

"I bet the old man is sitting down in hell somewhere and laughing at us," Trisha said, lighting a cigarette and blowing smoke rings. "Imagine, leaving nearly fifty percent of his estate to a daughter he couldn't find or didn't even know if she was dead or alive. What a joke!"

"Unless we have proof of her death," Jason reminded them both. "Then her share of the inheritance can be divided among the rest of us."

Zach's blood turned to ice as he noticed the cold hint of a smile curving Jason's lips. Just how far would any of his siblings go to get their hands on Witt's fortune? They all had their personal axes to grind. Jason loved money; Trisha had always wanted revenge against the family, and Nelson was ambitious to a fault.

And what about you? You're not exactly lily-white.

As for his brothers and sister, he was certain they would like to get what they wanted, and they would surely steal. But would they kill? His back teeth gnashed silently and his fingers clenched involuntarily into fists.

Trisha gulped from her drink and sighed. "Our father who art in hell. Truly one of the world's great bastards." She looked up sharply and her gaze met Zach's. "No offense, Zach."

Zach let the comment slide. The questions about his paternity no longer rattled him. Who really gave a damn?

"Just because he made a provision for London, doesn't mean we can't fight it," Jason pointed out. "Haven't you heard that wills are meant to be contested? We just have to prove that the old man was senile at the time he had the will drawn up. That shouldn't be too hard. After all, who in his right mind would leave millions of dollars to a girl who had been missing for nearly twenty years?"

"So why haven't you done anything about it?" Trisha said, squinting through her smoke. "You're the hotshot lawyer."

"Because Dad's attorney will swear that the old man was

as sane as you and I. Claims he's got proof that Witt hadn't lost any of his marbles."

"So it's his word against ours."

Zach hated discussing the old man's estate. It was necessary, of course; he wasn't foolish enough or rich enough not to care, but he really wished he could just wash his hands of the whole family. Greedy vultures, that's what they'd all become.

And what about you? You're here, aren't you? Hoping to keep the ranch. Hell, what a mess. Then there was Adria. At the thought of her, his blood heated and he rubbed his chin in frustration. He didn't like the idea of trying to buy Adria out, but he didn't have a better plan.

"So, the first order of business is getting rid of our latest London," Jason said. "Send her packing and try to break the will."

"I don't think she'll go for it," Zach said, his voice sounding a lot steadier than he felt. "It's more a question of pride and truth than money with her."

Jason shook his head and rubbed his chin. "It's always money, Zach. Haven't you learned yet that everyone has a price? Even Ms. Nash. We just have to find what it is."

Zach heard noises on the stairs and his nerves tightened. He could feel Adria's presence before she followed Nicole into the room. "Have you all met Adria?" Nicole said, forcing a smile on her tanned face.

Adria didn't seem the least bit intimidated. In fact, she looked as if she really did belong. Her hands were stuffed into pockets of a jean jacket trimmed in leather and she didn't bother to smile. She slid a glance in Zach's direction and he stiffened. For a second they stared at each other before she forced her eyes to meet Jason's steady gaze. "I got a message that you wanted to see me."

"I did. Come in and have a seat—" He pointed to the grouping of leather furniture positioned near the fireplace. "Would you like a drink?"

She hesitated for a heartbeat, but then she managed a thin smile. "Why not? Have you got any white wine? Chardonnay."

Jason moved to the bar, as if he were willing to do whatever she wanted. Zach considered leaving but before he could make his way to the door, footsteps sounded on the stairs and his mother and Nelson strolled into the room. Eunice took one look at Adria and for a split second her face drained of color, but she recovered herself. "So you're Ms. Nash," she said, extending her hand, though she appeared anything but friendly. Her eyes were cool, her mouth pinched at the corners, her skin stretched tightly over the bones of her face. "I'm Eunice Smythe."

Adria knew quite a bit about the woman whose fingers felt like dry parchment, but mostly she'd pieced together rumors. She would love to know the truth. There had been gossip that Witt had divorced Eunice because of infidelity with Polidori, though, of course, no one but Eunice knew the truth. Whatever had happened between Witt and his wife, it had cost Eunice. She'd been denied custody of her children in a time when a father's rights were virtually ignored.

"Well, Adria. Nelson tells me you think you're Witt's long-lost daughter." Eunice's smile was as cold as steel as she let go of Adria's fingers.

Jason handed Adria the glass of wine she really hadn't wanted. She held the stem in a death grip. Her throat was suddenly dry, her fingers damp with sweat. "That's why I'm here, yes," Adria replied. "To find out the truth."

"The truth," Eunice murmured as she studied Adria. "Sometimes so elusive." Without so much as a sip, Adria set her drink on a nearby table. "So let's get down to it, shall we?" Eunice settled into a cream-colored chair. "Nicole, would you be a dear and fix me a gin and tonic?" she asked her daughter-in-law, and when Nicole poured the drink and handed it to her, Eunice patted the younger woman's slim arm. "That's a good girl."

"Always," Nicole replied in a brittle voice as she shot her husband a glance that would have cut through granite.

Every muscle in Adria's body was strung tight; tension was thick in the air and she didn't know which was worse, being stared at by the dead animal heads mounted on the walls, or by the very living beasts that congregated around her. *You asked for this,* she reminded herself. *You knew it would be tough, so just hang in there!* Giving herself a mental shake, she sat on the edge of the couch, directly across the glass-topped coffee table from Eunice, and refused to give in to the impulse to stare at Zachary, to silently ask for his help.

Jason slid onto the couch next to her.

Zachary looked bored. He leaned against the stones of the fireplace, his features composed, his gaze fixed on her, his jaw looking as if it hadn't seen a razor for a couple of days.

Adria shifted a little and watched as Nelson slung a leg over his mother's chair, positioning himself near her. Nicole, after delivering the drink to her mother-in-law, caught her husband's commanding gaze and hastily said something about checking on her daughter before hurrying up the stairs. Trisha didn't join the rest of the group, but preferred to sit on a stool at the bar, where she smoked and drank and observed everyone from a distance. There was a bitterness to her, a hardness Adria couldn't comprehend.

"No one here believes you," Eunice stated flatly.

"I expected as much."

"So you came ready to accept defeat."

"I came for—"

"I know, I know." Eunice waved in the air, as if swatting a bothersome insect. "The truth. Listen," she leaned closer, "let's get past all this talk about the truth, all right? It's tedious. Noble, I suppose, but tedious just the same, and we all know it's a lie. What you really want is to be taken seriously enough so that the family scrambles around and offers you a decent amount of money to go back to wherever it is you came from."

"I didn't—"

"Cut the crap," Nelson said quietly. "We're prepared to pay you, but you'd have to sign a document—"

"Aren't any of you interested in the fact that I could, just could, be your sister?" Adria asked. "I know you're worried about the estate, but think about it, what if I really am London?"

"Doesn't make any difference," Trisha said through a cloud of smoke. "To us, you're a stranger, and if you fell off the earth, we wouldn't care." Her lips curved up just a little. "In fact, a few of us might celebrate."

"Trisha!" Eunice said sharply, then turned her attention from her daughter to Adria. "She's a little harsh."

"Look, I don't need this. I thought you called me here to talk to me, to ask me questions, to help me find out the truth, but I guess I was wrong." She stood and slung the strap of her purse over her shoulder. "Believe it or not, I didn't drive to Portland to wreak havoc on your lives, or steal your fortune, or hurt anyone in any way."

"Of course you did," Trisha said.

Adria's back stiffened. "I won't give up."

Trisha, with her cigarette dangling from the corner of her mouth, clapped her hands. "Bravo! What a fine performance!"

"Stop it, Trisha!" Zachary said so vehemently that Eunice's eyes narrowed on her second son.

Jason ignored the outburst. "We could make it worth your while."

"You still want to pay me off?" She picked up her glass and sipped.

"Mmm. Say twenty-five thousand?"

She almost choked on a swallow of wine. She had expected a bribe, but the amount staggered her. "I—I don't think so."

Jason's smile tightened. "We'd be willing to go up to fifty."

Nelson visibly blanched and when Adria shot a glance in Zach's direction, he returned her stare impassively. He was in on it! He wanted to buy her out, too. Her blood boiled silently because she'd told herself that he was different, that he would help her, that he, the rebel, *cared*. Obviously she'd been mistaken.

"If you'll excuse me," she said, setting her drink on the table with trembling fingers, "I think I'll go pack."

Jason was on his feet. "You don't have to move out of the hotel—"

"Of course I do. Staying there was a mistake. Only one of many." Her gaze swiveled once again to Zachary's and this time she saw a little spark of the fire in his gray eyes. She thought about their kisses in his Jeep, the anger and passion that had radiated from him. Had it all been part of the plan to break down her defenses? Would he stoop low enough to try and seduce her, just to scare her off? Sick at the thought, she squared her shoulders, turned on her heel, and marched up the stairs. As far as she was concerned, the battle lines had been drawn. The Danvers family could rot in hell for all she cared.

The locket glittered and spun, catching the light as it dangled from a worn gold chain. Cheap. A fake. Like the woman who owned it.

It had been a big risk sneaking into Adria's hotel room, but sometimes risks were necessary. And look what the spoils were—a cheap piece of jewelry and an even cheaper pair of panties. Oh, they were sexy enough. Black lace and not much of it.

Adria Nash was obviously into carnal pleasures, or perhaps she was a tease.

So much like Kat.

In the privacy of a hotel room, Katherine's killer clenched Adria's personal items in angry hands and tried to calm down. It was impossible. Unwanted memories of Kat continued to haunt and torment the one person who had so desperately wanted to bury Katherine LaRouche Danvers forever.

Even now, as Katherine's killer stood near the windows of a penthouse suite with a view of Portland's city lights, the panorama was lost beneath visions of long black hair that gleamed blue as it fell down an unmarred back, breasts that were full and high, long legs that promised men dangerous pleasures.

Kat.

Would she never die?

Would her image never fade?

Dear God, how long would this torment go on?

As long as the family is threatened. As long as there is a chance Kat's child is alive; as long as London walks this earth.

Rage coursed through the blood of Katherine's killer. The locket, clenched so tightly, cut into a palm, drawing blood that was wiped with the scrap of lace Adria Nash called underwear.

No, this job was far from finished. The threat still existed.

Because of Adria Nash.

Because of London.

But that would change.

Soon.

Very, very soon.

14

No one believed her. She'd told the front desk, the man in charge of security, and even Zachary Danvers himself that she'd felt someone had been in her room. Even though she'd insisted that she was missing her locket and probably a few other things as well, that they had been stolen, she'd been dismissed.

"You think I set you up to be ripped off?" Zach had asked when she'd called him.

"I'm just telling you what happened."

"While you were dozing in the Jacuzzi," he'd clarified, unable or unwilling to keep the disbelief from his voice.

"Yes."

"And you think someone—no, make that the Danvers family—is spying on you, is that it? That we put you into a room filled with all kinds of electronic surveillance equipment, then sent a burglar up when we caught you sleeping in the tub?"

"I know it sounds crazy, but—"

"But nothing. It *is* crazy, Adria."

"It happened, Zach."

"Fine. I'll talk with Security." His voice was filled with disbelief. He was placating her.

"I should go to the police."

"Please. Do. Tell them what you just told me. Have them search the room and dust for prints, if they're not too busy. Tell them they didn't take your credit cards or your money, that nothing but a few personal things were lifted—and while you're at it, you may as well let them know that you think you're London. Let them know that they can close the books on that open kidnapping file."

She'd gritted her teeth. "I'll think about it," she assured him as she'd hung up, but, of course, she wouldn't call the local authorities. Not yet. Not before she hired herself a lawyer and knew her legal rights. She'd talked to an attorney in Bozeman before she'd come to Portland, but decided not to have him take any legal action. Not until she knew what she was up against.

And now she did.

She was up against the entire Danvers clan. The proverbial brick wall. And that wall was covered with spools of barbed wire, the kind that was certain to cut a person to ribbons if they tried to scale the barricade.

So who would take the locket she'd gotten from her adoptive father on her thirteenth birthday? Or a pair of panties. A sick feeling curled inside her stomach and her skin crawled. What kind of a creep was she up against?

It may not be as bad as you think. Someone may be just trying to freak you out, to force you to back off.

Or whoever took the objects was a real whacko. Someone with several screws loose.

Either way, she'd decided to move out of the Hotel Danvers, away from curious glances, raised eyebrows, and the feeling that she was being spied upon. Away from the chance that whoever had been bold enough to break into her room would return.

Putting some distance between herself and the family was just as well, she told herself, as she found a room in the Orion Hotel just a few blocks away. The Orion intrigued her because it was the hotel where Zachary was supposed to have been beaten up and left for dead on the night London had been abducted.

The Orion had changed hands several times in the last few

years and had been updated. Whereas the Hotel Danvers had been refurbished to offer a charming glimpse of Victorian Portland, the Orion was modern with plush beige carpeting, recessed lighting, and walls tinged a subtle shade of gold. What it lacked in character, the Orion made up for in convenience with three restaurants, a pool, weight room, and sauna.

She pored over her notes until two in the morning and tried to shove all thoughts of her meeting with the family out of her mind. At least she knew where she stood and she didn't have an ally in the lot of them.

Even Zachary. Some rebel he'd turned out to be. When it came to the Danvers fortune, he was as greedy as the rest. He seemed anxious to be out of town and rid of her and away from the problems of the estate.

As she curled up on the queen-size bed, she wondered about him. He'd kissed her as if he meant it, and yet it had been nothing more than a test. She'd nearly been duped into thinking that he cared for her, but that notion was foolish. If she were London Danvers, then he was her half-brother and a romance was out of the question. If she wasn't London, then he'd expose her as a fraud and a romance would be out of the question.

Not that she wanted a romance, she told herself. She'd learned that lesson the hard way and she wasn't going to fall for Zachary. Not even if he wasn't related to her.

No, all she wanted was to find out who she was. She'd fight tooth and nail to discover the truth, no matter how deeply the Danvers kin had buried it.

As his Jeep crested the Santiam Pass, Zachary reached into his pocket for a cigarette, then frowned at himself and scowled at the twin beams his headlights threw on the asphalt slipping beneath the rig's tires. He'd stopped smoking years ago, but since he'd first set eyes on Adria, he'd felt a growing restlessness gnawing at him—a restlessness nicotine wouldn't satisfy. Nothing could drive away the feeling except one thing—sex with Adria Nash. His lips tightened at the thought and his jeans felt suddenly tight.

She was definitely off limits.

For Christ's sake, she could be your half-sister!

He gnashed his teeth and shifted into fourth.

The truth of the matter was that Adria or London or whoever the hell she was just happened to be the most attractive woman he'd seen in a long, long while. Beautiful, sexy as hell, with a quiet confidence and sharp tongue that should have repelled him, he found her more fascinating than any of the women he'd known. Even Kat. There had been a predatory edge to his stepmother that he hadn't liked and during the time she'd set out to seduce him, Zachary had felt manipulated. While in Kat's bed he'd felt primal and lost himself in her eroticism, but after the hot sex was over, he'd been empty, emotionally drained and left with the uneasy sensation that he was being used.

He'd tried to avoid women after Kat, but it had been difficult as the more aloof he'd become, the more female attention he attracted. The hell of it was, he loved sex. It was just that simple. He just didn't need the emotional entanglements that came with a night in a woman's bed, so he'd made a stab at celibacy. It hadn't worked and he'd eventually married.

He'd met Joanna Whitby shortly after Kat jumped to her death. In retrospect, the relationship had been doomed from the beginning. Zach, carrying a truckload of guilt around with him, had been devastated when Kat had committed suicide and Joanna had been there. With her magical hands, soothing words, and compliant body, she'd helped him forget. He'd married her. He hadn't even suspected that she was after her slice of the Danvers family pie, but of course that had been her motive. When he'd told her he wasn't interested in the fortune, she hadn't believed him. "You can't be serious," she'd said with one of her beautiful smiles. "Zach, that's crazy!"

"No more crazy than it is to sit around here and kiss up to the old man, just hoping that he cuts me into the will."

When she'd finally figured out that Zach wasn't going to beg Witt to leave him so much as a dime, she'd found a reason to divorce him and had moved on. Word had it that she'd remarried an older man in Seattle, a widower with no children, and now she was fixed for life.

Zach hoped so. He'd learned his lesson about what women really wanted out of life and it seemed to revolve around dollar signs. Adria wasn't any different. And she looked so damned much like Kat it was scary.

Jack Logan wouldn't give Adria the time of day. Retired from the police department, he lived in Sellwood, a small community wedged between southeast Portland and Milwaukie. His cottage was one block off Thirteenth, behind a warehouse that had been converted into one of the antique shops for which Sellwood was famous.

Adria had called and left messages on his answering machine and, when he hadn't called her back, she'd decided to visit him. But she couldn't get past the gate at the front walk where a snarling German shepherd stood guard.

Obviously the ex-police detective wanted his privacy.

She didn't have any better luck with Roger Phelps, a private investigator Witt had used in trying to locate his daughter twenty years ago. Phelps was retired, living in Tacoma, and when Adria had reached him by phone, he told her he never discussed his clients' cases. She'd explained who she was and he'd laughed, telling her to "join the club." Apparently he'd seen more than his share of would-be London Danverses when Witt had posted the million-dollar reward.

"Strike two," she told herself as she hung up the phone in her hotel room. Another reason she'd stayed at the Orion was in the hopes that there might be someone working in the old building who would remember back to the night when London Danvers had been kidnapped and Zachary Danvers had been nearly killed.

Most of the people who had worked there had long since left the employ of the hotel. Only a middle-aged Thai woman and a man who ran the magazine shop in the lobby remained. The maid wouldn't talk to her, explaining in halting English that she didn't understand, but the man who sold candy, cigarettes, and magazines enjoyed reminiscing.

"Sure, I remember," he said when she approached him. "Hell, I was right here in this very booth when I saw Witt's kid stumble out of the elevator. I knew right away somethin' was wrong with him. 'Course, I didn't realize who he was at the time, not until the next day, when the word hit the street." With a gnarled hand, he slapped a stack of newspapers under the counter. "The talk was fast and wild about a kidnapping or a murder of some big heist, but no one knew the real scoop.

"Rumor had it that the Danvers kid had been with some call girl. Room 317—no, that ain't right. 307. That was it, 307. The manager took the police up there and I guess they found booze and drugs and a pool of blood stainin' the carpet, but no whore and no sign of the two guys who were supposed to have roughed Danvers up."

"Who was the room registered to?" she asked, leaning over the counter.

"That was the hell of it. Get this. The name on the guest register was Danvers. Witt Danvers."

"Witt?" she said, stunned. "But—"

"Isn't that a hoot?" He cackled. "While Witt's up at his own hotel havin' the time of his life, someone steals his name and uses the room as a damned whorehouse." He scratched his head above one ear and turned his attention to a man in a dark suit who wanted a copy of the *Wall Street Journal*. After handing the guy his change, he turned back to Adria. "If ya ask me, Anthony Polidori was behind the whole setup. There was always bad blood between the Polidoris and the Danverses. Had been for generations. It just seemed to explode about the time Witt lost his little girl, and Zach Danvers, if you can believe what he says, claims the guys who roughed him up worked for Polidori."

The man's silvery eyebrows lifted behind the thick rim of his glasses. "Seems like it was more than coincidence."

She knew there had been some sort of feud between the wealthy Italian family and the Danvers clan, but didn't understand how the feud affected the kidnapping. After asking a few more questions and getting nowhere, she purchased a couple of candy bars and two magazines about Portland, then checked with the clerk at the desk for messages before heading up to her room.

On impulse, she stopped at the third floor and walked the corridor, pausing at room 307. So this was Zach's alibi. A tryst with an Italian prostitute. Adria smiled. He'd been little more than a kid at the time—seventeen. What was he doing with a whore?

Stupidly, she felt a touch of jealousy for the woman he had planned to meet. What could it possibly matter to her—she'd been only five at the time! *And his half-sister!* Damn it all, this was more complicated than she'd thought. She hadn't planned on being attracted to Zachary. She'd hoped he would become her friend, perhaps even her accomplice, and eventually prove to be her blood kin . . . but nothing romantic, nothing dangerous, nothing so sinful. For a second she thought of her mother and what she would have said had she known the path Adria had taken. *The wages of sin are—* "Stop it!" she whispered harshly to herself. She'd already convinced herself to forget Zachary. Aside from the fact that he might be her half-brother, he wasn't the kind of man to get involved with, a rawhide-tough man who dared cross the line to the wrong side of the law, who didn't give two cents about what other people thought, who ran the world the way he thought it should be run, rather than the way it was. A good man to avoid.

Except that she needed him. If she were ever going to get
to the truth.

Refusing to dwell on Zachary, she twisted the doorknob
and turned, but the bolt was drawn and she couldn't peek inside. Not that it would help. The room had probably been
redecorated three times over since the night Zach was beaten
to a pulp. How much of this story was true? How much fab-
rication? How much exaggerated by the old man in the
lobby?

Zach seemed to hold the key to what happened that night,
but he'd been evasive with her, suspicious of her motives.
Somehow she had to gain his trust. Not an easy task, she
thought, as she stepped into the Orion's mirrored elevator car
and slapped the button for the door to close.

As agreed, Jack Logan sat in the darkened booth of the Red
Eye Café, a small dive near the airport. It was a smoky bar
that he'd used before when he didn't want to be recognized.
He spied Jason Danvers and swore under his breath. The man
was dressed in a double-breasted suit, for crying out loud, and
he'd pulled up in his Jag.

"Why didn't you just put a neon sign on your back?"
Logan growled, nursing his glass of McNaughton's.

"What?"

"You stick out like a fucking sore thumb."

Danvers frowned. "I don't intend to be here very long."

"Neither do I."

Jason ordered a whiskey on the rocks and waited until the
waitress left the drink and picked up the bills. Ignoring the
drink, he reached into his jacket and pulled out the tape,
which he slid across the table to Logan.

"What's this?"

"I hope nothing." Jason filled Logan in on all the details.

"How many copies of this are floating around?"

"God only knows. She gave me one, and I gave a copy to Sweeny."

"None to the police?"

"Not yet. I thought you could check it out."

"Should go to the station."

"Too many leaks. I turn it in and it'll be on the six o'clock news."

Logan grunted. He couldn't argue with that logic. "I'll see what I can do, but she's been nosing around."

Jason froze. "What do you mean?"

"She's called my house a dozen times and even came up the front walk."

"You talked to her?"

"Not yet."

"Shit!" He ran a hand through his hair. "This is worse than I thought."

"You worried about her?"

Jason's gaze darted around the bar. "Hell, yes, I'm worried."

"Think she's London?"

"No!"

"But you're not sure."

"Nothing's sure, Logan."

"Looks just like your stepmother." The two men glared at each other for a second, sharing a secret neither wanted revealed, then Jason finished his drink.

"Just don't talk to her and find out what you can. If she goes public, we'll give the tape to the police."

"But not before."

"Nope."

"You say Sweeny's in on this?"

"In Montana right now. Checking out her story. He called yesterday."

"He's an asshole."

"Work with him on this, okay? Keep your ear to the ground and your mouth shut. If the police get wind of the story, let me know." Jason left a twenty on the table and swaggered outside.

"Bastard," Logan muttered under his breath as he quickly exchanged the twenty for a five.

Manny was right. The ranch could run itself. Zach didn't need to be here. Once again he wasn't needed. The story of his life. He smiled grimly to himself as he walked across the dusting of new-fallen snow to the shed where Manny was repairing a tractor. Tools lined the walls, a stained workbench stretched along a far wall, and the smell of oil and dust hung in the air.

Light flickered from fluorescent tubes and Manny, cursing to himself, was half lying under the tractor's engine. "Damned fool think," he muttered, working on the fuel line.

"How's it going?" Zach asked.

"Like hell." He gave the wrench another tug, then grunted. Satisfied with his work, he crawled out from under the tractor and pulled himself upright.

A full-blooded Paiute, Manny was a tall man with smooth, burnished skin, long braids beginning to gray, and a face usually devoid of expression. He found his black cowboy hat on the seat of the tractor and plopped it onto his head. "I thought I told you to stay in the city where you belong." Manny wiped a rag over his greasy hands.

"Couldn't stand it."

Manny flashed a grin that showed teeth rimmed in gold. "Don't blame you. The only reasons to go into town are women and whiskey. You can get those here."

He thought of Adria. Right now women were dangerous. Especially a woman claiming to be his half-sister. Whiskey was definitely safer.

Together they walked out of the shed. The sky was a gray shade of blue, the air crisp, and dark-bellied clouds collected to the west, hanging along the rigid skyline of the Cascades.

"Family business all taken care of?" Manny asked.

Somewhere in the distance a horse neighed.

"It'll never be," Zach said. If not Adria, then another imposter would show up. For the rest of his life Zach would meet women pretending to be London Danvers. He just hoped they didn't get to him the way this one did. He knew that one of the reasons he'd driven like a madman over the mountains was to put some distance between him and her, to run back here where he could clear his head.

"Got a buyer for the two-year-old steers."

"All of them?" Zach asked, trying to forget about the woman who claimed to be his half-sister.

"Couple hundred head."

"A good start."

"Mmm."

"Come on inside—I'll buy you breakfast and you can bring me up-to-date."

He spent the day at the ranch, reviewing the books, checking offers to buy and sell livestock as well as land, then rode through some of the fields. The water pump for the house and outbuildings was going out, the roof of one of the sheds was leaking like a sieve, there was a fight with the government over harvesting some of the ancient pine, and one of their regular customers who bought hundreds of head of cattle every year was delinquent on his payments. There had been an outbreak of a cattle virus in the next county and several ranchers in the area were concerned. Zach was supposed to attend a local meeting of the Cattlemen's Association in Bend, and order the feed and supplies to get the ranch through the winter.

"Same old, same old," Manny said as they drove through the fields and spotted a break in the fence where cattle could escape. It was true. Though there were problems at the ranch, they weren't insurmountable. Manny and the hands could keep the place going should Zach have to return to Portland.

He stopped by his office in Bend and found that work was

slow, as it had been ever since he'd turned his attention to refurbishing the old hotel. He made a few phone calls, met with a couple of realtors interested in starting a new resort development around a golf course, and conferred with his secretary, Terry, a petite, red-haired woman of thirty who was expecting her third child come February. Efficient to the point that she could run the office blindfolded, she knew Zach as well as anyone.

"So how's city life?" she asked when he walked back into the office. She was seated behind the desk, a pencil tucked over her ear, a neglected cup of coffee near the typewriter. She was studying a bank statement and little lines of worry crinkled her freckled forehead.

"Not great."

"Jason called." She sat back in her desk chair and it protested with a groan.

"Here?"

"He tried the ranch. You weren't in. Manny told him you'd come into town, so he tried tracking you down here. Said it was urgent that he talk to you."

"With Jason it's always urgent."

"He was more insistent than usual." She set her glasses on the desk, grabbed her half-full cup and stood. Rubbing a kink in her back, she walked to the coffeepot warming on the hot plate and lifted the glass carafe. "Want a cup? It's just decaf."

Zach shook his head. "Thanks just the same."

Pouring some of the weak coffee in to her mug, she asked, "So why does Jason think he needs you back in Portland—the hotel?"

"Yeah, that's probably it," Zach said, but he guessed that the problem was Adria Nash. No doubt he'd have to drive back to the city. Resentment boiled through his blood. He didn't want to see Adria again, didn't want to deal with all the conflicting emotions she inspired.

He grabbed the handle of the coffeepot and poured himself

some of the tasteless decaf as the telephone rang and Terry answered.

With a sweet smile, she said, "He'll be with you in a second," and snapped the hold button. "It's your brother dear again and he's fit to be tied."

"Why?"

"Something about 'the shit hitting the fan'." She went back to the bank statement and Zach walked into his office. Kicking the door shut, he reached for the phone and sat on a corner of the desk.

"Hello?"

"Where the hell have you been?" Jason demanded, and Zach couldn't miss the agitation in his voice.

"What's the problem?"

"You know what the problem is. It's Adria! I think she's going to run to the papers with her story."

"She told you this?"

"In so many words."

Zach felt his shoulder muscles pull together into hard, tight knots. "What happened?"

"I called her. Offered her a little more money."

"And she got pissed."

"Beyond pissed."

"Christ, Jason, you never back down, do you?" He was on his feet without even thinking about it.

"Just get back here."

"And clean up your mess."

"Do whatever it takes, Zach. You're in this as deep as the rest of us!"

Anthony Polidori didn't like his breakfast disturbed. In his later years, he felt as if an intrusion upon his meals or his sleep was a personal affront and he left strict instructions with everyone in the household that he was not to be interrupted. Even by his son.

He sat in the bay window of the morning room overlooking the river and picked at his croissant with idle fingers as he scanned the newspaper for sports scores from the day before. The day was bright for late October, and he wore sunglasses to protect his eyes.

Mario sauntered into the room carrying a mug. His hair was disheveled and he hadn't yet shaved. He looked like hell as he poured himself a cup of coffee from the silver carafe on the table. Mario was uncivilized—he had no manners.

Anthony didn't bother hiding his irritation. He folded the sports section of the *Oregonian* and set it by his glass of juice. "What is it?" His son wasn't usually up by noon.

"Big news." Mario flashed his killer smile—the one that got him into all the trouble with the women. He walked to the glass wall facing west and watched a barge being pushed upriver by a tugboat.

"It must be, to get you out of bed while the sun's still up."

Mario snorted, then plopped into the wrought-iron chair opposite his father. "I think you want to hear this."

"I'm waiting."

"Looks like there's a new lady in town."

"This is news?"

Mario slowly poured a thin stream of cream into his coffee. "Could be. Claims she's London Danvers."

Behind his sunglasses, Anthony's eyes narrowed thoughtfully. "This isn't news. It's predictable."

Mario's dark eyes twinkled and he reached over and stole the fruit cup his father always saved for the last part of his meal. Annoyed, Anthony motioned to the maid, who had already anticipated his request and was scurrying off to the kitchen.

"There's always someone claiming to be London."

Mario rubbed the stubble on his jaw. "But you should see this one. She's the fuckin' spittin' image of her old lady. Katherine—wasn't that her name?"

Anthony's spine stiffened a bit. He didn't like foul language—not at the table, and he wasn't in the mood to be jerked around by his son. It was hard to read Mario these days. "So she resembles—"

"Not only resembles—the way I hear it, she's a mirror image!"

Anthony set down his fork as the maid brought a second cup of fruit and a plate for Mario. He was enjoying himself, grinning as he sliced into a fat sausage, ignoring all sense of decorum as he set his elbows on the table.

"Maybe I should meet—what's-her-name?"

"Adria Nash. Hails from some hick town in Montana. I've got a couple of guys working on it."

"How'd you find out about her? I haven't seen a word in the paper or heard anything on the news."

"She hasn't gone public yet, but probably will. One of our men spotted her at the grand opening of the hotel. She came in with Zach Danvers, then made the rounds meeting the 'family.'" Mario took a sip from his cup. "Jason nearly hit the roof."

"I'll bet," Anthony said dryly. "How authentic is she?"

"Could be the real thing." Mario skewered his father with a hard look. "You know, lots of people think you kidnapped the girl."

Anthony picked up the remainder of his croissant. "If I'd taken her, do you think she'd be walking up to the Danvers family right now and announcing that she was their long-lost sister?" He saw his son blanch and felt a glimmer of satisfaction. "What does Trisha think? Is she worried?" he asked coldly.

A small muscle worked in the side of Mario's cheek. "How should I know?"

"Aren't you still seeing her?"

"You took care of that a long time ago," his son said with more than a trace of bitterness.

"Trisha Danvers is like the rest of them. She doesn't give up. Not ever. When she wants something, she goes for it, and, my boy, she wants you. She always has, and she also used you to get back at her father. You were a pawn, son."

Mario's eyes sparked with a deadly rage.

Anthony snapped his newspaper open and wondered about the woman who called herself London Danvers. He'd have to find out everything there was to know about her. "Maybe we should invited Miss Nash over," he said, flicking a gaze over the top of the paper. Mario had elbowed his plate aside and was brooding.

"Why?"

"For old time's sake."

"Witt's dead. What could it mean to you?"

Anthony didn't bother answering. How could he explain to his son that feuds never ended? No matter how many of the players died, the vengeance continued and festered. As long as there was anyone named Danvers left in Portland, Anthony wouldn't be satisfied.

He was pleased with the news that another London Danvers had shown up.

Adria knocked on the door of the small apartment in Tigard, a suburb just over the west hills of Portland. Within minutes she saw a dark eye in the peephole and quickly the bolt was thrown. The door opened and a small Chicano woman with graying black hair twisted into a bun and incredibly white teeth stood over the threshold.

"Mrs. Santiago?"

"For the love of Mary," the woman whispered, crossing her ample bosom. "You are the image of the missus."

"Could I come in?" Adria asked. She'd already called the woman, Maria Santiago, who had worked for the Danvers family until her retirement shortly after Witt's death. She'd explained her business and Maria had reluctantly agreed to see her.

"Please, please—" Maria stepped out of the way and waved her inside the tiny rooms. "Sit down."

Adria perched on the edge of a floral couch that was worn around the edges and Maria settled into a rocker by the window and put her feet onto a stool.

Adria had already explained on the phone why she was in Portland. She'd sketched out her story, explaining that she was adopted, that she wanted to find her roots, that all the records were destroyed, and Maria, obviously lonely, had offered to speak with her.

"I don't mean to ask you to break confidences," Adria said, "but there's just so much I don't know about the Danvers family. I thought you could help me."

Maria rubbed her chin and stared out the window to the parking lot. "A few years ago, I would not have said a word," she admitted, "but then, the mister, he died, and Jason, he fired me. Now—" She rubbed her hands anxiously together. "What is it you want to know?"

"Everything."

"Ahh. That would take some time. There is so much."

Adria couldn't believe her good luck. She smiled at the pleasant little woman. "I've got the rest of my life," she said and sat back to listen.

It was nearly ten o'clock by the time she returned to the Orion and her head, as well as her tiny tape recorder, was filled with facts about the Danvers family, secrets, and the answer to some mysteries, including the feud with the Polidoris.

She considered celebrating with a glass of wine and a hot bath in the hotel room because tomorrow she'd have to move to a cheaper, and less high-profile, place. After settling in, she had other important business to attend to. Since the Danvers family wouldn't recognize her, it was time to go to the police and press. As soon as she found a more permanent address, she'd contact the authorities and grant an interview with someone from the local newspaper to start the ball rolling. Then, of course, she'd have to speak with the lawyers for

Witt's estate. She wasn't looking forward to any of the interviews, but she'd get through them.

She'd be called a gold digger, a fraud, an opportunist, and an imposter. Lawyers would call her, attorneys with "her interests" at heart. She wasn't interested. Not yet. The press would make her life a circus. The Danvers family would go after her with all the money they had behind them. They would try to dig up any rumors that might discredit her and they would look into her past, digging, always digging and looking for any glitch in her story, any inaccuracies in their attempts to disprove that she was London.

That's what she wanted.

And what about Zachary?

Oh, Lord, yes. What about Zachary?

In her room, she stripped off her clothes, poured herself a glass of Chablis, then slid into a tub of hot water. She sipped her wine slowly and considered her half-brother.

Sexy.

Smart.

Rough.

Big trouble.

Zach Danvers was a man to avoid unless she wanted to lose her heart.

15

Half an hour later, as she eased out of the tub and buffed her skin dry with one of the Orion's thick towels, Adria wondered about her mission—her quest to find her true identity. Was she London Danvers? Did it matter if she was? Did she really want to be related to any of those people—the Danvers kin? None of them appealed to her.

Except Zachary.

Not that she trusted him. He was no better than the rest, but she couldn't wedge his image out of her mind. Rugged, whereas his brothers took pride in being polished; outwardly irreverent, while Nelson took pains to look as if he played by the rules. Zachary was arrogant because he didn't give a damn; Jason was arrogant because he thought he deserved the money and power into which he'd been born.

Zachary was different.

Because of the blood flowing through his veins? Because he could be a Polidori? She grimaced at the thought, but found it intriguing. Her relationship with him would be easier to understand if he wasn't part of the Danvers family. She rubbed the mist from the mirror with the edge of the towel and wondered about Zachary, what kind of man he was, what it would feel like to have him take her to his bed. . . .

The thought was like a cold slap in her face. What was she doing fantasizing about a man who detested her, a man who could be her half-brother? Giving herself a swift mental kick, she stared into her reflection and told herself that she had to think of him as her brother: her irritable, woman-hating, problem of a half-brother who was, without a doubt, her sworn enemy.

Just like the rest of the clan.

She slipped into a T-shirt and climbed into the bed. The sheets were crisp and clean, but didn't have the same country-fresh scent of those that were dried on the line at home. In Belamy. Funny, for years she'd wanted to escape. City lights had beckoned her young heart, but duty had kept her tied to the only town she'd ever called home. Not that it mattered, but the harsh Montana grassland didn't seem so loathsome anymore, and for the first time in years she thought of her hometown and felt the pull of her heartstrings.

But she wasn't running back to the safety and boredom of Belamy. Not when she'd come so far. *When the going gets tough, the tough get going,* she reminded herself as she plumped a pillow.

Closing her eyes, she heard the hum of traffic, an occasional shout and, every so often, the distant cry of sirens. She wondered where Zachary was, and then, irritated that she'd allowed him into her mind, she rolled over and tried to force him from her thoughts. What did she care about him, anyway? She was too smart to get involved with him. Even if he might not be her half-brother, even if he hadn't been somehow involved with her mother, even if his last name wasn't Danvers, he wasn't the kind of man she could trust, let alone fall for.

Fall for? As in "fall in love?"

No way—nohow. He was just forbidden fruit, that was all. Seductive because he was taboo. Erotic because he was so wrong for her, so very wrong.

And yet, there he was—his image teasing her mind. She imagined his crooked, irreverent smile flashing against his rock-hard jaw, remembered how it felt to have his lips pressed hard and wanting against hers, could envision the play of light in his gray eyes, or remember the feel of his hands against her skin.

For God's sake, stop it!

Forget him. He's not someone to be attracted to! He's the enemy! Just like the rest of his family! Think, Adria. Use your brain and be smart.

Somewhere down the hallway she heard the *ding* of the elevator and the rattle of a service cart. The heater rumbled as she drifted off to sleep fitfully. She dreamed—erotic, pulse-pounding fantasies of sweat-slickened bodies, wildly beating hearts, lips that caressed the most intimate of spots and fingers that whispered over fevered flesh. In her mind's eye, she saw him hovering above her, his naked skin gleaming gold in the light of a dying fire, his hair wet with sweat and his eyes dark with a deep secret.

She wanted him so badly, and yet, there was something more, someone else in the room with them, a faceless presence, menacing and dark, lurking in the shadows.

There was a rustle and quick footsteps.

"Who's there?" she cried, her gaze searching the murky corners, her heart pounding in fear. She looked back for Zachary, but he was gone and she was alone. "Zach!" But her voice only echoed back at her, bouncing off unseen walls.

Again the rustling and her skin prickled in dread. "Zach! Where are you?" She got up and started running, her legs heavy, her body naked. She was in an alley, fog surrounding her, something chasing her, footsteps pounding along the wet pavement.

"Zach!" she yelled, desperate, certain she could feel the breath of her attacker. "Help!" She ran. Faster, her bare feet slapping the uneven asphalt. Oh, God, where was he? If only she could duck around the next corner—

Too late! Whoever was after her was closing in. She could hear his breathing, feel him closing in. A hand reached out and touched the back of her neck . . .

Adria's eyes flew open. It was dark. Her heart was jack-hammering, her body drenched in sweat. For a second she didn't know where she was and then she remembered . . . the Orion . . . safe . . . the door firmly locked.

Then why did she still feel unnerved, her breathing shallow, her teeth on edge? It was a dream. Just a dream. No big deal. She let out her breath slowly and climbed to her feet. She'd go into the bathroom and get a glass of water and . . .

She saw it then. A slim envelope slipped under the door. *Probably just the bill,* she told herself, but knew better.

Every nerve strung tight, she crossed the carpet and picked up the envelope. It was blank. Sealed. Carefully she slid a nail under the flap.

Inside was a simple note: *You have a package at the front desk.*

"What?" She opened the door but the hallway was empty. Something felt wrong about this. Very wrong. *Don't jump to conclusions.* Crossing to a small table near the bed, she punched the number on the telephone for the front desk.

"This is Adria Nash," she said when a female voice answered. She gave her room number and asked, "Do I have a package?"

"Let me check." There was a *click* and a few minutes of nondescript music before the woman returned. "Yes, Ms. Nash, you do have a package. I'll send it up."

"Wait a minute. Do you know who sent it to me?"

"No—I'm sorry. It was in the business office. Probably came by courier. I'll check the log and get back to you."

"Thanks." Adria hung up and within two minutes a bellman was standing on the other side of the door and handing her a thick, padded manila envelope with her name written in block letters. She tipped the man and before she could open the bulky package, the phone rang.

"Ms. Nash, this is Ellie at the front desk. I don't know how to explain it, but there is no record of anything coming in for you. Maybe someone forgot, but usually the staff is on top of this kind of thing and keeps a precise record of when the delivery was made and by whom."

Adria stared down at the bulky envelope in her hand and she felt her insides curdle. Whatever was inside was soft. "The hotel apologizes and I hope this doesn't inconvenience you."

"No . . . it's all right," Adria said, though she sensed, feeling the awkward package, that it was anything but okay. "If I have any more questions, I'll come down."

"Thank you," Ellie said as Adria hung up.

Don't open it. What if it's a bomb?

That was ridiculous. A bomb? No way. And yet . . . should she call the police?

"Oh, for God's sake, you're letting your imagination run away with you." Angry with herself, she found a nail file and ripped open the package. Nothing exploded. Nothing jumped out at her. But as she peeked inside, her heart froze.

There, zipped inside a plastic bag, was a dead rat, one beady eye visible through the sheer covering. Adria dropped the package as if it were red-hot. "Oh God, oh, God, oh, God," she whispered, a hand clamping over her mouth.

Who would do such a thing?

Bile burned in the back of her throat.

Was it a warning?

Or just a chance for some pervert to get his rocks off by trying to scare her?

"Mission accomplished," she said, calming a little. Gritting her teeth, she grabbed a tissue from the bedside table, and kneeling, gently pulled the plastic-enshrouded rodent from its manila coffin.

There was a note inside, a message from the pervert who'd left this for her. With shaking fingers she withdrew the single piece of paper that read: BACK OFF BITCH!

"Oh, God," she whispered. Through the plastic, she noticed something sparkling, catching in the light, and she nearly threw up when she recognized the chain and locket wound around the dead rat's neck and body.

The fragile piece of jewelry her father had given her was sealed tight with the furry little body.

"Bastard," she said, gagging.

To retrieve the necklace, she'd have to unwrap the dead animal and wash the chain and . . .

Don't touch it! Don't touch a thing! You have to go to the police! You have to tell them what's going on. They can fingerprint everything and check for clues. Otherwise, whoever is behind this will continue to terrorize you—or worse.

Letting out her breath, she straightened, leaving the package where she'd dropped it on the floor. She opened a window and let in the fresh air.

Think, Adria, think. Scraping her hair away from her face with tense fingers, she pulled herself together.

Slowly she began to calm. She'd grown up on a farm. Dead animals and all kinds of rodents—rats, mice, shrews, squirrels, and the like—were something she and the barn cats had dealt with. The rat's corpse didn't frighten her, but the intent behind the package did, and the fact that someone had broken into her room at the Hotel Danvers, violated her personal space and taken items, then took the time to kill a rat and send it anonymously, was terrifying.

She reached for the phone. She could call the police. Or hotel security. Or Zach.

Which is probably what the sicko expected. Whoever he was, he was counting on her running scared and calling the authorities. Whether she wanted to or not, she had to wait . . . at least until she figured out what was going on.

For now, she'd bide her time, but be on her guard.

Whoever was behind the depraved prank wasn't going to get the better of her.

But he could be dangerous. This might be just the start of something worse. The more you push the Danvers clan, the more the clan will push back.

She considered the members of the family. Was it one of them? Or someone else, someone she hadn't yet met? Someone connected to the Danvers family who didn't want London to surface?

Whoever it was behind the stupid little charade was going to get a surprise. Adria wasn't backing down. Gingerly, using the tissue, she slipped the plastic bag into the envelope and opened the refrigerator of the minibar. Quickly she removed several bottles of beer and soda, then placed the envelope inside. She'd put the DO NOT DISTURB sign on the door and figure out her next move.

Wedged between the pool tables and the rest rooms, the phone booth was located in the back corner of the tavern. Sweeny waited as the phone rang in Portland. He needed to report to Danvers, but first things first.

Foster's voice boomed over the line. "You have reached the offices of Michael Foster. I'm away from the phone right now, but if you leave your name and number and the time you called, I'll get back to you—"

"Bullshit!" Sweeny growled. The beep shrilled in his ear. "Foster? You there? It's me, Sweeny. Pick up the goddamned phone." He waited, but no one answered. "Hell," he ground out. "Look, I know you're there, so pick up. I've got a job for you. One that pays well. If you're interested . . ." He waited but still no answer. Drumming his fingers on the edge of a tattered copy of the yellow pages, he finally decided to give up. "I'll call later." As he slammed down the receiver, he tried to shake off his bad mood, but it lingered, like the cold-blowing wind that seemed to forever cut through this town.

He settled into the bar, drank his beer, and listened to some country-western ballad where the guy was all choked up over some dead woman. Christ, what a miserable place. A few of the locals came in, smiled and chatted with the bartender, and climbed onto their usual stools. Just like *Cheers* on television.

Sweeny could name them all—Norm, Cliff, Sam . . . Rather than gawk at the hicks, he turned his attention to a television positioned over the bar where a baseball game was in progress. He didn't even check the score.

His bones ached from the job he'd done the night before. After he'd driven to the farm where Adria Nash had been raised, he'd talked with the people who'd leased the place, but he hadn't learned much. Either the couple was tight-lipped by nature or they'd seen through his story of being an insurance agent interested in selling fire insurance on the house and outbuildings. He'd never even gotten inside. The woman had kept the screen door closed and locked and had spoken tersely through the torn steel webbing. After striking out at the farm, he'd driven to the only bank of storage units in town, bribed the kid who was the night watchman and broken into Ms. Nash's unit. Sweeny, sensing a bonanza, had spent hours in the cramped space, moving boxes, climbing over old, taste-less furniture, and digging through pile after pile of crates until he'd hit pay dirt and come up with the family Bible as well as copies of tax returns that proved how broke Adria Nash really was. No wonder she was after the Danvers money. The tax files and the Bible were now sitting securely back in the storage unit. He'd taken copies of the returns and the family-tree section of the Bible, including any pages with notations on them, then slipped the kid watching the storage place a fifty, and replaced Adria's property in the packing crates. She'd never be the wiser.

But he was still stuck in this frigid hellhole. He downed an-other beer and checked his watch. Hauling his briefcase, he strolled back to the phone booth. This time, Foster was there. The computer nut picked up on the second ring.

" 'Bout time," Sweeny grumbled.

"Oswald. Always a pleasure." Foster didn't bother hiding the sarcasm in his voice.

"Yeah, right."

"Okay, so I got your message. What's up?"

"It's a piece of cake. I want you to find some people for me. The first one has several names. She goes by Ginny Slade, Virginia Watson, or Virginia Watson Slade. She's somewhere around fifty, give or take a few years, I think, and was married to Bobby or Robert Slade."

"That's it?" Foster asked.

"What more do you need?"

"Watson and Slade aren't uncommon names. How about a location to start with—you know, something like east of the Mississippi?"

"Just a minute." Impatiently Oswald opened his briefcase and pulled out his copies of the family tree from the Bible. "Okay, let's see," he said, running his finger down the page. "Looks like Virginia was born in Memphis, Tennessee. She and Bobby were married in the First Christian Church in June of 1967. Other than those specific dates, all I know is that she cruised through Montana at one time and gave up her daughter, probably named Adria or something like it, for adoption. An old couple—Victor Nash and his wife Sharon—adopted the kid sometime in late 1974, I think, though I can't find any reference to a specific date and no official papers were filed."

"That all?"

"Not quite," Sweeny said, loving to spread news meant to shock. "Get a load of this—we suspect this Virginia Watson Slade might have been the governess for London Danvers."

There was a long, low whistle on the other end of the line. "Ginny Slade."

"Bingo."

"So why're *you* involved? No, let me guess. The kid's shown up and is demanding her part of the fortune."

"You got it."

"Could be interesting."

"See what you can come up with."

"Where can I reach you?"

"I'll call you. Need anything else?"

"How about a social security number?"

"Right." Sweeny sorted through his notes on Ginny Slade. "Got it," he said, and rattled off the series of numbers she'd used when she was London's governess. He explained a little more about the case and hung up, satisfied that Foster would come up with something. He was a computer hacker from the 80s who'd found a way to put his skills to work. Sweeny didn't really know how he operated, if he broke into the IRS's files or had someone in the government working for him, but Foster was part of a national service where people who had been lost were found—even people who didn't want to be located. He'd get the job done one way or the other.

Satisfied, Sweeny snapped his briefcase shut. He felt better. Another drink and he'd call Jason Danvers.

Adria glanced over her shoulder but she didn't see a familiar face in the stream of people that passed by the front door of the Orion. She told herself that she was being paranoid, that no one was following her, but she couldn't shake the feeling that someone was watching her. And the dead rat in her mini fridge served to remind her that *someone* did know where she lived and where she went. All day, while she scouted around town looking for a more permanent residence, she'd felt as if a pair of eyes had been boring into her back, watching her every move.

She'd half expected to run into Zachary again, but he hadn't shown up and it wasn't his style to stay in the shadows. He might follow her, as he'd done before, but he'd end up confronting her again.

So who? she wondered as she swept her gaze along the street again. She didn't see anyone hunched over a newspaper, or lounging near a telephone booth, or quickly ducking into storefronts when she glanced behind her. The person who had sent her the package had put her on edge. She was jumping at shadows. Before leaving the hotel earlier, she'd checked with the bell captain, Security, and the business office. No one had re-

membered anyone leaving a package for her. Whoever was behind it had been very careful. And so would she be.

Waving to the old man behind the magazine counter, Adria
dashed into the hotel and asked for messages at the front
desk. She was handed one note from the switchboard and a
stiff white envelope with her name scrawled across the linen
surface, not in block letters this time but flowing script.
Rather than read the messages where anyone lounging in the
lobby could see her, she took the elevator to her floor.

In her room, she kicked off her shoes, cast a glance at the
closed refrigerator, then she scanned the notes. The telephone
call was from Nelson Danvers, who wanted to speak with her
"urgently." Good. Progress, she thought. But she could let
Nelson wait a little longer.

The invitation in the linen envelope wasn't expected. She
pulled out the handwritten card, and read the offer:

> *Mr. Anthony Polidori requests the honor of your pres-
> ence tonight at dinner, seven o'clock at Antonio's. A
> driver will pick you up in front of the hotel.*

No telephone number. No address. Just a note left at the
front desk of the Orion.

Adria read the words over again. Why would Polidori want
to see her? Obviously he'd heard that she was in town claiming to be London Danvers, but how? And how did he know
where she was staying? She felt goose bumps crawl up her
back and she walked to the window and stared out at the
street, wondering again if even now she was being followed
or if anyone was watching her room.

She saw no one leaning against a lamppost while staring up
at her window, no malicious figure darting into the shadows.

"Relax," she told herself as she tapped the edge of the card
on her lips and walked to her closet, where she eyed her meager wardrobe. What would it hurt to meet Polidori? Should she

take him up on his offer or would that be playing into his hands?

She smiled to herself because she was starting to think like a Danvers. She had no reason to fear the Polidoris; in fact, talking with Witt Danvers's sworn enemy could be enlightening. According to everyone in the family, he was the most likely suspect in the kidnapping of London. So why would he want to see her?

She changed into a simple black skirt and top, clamped her hair back, and slipped her arms into a jacket.

By the time she hurried out of the elevator in the main lobby, the limo had arrived and a driver helped her into the shadowed interior. She wasn't alone. Two men sat across from each other. The short, older man in an elegant gray suit and dark glasses greeted her. "Ms. Nash," he said, taking her hand as she slid onto the seat beside him. "Welcome. Welcome. I'm Anthony Polidori. My son, Mario."

"My pleasure," Mario said smoothly. He was tanned and good-looking, with even features, curling black hair cut longer than fashionable, and eyes the color of obsidian.

"I was surprised to hear from you," she said, deciding not to play games.

Anthony smiled and tapped his son on the knee with his cane. "She was surprised." He patted her arm as the limousine pulled away from the curb. "You've not heard of the feud between the Danvers family and my own?" His voice was skeptical.

"A little," she hedged, not wanting to give anything away.

"I bet." For a few seconds he seemed lost in thought and only the soft sound of classical music filled the plush interior of the car. "Mario, where are your manners? Ask Ms. Nash if she cares for a drink."

"Later, maybe," she said, but Mario ignored her and poured a glass of wine from a bottle chilling in an ice bucket.

"Please, be our guest," Mario insisted. Probably in his late thirties or early forties, Mario wore his good looks like an ex-

pensive suit. He seemed to pose as he sat across from her.
As he handed her the stemmed glass of chilled wine, his fingers brushed hers for just a fraction of an instant but his gaze
touched hers briefly before he removed his hand.

Staring out the tinted windows, Anthony clucked his
tongue. "It's sad, this feud," he admitted, "but it can't be
helped. It goes back for generations, you see. Starting with
Julius Danvers and my father."

That much Adria understood. Maria, who had worked for
the Danvers family for years, had told her of Stefano Polidori
and how he became the rival of the Danvers family.

The original patriarch of the Danvers family, Julius Danvers, made his money and the beginning of the family fortune
in the late 1800s. An immigrant logger who had the foresight
to acquire all the timber-rich land he could beg, borrow, buy,
or, in some cases, steal, he not only founded a company to
harvest the raw timber that was abundant in the state, but also
built a chain of sawmills that eventually stretched from north-
ern California to the Canadian border north of Seattle.

It had been rumored, but never proven, that Julius was a
mean son of a bitch who was willing to kill any man who
tried to thwart him in his quest for unrivaled power in the
timber-rich Pacific Northwest. His guilt in several "logging
accidents," which took the lives of some of the men not particularly loyal to him, was always assumed, but never proved.

Already a wealthy man by the turn of the century, Julius diversified into shipping and hotels, spreading the family
fortune into new industries. He opened the elegant Hotel
Danvers in downtown Portland in time for the Lewis and
Clark Exposition of 1905. The hotel, rumored to be the most
lavish in Portland, became home to the elite who traveled to
the city on the Willamette River.

Though Julius never finished the ninth grade, he was also
instrumental in establishing Reed College, the first college in
Portland, where his children attended school and earned
diplomas as well as social standing.

Julius was famous for his hard, cruel streak, and it was generally thought that he'd won favors from politicians, judges, and policemen, thereby having more than his share of important men hidden deep within his gold-filled pockets. Julius was careful to align with the powers-that-be in the city and state in order to assure that nothing would ever stand in the way of his ambitions or threaten his family.

His biggest competitor was Stefano Polidori, an Italian immigrant, one of the few in Portland, who had started his career by working on a truck farm in southeast Portland. Stefano had sold vegetables from a cart and later a truck, saving every penny and eventually buying several farms as he could afford them. As the city and his business grew, he opened a highly successful open-air vegetable market and later a restaurant. Eventually he had accumulated enough money to build a hotel that rivaled the Hotel Danvers in turn-of-the-century charm.

The Polidori family, too, became rich, and as Stefano added to his fortune and diversified his investments, he stepped on Julius's toes by outbidding him on prime real estate along the river or by convincing conventioneers that his hotel was better able to serve their needs than the Hotel Danvers.

Stefano and Julius became bitter rivals.

Julius couldn't believe Stefano could do anything more than sell tomatoes and lettuce from a cart. But Stefano was as shrewd and tough as his fiercest competitor. Like Julius, Stefano used his wealth to purchase rungs on the gold-plated social ladder of Portland.

The rivalry and hatred between the two men and their families deepened as the years passed.

"I've heard about Julius as well as your father," Adria ventured as the limo turned into the parking lot of the riverfront restaurant.

"Stubborn men, both of them." Anthony sighed loudly. "We all blamed Julius for my father's death, you know."

She'd read of the fire, of course. It had been a major news story in 1935. The cause of the blaze had been a grease fire that had started in the kitchen, but some journalists wondered if Stefano's death had truly been an accident, or if Julius Danvers had somehow masterminded the blaze that had burned the hotel and surrounding buildings to the ground.

Upon his father's grave, and in full view of the press, Anthony Polidori, the new patriarch of the family, had sworn vengeance against the murdering Danvers family.

"Here we are," he said, motioning to the restaurant. "A friend of mine owns it." The door of the limo was opened by the driver and Anthony, barely using his cane, walked down the plank docking leading to the front doors.

As they entered they were greeted loudly by the maître d'. Voices from the kitchen staff and waiters shouted out greetings as well. In this Italian restaurant, Anthony had no enemies.

"So good to see you," the maître d' enthused. "Your table's ready. Please come this way." They were led up a short flight of stairs to a private, glassed-in room on the second story that offered a 360-degree view of the bridges spanning the murky Willamette River.

"Beautiful, isn't it?" Anthony asked.

"Very." Adria nodded as the maître d' pulled out a chair for her.

"The Willamette River is the lifeblood of the city." Anthony gazed through the windows as if he could never get enough of the panorama of the Willamette River and the skyscrapers rising off the western shore.

Without waiting for him to order, a slim waiter brought wine and crusty Italian bread. "The usual?" he asked as he poured three glasses.

"For all of us," Polidori responded.

"Why did you want to see me?" she asked as the waiter disappeared.

"Haven't you guessed?" Anthony's dark eyes twinkled devilishly and he chuckled.

Mario came to the rescue. "It's because we know you've come to Portland for your birthright. That you're claiming to be London Danvers."

Adria took a sip of the Chianti. "Why would you care?"

"Try the bread," Anthony ordered, ignoring her question for the moment. "It's the best in the city. Probably in all of the Northwest." He reached for a slice himself.

"Does the Danvers family still bother you?"

She was rewarded with one of his smiles. "I always care what happens to the family of my old rival." He glanced up at her and dusted the crumbs from his fingers. "It was a shock to me when the little girl was abducted and yet I was considered a suspect." Shaking his head at the folly of it all, he added, "Despite my protests and alibi, Witt and his henchman, Jack Logan, seemed to think I had something to do with the girl's disappearance. Even Mario, though he was in Hawaii at the time, was regarded as a suspect. The fact that the second son, Zachary, claimed he was roughed up by some Italians immediately put my family at the top of the list of possible kidnappers. Never mind that the two men whom he claimed to have attacked him had airtight alibis and were seen at several restaurants around the city." He wagged a finger in the air. "Didn't matter. A *Danvers* had made the accusation and in this town that makes a difference—a big difference." He raised his palms to the ceiling. "So, I would like to clear the Polidori name. And, if you are indeed London, I would like to help you." He bit into his bread and sighed happily, as if he'd forgotten the conversation, but Adria knew differently. When she didn't respond, he said, "I doubt the Danvers family is eager for you to be their half-sister."

She hedged. "There's been a little resistance."

Mario snorted a laugh at her understatement. "A little? Come on."

Waving off his son's sarcasm, Anthony said, "Of course, I know nothing of your financial situation, but it's no secret that the Danverses are exceedingly wealthy and influential. If they decide to fight you on this—and believe me, they will fight you like wounded wolves, with everything they've got—I'm willing to help you."

"Help me?" she said, not sure she understood correctly.

"Absolutely."

Mario leaned back in his chair, his dark eyes squinting thoughtfully in her direction. He steepled his fingers beneath his chin. "Our family has some power in this town, too. In fact, we think our lawyers are the best in the city. If you need legal help, or a loan—"

"I don't think that would be such a good idea." It was beginning to sound as if they wanted her in their camp and she suddenly felt anxious.

"Do you want to prove you're London or not?" Anthony asked and his dark eyes gleamed with a frosty inner light that was as cold as death.

"Of course."

"Then you should take my offer."

She wanted to turn him down flat. Though he and Mario were both trying their best to be charming, she felt as if he was attempting to orchestrate the conversation and push her into a position where she'd be in debt to him forever. However, she wasn't foolish enough to reject his offer outright. Not yet. She'd learned that patience was a virtue, though sometimes hard to attain. The fact of the matter was that she was in no position to turn away help of any kind. Though the Polidoris had axes to grind with the Danvers family, she needed allies in her search—any allies she could get. She had only to think of the dead rat to remind herself. "You're very generous."

"Then it's settled."

"Not quite. You know, most of the family still thinks you were behind London's kidnapping."

Polidori's smiled faded. He studied the red wine in his glass. "I had nothing to do with the kidnapping. I would never hurt a child. Anyone's child."

"What about Robert Danvers?" she asked the old man.

Polidori snorted. "Julius's oldest son had a boating accident, if I recall."

"Some people think you arranged it."

"People like to make something of nothing."

She plunged onward. "Julius had three children. Only one—Witt—survived."

With a long sigh, Anthony said, "Julius's second boy, Peter, was killed in the war." He frowned. "I had nothing to do with that, either, you know. Though I'm sure the Danvers family would like to think I was in league with Mussolini and Hitler, I didn't hire the Nazis to shoot Peter's plane down. Nor did I do anything to the boat that Robert was driving on the river the summer he was killed. The way I heard the story was that he'd been drinking heavily and came too close to the shore of the Columbia. His boat crashed against the rocks. In the accident, his neck was broken. He was killed instantly."

"An accident that left Witt as the only Danvers heir."

"Precisely. Look, if I was so vile as to have arranged all these deaths, why wouldn't I kill Witt as well?"

Adria considered, then decided to gamble. "Maybe you wanted him to twist in the wind a little. There are rumors about your rivalry with Witt. It isn't out of the question to think that you might want to watch one of Julius's sons face a little pain in his life." She didn't mention Anthony's affair with Witt's first wife, Eunice, but it hung on the air between them—suspended by invisible threads of innuendo.

Anthony shook his head. "You think I'm some big Mafia don, is that it?" he asked and exchanged looks with his son.

"I don't know you at all," Adria pointed out. "In fact, I wasn't sure I should come here."

"And why is that?"

Leaning closer to him, she said, "Because, Mr. Polidori— I thought you might have wanted to talk to me to get information on the Danvers family for your own purposes."

"You don't trust me."

"There's a reason you asked me to dinner and I don't think it's because you think that I've had a lack of Italian cuisine while growing up in Montana."

One graying brow lifted. "I'm just curious, that's all."

"Why?"

"It is rumored that if London Danvers does appear, she'll inherit a good portion of Danvers International."

Here it comes.

"Many of our business interests are in direct competition with the Danvers Corporation and I was hoping, should you come to inherit part of the fortune, that you might be willing to sell off some of the smaller industries." Resting his elbows on the table, he propped up his chin. "I'm specifically interested in the Hotel Danvers."

Her heart dropped to the floor. The hotel? She thought of the ballroom with its glorious chandeliers, the old elevator, the time and money put into renovating the old building to its original state.

"You brought me here to . . . what? Bribe me?" She shook her head and laughed at the pomposity of this man, who, though he was loath to admit it, was very much like several members of the Danvers clan. "I'm afraid you'll have to take a number and stand in line. A few people in the Danvers family are already in a bidding war. They seem to think that I can be bought off."

"Can you?" he asked.

"No."

"Ahh . . . an *honorable* woman. With *noble* intentions." His eyes flickered dangerously.

"I just want to find out the truth."

16

Zach smelled trouble. It sizzled in the air, like electricity before a lightning storm, and drew him back to Portland.

Jason's panicked phone calls hadn't caused him to climb into his Jeep and head west over the mountains. Pressing business worries weren't the reason. Nor had his concern that he'd lose the ranch if Adria proved to be London been his impetus. No, the reason he'd driven like a madman across the mountains had been something more basic, more primal, an urge deep in his guts that he couldn't suppress and didn't want to name.

"Idiot," he ground out as he glowered through the raindrops drizzling down the windshield. The lights of Portland shone like tiny beacons, leading him closer.

To what?

Adria.

He ground his teeth together and his fingers clenched the steering wheel, gripping hard. He didn't even know where she was staying.

It was after ten by the time she returned to her hotel room. She kicked off her shoes. Rubbing one foot, she sat on the bed and glanced at the mini refrigerator. Didn't want to go there. She picked up the receiver with her free hand. As she dialed the number Nelson had left with someone at the front desk, she cradled the receiver between her shoulder and ear.

The phone rang five times and she was about to hang up when he answered.

"Nelson Danvers."

"This is Adria," she said. "You called?"

There was a pause on the other end of the line. "Yes, I, uh, thought we should meet. You know, to talk, to get to know each other. I was hoping maybe tonight if you can make it. I'd be willing to come downtown and meet you in the bar of your hotel."

She glanced at the clock. Why not? It was early and she wasn't the least bit tired. In fact, the dead rat and then her dinner with the Polidoris had set her nerves on edge and she needed to calm down. She told him she'd meet him in twenty minutes and hung up before she noticed the note—a single piece of paper folded, with her name scratched on the back—lying on the bureau. Oh, God! No one had slipped this piece of paper under the door.

Dread settled in the back of her throat.

Hands shaking, she snatched up the note and opened it. DIE BITCH.

A chill slithered down her spine. Her skin crawled in apprehension. Her lungs were suddenly tight and she nearly dropped the paper onto the floor.

Pull yourself together!

Taking in a deep breath, she decided that the message didn't bother her as much as the frightening fact that someone had delivered the simple piece of paper to her locked room. The same person who had let himself into her room at the Hotel Danvers, the same creep who had left the dead rat and locket downstairs. Her stomach turned at the thought. He knew where she was staying and worse yet, could come and go as he pleased, while she was away or while she was sleeping.

Panic tore through her but she tamped it down. Yes, she would have to go to the authorities and soon, but for now she couldn't let some chickenshit letter-writer get to her. She reminded herself that she didn't scare easily. She'd grown up on the farm and her father had taken her hunting, fishing, and even rock climbing in the Bitterroots. She'd skinny-dipped in Flathead Lake and branded cattle, smelling the searing flesh, hearing the cows bawl, as she learned to be tough. She'd shot the rapids as well as her .22 and she'd watched as her favorite horse had to be destroyed after shattering his leg. She'd faced the threat of losing her home and the death of all her loved ones and, by God, she wasn't going to let anyone get the better of her. Not by writing silly little notes. Damned coward. She folded the stupid threat and tucked it into her purse with the other one that she'd crumpled, then smoothed flat and decided to keep. Maybe she'd show them both to Nelson and see what he had to say.

Within ten minutes, she was downstairs in the bar, at a private table near windows that looked onto the street. She watched the steady stream of traffic moving slowly between red lights. Pedestrians carrying umbrellas and wrapped in winter coats with the collars turned against the wind dashed along the sidewalks. Always in a hurry.

She hadn't planned to order a drink, but receiving the package and note had definitely changed her mind. She was sipping a rum and Coke when Nelson appeared. She almost didn't recognize him, as she'd always seen him impeccably dressed in expensive suits. Tonight his hair was uncombed, windblown and damp from the rain, and he wore a wool sweater, black jeans, and a black leather jacket that looked brand new, as if he'd bought it for the occasion.

Whereas Zachary was rough-and-tumble and wore his I-don't-give-a-shit attitude comfortably, Nelson seemed out of place in clothes a little too fashionable to be casual. An enigma.

Nelson glanced nervously around the room before he spied her. Relief crossed his face as he threaded his way quickly through the tables. He seemed paler than she remembered, less self-assured, and there was a little-boy quality to him that she hadn't noticed before.

"Adria!" His face broke into a warm smile as he dropped into the chair opposite her. The waiter was there immediately and he ordered a Scotch on the rocks. "You must think it's strange that I called you," he said, wiping a few drops of rain from his jacket.

"I expected it."

"Did you?"

"You're just the first. I'd guess that everybody in the family will want to have his or her say. You know, try and convince me that it's in my best interests to leave town."

His smile didn't even falter, though she thought she saw a flicker of ice in his warm blue eyes. "Well, I hate to say it, but it would make it a helluva lot easier on you."

"Mmm. So I should just turn tail and run?"

"Not exactly."

"And then I'd be back to square one."

"Is that so bad?"

"I think so, yes," she said, her temper frazzling. "Do you know, have you any idea, how many years I've been trying to find out who I am? Where I came from?"

The waiter brought his drink and Nelson fingered the glass. "So it doesn't matter if you're London, as long as you find out who you are."

"I *am* London."

He eyed her speculatively. "Okay, *London,*" he said with just a hint of sarcasm, "what is it you want from us?"

"I already told you—recognition."

"And, with the recognition, your inheritance."

"Look, Nelson, I don't expect you or the rest of your family to roll over and take me in with no questions asked. That wouldn't make sense."

"No . . ."

"And I realize I'm not the first one to make the claim that I'm your half-sister."

"Not by a long shot."

Adria spread her hands over the table, as if in supplication. "All I want is a chance. I don't know what your family's doing, but I imagine everyone is trying his damnedest to prove me a fake. I figure you've got a team of lawyers and investigators working on this day and night." His eyes shifted away from hers and she knew she'd been right about one thing. She was being followed, by some detective hired by the family. A knot tightened in her stomach, but she managed to appear calm. "So if you get any information that conclusively says I'm *not* London Danvers, just let me know and I'll back off. I'll take blood tests, lie detector tests, DNA tests, anything, to help sort this out. Give me a call when your PI reports back to you."

"How do you know about—?"

"Only makes sense." She sat back against her chair and regarded him coldly. "It's what I would do if the situation were reversed.❦

"You could go away from this empty-handed."

"That's not exactly a news flash." She stared at him steadily and he blinked before finding interest in his half-empty glass. "I just have to know the truth, Nelson. Maybe you aren't interested in that, but I'd say it's a shame if the public defender wasn't looking for it around each and every corner."

He took a quick swallow of Scotch and Adria thought that he, of all the children, looked the most like his father. Witt had been a bigger man, but he had the same startling blue eyes, aristocratic, straight nose, thick hair, and square jaw. Aside from the similar facial features, the resemblance ended, however. Nelson was decidedly different from Witt—or at least what she imagined Witt to have been from all the articles and newspaper reports she'd read of him, the pictures she'd seen. Witt Danvers had been imposing and ruthless and cruel. Nelson seemed to have a gentler side to his character and Adria guessed there had been little, if any, gentleness in Witt Danvers. Whatever tenderness had been trapped in his black soul had been given only to his youngest child: to London. His little treasure.

She felt suddenly sick and surprisingly empathetic for this man sitting across from her. All Witt's children bore emotional scars that might never heal. But she wouldn't learn anything if she showed any sign of weakness, if she let her emotions get the better of her. "What if I do turn out to be London?" she asked, lifting an eyebrow. "What would you do then?"

"I don't know . . . it's impossible to even consider it. She's been dead too long . . . at least dead to me. Us. The family."

"If I do turn out to be dear little London, you'll have to see me day after day and have to deal with me regarding all the family business, won't you?"

"I don't work for the company."

"You're on the board of directors. You aren't high-profile, but you're involved. Sure, Jason pulls all the strings, but you and your sister are always hovering in the wings." When he didn't respond, she plunged on, determined to make her point. "I could be helpful to you, you know. I read somewhere that you'd like to go into politics. If you assisted me in uncovering the truth, it would look good on your record, wouldn't it?" She winked at him, as if they were co-conspirators. "The headlines could be a veritable bonanza of goodwill—which wouldn't hurt you in the final ballot count. I can see them now: DANVERS BROTHER FINDS LONG-LOST SISTER; or NELSON DANVERS PROVES WOMAN IS HIS HALF-SISTER. CANDIDATE FINDS LONG-LOST RELATIVE. It could go on and on."

Nelson's eyes grew wary.

"Then again," she said, with a lift of her shoulder, "if I really do turn out to be London, I could throw a monkey wrench in all your ambitions. You're probably banking on getting your share of the fortune." She clucked her tongue and wondered what it was about him that made her second-guess herself.

"You know, Adria, I came here hoping that we could settle things. I don't need to be threatened."

"Glad you brought it up, 'cause neither do I." Reaching into her purse, she retrieved the nasty little notes she'd received and slapped them onto the table. "Someone has been sending me notes and . . . gifts, if you would call it that."

The color seeped from his face. "Who gave these to you?"

"Don't know. Notice that they're not signed. The mark of a true coward."

"How'd you get them? Were they delivered?" he asked, a muscle ticking near the corner of his jaw.

"One turned up on my bureau. The other, a nasty little surprise, was left at the desk. Not many people know that I'm a guest here, Nelson, but obviously you did, so I assume the rest of your family does as well. My guess is that the guy you've got following me reports back to you and you all know when I'm out of my room." She glared at him. "Give the family a message—it won't work. I won't back off. I've been told that I've got a stubborn streak that becomes obvious when people try to force me into doing what they want." She leaned across the table, bringing her face closer to his. "The bottom line is this—the more you push, the harder I'll push right back. These"—she pointed to the letter—"are a waste of my time, and the package just evidence that someone needs to see a shrink."

"I have no idea where those letters came from," he said, blinking hard, as if trying to put his thoughts in some sort of order. "And a package—what was in it?"

"Believe me, you don't want to know. Why don't you give your siblings a message for me, okay? Tell them to knock it off. I'm about ready to go to the police and the press as it is and this is just one way of pushing me right through the open doors of the *Oregonian*. I know of several columnists who would have a ball with this story and probably a dozen freelance reporters who would cut off their right arm if they could create a little controversy in this town. They'd love to shake up the social strata a bit by writing an exposé of some sort on the Danvers family." She took a long drink from her glass. "What do you think?"

"What I think, Adria," Nelson said, his voice surprisingly low and calm, "is that you're just like all the rest. A fraud."

"And what I think is someone in the family is running scared." She tapped a fingernail on the letters. "Really scared."

"You don't even know that they're from the family."

"Who else?"

She folded the notes and put them in her purse. She didn't like pushing so hard, but she had no choice. Someone in the family had decided it was time to play hard ball. Was it Nelson? She didn't think so, but she didn't know much about him. If Nelson were really her half-brother, she'd feel sorry for him, wearing his expensive suits during the day, and his new black leather jacket at night, while holding on to a job he didn't want just because he was a part of the political game started long ago by his father. She suspected that even though good old Witt was in the grave, Nelson was still trying to prove to his father—or to himself—that he was truly worth something after all.

"Is there anything else you wanted to know?" she asked.

"Why don't you just leave us alone?"

"I can't."

"This is your mission, right?"

"You got it, Nelson." Since the conversation wasn't going anywhere, she stood. "Look, this doesn't have to be a battle," she said.

"Of course it does." He stared up at her and his eyes seemed suddenly lifeless. She wanted to wiggle away from his dead gaze, but she didn't. "If you know anything about our family, you know it does."

"As long as we understand each other." She motioned toward the bar. "Don't worry about the bill. I charged it to my room."

Nelson watched as she walked briskly out the double glass

doors. He'd made a mess of things. He'd hoped to befriend her and weasel a little information from her, but she'd turned the conversation around and he'd been nearly tongue-tied. He was usually calm around women, immune to them for the most part, but occasionally he found one who could rattle him and Adria Nash, whoever the hell she was, had done more than her share of rattling.

He had the horrible premonition that she was London. Not only her looks, but her manner spoke of arrogance and power. He'd expected a shy little hick from Montana, a girl interested in scamming a few bucks and beating a hasty retreat, but there was more to her than met the eye and that scared him shitless.

Straightening his collar, he caught his reflection in the beveled mirror over the bar. Another murky gaze met his and locked and Nelson felt the back of his throat turn to cotton. There was passion in that stare—unreined, raw sexual energy that hit him with an intensity that knocked the breath from his lungs. He felt the same dark stirrings he'd tried to deny for years, held the stranger's gaze for just an instant, and turned quickly on his heel. He didn't have time for any one-night stands. Besides, they were much too dangerous. He had his career to think about and he couldn't, for the sake of one wet tongue sliding down his spine, give in to the dark desire that had been his curse for as long as he'd been interested in sex. One night could put his entire future in jeopardy. Especially now.

Ignoring the heat that crept into his loins and brought a sheen of perspiration to his upper lip, he left the bar and hunched his shoulders against the cool October breeze. Briskly, before he gave in to the sexual demons still burning through his mind and he turned around to meet with the sensual stranger, he walked the few blocks to the Hotel Danvers where his car was parked. Without a second's hesitation, he called Jason from the cellular phone in his Cadillac. "I just met with Adria," he said, looking over his shoulder as if he expected someone—the potential one-night stand, perhaps—to be staring through the windows. "I'm on my way to your house."

"Great!" Jason slammed the phone down and rotated the kinks from his neck. It had been one hell of a day. He'd been in meetings all day, but his mind hadn't been on business. No. He hadn't been able to stop thinking of Adria Nash—the proverbial fly in the fucking ointment.

How could the family get rid of her? There was something about her that got his blood up and he imagined himself either knocking her senseless or making love to her or both. He got hard just thinking of shoving her onto the bed and giving her the fuck of her life. "Get a grip," he muttered. Even thinking about a sexual involvement with her was a ridiculous, treacherous notion and had probably started because she reminded him of Kat. Guilt, ever his companion, ate at him.

He was waiting for a call from Sweeny and he'd already had a run-in with Kim, who was making demands upon him, begging him to get the divorce he'd so foolishly promised her. He didn't need the added aggravation and now Nelson was losing it. The kid was about to go around the bend with this Adria/London thing. Usually even-tempered, Nelson was coming damned close to becoming unhinged. Jason checked his watch and frowned. "Come on, Sweeny," he said before pouring himself another drink and tossing it back.

Ten minutes later the phone rang. Jason picked up the receiver on the second ring and heard Sweeny's nasal drawl. "I've done as much checkin' in this shit hole as I can," Oswald announced without so much as a greeting. "Our friend Ms. Nash has been a busy woman. After discovering the tape from her father, she checked out every library book in the county on the timber business and the hotel business as well as shipping and real estate."

Every muscle in Jason's body tightened. *Danvers International.* "So she's done her homework."

"Hell, yes, she's done her homework, even got herself some goddamned extra credit, if you ask me. She ordered books from other libraries all across the Northwest—Seattle, Portland, Spokane, Oregon City, and newspapers, too. Contacted all the majors in three or four states. As I said, the lady's been busy."

Jason's insides seemed to congeal. He'd hoped she was a bimbo, a low-class gold digger out for a quick buck.

Sweeny was still saturating him with the bad news. "Now you have to remember that she graduated with honors from the college she attended. Summa cum laude."

"Christ!"

"This gal isn't another one of your look-alike airheads. She's got brains and it appears as if she wanted to know everything she could about you, the family, and how you go about making your money."

Jason sagged against the wall and stared out at the night. He felt as if the floorboards were shifting beneath his feet.

"If you look through your list of stockholders, you might find that she owns some stock in Danvers International— not much, mind you, just a hundred shares, enough to get all the information you send to your investors."

Jesus! Jason resisted the urge to clear his throat. "Anything else?" he asked, his jaw clenched so tight it began to throb.

"Oh, yeah. A lot. And nothing you're going to want to hear. She's got the right kind of blood. A negative. Not all that uncommon, but since Witt was O negative and Katherine was A positive, their daughter could very well have been A negative. I never found any records where London was typed, but A negative would certainly have been in the ballpark. It's just too bad that old Witt or Katherine aren't around so that we could do a DNA test. Kind of a break for her that she had to wait until both London's natural parents were cremated, don't you think?"

"Damned convenient for her."

"So far, it looks like she's got you by the short hairs," Sweeny said, and Jason heard the note of satisfaction in the oily man's speech.

Jason took in a deep, calming breath. "So tell me the good news," he said, praying there was a chink in Adria's story.

"She's broke."

"How broke?"

"Broke as in drowning in red ink. Even though she's leased her farm, looks like she'll have to sell it and she's still got hospital bills hammered up her ass. A chunk of Danvers change would definitely keep the wolf from the door."

That news was encouraging. In a legal fight, Ms. Nash would lose unless she came up with some egomaniac of a lawyer, some renegade who wanted a piece of the Danvers fortune himself and was willing to work on a contingency with no money up front. Jason had a lot of friends in town, attorneys who wouldn't dare go up against the Danvers family in a court of law, but there were plenty who would—on a contingency basis, just for the challenge and fame of it all. "Okay, what else?"

"That's it for now, but I plan to come up with something when I get to Memphis."

"What's there?"

"Hopefully, Bobby Slade."

"Virginia's husband?" Jason began to feel a little ray of hope. "You found him?"

"I think so, and a word of advice to you. You'd better get down on your knees and pray he's got A negative blood running through his veins. Would help cast a big shadow over her story. Oh, and there's one more thing you might like to know. Earlier tonight, our Ms. Nash was picked up at the Orion Hotel in a stretch limo."

"By whom?"

Sweeny hesitated a beat and Jason had the sickening feeling that he was being strung along. "Well, that's the kicker," Oswald Sweeny finally drawled. "Seems as if your good friend Anthony Polidori took her out to dinner."

* * *

"Listen," Nelson said, tossing his jacket over the back of a chair. "I'm telling you she's a wild card. There's just no knowing what she's going to do next. She's said she'll go to the press, do whatever it takes to get what she wants and I believe her. She wasn't just jacking me around."

Zach stood near the fireplace, resting his hip on the Italian marble, feeling uncomfortable in the formal living room—the room he'd never been allowed to walk through as a child. Decorated in white, with touches of black and gold, it was a cold room and he would've preferred to be anywhere else in the world, rather than cornered here at the old family home with his brothers and sister.

Now, his eyes narrowed on Nelson. The youngest Danvers brother was known to exaggerate and for that reason he'd probably make a good politician.

Nelson had been pacing the length of the living room, nervously eyeing Zach ever since his middle brother had shown up.

"What do you think we should do?" Zach asked, unable to read his younger brother. Zach had never understood him, not even when Nelson was just a kid.

"Shit, I don't know what we should do! That's why I'm here."

"You'll make a helluva mayor, Nelson," Zach remarked before lifting his bottle of Coors to his lips.

"Governor," Nelson clarified.

Trisha flicked a lighter to the end of her cigarette. "So what would you do, Zach?"

"Leave her alone. Let her play out her hand."

Through a cloud of smoke, Trisha laughed. "Just because you don't give a rat's ass, doesn't mean the rest of us don't."

"You've got a better idea?"

"Hire a hit man." Trisha crossed her legs and settled back into the plump white pillows of the couch.

"Don't even say it!" Nelson bit out.

"Christ, don't you know when I'm joking?" Trisha rolled her eyes, but Zach noticed something darken her gaze, something she quickly disguised.

Nelson faced his sister. "No one knows when you're joking, Trisha. Not even you."

"Clever, Nelson. Clever."

Nelson shoved both hands through his hair. "We'd all better be careful. She's already received a couple of threatening letters and some damned package that she wouldn't say too much about."

"How nice," Trisha purred but Zach felt every muscle in his body grow instantly taut.

"What do you mean?"

As Nelson related his conversation with Adria, Zach's insides grew cold. Someone was threatening Adria? But who? Only the people in this room, his mother, and the Polidori family knew she was in town. No, that wasn't right; there were all the people who worked for the family, servants who could have overheard phone calls, and then there was the private investigator and anyone else Jason had put on the payroll.

Trisha, her expression unreadable, crushed her cigarette in a crystal ashtray. "Have any of you thought about the fact that Adria could just be who she claims she is? Maybe she is London and if she is, we're all up shit creek without our proverbial paddle."

"London's dead," Jason said, cutting off further speculation.

"How do you know? How do any of us know?" Trisha asked.

"We all know it. She obviously died years ago, or maybe there's a one-in-a-million chance that she's living somewhere, oblivious to the fact that she's a Danvers."

"Or maybe she just found out who she is," Zach drawled, narrowing his eyes on his family.

"It's all just a pain in the ass," Trisha said as she climbed off the couch. "You know, I hate it when this happens, when someone comes in with all that crap about being London— Witt Danvers's little princess. That's what he called her, you know." She turned her shadowed eyes on Zach. "You remember, don't you? She was all he cared about. The rest of us could have dropped off the face of the earth and he wouldn't have blinked an eye. But because it was London—it was a really big deal!"

"She's got to be dead," Jason said.

Zach couldn't help rising to the bait. "Maybe one of us killed her."

"Jesus, Zach, listen to you. Don't even think about it." Nelson shoved the sleeves of his sweater to his elbows as he looked from one of his siblings to the other. "Look, arguing among ourselves isn't doing any of us any good. What we've got to do is find a way to discredit her. She assured me that if we found out the truth and proved to her that she *wasn't* London, she'd take a hike."

"And you believe that?" Trisha asked with a low-throated chuckle. "Jesus, Nels, you really are a dumb shit, aren't you? The more I think about it, the more I think you're the perfect public servant."

"Knock it off," Jason ordered. "I've got Sweeny checking her story and he's got a man following her. If she's got an accomplice, we'll hear of it."

"Sweeny?" Zach said, disgusted. He'd suspected that Jason would have Adria followed, but Oswald Sweeny was lowlife trash who would sell his own mother if the price were right.

"He'll get the job done."

"He's a fucking creep," Trisha said.

For once Zach agreed with his sister, but he didn't have time to argue with Jason's choice of private investigators.

Zach turned his attention to his younger brother. Nelson seemed incredibly nervous—like he was on speed. "Are the notes legitimate threats?" he asked, forcing himself to think logically. On one level he wanted to tear his siblings limb from limb for all their disparaging remarks about Adria, and yet, he was a fool to think he could trust her one little bit.

Nelson eyed him curiously. "What're you getting at?"

"Could she have written them herself?"

"What for?" Nelson asked.

Zach peeled the label off his beer. "Public sympathy."

"You are perverted, aren't you?" Trisha said.

"Wait a minute. Why not?" Jason asked, warming to the subject. "She's clever enough to have written the threats herself. Shit, yes, that's probably just what she did." There was genuine admiration in his eyes.

"Or else she might be in serious danger," Zach said aloud and that thought chilled him to the bone. "Why don't you tell me where she is?"

"She's got a room at the Orion," Nelson supplied. "Don't know the room number."

The Orion. He hadn't been in that hotel since the night of the kidnapping, had never been able to drive past its cold concrete exterior without feeling a time warp that dragged him back to the horrid night when he'd been beaten, left for dead, and ended up a suspect in his kid sister's abduction. "Who knows she's there?"

Nelson bit his lower lip. "Probably half the people in Portland by now. Hell, Zach, didn't you hear me? She's talking about going to the police and the press! Do you know what will happen? It'll be a circus—"

"Why do you care?" Trisha asked Zach as she reached for another cigarette. "As I said, you've never given a good goddamn about the family."

"Still don't."

"But you've got a bug up your butt, don't you?" She flicked her lighter to the end of her filter tip. "You know, Zach, if I didn't know better, I'd think you were interested in Adria. Romantically speaking."

He didn't bother answering.

"Just like Kat. Couldn't keep your hands off her, even though you knew it was suicide." Trisha studied the glowing tip of her cigarette as if it held all the answers to the universe. "I'd hate to think this copy-Kat's got her claws into you already."

Zach forced a cold smile. "Hell, Trisha, and here I thought you were the only one with claws."

She glowered at him through smoke.

Jason said, "I still think the best idea would be to hide her away somewhere like the ranch."

"Forget it." Zach told himself he wasn't interested.

"Could give you a chance to be alone with her," Trisha taunted. "At the ranch. Just like Kat."

Zach's fingers tightened around his Coors and Jason, his mouth set and grim, held up a hand. "Time for a truce, you two. Get ahold of yourself Zach. You know who the enemy is here."

Yeah, Zach knew. But he didn't like it. Jason was still suggesting that he convince Adria to leave Portland and go to the ranch with him.

The trouble was, Zach was beginning to agree.

17

From the outside, the Orion Hotel looked the same as it had years ago when Zach, determined to lose his virginity, had crossed the threshold. Inside, things had changed. The main lobby had been remodeled. Glass tables and floral couches were positioned away from the desk and spiky-leaved palms seemed to grow out of the terra-cotta floor.

Ignoring a sense of déjà vu that made his skin crawl, Zach walked straight to the desk where two clerks—a man and a woman in their early twenties—were manning the night shift. "Would you ring Ms. Nash's room?" Zach asked. "Tell her she has a guest in the lobby." The two exchanged glances and the woman checked her watch.

"Is she expecting you?"

"No."

"It's late—"

"She won't mind."

Polished fingernails flew over the keyboard of her computer. "Let me see if she's asked not to be disturbed . . ." She studied the monitor, gave a little shrug, and lifted the phone receiver to her ear. "What's your name?"

"Zachary Danvers."

"She knows you?"

"Yeah."

"It'll be just a minute."

"I'll wait in the bar."

* * *

As the telephone jangled for the third time, Adria reached blindly for it and glanced at the clock. Twelve-thirty. She'd been asleep for less than an hour, but the clouds of slumber had been heavy and hard to part. Fumbling for the receiver with one hand, she pushed her bangs out of her eyes with the other. "Hello?"

"Ms. Nash, this is Laurie at the front desk. I'm sorry to disturb you, but you have a visitor. Mr. Danvers is here to see you."

"Who?"

"Zachary Danvers."

"Zach?" The fog cleared from her mind as the apologetic clerk conveyed Zach's message. Her heart skipped a tiny little beat before she realized that he'd been called in by the troops. It was time to circle the Danvers family wagons as Adria had threatened to go to the press. She wondered how he'd try to convince her to take a hike.

She threw on a pair of jeans and a bulky sweater. Unable to control the wild black curls, she clipped a barrette over her hair at the base of her neck and grabbed her purse.

"Ready for round three," she told herself as she thought of Polidori and Nelson Danvers and the damned dead rat wearing her locket! Suddenly she'd become popular. Too popular. And too many people knew where she lived. It was time to move to cheaper, more private quarters.

She saw Zach the minute she entered the bar. Despite the soft lights and the dark interior, she noticed him at a table in the corner.

His jean-clad legs were stretched out in front of him and he rested on the small of his back. His blue work shirt was pushed high on his forearms and he was watching the door with hawklike eyes that followed her as she made her way to the table.

She'd forgotten how formidable he was: the cruel set of his mouth, the thick black brows, his face—all sharp angles and planes—and eyes that seemed to see through any facade.

Nursing a beer, he didn't say a word as she approached, didn't offer the hint of a smile or indicate in any way that he was glad to see her. In fact, he almost scowled as if irritated by the sight of her.

"Do you know what time it is?" she asked, dropping her purse onto the table.

He shrugged. "After midnight."

"If you're here to offer me a bribe, forget it."

"Sit down, Adria," he suggested. "I heard you've been getting some nasty mail."

"Bad news travels fast." She settled into a chair.

The waiter came and she started to decline, then decided she could use a drink. Zach's presence always unnerved her. It was his attitude, she supposed. All male ego and raw sexuality, as if he knew he was attractive to females, the kind of cynical man most women considered a challenge and itched to tame, the kind of man she should stay away from—a lonesome cowboy who was up to no good. "I'll have a glass of chardonnay, please."

"Tell me about the letters."

"Not exactly love notes," she said and pulled a plastic bag from her purse. She slid it across the table and he read the short messages through the plastic.

"Someone means business." His mouth was grim, his eyebrows pulled together.

"Someone named Danvers, unless I miss my guess."

"Nelson said you got a package, too."

"That I did." Her wine came and she took a long sip.

"From the same guy?"

"I imagine."

"What was it?"

Oh, Lord. "A personal gift," she said, watching his reaction. "A dead rat with—"

"What! Someone sent you a dead rat?" His face drained of color.

"—with a necklace around its throat and body, the very

locket and chain that was stolen from my room when I was staying at the Hotel Danvers and this note." She pointed to one of the plastic encased letters.

"Jesus Christ, Adria, are you kidding?"

"About this? Nope." She shook her head.

"And you didn't call the police?"

"Not yet."

"Where is the damned thing?"

"On ice."

"What?"

"In the mini fridge in my room." He looked as if he didn't believer her. "You want to see it?"

"Damned straight." His countenance had changed from shock to anger and he slapped some bills onto the table and followed her out of the bar, past the front desk and to the elevators.

"This is friggin' nuts," he growled as she unlocked the door to her room, stepped inside, and walked to the minibar.

"You're telling me." She opened the refrigerator door and Zach, bending on one knee, looked inside. "Son of a bitch," he whispered. "Son of a goddamned bitch." He didn't touch the bag, but said, "You have to tell the police about this, Adria." He motioned toward the package. "This isn't just a simple threat scratched on a note and slipped under the door."

"I was just waiting."

"For what? The sicko to come after you? No. There'll be no waiting." He crossed to the bed and swept the phone from its cradle. "Either you call or I will. But this has gone far enough!"

"Just hold on a sec. I said I'd call the police and I will, but . . . but let's go back downstairs and finish our drinks. Think about this calmly." She suddenly needed to get out of the room.

"There's nothing to be calm about. This is serious, Adria." Using a handkerchief, he pulled the plastic bag with its grisly contents from the refrigerator. "Is this what it came in?" he asked, motioning to the torn manila envelope on the desk.

"Yes."

"Then let's put it back." He started to stuff the rodent carefully back into the packet.

"Wait a minute. What are you doing? We have to save it."

"I've got a friend who works for the police department. A detective. He'll know what to do with it."

"I don't think this is a good idea."

"It's better than anything you've come up with. You don't want to go to the cops, fine. Let's handle this discreetly."

"I'll have to fill out a report."

"Yeah. Eventually. But come on, do you really want to spend another night with this guy?" He hitched his chin at the envelope where the rat was now tucked.

"No, I guess not," she admitted, but she didn't know if she could trust him.

As if he could read her mind, he said, "Believe me. I'll talk to my friend ASAP. Come on. I'll buy you a drink."

"I don't like being manipulated."

"I'm just trying to help." His gaze held hers for a second too long. "You've got to trust someone, Adria. And you're the one who came looking for me a few days back. Not the other way around."

That much was true. "Fine," she said with a quick nod. "Have your friend in the department call me. I would like my necklace back."

Zach lifted a dark brow. "You'd wear it again?"

"I don't know. But I'd like the option."

Carefully, he tucked the envelope into his jacket pocket and walked to the door.

"We need to stop downstairs at the front desk. Get new keys . . ."

"As if that will stop anyone," she muttered, and hated feeling a little more secure because Zach was around. Which was just plain stupid. He was a Danvers. One of them. She shouldn't trust him one little bit, but she didn't argue when the elevator landed on the first floor and he helped her get a new room key at the front desk. He also impressed upon the woman behind the counter that no one, not even a member of the staff, was to go into Adria's room.

"I don't think your speech is going to help. Whoever wants to get into my room will find a way," she said as they crossed the foyer to the bar.

"Over my dead body," Zach whispered and held open the frosted glass door. Inside he chose a booth near the windows that had a view of the door. Zach could watch people on the sidewalk near the exterior door and he could also watch anyone slipping into the bar through the vestibule. Not that there weren't hidden service entrances and back doors where someone could slip inside.

Adria had never felt more vulnerable in her life. And yet, silly as it was, Zach's presence was comforting. If only she could trust him.

You can't trust anyone, Adria. Remember that. Remember the notes. Remember the package that is now in Zach's pocket. Don't let your guard down for a second.

A waiter deposited their drinks and Adria tried to sip her wine, but she couldn't enjoy a swallow, not with Zach so close, his eyes trained on the doorway, his jaw hard and set. Not with everything that had happened in the last twenty-four hours.

Zach glanced around the small establishment, his gaze scouring the patrons settled into dark, paneled booths or perched upon stools at the long, polished metal bar. "I don't like this," he said, ignoring his beer as laughter broke out from a corner table.

"That makes two of us." But along with a case of nerves, she was furious. No one had the right to terrorize her. "Look, I'm not going to let that bastard, whoever he is, stop me. That's what he's trying to do, you know. I guess he thinks I'll just shiver in my boots and hurry on back to Montana."

Zach's mouth twitched.

"Well, it's just not happening. He's made me too angry. Instead of running scared, I've decided to notch things up a bit. Turn up the heat."

He watched her over the rim of his glass.

"I'm going to go to the press and I'll start with the newspapers."

"Fine." His eyes crinkled at the corners.

"Don't you care?"

"What? About the bad press? Hell, no. What I care about is that you don't get hurt." His gaze drilled into hers and she had to look away. "Call a damned press conference for all I care, but watch your back. Better yet, have someone watch it for you." He took a long pull on his beer and his eyes narrowed on her in a way that made her stupid heart skip a beat. "You know what you need?"

She nearly groaned. "No, but I have the feeling you're going to tell me."

"A bodyguard."

"What? You're joking, right?"

"Not a bit."

He was suddenly so serious, she nearly laughed. "Give me a break. I can take care of myself. Remember, I grew up on a ranch in Montana and—"

"And you're getting threatening letters."

"From a coward."

"Who plays with dead animals. Wake up, Adria. This is serious."

She felt a chill as cold as midnight pass over her skin and swallowed hard. "So . . . Danvers . . . Are you suggesting that *you* become my bodyguard? Are you applying for the job?"

He didn't reply but gazed straight back at her with such an intensity she felt as if her diaphragm had slammed up against her lungs. Breathing was suddenly all but impossible.

"Don't you think it would be stupid of me, I mean really stupid, to have someone named Danvers protecting me?"

"You can't fight the world alone."

"Not the world, Zach. Just the Danvers family."

"They're powerful."

"You mean *you're* powerful, don't you? You're part of the family whether you like it or not."

He hunched over his beer. "For the record, I don't like it."

"But you're tied to them, aren't you?" she said. "Because of Daddy's money."

His arm shot across the table and he clamped his work-roughened fingers over her wrist. His words came out in a low, menacing growl. "Listen to me, lady. I'm trying to do you a favor here and all you're doing by fighting me is pissing in the wind."

"I don't want any favors." She inched her chin up but she couldn't ignore the five warm impressions where his fingertips pressed against the sensitive skin of her inner wrist. Her throat seemed as dry as smoke and his gaze lowered, resting for what seemed an endless second on the pulse throbbing above her collarbone.

"I'm trying to help you. After the threats you've been getting I'd think you'd take a hand when it's offered."

She wanted to believe him, but she knew that he was probably lying, that he'd been sent on a mission to render her harmless. He'd come from the family—whether he admitted it or not—and that thought, of the Danvers kin deciding how to manipulate her, caused her temper to ignite. For as long as she could remember, someone was trying to dictate to her, bend her will, and this time, by God, she wasn't giving in an inch. Gritting her teeth, she yanked back her arm and scrambled to her feet. "Back off, Danvers. I know I'm on my own here, so you don't need to be playing the part of the hero."

"Is that what I'm doing?"

"You tell me."

He watched her storm out the door, noticed the curve of her hips and the stiff set of her back. Her legs were thin, but not skinny, and he wondered what they'd feel like wrapped around his waist.

"Shit," he muttered under his breath, disgusted at the direction of his thoughts.

No matter what, he intended to camp out on her doorstep. Dropping some bills on the table, he took out after her. He stepped into the lobby just as the elevator doors were closing, but that suited him just fine and he paused, leaning against a pillar to watch as the elevator's indicator lights mounted over the closed doors, blinked on in succession, then held steady for several seconds at the fifth floor. There were no other stops as the car descended. Without a second's hesitation, he waited for the doors to open and rode the empty car back up. He'd sit out in the hallway if he had to, but he'd damn well see for himself if there was anyone set on stalking her.

The elevator bell rang softly as it reached the fifth floor. Zac stepped into the empty corridor and spied a house telephone. He made a quick call to Len Barry, his friend on the force. Len agreed to stop by for the package burning a hole in Zach's jacket pocket. After hanging up, Zach found a chair and fake tree nestled against windows at the corner of the hallway, with a view down both wings. He settled into the low-backed chair to wait.

Adria slowly counted to ten. Zachary's taunts had followed her up the elevator shaft. His arrogance disturbed her—the way he tried to order her around made her want to kick at something. He and the rest of the family acted as if she just wanted to rip off all their money. She unclipped her hair and threw the barrette onto the bed in frustration. "Bastard," Adria muttered and caught herself as the word rolled easily off her tongue.

There was more than a little truth to the name, wasn't there? If she looked inside herself, really looked, she knew she'd discover that a part of her wanted Zach to be sired by another man—any man other than Witt Danvers, whom she believed to be her own father.

Because, damn it, she found Zachary sensual and disturbing and like no man she'd ever met before. Was he trying to help her? Or had it all been an act?

Her head began to pound. Was Zach really Witt's son? Oh, who cared? Did it matter? All she needed to know was if she was really Witt's daughter. Zach's paternity wasn't something she needed to think about. Zachary Danvers wasn't anyone she needed to think about.

She picked up the newspaper lying in sections on the small table in her room and snapped it open. With furious fingers, she flipped through the pages and stopped at the section marked Rooms For Rent. Tomorrow, first thing, she'd find a new place to live, then she'd waltz into the *Oregonian* and tell a tale that would leave the reporters hustling as they scrambled to get her story into the next edition. Later she'd talk to the television and radio news stations.

If the Danvers family wanted to play hardball, so be it. She was more than ready to pitch them a curveball the likes of which they'd never yet seen.

Trisha parked in her usual spot, between the garage and the cabin in the woods of the Polidori estate. A gardener's cabin that was supposed to be unoccupied, Mario had converted the little vine-covered cottage that had served as their secret rendezvous for over twenty years. Her heart was beating a light little tempo and she chided herself for being foolish as she ducked under the dripping clematis and knocked softly on the front door before turning the lock.

He was waiting for her. Backlit by the lights in the kitchen, he strode across the dark living room and her breath caught in her throat. Though she'd grown cynical and callous over the years, the sight of Mario never ceased to cause a wave of anticipation to race through her blood.

He was bare-chested—his jeans hanging low over his hips.

"You're late," he said in the smoky voice that had always caused her bones to turn liquid.

"Problems at home."

"Forget them." He reached over her shoulder and pushed the door so hard that it slammed in the casing before the lock latched. His arms surrounded her and his lips crashed over hers—hot, hungry, possessive. Trisha shivered in anticipation and closed her mind to everything but this one vital man. She needed a few hours to forget about Adria and London and the whole sordid mess.

If Adria could prove she was London, all of Trisha's dreams would be shattered, her life destroyed.

Unless she could be stopped.

Adria nearly jumped from the bed when the alarm jangled at six A.M. She felt as if she'd barely drifted off after a night of tossing and turning and worrying subconsciously that someone was sneaking into her room. Sleep had been nearly nonexistent and her mind had swum with images of rats with big teeth, strangers hiding in the shadows, and Zachary— sometimes as her enemy but more often than not as her lover. Over and over again she remembered the night in the Jeep when he'd kissed her with a raw animal passion that made her insides turn to hot, soft wax. Because of the fear she felt, be- cause she knew she was being followed and watched, because someone was out to terrorize her, she was more drawn to Zachary Danvers.

It was ridiculous, of course. She couldn't want him. Her fantasies were only because he was the sexiest man she'd been around in a long while and the simple fact that he was forbidden fruit—a rough man she couldn't have.

"Character flaw," she told herself as she brushed her teeth and saw her tousled-haired reflection in the mirror over the sink.

She stepped under the hot spray of the shower until she was

awake. Today was the day she was going to the papers. A knot of dread twisted her stomach at the thought. She had hoped it wouldn't come to this, but she'd been foolish. Talking to the press was inevitable.

But first things first. She needed a permanent residence. She dressed quickly and, armed with yesterday's paper, she walked out of the room and stopped dead in her tracks. Her heart jolted and she could barely find her tongue as her gaze collided with Zachary Danvers's interested gray eyes. Still in the clothes he'd worn the night before, his long legs stretched out in front of him, his chin shadowed with more than a day's growth of beard, he rubbed the crick from his neck and gave her a crooked smile.

"Mornin'," he drawled, as if they saw each other at the crack of dawn each and every day.

"What're you doing here?" she managed to ask.

"Waitin' for you."

Another jolt. "Why?"

"I thought someone should hang around, you know, and scare away the bad guys."

"Did you?"

"You didn't have any trouble, did you?"

"And that was because of you?"

He shrugged. "Only a few people saw me. The early risers this morning. Jogger and guys with briefcases off to important meetings." He stretched, his tall body seeming to grow longer and leaner as he reached over his head, then winced as the cramps left his muscles. "So, no one bothered you?"

"No one called, but I asked the desk to take messages."

"Maybe I could buy you breakfast."

She slid a glance in his direction. They were alone in the elevator and he seemed to fill it with his presence. For once there wasn't a trace of hostility in his eyes and she was tempted to let down her guard a bit even though he had the innate and maddening ability to make her see red at the drop of a hat. Be that as it may, she needed one friend, one contact in the family, someone who didn't outwardly hate her, and yet being close to Zach was dangerous on an entirely different and deeper emotional level.

As the elevator ground to a stop and the doors whispered open, Adria stepped into the lobby and let out the breath she hadn't even realized she'd been holding. She paused at the desk to ask for her messages. The clerk offered her a plastic smile. "You're a popular lady," he said, handing her a stack of eight or ten pieces of paper.

"What's this?" she asked aloud as she fingered the pages: Mary McDonough from KPTV news, Ellen Richards with a local magazine, Robert Ellison, a reporter for the *Oregonian*. Her throat tightened. "Looks like the cat's out of the bag," she said to Zach just as a short balding man pushed himself out of a chair half hidden by large-leafed ferns.

"Are you Adria Nash?" he asked with a smile. Beside her, Zach tensed. "I'm Barney Havoline with the *Portland Weekly*." He shoved a card at her and she checked it quickly, her fingers curving over the crisp edges. "I'd like to ask you a few questions." He didn't wait for her to answer, but rushed on, "I heard that you're in town, claiming to be London Danvers. Is that true?" He clicked on his microphone and grinned at her as if she were his long-lost friend.

Zach took a step closer to her.

Adria managed a thin smile. "That's essentially true, yes."

"And how do you know you're the Danvers heiress?"

"I found out from my father."

"Witt Danvers?"

"No, my adoptive father. Listen, Mr. Havoline, I don't know how you found out why I'm in town or where I'm staying, but—"

"Can you prove you're London?"

"—I was planning to call a press conference later in the day and explain everything."

He flashed her a smile and she was aware that several patrons of the hotel were staring at them; even a bellboy had stopped to watch the unfolding drama.

"Really," Havoline insisted. "This will take just a little while. I only have a couple more questions."

"She said *later*," Zach cut in, stepping between the pushy reporter and Adria.

"But we're here now," Havoline insisted. "I could buy you both a cup of coffee or breakfast . . . and who are you?" he asked, before his eyes met Zach's and the light dawned on his face.

"Your worst nightmare." Zach's expression had turned murderous.

"What—"

"Get out."

"Zachary Danvers." The reporter's eyes gleamed as if he realized he had more of a story than he'd first guessed. "So this woman could be your long-lost—"

"I said 'get out'!"

"Not just yet. I've got a few more questions?" He tried looking over Zach's shoulder to catch Adria's eye, but a huge hand clamped over the lapels of his jacket and propelled him past the magazine stand toward the entrance. "Hey, you can't do this! I've got rights!"

Zach shoved Havoline through the glass doors and he stumbled onto the street. "I'll sue you, you bastard!" he yelled, brushing off his jacket as a news van for a local station pulled up to the front doors.

"Hell," Zach muttered and clamped his fingers over Adria's arm. As reporters climbed out of the cab, he spun her around and half ran back to the desk. "We need to leave," he told the clerk who had witnessed the entire scene. "You must have a back way out so we don't have a mob scene here in the lobby."

"I don't know—"

Another van from a rival station pulled up and reporters started through the doors.

"Now!" Zach ordered and the clerk called over a security guard.

"Give these people an escort out and have Bill come up to handle the rest."

"This way!" The guard, a burly black man with a grim I've-seen-it-all expression, ushered them to the back of the lobby and through a set of double doors toward the kitchen. Excited voices drifted after them and Adria ducked gratefully into a stainless steel elevator. She wasn't ready for the press. Not just yet. She needed time to prepare a statement, time to get herself ready for all the questions and accusations that were sure to be hurled her way.

Minutes later they were on the street and walking the short distance to the Hotel Danvers, where another crowd had gathered. Holding her arm fiercely, Zach guided her to a private entrance, through a tangle of hallways, down to the parking garage and into his Jeep.

"Where are we going?"

"Does it matter?" he asked, throwing the rig into gear and backing out of the narrow parking space.

"I think I have the right to know."

"You got yourself into this mess. I could just leave you here to the piranhas."

"I didn't call the press."

"Like hell." Zach aimed the nose of the Jeep toward the exit of the parking lot.

"You don't believe me?" she said, disappointed as they sped out of the lot and joined the sludge of traffic clogging the city streets.

"No," he admitted, glancing in her direction. "But if it's any consolation, I haven't believed a word you've said since you blew into town."

18

Her face was a mask of calm resolution. Her chin was thrust forward with determination and her eyes, so blue, moved from one reporter's face to the other. As the clouds overhead threatened rain and the cool wind caused the leafless tree branches to sway, Adria stood on a small rise in the park walkway blocks and addressed the throng of reporters. Her cheeks, stung by the wintry wind, were pink, her smile sincere, and Zach guessed that she'd had years of public speaking in college.

So far, her hastily convened press conference had gone well, and along with the reporters, a few passersby listened to her strong voice. " . . . that's why I'm here. To uncover the truth. To find out for myself if I'm really Witt and Katherine Danvers's daughter." Six microphones were thrust in her face while photographers snapped still pictures and shoulder-held minicams rolled. The wind teased at her hair, whipping it across her face, and traffic continued to flow, the sounds of engines running, tires throwing up water, and hydraulic brakes squealing as a backdrop.

A pushy reporter with thin lips and a pointed nose asked, "Do you have any proof, aside from this tape of your adoptive father, that you're London Danvers?"

"No, not really—"

"Isn't that a little thin? Home video cameras are a dime a dozen now. Anyone could put together a stunt like this."

Zach's eyes narrowed on the man and he hooked his thumb

into his belt loops just to make sure he didn't start pushing the little bastard around.

"It's not a stunt," Adria replied firmly.

"You don't think. But you don't know. You have no idea what your adoptive father's motives were."

A red-haired woman with a deep voice asked, "What happened to Ginny Slade?"

"I wish I knew."

"Why didn't she demand ransom?"

"Again. I don't know," Adria said, as a truck roared past, sending pigeons scattering through the park and trailing a plume of blue exhaust.

"What about the million-dollar reward that Witt left for anyone who found his daughter? Wouldn't Ginny have wanted a piece of that?"

"I can't speak for her."

Another woman asked, "At the time of the kidnapping, some people thought a local businessman, Anthony Polidori, was behind the plot. Witt Danvers always maintained that Polidori was involved."

"I don't know who was behind it."

"Polidori was harassed by the police but he swore he was innocent."

"I can't comment on that."

"Who was behind the kidnapping?"

"I don't know—"

"What about you, Mr. Danvers? What do you and your family think?"

Zach responded by skewering the woman with a gaze meant to strike fear into her heart. "I have nothing to say.

"But you're here, with a woman claiming to be your half-sister."

He felt his blood beginning to boil. "This is her circus, not mine."

"So that's what you think about it?" the woman pushed, obviously pleased to get a rise from him. "What about the rest of the family?"

"You'll have to ask them."

"They're not here. You are. What do *you* think?"

"I have no comment."

"Weren't you one of the prime suspects at the time?"

Zach's eyes flashed. "I was seventeen, for Christ's sake," he said, then forced a lid on his temper. "You'll have to ask the police that one." He grabbed the crook of Adria's arm and if he could, he would have bodily carried her away from this ridiculous sideshow. Reporters were jackals. The whole lot of them. He'd learned that firsthand when London had been kidnapped.

"What do the police have to say?" the redhead asked.

Adria shot a glance in Zach's direction. "Nothing yet." She didn't add that, at Zach's insistence, she'd spent the last three hours at the station, explaining her story, giving the police a copy of the tape, showing them the threatening notes. "Thank you all for coming. If you need to get hold of me, please leave a message at the front desk of the Orion Hotel."

"The Orion? Why not the Hotel Danvers?" a man yelled.

"Hold on a minute—"

"Just a few more questions—"

Zach's fingers clamped firmly around her elbow and he propelled her to the Jeep. "Damned zoo," he ground out as he helped her inside, then slid behind the wheel. Glancing in his rearview mirror, he spotted more than one of the hungry reporters dashing to their cars and vans, hoping, no doubt, to follow them. *Good luck,* Zach thought humorlessly. He knew the city like the back of his hand and had spent most of his teenage years trying to outrun the law. He slammed the rig into first, popped the clutch, and took off. A few cars gave chase and he had to suppress a grin of satisfaction.

"I think it went well, don't you?" Adria asked.

"It was a fiasco."

"Spoken like a true Danvers."

He braked around a sharp corner and the tires skidded.

"We're being followed?" she asked.

"Yep." He glanced in the side-view mirror, frowned, and turned down an alley that opened onto Burnside. "Some of the vultures weren't finished getting what they wanted." He sped across the bridge over the dark Willamette, heading east toward the mountains, then doubled back on the freeway, crossing the river again and turning south, continuously checking his rearview mirror until he was satisfied that the cars shifting from lane to lane behind the Jeep weren't giving chase. "You've really stirred up a hornet's nest now."

"It's time."

"You shouldn't have called the press in the first place—"

"I told you I didn't."

"Well, someone did."

"Yes," she agreed, her thoughts whirling as they left the city. "Someone did." *Who?* Someone from the Danvers family? Anthony Polidori? The stalker who had left her the ugly notes? Someone who had overheard one of her conversations? Trisha? Jason? Nelson? *Zach?* A headache thundered behind her eyes and she realized that other than some dark, bitter sludge the police department called coffee, she hadn't had anything to eat all day.

"You'll have to check out of the Orion."

"I know."

"You have another place to stay?"

"Not yet."

"Jason thinks you should move to the ranch."

"With you?" she asked.

"I suppose."

The Jeep's interior seemed suddenly close, the atmosphere thick as she considered what life would be like living far removed from the city—with Zachary. How would she stand every day cooped up with him? She glanced at his profile. Her heart began to beat more loudly. Of course, she couldn't accept his proposal—she had work to do, here in the

Willamette Valley. This was just another ploy by the family to derail her from her goal. "I don't care what Jason thinks."

"It wouldn't be a bad idea. You'd be safe."

Alone with Zachary Danvers? Safe? She didn't believe it for a minute. Zachary was dangerous on too many levels to count. She was never safe with him. "You'd like that, wouldn't you?" she said, touching the inside of the passenger window with her finger and erasing the dew that had collected on the glass. "Then I'd be trapped in a place where the family could watch me, tape my phone conversations, and monitor me twenty-four hours a day. Thanks, but I don't think so."

He eased off the freeway and found a truck stop. A diner with a flickering neon sign that advertised breakfast was served around the clock was set back from the road. Zach parked close to the front door. "Come on, let's eat something and then you can decide." He reached across her and opened the door on her side of the Jeep. The feel of his body, warm and hard, leaning over her thighs had a definite effect on her pulse rate. *Stop it!*

As if he felt it, too, his gaze found hers and for a ridiculous heartbeat she thought he might kiss her again. His eyes darkened for a second, searching hers, and his breath fanned her face. He smelled of leather and coffee and musky male and his jaw was nearly black because he hadn't shaved.

Earthy and raw.

Primal and wanton.

Passionate and wicked.

Zachary Danvers was all these and more. She licked her dry lips and held her breath. Waiting . . . sensing he could read her thoughts. "What the hell am I going to do with you?"

"I'm not your responsibility."

"Aren't you?" One dark brow lifted.

Her spine stiffened in defense. "Look, Zach, I guess I should thank you for helping me out today, but I don't really need a baby-sitter."

"You might be surprised." He sent her a smile that cut past all her facades. Pure male animal. He hopped to the gravel and she had to scramble out of the Jeep and hurry to catch up with him.

She wanted to tell him to get lost and leave her alone, but she couldn't. He'd been nearby when she'd needed him and when she'd decided to hold the press conference, he hadn't argued with her, even helped her pick the spot and stayed with her throughout the entire, nerve-fraying ordeal. She didn't know his motives, but she doubted they were pure. She'd just been thankful to have his strength, his presence during the press conference, though she was certain she could have handled the situation herself and she believed that he was probably sticking to her like glue in order to spy on her for his family. But why then did he insist she go to the police station with her complaints? Maybe he had no choice and felt backed into a corner since the word was out on the street that another woman claiming to be the little lost daughter of Witt Danvers had shown up in Portland.

They walked into the diner. Country music could be heard over the buzz of conversation and sizzle of the grill. They sat in a booth near the window.

Within seconds, a waitress poured coffee and promised to be back for their orders. Adria picked up her menu and tried to concentrate on the daily special, but having Zachary seated directly across from her was a distraction—the kind of distraction she didn't want.

Once they'd ordered, Zach drained his coffee and settled onto the small of his back. "You'd better tell me what you're planning, Adria," he said, staring at her with eyes that seemed to see into the darkest corners of her soul, "because from here on in, it's not gonna be much fun."

"And that's why I'm here. To uncover the truth. To find out if I'm really Witt and Katherine Danvers's daughter . . ." Her voice was clear. Strong. Her chin thrust forward as if she wouldn't back down.

Hell!

In a private room, Katherine's killer stared at the television screen with its flickering images of Adria Nash.

Why didn't she back off? Why in the world would she actually call a press conference? Now all of Portland—no, make that all of the whole damned country—was watching!

Rage boiled up inside.

What if she really was London? Jesus, she looked so much like Kat it was eerie.

Pictures of Katherine Danvers skated through her killer's mind.

Kat, young and successful, assured of her sexuality, walking up to Witt on the street.

Kat, a bit older, the gold band on her finger flashing the fact that she was Mrs. Witt Danvers.

Kat, pregnant and still sexy, her once-taut belly rounded. Smug pride had lifted her sharp chin because of the baby growing within her. Now she was tied to Witt and the Danvers fortune irrevocably.

The killer blinked, felt sweat beading, then dripping onto the plush carpet.

Calm down. Don't let it get to you.

But the images on the television only brought others to the fore, mental pictures that could never be forgotten. Pictures that burned and flashed painfully.

Flash!

Kat with the baby, the darling, and Witt doting on them both, as if he didn't already have a family, as if he didn't have four other children, as if this one precious piece of flesh was more important than all the other ones put together.

God, it had been sickening. Horrible.

Inside, Katherine's killer was shaking. Remembering.

Flash!

Kat getting her figure back, toning up any remaining fat from her pregnancy and showing off her figure, in a sleek, one-piece swimsuit.

Flash!

Kat, black hair gleaming and pinned high on her head, holding court with the elite of Portland. Playing bridge. Attending charity auctions or balls in her tight dresses . . .

Flash!

Kat flirting with anything in pants.

Flash!

Kat naked . . . her body gleaming . . . the shower . . . oh, God, how vulnerable she'd been after London had been stolen from her—how easy it had been to place the pills in her drink and then, when she was disoriented, when she'd stumbled outside, give her a shove over the wall.

Flash!

Kat falling over the wall, recognition dawning as their eyes met, fear contorting her beautiful features . . .

Then the sound. The sickening sound of bones cracking and muscles thudding hard against the pavement below.

It hadn't been hard.

It could be done again.

"Just a few more questions," a reporter was insisting but the camera was no longer trained on Adria. The focus had been shifted to the rock-hard countenance of Zachary Danvers and he was pissed. A vein bulged in his neck and his eyes were so dark they were nearly black as he forcibly propelled Adria away from the crowd.

Of course he'd be there. Zachary had always been a sucker for a beautiful woman. Hadn't he, like so many other men, been enthralled by his stepmother? Hadn't he risked Witt's wrath to be with her?

And now he was with a woman who could be a carbon copy.

Like father. Like son.

Fools both.

It was time to do something.

Something permanent.

But first . . . a scare.

Katherine's killer smiled and clicked off the television.
Flash!

In a glimmer of the future there came an image of Adria, the pretender, lying in a pool of her own blood, her bones broken, her neck and head turned to an impossible angle, her eyes staring sightlessly upward.

Even in death, she would resemble the woman she claimed was her mother.

The intercom beeped.

"I know you said you didn't want to be disturbed, Mr. Danvers," Jason's secretary, Frances, said in her most annoyed voice, "but your brother is on line two and he insists on speaking with you right now. I tried to get rid of him—"

"It's all right. I'll take it."

Jason crossed the thick forest-green carpet and picked up the phone. Nelson's voice was agitated and high-strung. "Channel Two. The news." A click signified that he'd hung up.

Like a hangman's noose, dread took a choke-hold on Jason's neck. He grabbed the remote control, pointed it at the television in the opposite corner of his office, and, with a sick feeling, dropped the telephone receiver back into its cradle. The television flickered on. As Jason stared at the program in progress, his worst fears crystallized. She'd done it. Adria Nash had held her own goddamned press conference in the middle of the park blocks and standing to her side, sometimes in the camera's eye, often not, was Zach. Good old pain-in-the-ass Zach. A day's growth of beard discolored his chin and his eyes were dark and unreadable. He was wearing clothes that were mussed and he looked like a damned range cowboy, but he didn't seem to care that the cameras weren't being particularly kind.

Jason swore loudly. A tic started beneath his left eye as he watched, transfixed.

God, she was beautiful. Standing straight, her wild black hair tossed in the wind, her eyes clear and blue, she looked so damned much like Katherine, Jason could barely breathe. He remembered Kat's sexy little come-hither smile, her teasing laugh, the mischievous light in her gaze. At first she'd only had eyes for Zach, even though Zach had been a kid at the time, but later, after Zach had been banished from the family, when Witt had discovered his errant son in bed with Kat at the ranch, things had changed. Kat had finally begun to notice Jason.

It had started slowly at first. A smile. A wink. A naughty little joke. A finger touching the back of his neck that lingered a second too long. Witt's long absences on business trips didn't hurt, either.

The first time had been on a cold winter night with the wind howling through the attic. The electricity had gone out and Jason and Kat had been alone in the house. She'd feigned being frightened and he'd wrapped his arms around her to settle her down and to keep her warm. When she'd tilted her face up to his, it had been the most natural act in the world to kiss her, to touch her, to rip her robe from her and to claim her like a wild buck stealing another's mate. She'd been an untamed one, her passion pent up from years of frustration.

After their first night together, they'd begun sneaking around, experimenting with drugs, getting high on coke and marijuana and sex. Even thinking of her now, he was harder than he'd been in years. His wife, Nicole, was and always had been frigid. Kim was a hot little piece, frantic to please him, willing to play out all his fantasies, but she kept pressuring him to file for divorce and she'd never had the raw sensuality, never shown the primal lust for sex that had set Kat apart from all his other lovers. While Kat enjoyed sex, Kim tried too hard to act as if she were enjoying it. Even though she'd do anything he asked, Kim's responses seemed forced and inhibited.

There had been no one to equal the pure nymphomania and narcissism of Katherine LaRouche Danvers.

And this Adria woman—whoever the hell she was—looked so damned much like Kat it scared him—and excited him.

She was fielding questions and smiling, for God's sake, handling the crowd deftly. Jason leaned his hips against the desk. He'd already realized that Adria Nash was an enemy to be reckoned with. She couldn't be taken lightly. Nor was he. He'd seen through her scam from the minute he'd set eyes on her. She wouldn't get away with it. He'd stop her dead in her tracks before she claimed one cent of the Danvers assets. He wondered fleetingly what she was like in bed. Sexually charged like Kat or dispassionately accommodating like Kim?

He frowned at the thought of his mistress and her increasing demands. He couldn't divorce Nicole. Wouldn't. His wife, though a limp dishrag in bed, was shrewd. She'd take him for half of everything he owned, which, he hoped, would soon be the largest fortune in Portland. Somehow he'd have to find a way to keep Kim appeased—as well as deal with Adria Nash.

Through narrowed eyes, he watched the end of the segment, listened to the two anchors speculate on the possibility that the missing heiress had stepped forward to claim her fortune, then felt his insides tense as old footage taken the night London had been kidnapped rolled across the screen. His guts twisted at the sight of his father and Kat, and there was a photo of little London. An artist, using the latest computer technology, had provided a simulated portrait of what the girl could look like and the features weren't far from Adria's. Dread settled like lead in his spine.

But there was no way she could be London! It was damned impossible.

He clicked off the television as the intercom beeped again. "I'm sorry, Mr. Danvers, I really am, but Mr. Sweeny insists that you'll want to talk to him. I tried to tell him you were busy and he used the most foul language—"

"It's all right, Frances. I'll take it."

"Line two again."

"Got it." Jason's palms began to sweat. He picked up and braced himself for Sweeny's news. "Jason Danvers."

"You told me to call you when I got to Memphis and I'm here," Sweeny said, his voice sounding smug.

"You've found Bobby Slade?"

"I've found a whole mess of 'em. Robert E. Lee Slade seems to be a family name or somethin'. It hasn't been easy, but I got the list narrowed down to a few prime candidates."

"Just be sure you end up with the right one."

"Piece of cake. Oh, by the way, thought you might like to know that your girl Adria's been busy."

Jason's fingers tightened over the receiver. "Has she?"

"Yep. I found out from an insider in the Polidori house that she's big news over there. The old man thinks he can use her if she is London because, as you probably already know, he's interested in buying out big chunks of Danvers International."

"Go on," Jason said through clenched teeth.

"Well, that's about it. Except that the younger Polidori seems to be very interested in her."

"Mario?"

"Mmm, could be messy, don't you think? Your sister's still seeing him."

"I know," Jason ground out. Trisha would never learn.

"Fun family you got there, Danvers. I'll call you when I have more."

Click.

"Wait!" Jason said, hating to be dismissed by the slimy detective. Sweeny's information usually was good and if he'd managed to make an informant out of one of the servants in the Polidori house, then Jason felt as if his money had been well spent. But he wanted to know more. Lots more.

The noose around his neck tightened a notch.

Glancing at his watch, he frowned and yanked his briefcase from the top of the desk. In the reception area, Frances was talking on the phone. He headed to the elevators, but she flagged him down. "It's Guy in Security," she said, hanging up.

"Seems we've got a siege of reporters downstairs wanting to talk to you or someone in the Danvers family. And these"—she held up a small pile of messages—"are all from reporters and columnists from all over the country. They want to talk to you about London." She raised her eyebrows over the tinted lenses of her glasses. "Do we have a new one again?"

"Yes, and a very convincing one," Jason said, unable to hide his irritation.

"Oh, dear." Her small lips pursed in her fleshy face. Frances Boothe would lay down her life for Danvers International. "Well, Guy said you might want to avoid the lobby."

"I am," he said, flashing her a not-to-worry smile. "They won't expect me to be going off the roof. Anything else?"

"Miss Monticello called twice. Wanted you to call back."

Jason's fingers clenched over the handle of his briefcase at the mention of Kim. She could stew for a while; it wouldn't hurt her to wait for him. Now that Adria had gone to the press, Kim held nothing over his head—except his affair. Frowning to himself, he dashed down the hall with two vice presidents. They were both talking to him at once, two yesmen who cared more about Danvers International than they did their own families. He managed to respond automatically as they rode the elevator to the helicopter pad on the roof.

The chopper was waiting and Jason was grateful for the roar of the whirring blades that drowned out conversation for the next few minutes. As the helicopter lifted off and he looked down at the city he felt a premonition of doom. At one time he'd been certain he would be the crown prince of Portland. Now, because of Adria Nash, he wasn't so sure.

It was time to show Ms. Nash what she was up against. Really up against.

Zach glanced at Adria. She was huddled in the far corner of his Jeep, staring at the middle distance through the windshield, but, he guessed, seeing nothing as cars sped around them. She acted as if she didn't know he was in the rig with her, and he couldn't forget how close she was. Whenever he was with her, his instincts seemed to sharpen and his nerves were strung tight as bow strings.

Her lower lip protruded slightly and her fingers drummed impatiently upon her leg. Her hair was loose and windblown and fell down one shoulder in thick, unruly curls. Beneath her jacket he noticed the outline of her breasts and he wondered if her resemblance to Kat stopped at her face or continued beneath her clothes . . .

Angry with himself for the single-minded track of his thoughts, he switched on the headlights and pulled out of the parking lot of a restaurant where he hadn't been able to keep his eyes from gazing at the curve of her cheek, the precocious little dimple when she smiled, the smooth column of her throat, and the roundness of her breasts.

He'd been hard half the day, silently cursing himself for feeling like a sex-starved teenager all over again. It was more than just her looks that attracted him; her mind was just as sexy as the rest of her.

Adria had given one interview after another and though Zach had disapproved, he didn't have a death wish and didn't do anything as stupid as try to stop her. He'd stood in the shadows, watching her handle the reporters' questions deftly, though she couldn't have missed the innuendoes that she was just a cheap fortune hunter out to steal a dead man's money. She had managed to stay calm, even injecting a little humor into the situation. From the newspaper-reading and television-watching public's point of view, Adria Nash was going to look good— damned good—and if the Danvers family didn't accept her as an honest woman searching for the truth, they would have one hell of a public relations problem.

Zach snorted in disgust. Public relations and public image were Nelson's department. The kid was certain to be sweating. "Okay, where to?"

"I guess back to the hotel."

"You'll have reporters swarming through the lobby," he predicted. "Your phone will ring off the hook."

She smiled a little. "I'll leave that to Security." Stifling a yawn, she added, "Besides, I think I can handle them."

"It's your funeral," he growled, and she even managed a laugh as he drove to the Orion Hotel. She was tougher than he'd first thought and as she'd so vehemently claimed on more than one occasion, she didn't run scared easily. Her tenacious and independent spirit had earned her his grudging respect. "The press can be ruthless."

Her gaze slid in his direction. "I'm used to it." For a split second he read something more in her eyes than her usual hostility, a dusky look that caused a forbidden quivering deep in his gut. "Don't worry about it, Zach. I'll be fine."

Silently cursing the lust that continually teased the corners of his mind whenever he was around her, he parked near the hotel. "Let's go," he said gruffly, hustling her through the gathering mist to the hotel. Their footsteps rang on the wet sidewalk and Adria ducked her head against the wind.

He expected to be crushed by a throng of scandal-hungry reporters, but the lobby was nearly deserted. Only a few people, carrying raincoats and umbrellas, were hurrying in and out of the restaurant and bar.

Adria relaxed a little. It had been a long day and she'd been on edge, if not because of the reporters and their questions, then because of Zachary. He'd been apprehensive, his gray eyes brooding as he'd watched the crowd and tersely answered the few questions cast in his direction. She'd felt his tension hovering in the air, noticed the muscles of his neck flex when a reporter asked a particularly pointed question, and knew the minute he turned his gaze on her. He was with her most of the day, only leaving her for about an hour when she was in an interview with a woman reporter from the *Oregonian*.

She found it impossible to believe that he was her half-brother. He was just too sexy, too darkly sensual, to be related to her. Surely she wouldn't find him so attractive, so danger-ously alluring, if in fact the same blood ran in their veins. As if he read her thoughts, he turned his eyes on her and she saw it, that tiny flicker of passion that he tried vainly to hide.

Her throat closed in on itself and time seemed to stand still.

She felt as if she and Zach were the only two people in the world. One man. One woman. Licking her lips nervously, she noticed that his gaze was drawn to the movement at her mouth. He swallowed hard.

"Miss Nash?" The clerk at the registration desk was trying to catch her attention.

"Oh, yes," she said, glad for the interruption. Clearing her throat and praying she wasn't transparent, she asked, "Are there any messages for me?"

"Does it rain in Oregon?" the desk clerk asked dryly, try-ing to make a joke as he handed her a thick stack of small papers that filled her fist. She flipped through each missive quickly. Some of the people were reporters, others she didn't recognize at all, probably just the curious, starstruck that someone dared claim to be London Danvers.

They walked to the elevators and Zach cast one final look over his shoulder before he touched her arm. "You don't mind if I come up to your room and see if your friend left any more gifts?"

Adria's heart nearly missed a beat. She hesitated and bit her lip. *This is stupid—just plain stupid, Adria. You've always been a smart woman, so don't blow it now! Think, for God's sake! Being alone in a hotel room with Zachary is asking—no, begging—for trouble so deep you're sure to drown! He's asking the impossible!* With a lift of her shoulder as she punched the elevator call button, she replied, "Whatever you want." Oh, God, had she really said that?

They stepped into the elevator car and the atmosphere seemed close, making breathing difficult. Zachary placed both hands on the back rail, leaning his hips against the smoothly polished brass, not attempting to close the distance between them.

She shouldn't be thinking about Zach like this. She didn't have time to get involved with a man; she had to remain focused and, until she knew if he was her half-brother, the only sane thing was to stay away from him.

Which seemed impossible.

Well, at least quit thinking of him in any way the least bit sexual, she told herself as the car stopped and the elevator doors parted. *He's the worst candidate for a lover for you. The absolute worst! For God's sake, use your head, Adria!*

Trying to ignore Zach, she stepped into the long hallway. It was deserted and quiet. Almost too quiet. Too empty.

Don't let your imagination run away with you.

She attempted to shake off the feeling that something was out of place, just not quite right, but as Adria reached for the door, she felt more than a second's hesitation. Dread made her hand pause, her key extended. Silly as it was, she had the eerie sensation that someone or something evil had been here recently, and a frisson of fear swept down her spine.

Which was ludicrous. She'd just had a long day and the notes and package she'd received earlier were getting to her— that was all. Still, she hesitated before inserting her key.

"Something wrong?" Zachary asked, so close she could feel his breath against the back of her neck.

Don't be silly.

"No, of course not."

He lifted a dark brow, encouraging her. "You want me to go in first."

That did it. "No, Zach, I think I can manage," she said sarcastically. "Relax with the bodyguard tactics, okay?" Managing a thin smile, she pushed her key into the lock and shouldered open the door.

She took one step inside.

The room was freezing, the air conditioner rumbling.

Adria's gaze fastened on the full-length mirror near the

closet. Her blood turned to ice. "Oh, God," she whispered, biting back a scream.

"What?" Zach demanded, striding past her, only to stop short as he viewed the scene. "Jesus!"

The mirror was cracked and smeared with blood, as if someone had put a fist through the glass. Upon the splintered pieces, a large, mutilated photograph of Adria had been taped. Her head was severed from her body, the bloody crack in the mirror slicing across her neck. Her eyes had been cut out and rimmed in blood, the mirror behind streaked red, so that when she looked at the image she saw the reflection of her eyes cast in blood.

Adria began to shake. "What kind of monster would do this?" she whispered.

"Someone who wants you out of the picture." Zach wrapped an arm around her shoulders. "Don't look at it."

She couldn't drag her gaze away. Fear congealed inside. "This is crazy," she whispered. "Certifiably nuts."

"You got it."

"Someone hates me."

"Very much, and you've got him backed into a corner."

"Oh, God."

"You could just give up, you know," he said, his chin resting on her crown, his arms wrapping around her. "Forget all this London stuff. The family would pay you—"

She pushed away from him. "Is that what *you* want? Are you . . . are you some part of this sickness?" she demanded, her mind racing. Was Zach here at someone's behest, to be her savior, to talk some sense into her, to make sure she was being driven away?

"I want you to be safe."

"And leave."

"Adria—"

"It won't work. I think I told you before, I don't scare easily."

"This isn't a little prank."

"I know. But I'm not backing down." Though she was trembling, she set her jaw. "I can handle this, Zach," she said and wrapped her arms around her middle. "Sick, twisted bastard. He won't get away with it. I won't let him."

Zach eyed her a second, then quickly checked the bathroom and closets. Both seemed okay. They were alone. "Whoever did it is gone, but not by much, the blood isn't completely dried. Maybe he got careless, maybe he left a fingerprint or hair or something."

"Bastard," she muttered, her insides turning to jelly. Despite her brave words to Zach, she wanted to fall into a million pieces, to throw in the towel, accept defeat and leave. Who the hell cared if she was London Danvers? It wasn't worth it. Not when she was dealing with a psycho. And yet she couldn't. Not when she was close enough to have obviously scared the living hell out of the bastard.

"I'm calling the police first and hotel security second." He checked out the room, then strode to the bedside phone.

"Wait a minute." She reached for his arm.

"Like hell! This is serious, Adria. Whoever is doing this to you is sick. First the rat, now this." He picked up the receiver.

"Whoever is doing this is running scared," she pointed out, trying to keep from panicking, which was damned hard to do. She was safe, she reminded herself. She was with Zach.

But isn't he part of the family? Hasn't he encouraged you to back off—even suggested taking a payoff?

The back of her throat turned dry. Could she trust him? And if not Zach, then whom? "I just need a minute to think and . . . and sort this out and—"

"Stop! Don't even go there." He glared at her. "You don't get it, do you? This isn't a kid's prank. Some major pervert is on your case. He's obviously unhinged. No telling what he'll do next."

"I'm . . . I'm not afraid," she lied.

"Like hell. You're afraid and I'm afraid. Don't give me any

of that crap. Look, I didn't fight you when you wanted to go to the press, and I stood by like a friggin' wooden Indian while you gave your interviews. But I'm not gonna have something happen to you just because you're too bullheaded to back off when some major nutcase is threatening you."

"You want me to back off?"

"Hell, yes!"

"That's what *he* wants. What *he* expects."

"Fine. Who cares?"

"I do."

He glared at her. "Then you're not as smart as I give you credit for." He crossed the room and grabbed her shoulders before thrusting his face next to hers. His nostrils were flared and his eyes narrowed. "You're getting out of here tonight."

She decided not to argue. She couldn't stay in this room a second longer than necessary. "I get the message," she said, her nerves beyond frayed. "And you're right, I *am* afraid. What happened here tonight scares the hell out of me."

"It should."

"But," she admitted, "I'm trying to stay as calm as possible—which isn't easy."

"Amen to that."

"So how does he get in here?"

"With a key—someone on the staff," Zach said, thinking aloud as he took another quick look around the room. He squeezed her shoulders gently, then let go. "Either way, it doesn't matter. You're not safe here."

She didn't try to stop him from calling the police. He was right; she knew it. Len Barry wasn't on duty, but another detective, Celia Stinson, arrived and took charge by sealing off the room and calling in a crime-scene team. The hotel security officer wasn't happy, but Stinson didn't seem to care as she gave orders, took notes, and listened to what Adria and Zach had to say. Then, after hearing about the notes, dead rat, and observing firsthand the magnitude of the stalker's depravity, she advised Adria to move. Pronto.

"And I'm not talking about just down the hall," she said, eyeing the cracked mirror, picture, and smeared blood as a photographer took pictures of the scene and another officer was dusting the room for prints. Still another was carefully vacuuming the carpet. "This creep means business. And he's dangerous. Go to another hotel, preferably far away."

Adria provided the detective with a statement and a list of people she thought might be trying to terrorize her. Most of them were members of the Danvers family.

Who would try to terrorize her?

Jason?

Trisha?

Nelson?

Someone she didn't know about? Someone who was afraid that she really was London Danvers.

Adria glanced at Zach and prayed that he wasn't a part of this . . . surely he wasn't. His fear and anger seemed too sincere.

But who? Who was so desperate? So determined? So deadly?

From the corner of her eye, Adria caught her reflection in the cracked, bloodied mirror and her heart nearly stopped. Her hair was disheveled, her face pale, her image distorted.

For the briefest of seconds Adria felt as if she'd been given a glimpse of the future and witnessed her own death.

19

Hell.

That's what the last three days had been: pure hell.

So far the police hadn't located the perpetrator who had terrorized Adria. The crime scene at the Orion Hotel had given up no fingerprints nor any other substantial evidence. Zach had spent most or his time with Adria, either dealing with the media circus that her announcement had created or camped out on her doorstep at the run-down hotel in Estacada, miles away from the city. He'd taken the room next to hers and insisted they keep the connecting door unlocked should she need help. Every night since then he'd spent hours looking at the unlocked door and thinking about her—how warm and innocent she would look with her hair fanned around her face, her dark lashes curled over her rosy cheeks, and her breasts visible over the edge of the sheets. The image had nearly driven him out of his mind.

He'd even given in once, opened the door and looked in, watching as she lay sleeping. Moonlight had spilled through the window and she'd sighed, her lips parting gently as she rolled over. Her eyelids had fluttered for a second and he'd stood still as death, but she hadn't awakened and he'd somehow found the strength to turn away from her. He'd gritted his teeth, slept little, and spent more time taking cold showers than he wanted to admit.

So far, it seemed, no one knew where she was staying. He hadn't told a soul and unless she opened her gorgeous mouth, she should be safe. She had talked about more permanent quarters, but he'd managed to convince her that mobility was important should her personal nutcase find her and force her to leave in a hurry.

Now, as he stared across the table of the little out-of-the-way tavern where he hoped neither of them would be recognized, she was smiling up at him with a wicked little glint in her eye.

"You're paranoid," she accused over clam chowder.

Men in work clothes bellied up to the bar, where peanuts, pretzels, and popcorn were offered for free and the television was tuned in to a basketball game. From the sounds of the crowd, the Portland Trail Blazers were ahead.

"Family trait." He pushed his platter aside. "Guess you can't be part of the Danvers clan if you don't have it."

"Guess not," she said with a teasing smile that caught on the strings of his heart. Hell, but he was becoming a fool over her.

She looked suddenly guilty, as if she'd been keeping something from him. "I got a phone call," she admitted. He waited for the rest of it and guessed that she'd spent hours, maybe days, deliberating on whether or not she should confide in him.

"Who called?" he asked as his patience gave out. He felt the brackets near the corners of his mouth deepening.

"Mario Polidori."

"He knows you're here?" Zach's smile faded and his entire countenance turned to stone.

"Probably a lot of people do," she pointed out as she waved the end of her spoon at him. "Your family's having me followed, I'm sure of it. And they're probably not the only ones. With all the interest in the media . . ."

"Christ!" He rubbed the back of his neck in agitation and his gut wrenched—a sure sign that he expected trouble. He didn't often foresee it and find out that somehow trouble had managed to slip him by. Why hadn't she told him earlier? They could have moved to another spot somewhere farther up in the hills—or toward the beach. Somewhere safe. "Anyone else call?"

She shook her head and her wild hair brushed across her shoulders. "Just Polidori."

"What does he want?"

"To talk to me, obviously." She let her spoon clatter back in her empty bowl. Should she tell Zach about the Polidoris's offer? She considered it, but decided to hold her tongue. What good would it do? Knowing that the Italian family was looking for ways to buy chunks of Danvers International would only serve to make him more angry and suspicious than he already was. And she didn't need to be on the receiving end of his particularly bad temper. Since she, if she did prove to be London, had no intention of selling the hotel or any part of the vast businesses to Polidori or anyone else, it seemed a moot point.

"Stay away from him," Zach advised.

"Why?"

"There's bad blood."

"Oh, don't give me that old feud thing." Someone turned on the jukebox and the notes of a country ballad drifted through a cloud of smoke.

"It exists, Adria. I've got the scars to prove it." Her gaze shifted to the fine line cleaving along the side of his face. It was barely visible, but seemed to serve as a constant reminder to him. No doubt he was still convinced that his attack at the Orion had been orchestrated by the Polidori family.

Near the bar, there was a roar of approval from the patrons watching the basketball game. Hoots and hollers filled the room, obscuring the announcer's voice and drowning out the music. The Blazers must have found the bucket again.

"Why don't you fill me in on the details of the feud," she suggested once the din died down and some drunk offered to buy the house a round. "Then I'll decide if I want to meet Mario."

"The feud," he said, obviously reluctant to talk about it.

"I know some of the story already."

"I'll bet."

"Come on, Zach. Tell me about it."

Gazing at her thoughtfully, he rolled his long-necked bottle of Henry's between his palms. He frowned silently, then shrugged.

"Okay, why not? You probably know most of the gory details anyway. It's always been there—ever since I was a kid—This . . . intense hatred of a family I'd never even met. You've probably read about most of it," he said, and she nodded, deciding it best not to mention talking to Maria Santiago.

The waitress came with a fresh bottle of beer for Zach and after she'd swept away the empty bottle and glasses, cleared the platters and bowls, slapped a bill on the table, and left balancing her precarious load, Zach told the story of the Polidoris and Danverses. His version was about the same as she'd heard before.

Zach scowled. "It's all such a waste." He downed part of his beer, left the rest and paid the bill. They walked outside. The night was cool but clear and a million stars glittered in a soft ebony sky. Fir trees loomed like ancient sentinels around the old tavern and the sounds of a creek splashing over smooth stones cut through the still night.

Her defenses were down as she climbed into the Jeep. It seemed right to be with Zach and she wondered at the fact that she'd met him only a short while ago—or had she? A part of her felt as if she'd known him all her life.

He drove her into the foothills of the mountains on a zigzagging course that followed the Clackamas River. At a wide spot in the road he parked and helped her down a seldom-used trail that led to the water's edge. Even in the darkness, she smelled the clear water mixed with the scents of damp earth and fir trees, and felt the force of the river as it roared and surged through the cliffs.

A cool breeze sped down the canyon as if riding on the back of the river and Adria felt its breath upon her face. She shivered, rubbed her arms, and Zach slipped out of his denim jacket, then tossed it over her shoulders, his fingers never touching her. "I thought you might like to see this," he said, as if he needed a reason to explain himself. "Whenever things are cloudy or unfocused for me, I usually spend some time where the power of nature is the strongest. Sometimes it clears things up. If I'm near the coast, I walk on the beach and stare at the breakers. If I'm on the ranch, I ride into the mountains to the creeks that feed into the Deschutes River, and if I'm in the city, well, I usually drive up here."

"Alone?" she asked and his smile slashed in the night.

"Always."

A night bird cried plaintively and the forest with its ancient trees seemed to close around them, separating the rest of the world from this little stretch of water. "You were telling me about the feud," she prodded and she saw the tension return to his hard features.

"It just goes on and on, doesn't it? Good old Witt—the great man you hope to prove is your father—was as tough and single-minded as his old man. Witt was willing to do whatever he had to in order to preserve the Danvers fortune and name."

"You didn't like him."

"Never," Zach admitted.

"But you respected him?"

"I hated the son of a bitch." Zach stared at the river and in the pale moonlight, Adria could see his features, stark and harsh, set without a trace of remorse.

"What about your mother?"

He snorted, his lips thinning thoughtfully. "Eunice . . . she's something. Complex," he said as if weighing his words. "She says one thing and does another."

Adria had heard the story of Eunice Patricia Prescott Danvers Smythe. As a young woman, Eunice had been the socially correct choice as a bride for Witt Danvers. Only child of rich parents, she had her own money, a quick wit, and regal bearing, though it was reported she had been cursed with a mind of her own. Some people had thought her spoiled and disdainful and a woman scorned. There were sketchy references to other women in Witt's life, especially when he was younger, and Maria, the maid, had admitted that Witt's affairs had been whispered about around town as well as into Eunice's ear. Though she'd borne him two children, a son and a daughter, Witt hadn't been satisfied with his willful wife and had spent many nights out.

Maria had mentioned that she'd overheard an argument in which Eunice had accused Witt of impotence, but it had to have been just the vindictive words of a bitter woman for it hadn't proved true. Eunice had given Witt two more children, Zachary and Nelson.

From the beginning, there had been speculation about Zachary's paternity. Zachary was still staring across the dark, angry river.

"Your mother seems to care about all of you," Adria said tentatively.

"My mother left us."

"Because she had no choice."

His jaw worked. "That's what she claimed." He bent down, gathered up a rock, and hurled it over the river with all the pent-up fury in his muscles.

"You expected her to stay with your father?"

"No," Zach said, his lips compressing in the darkness as he reached for another stone and flung it over the canyon. Then, as if sensing the futility of his actions, he walked to the base of an ancient fir tree and leaned against its rough trunk. "I expected her to take us with her."

"But she couldn't—"

"She wouldn't, you mean. Back then, divorce courts and judges usually favored the mother, even if the father was as powerful a man as Witt Danvers. But Eunice was too scared to go public, too interested in saving face and getting as much money from Witt as her attorney could wangle. She had a lifestyle to maintain. The truth of it is, even when we kids were young, Eunice spent more time at the MAC club working out and socializing than she did with us. And then, once my father decided to divorce her, she didn't want her reputation ruined by the fact that father was a womanizer and she'd had an affair with Polidori—" He cast a hard glance in Adria's direction, assessing her reaction. "You didn't really think I was naive enough not to know what people thought or deaf enough not to have heard the talk." His smile was as cold as the bottom of the river. "For as long as I can remember, I've heard people conjecture that I was Polidori's son. It's just not true."

She moved closer to him and stood beneath the drooping boughs of the massive tree. The smells of damp earth and spring water mingled in the air and carried with them the underlying scent of musk, unadulterated and male. The night was seductive as it folded, like a gentle black cloak, around them. "Even then there were blood tests. You could have proved that you were—"

"Are you kidding? Witt Danvers go to a doctor to prove that he had fathered his own son?" His voice was harsh, barely audible over the rush of water cutting through the trees. "You don't have any idea what kind of man he was. A mean bastard who thought nothing of slapping his wife around, or controlling his kids with a belt, or buying up smaller businesses on the verge of bankruptcy for a song. He clear-cut forests, stripping the land bare, never once thinking about reforestation or erosion or anything but how the chain saw could bring him more money. Without batting an eye, he closed sawmills and logging camps, putting families out of work and never gave a damn, not if the bottom line told him there was a chance to make more money elsewhere. He was unbending and ruthless and proud of his power. He would never, *never* have submitted to paternity tests. You have to understand, Adria, that he didn't care about anyone or anything except himself, the bottom line, his own damned pride, and London—hell, yes, he cared about London." He turned and the moonlight caught in his furious eyes.

"You didn't like her."

"She was just a kid," he said, staring at Adria's face, his eyes moving slightly as if he were trying to find a flaw in her features, looking for certain proof that she couldn't be the little girl he remembered. Adria's heart kicked into double time and she found it suddenly hard to breathe. One of Zach's fingers touched the side of her face, stroking her cheek as he stared at her. "London was precocious, stubborn, and smart as a whip. She had Witt wrapped around her little finger and she knew it. She followed me around like a damned puppy. I didn't need it, but I wouldn't say I didn't like her. In fact I thought it was kind of funny the way the old man made a fool of himself over her." He reached up and captured a strand of Adria's hair. Her throat, suddenly scorched, closed in on itself. "I don't know if you're London," he said slowly, his teeth flashing white in the darkness, "but if you are, it's gonna make things a helluva lot more complicated." He paused for a heartbeat, his eyes locking with hers. She swallowed hard and her pulse pounded in her throat.

In that forever instant she knew he was going to kiss her.

She gave a small sound of protest as he slowly lowered his head, but she didn't stop him. His lips found hers in the darkness. Warm, anxious, burning, they molded over her mouth with a possession that was frightening.

Her heart drummed in her ears as his arms closed around her, dragging her close, forcing her to feel the heat of his blood, the fire in his loins.

Hot and hard, his body pressed hers and his tongue slid between her parted lips.

A pool of desire began to swirl deep within her.

She wound her arms around his neck, feeling the brush of the hair over his collar on the back of her hand, tasting the salt on his skin, smelling his musky scent, feeling the bulge in his jeans where he held himself so intimately against her.

He reached beneath her sweater, touching her abdomen before scaling her ribs with hard, work-roughened fingers.

"God, you feel good," he moaned as he slipped his hand beneath the flimsy lace. She groaned, wanting more, knowing being with him was a mistake.

"Adria," he ground out as the tip of one finger brushed against her taut, waiting nipple. He kissed her again, harder still. He shoved the jacket off her shoulders and pulled her sweater over her head.

Cool air swept up her abdomen. His mouth moved slowly and sensuously along her jaw and her neck, his tongue licking a hot path to the circle of bones at the base of her throat where her pulse hammered impatiently.

Adria sagged against the tree.

When he lifted his head and stared into her eyes, her bones turned to water. "I want you," he whispered, his voice as tortured as the wind racing through the trees.

"I know."

"We can't do this."

"I know."

His hand cupped a breast and she closed her eyes and threw back her head, telling herself that she wouldn't, couldn't make love to him, but as his mouth surrounded her nipple, her will vanished as quickly as if it had been ripped from her by the angry wind before being carried far away. His supple tongue and lips suckled through the wet lace of her bra and her knees gave way. They tumbled to the ground, disturbing the thick carpet of needles beneath the tree. The river rushed at a furious, wintry pace, and Adria cradled his head closer, her fingers twining in the thick strands of his hair.

Dangerous thoughts mingled with reckless abandon. *Why not make love to him? You don't know if he's your brother . . . you don't know if he thinks of you as Kat.*

"Adria, for the love of God," he said hoarsely and buried his face in her abdomen. His breath was a tempting desert wind, trickling past the waistband of her jeans, touching the most feminine part of her. She kissed his crown.

He drew in a long, shaky gulp of air, then rolled away from her.

"Zach—"

"Leave me alone."

"But—"

"For Christ's sake, get dressed," he ordered, not even looking over his shoulder.

"It's all right."

"It's *not* all right. Put your damned clothes on and pretend this didn't happen." He jumped to his feet, kicked the flashlight toward her, and started hiking up the path in the darkness.

Damn the man! He could be so maddening! Scrambling into her clothes, she refused to feel an ounce of remorse. She hadn't tried to seduce him and what had been simmering between them for over a week was just starting to ignite. She knew she had to tread carefully, and that deep down, he was right. She couldn't make love to a man who could be her half-brother, but she'd be condemned to hell before she accepted sole responsibility for the desire that sizzled between them. Grabbing the flashlight, she marched up the path, muttering under her breath as the small beam bobbed ahead of her and the rush of the river faded into the distance.

As she rounded a final bend in the trail, she spied the Jeep, headlights splashing twin beams on the grizzled bark of a huge trunk. Someone had carved initials into the rough bark, surrounding their art with an imperfect heart. How ironic.

As she climbed into the passenger's side of the Cherokee, she shot a furious glare in his direction.

"That was a mistake," he said.

"You'll get no arguments from me."

"Good."

"Just don't act as if I started it."

"It just happened, okay? It won't happen again." But even as the words passed his lips, he knew they were a lie. There was no way in hell he could keep his hands off her.

* * *

Later, Adria saw no reason to tell Zach she was going to meet Mario Polidori. Zach had been furious when she'd mentioned that Mario had called. She decided she'd had enough with his overprotective attitude. Half the time he acted like her older brother, the other half he seemed as if he wanted to be her lover.

Warring emotions battled inside her and she decided she needed to get away from him to clear her head, to set her sights back on the path of her quest. She had to find out if she was London. If she was, she'd fight the entire Danvers clan to gain her birthright; if she wasn't . . . then she'd leave. Or she'd become Zach's lover. Either way, she was risking emotional suicide.

She parked her battered car on the street near the old vegetable market where Stefano Polidori had first made his fortune. Located only four blocks from the Hotel Danvers, the market was now closed, and a new high-rise office building was being considered for the property.

Mario was waiting, leaning against a lamppost near an Irish pub. "I had just about given up on you," he said.

She was uneasy, but managed to hide her case of nerves. "I said I'd be here."

"I know, but I thought your friend might have persuaded you to stand me up." He straightened and offered her an engaging, brilliant smile.

"My friend?"

Mario held the door to the bar open for her. "Zachary Danvers. Your brother."

Adria's stomach plummeted.

"Hasn't he been playing the part of bodyguard?"

"He's not playing anything," Adria said as Mario followed her into the smoky interior. Laughter and loud conversation filtered out from the bar. Glasses clinked and pool balls clicked and darts zipped through the air. A jazz band was playing from a makeshift stage, but most of the music was drowned out by the raucous patrons.

Without asking, Mario ordered two Irish coffees before he got down to business. "My father and I were wondering if you had thought about our proposal."

"A little," she hedged as a slim waitress slid two glass mugs in front of them. "And the truth of the matter is that I can't make any deals with you or your father." With a thin plastic straw she stirred the green drizzle of créme de menthe into the whipped cream floating on her coffee.

"You don't know that."

"What I don't know is who I am. But if I do find out I'm London, then I won't be making any big demands on the company."

His dark brows lifted in surprise. "You would own over half of it."

"I'd still be the outsider."

"But—"

"Where I come from, Mario, you look before you leap and I can tell you this straight out—I don't have plans to sell or change anything at Danvers International. In fact, unless I find glaring incompetence, I probably won't make any big waves."

"That surprises me." He sipped his drink thoughtfully, his dark eyes assessing.

"I believe in the old adage 'if it ain't broke, don't fix it,' " she said, thinking of the long, hot summer days under the blistering Montana sun and how many times her father had said those very words to her. Her father. The man who had raised her, who had often placed a hand on her shoulder in a tender gesture reserved for her. She missed him now and knew that even if Witt Danvers proved to be the man who had sired her, Victor Nash would always be her father.

"Tell me more of yourself," Mario suggested, but Adria only smiled.

"It's boring. Really. I grew up on a Montana farm. Worked all week, went to church on Sundays. End of story."

"I doubt it," he said slyly.

"Why don't you tell me about you and your family—it has to be a lot more interesting than hauling hay and making jam."

"You're playing with me."

"No, I honestly want to know," she said. "Come on. What was it like growing up as Anthony Polidori's son?"

Mario's smile widened and his dark eyes sparkled. "It was hell," he said mockingly. "Servants, chauffeurs, two houses in Portland, a condo in Hawaii, and a villa in Mexico. No child should suffer as I did."

Adria had to laugh.

He told her interesting stories about private Catholic schools and nuns with quick tempers and long rulers that they were ready to rap against the palms and knuckles of those children whose piety wasn't convincing. She heard about his mother's early death, probably from the frustration of dealing with her hardheaded son and husband, and his own run-ins with his father.

"But you seem close now," Adria observed.

"I was younger. Rebellious. Horny." He shrugged. "You must know how that is . . ."

"Do I?"

"Your turn, Adria. Tell me about you."

Staring into his dark eyes, she experienced a sudden rush of insight. No matter how she felt about him, this man would like to seduce her. "Why did you ask me to meet you?"

"There was the business about Danvers International," he said, seeming amused that she would so quickly draw away from him. Obviously he liked a challenge. "But also, I wanted to meet you and get to know you better." He took a swallow of his drink, frowned, and added sugar.

"Okay, but let's get one thing straight," she said. "I'm not a pushover." She didn't trust him but knew he could supply

her with information on the Danvers family that might help
her cause.

"I believe it." He motioned to the waiter and indicated that
he wanted another round. "I think we could learn a lot from
each other." His smile was decidedly wicked.

Trisha watched from the shadows of the alley across the
street. She saw Mario with Adria and jealousy swarmed
through her. Angrily she thought of how much she'd given up
for him, how much she'd loved him, how much they had shared
and suffered together. Obviously, it meant nothing to him.

Tears burned her eyes. She prided herself on her tough exterior, her ability to hide the pain that never seemed to go
away, even with drugs and booze.

With trembling hands she lit a cigarette and drew the smoke
deep into her lungs. She should have ended her affair with
Mario years ago, but she never had been able to completely forget him. Just when she was certain he was out of her system,
that she was over him, he'd call or send a single flower and she
would run into his waiting arms. Even during her brief marriage
she'd carried on with Mario in secret, lying to her husband,
cheating on him, cuckolding him because she couldn't give up
her most deeply imbedded vice: Mario Polidori.

She'd been only a girl when she'd met Mario and it had
been a thrill to see him behind her father's back, behind *his*
father's back. He'd introduced her to wine and marijuana and
in return, she'd given him her virginity in the backseat of his
father's red Cadillac Eldorado. Her interest in art had waned
and she'd skipped lessons just to meet with him at the river,
in a room rented by the hour, in a farmer's field, wherever
they could be wild and free and laugh at their stodgy old fathers and their silly feud.

The lump in her throat turned hard as she stared past the
café curtains of the Irish pub. Mario tossed his head back and
his teeth flashed as he laughed. Trisha's stomach wrenched

and her fingers balled into fists of frustration. She wouldn't stay here and watch him humiliate her with that woman—the phoney claiming to be London.

At the thought of her half-sister, Trisha felt she might be sick. It would be hard losing Mario to someone pretending to be London. London, who had managed to steal all their father's attention. London, born to be a beauty. London, the princess, the treasure of the Danvers family.

Nauseous, Trisha turned away from the damning view and headed back to her car. Tears came unbidden to her eyes and she silently swore that Mario would pay and pay dearly for this slap in the face. Tossing her cigarette into the darkness she ran to her car and tried to erase the image of Mario laughing and joking, sharing a drink and a smile with the imposter.

No doubt he would try to seduce Adria. Mario believed himself to be a great lover and Trisha certainly couldn't argue with his skill in bed. Unfortunately, his appetite was insatiable and he'd never been faithful to her, not even when Trisha had turned up pregnant. She remembered that night with soul-jarring clarity.

She'd finally worked up the nerve to tell him about the baby after they'd made love in the motel near the airport.

His body was still dewy with sweat and she'd stretched out beside him, running her fingers down the sleek muscles of his arms.

"I have a secret," she'd said as he reached for a pack of Winstons.

"Do you?" He struck a match, lit up, and blew smoke from the corner of his mouth. With a smile, he asked, "What is it?"

"Something special."

"Oh, yeah?"

"You're going to be a father."

Silence. Dead silence.

"In September," she'd rushed on as his eyebrows pulled together and smoke drifted from his nostrils. Then he smiled—that winning, cocky grin, and she knew everything would be all right.

"A father. Me? Yeah, right." His words were filled with sarcasm as he laughed. Slapping her on her naked rump, he added, "Good one, Trisha, you nearly had me believing that you were knocked up."

Her back stiffened and she felt the sting of tears behind her eyes. She'd fantasized that he would smile and twirl her off her feet and promise to marry her when she told him of the baby. She'd even been silly enough to believe that their love—and this baby, this precious, precious baby—might put an end to the horrid feud that existed between their families. Love would conquer over hatred.

"You're kiddin', right?" he said when he saw the tears filling the corners of her eyes.

"I'm going to have a baby, Mario," she said angrily as she'd climbed out of bed and threw her sweater over her head. "Your baby."

He stared at her for several long seconds, the cigarette dangling neglected from his lips, the ash growing. "No—"

"It's true! Whether you like it or not, we're going to be parents!"

"Oh, God, Trisha, how could you do this?" he'd whispered, his dark complexion turning pasty white. He rubbed his forehead as if he were trying to erase the entire conversation.

"I didn't do it. *We* did."

"But are you sure?"

"I had a test at the free clinic."

"Fuck." He fell onto the mattress and cradled his head in his hands. "How could this have happened?"

"You know how it happened."

"This couldn't have come at a worse time. My old man's—"

"For crying out loud, Mario. I didn't plan it. Sorry if it's inconvenient for you," she snarled, hurting inside. The room shook as a great jet roared through the sky and Trisha felt like dying inside.

Jabbing out his cigarette in a tray, he looked up at her. As if finally realizing how distressed she was, he opened his arms and motioned for her to join him on the bed. "Come on, Trisha. It's not the end of the world."

"It's a miracle," she said, defensive of her unborn child. "A miracle."

" 'Course it is."

She didn't trust him and tears threatened to overtake her again. "You aren't happy."

"Sure I am" he said, though his voice sounded glum. "I . . . I was just shocked, that's all. Hell, it's not every day you get news like this." He patted the bed beside him and she sat on the edge of the stained mattress. His strong arms surrounded her and she wanted to trust him again—to believe in their love. His breath, smoky and warm, teased her ear. "You want this—this baby?"

"Don't you?"

"Oh, sure. Sure."

She relaxed a little, though she wished she'd heard more conviction in his voice.

"I guess this is the part where I should ask you to marry me, huh?"

Sniffing back her tears, she nodded. "I think that's the proper thing to do."

"Hey, well, proper. That's me. Okay, then I'm askin'. Trisha, will you marry me?"

"Of course I will," she'd vowed, throwing her arms around his neck and tumbling into the bed with him. "I love you, Mario. I've always loved you and I will love you until the day I die."

"That's my girl," he'd said, kissing her and patting the top of her head as if she were a child.

Two weeks later they'd broken the news to their parents and both Witt and Anthony had hit the roof.

According to Mario, Anthony had called his son a dumb fuck and forbade him from ever seeing Trisha again. If Mario wanted to fall in love and get married, there was always that nice Lanza girl who lived in the neighborhood; and if he wanted to be so stupid as to knock someone up, Mario should have his head examined. He'd been told to quit thinking with his cock and start listening to reason. Anthony had warned his son never to see Trisha again, and Mario agreed.

But Mario had broken that promise. The next week Mario told Trisha about the scene with his father. To Trisha, Mario had seemed spinelessly relieved.

Witt had been working in his den and had been even more furious than Mario's father. When Trisha broke the news to her father, Witt had turned crimson and been consumed by a rage so deep, Trisha feared for her life.

"You'll never marry Polidori," Witt had vowed, rounding the desk and kicking an antique vase that had shattered into a million pieces.

"You can't stop me!" Trisha could be just as bullheaded as her father.

"You're underage, Trisha. Sixteen, for crying out loud! We could have that bastard up on statutory rape."

"He loves me, Dad. He wants to marry me."

"Over my dead body," Witt insisted. "This is one helluva blow, but we can still take care of things. There's still time."

"What do you mean?" she had asked, refusing to understand. But her stomach had begun to flutter in anxiety.

"I know a doctor who'll—"

"No!" she'd screamed. "I'll never have an abortion! Oh, God, Dad, you can't be serious!" Panic screamed through her blood. Lose the baby? No! She'd run away before she'd let her father snuff out the life of her unborn child. Protectively she held her middle.

"Either you take care of this my way or the boy gets arrested," Witt insisted, his face twisted in hatred. "And don't mess with me, Trisha, 'cause there's nothing I'd like better than to see Polidori's only son in jail."

"You wouldn't—"

Witt's lip had curled and his blue eyes had gleamed with pure malice. "He defiled you, Trisha. Raped you and got you pregnant. He used you—like some common slut. And if you think I'll allow you to have Polidori's child, you can think again."

"I won't—"

Witt had raised his hand, intending to strike her, and Trisha let out a bloodcurdling wail.

"I'll handle this." Kat had hurried into the room, as if she'd been hovering in the hall, waiting for the right moment to appear. She'd stared at Trisha with chilling calm. For the first time Trisha felt fear.

"She's my daughter," Witt protested.

"And you're out of control." Kat's lips had compressed. "I said, I'll handle this, Witt. It's women's business."

"I'm not backing down," he'd growled and stalked out of the den, kicking the door on his way out.

Quietly, Kat had shut the door and the lock clicking into place was like the knell of doom. Trisha's eyes filled with tears because she knew she'd already lost. God, she'd hated her stepmother.

"Come on, Trisha, let's talk sensibly about what's going on here," Kat said. "I know you're upset and your father, well, he is, too. It's just because he loves you so much."

"Bullshit!" Sniffling, Trisha had backed up, her shoes crunching on the broken shards of glass.

"He does. In his own way. But he hates the Polidoris as much as he loves you and he's serious when he says he'll press charges. Mario will probably spend time in jail and how good would that be for you and your baby?" Kat's smile was patronizing and cold as death.

Trisha had begun to sob brokenly, already giving in to the

steady, unrelenting pressure her family was sure to put on her.

In the end, Kat had convinced her that the only reasonable thing to do, the best thing for all concerned, was to abort the baby, and the next day, before Trisha could change her mind, Kat had shuttled her off to a private clinic where she'd given up the only person—the only thing—that had meant anything to her.

She'd never gotten pregnant again. She'd lost the baby and Mario's love. Though he claimed to still care for her, their relationship had never been the same. They had lost what little innocence they'd once shared. Because of Witt. Because of Kat. God, she'd hated them both.

Now, so many hateful years later, she rested her head on the steering wheel of her sports car. At least her father and Kat were dead. They deserved their ends. But, Trisha and Mario were still illicit lovers, running through the shadows to private rendezvous of hot sex with no strings attached. Trisha tried to hide the fact that she still loved him, even from herself, but then something always happened to awaken all her old, long-buried emotions, as if that little bit of life that had been so frail, existed for so little time, had linked Trisha to Mario forever.

Love, coupled with the possession and jealousy that came with it, always resurfaced. She would love Mario Polidori until the day she gave up her last breath. Tonight, watching Mario with Adria, Trisha had felt the old pangs of pain and loss, love and jealousy. She sniffed loudly and her hatred grew white-hot, settling in the pit of her stomach and burning.

Mario had been with Adria.

Beautiful Adria.

So much like Kat.

Too much like London.

20

"I'm going out," Jason said as he paused at the door to his wife's bedroom.

"Now?" Sitting in her robe, brushing her hair, Nicole caught Jason's reflection in the mirror and she wondered why she'd ever been foolish enough to think that he loved her. She glanced at her watch. "Why?"

"Late meeting."

"It's nearly midnight," she said, hating the wheedling sound of protest in her voice.

"I know."

Closing her eyes, she tried to pull together whatever it was that kept her going. She set her brush down and said calmly, "You know, Jason, I should just divorce you and get it over with. Then you wouldn't have to lie anymore."

"I'm not—"

She held up a hand before opening her eyes. "Please. Give me some credit, will you?"

When she looked up, Jason was smiling that waxen, tight little grin that she'd grown to hate over the years—the smile he seemed to reserve just for her. "The skillet suddenly too hot for you, darling?" he said, and her insides revolted at the endearment.

How far they'd drifted apart over the years. Too far to ever find each other again. "What's too hot isn't the skillet, or the fire, it's that damned little mistress of yours," she said evenly though her insides churned. She'd thought she'd quit loving him years ago, but still the lies hurt.

At least he had the decency to blanch.

"She called here. Kim, isn't it? The little blonde with legs that won't quit and no breasts?" Nicole applied a little night cream to moisturize her face and hopefully forestall a few of the determined little lines that remained on her skin as the years crept by. "You really didn't believe I didn't know, did you?"

He seemed to puff up a bit—like he used to do when he practiced law and stood in front of a particularly recalcitrant witness on the stand. "I don't know what you're talking about."

"Come off it, Jason." She wiped off the excess cream. "Contrary to what you would like to think, I'm not stupid. And I know what's going on with this London thing. You're running scared, aren't you?" She tossed her pale hair over her shoulders and removed her earrings, diamonds that sparkled in the soft lights arranged over her vanity. She'd picked out the earrings herself, though Jason had bought them for their fifth . . . or was it their sixth? . . . anniversary. "This new little London, she just could be your sister."

"I don't think so."

Sometimes, when the pain wasn't too great, when she could distance herself from him, it amused her to watch him lie. He did it so well, with such grace and such . . . conviction, as if he really believed himself.

"Zachary wouldn't be hanging around if it weren't serious," she said. "Nelson looks like he's hiding something, Trisha's worse than ever—I shudder to think what she's on these days—and your mother, usually so remote, she seems to have taken a sudden interest in the family. Oh, you're worried," she said, dropping her earrings into a velvet case and snapping it shut. "All very worried."

"And you're not?" He walked up behind her and placed his hands lightly around her throat. Their gazes locked in the mirror and she tilted her chin up a fraction as she felt him squeeze, ever so slightly. It would be so easy for him to cut off her wind and strangle her, but Nicole wasn't afraid. She slid a meaningful glance to the framed eight-by-ten picture poised on the corner of the vanity.

Their daughter, Shelly, laughing, her hair windswept in the breeze rising off the ocean that day, gazed back at her. Shelly was the one thing that both she and Jason cared about. The only thing.

Jason's gaze dropped to the picture and his fingers relaxed.

He would never do anything that might cause him to lose his daughter, for, as overly doting as Witt had been with London, so was Jason with Shelly. In his eyes, his daughter could do no wrong. The little imp had him wrapped around her slim little finger.

"You know, I'd hate to see anything happen to us," Nicole said softly, though there was a steel thread running through the words. "It would be devastating to Shelly."

Jason's smug smile faltered. "Kids are survivors."

"Are they?" she asked pointedly. "What about you?"

"I'm doing okay."

"Are you? I'm not so sure. Then there are your brothers and sister . . ."

His gaze met hers again in the mirror. "Zach always seems to land on his feet. The others . . . who can say?" He turned away from her and started for the door.

"I won't be publicly humiliated, Jason. If your little girl-friend wants to get down and dirty, I won't be a part of it and neither will Shelly. Either stop seeing that little bitch or control her—I don't really care which." That was bending the truth a little; she did care—it bothered her to think that another woman, a younger woman, could turn his head, but she was shrewd enough to understand that Jason needed more than just a wife. He needed to be adored and fawned upon and he always needed a hot little number warming his bed and stroking his male ego.

The thought made her sick, but she'd live with it. For Shelly.

As long as one of his slutty little mistresses didn't go public. Nicole had never before been concerned, not really, but she was worried about this Kim. It took nerve—hell, it took brass balls—to call up Jason Danvers's wife and start issuing orders.

Things had changed since Adria Nash had waltzed into town. And not for the better.

She heard a pounding on the front door and her heart leaped to her throat. Now what? For a foolish split second her fears took hold and she thought Kim had become desperate enough to show up here. Jason probably had given her the code to the gate and the little slut had just enough nerve to confront her lover and his wife.

Shelly! Her thoughts flew to her daughter. She couldn't let Shelly meet the woman! Grabbing the satin robe left at the foot of her bed, she slid her arms through the sleeves and hurried down the hall, looping the belt; damned if that little tramp would meet her daughter. Jason was two steps in front of her and he opened the door, letting in the slice of wintry cold wind that preceded his brother.

Zachary, in jeans and a denim jacket, looked out of place in the house where he'd grown up. He was tense and the restless energy that Nicole had come to associate with him was evident in the way he paced the room, the manner in which his eyes took in everything at once, the feel of electricity that he generated. His hair was a little too long, uncombed, and he looked as if he could use a shave—like he'd just come in off the range. He was so innately sexy that Nicole tried to avoid looking in his eyes for fear she would see the promise of sweet seduction lingering in those hot gray orbs.

She offered him a chair, but he shook his head and stared at his brother. "I want Sweeny's number."

"I was just on my way out—" Jason said.

"Now?"

"Late meeting."

Zach didn't press it, as if what Jason did with his own time was his business. "Fine. Go out Just give me the number."

"Sweeny's out of town." Now it was Jason's turn to be nervous.

"Then tell me where he can be reached." There was a desperate edge to Zach's voice, one that dared to be defied.

"He's in and out—you'll never catch up with him," Jason said, and his voice sounded strangled. Out of control. All that practiced courtroom poker face shot to hell. He was lying again, Nicole surmised. And the untruths seemed to come harder when they were told to his steel-jawed brother. Would this chain of deception never end?

Zach's eyes grew dark. "Give me the number, Jason, or place the damned call. I want to talk to him."

Jason backed off. "You look like you could use a drink. I've got a bottle of—"

"I don't need a drink," Zach snapped. "Just give me the number."

Jason eyed his brother and finally relented. "All right. Come on. In the den." He checked his watch. "You know it's nearly two o'clock in Memphis."

"Good. He should be in."

"Sweeny could be asleep."

"Then it's time to wake up," Zach said, unable to tamp down the raw, naked tautness that had been with him ever since he'd kissed Adria and held her in his arms. He was frightened for her. Afraid that whoever was stalking her would up the ante. But he couldn't confide in his family. Not when one of them could be the sicko. And there was the other problem of his feelings for Adria. Her lips had offered such sweet promise, her head thrown back in absolute abandon, her breasts straining against that little scrap of a bra. He'd come close to making love to her, so damned close, and it had been all he could do to break it off. She'd been willing and soft, her body yielding to his. He'd argued with himself as he'd kissed her, sworn at himself when he touched her breasts, and nearly lost all reason as she'd cradled his head to her nipple. He'd never been so hard in his life. Never wanted anything more. Never been so repulsed by his own desires.

Just thinking of it now caused the beginning of an erection to swell in his jeans. He stuffed one hand into a front pocket as Jason showed him the numbers scratched on a pad across the desk. Cradling the receiver with his shoulder, Zach punched out the numbers and waited impatiently, tapping the fingers of his free hand on the corner of the desk. "Come on, come on," he muttered as Jason closed the door to the den.

Sweeny's groggy voice answered on the seventh ring. "Yeah."

"This is Zachary Danvers."

"Jesus, do you know what time it is?"

"What've you found out?"

"I was gonna call Jason in the morning."

Zach glanced at the clock. "You're in luck. It is morning and Jason's right here."

"You're a fucking prick, Danvers." The voice cleared and he heard the sound of a lighter clicking. "Okay, it's not much, but a start." Zach's stomach twisted. If Sweeny confirmed the fact that Adria was a fraud, then she was little more than a cheap hustler—a gold digger. But if he'd discovered she was London . . . hell, that would be worse because he'd be related to her. His heart drummed frantically in his chest. Either way, he was bound to lose. "It's kind of been like lookin' for a needle in a haystack," Sweeny was saying, "or trying to find that damned guy in the puzzle, you know what I'm talking about? The guy in the red stripes? Where's Whosit?"

"Waldo," Zach said tersely.

"Right. That's it. Anyway, I narrowed it down and it looks like the guy who was married to Ginny Watson moved to Kentucky a while back. Lexington, in the seventies sometime, near as I can tell. I'm gonna visit him tomorrow."

"You got his phone number?"

Zach heard nothing but silence for a few seconds.

"Well, do you?"

"Sure, I got it, but I figured a visit in person would be better. Seeing people face-to-face makes it impossible to hang up."

"I want to speak to him."

"Easy, boy. You'll get your chance," Oswald said smoothly. "Just let me break the ice. I'll call you as soon as I have more news. I'll leave the message with Jason."

"Where will you be staying?" Zach demanded.

"Where will I be staying? That's a good one. Maybe at the Ritz? Or how about the Hotel Danvers? You got one over in Kentucky? Shit, how'm I s'posed to know?" He hung up and the phone clicked loudly in Zach's ear.

"What was that all about?" Jason asked, pouring two glasses from a bottle of Scotch he kept in the bar. His eyes were trained suspiciously on his brother.

"I'm just tired of waiting around and I don't trust Sweeny."

"Neither do I, but he keeps his mouth shut and if he finds out something, he'll let us know, but it'll cost. Now, where's Adria? Are you hiding her somewhere?"

Zach didn't answer and his older brother's lips curved into a hard little smile. "Keeping her all to yourself?"

"I thought you wanted her low-profile."

"She's already been on the news and in the papers. Hardly low-profile." Jason walked to the desk, opened the drawer, and flipped out clippings and copies and faxes. "She's made the national news, you know . . . and I mean more than just the little blurb that was reported through the AP. The networks are beginning to call and even a few papers back East are showing a little interest. Every time I turn on the television, someone seems to be talking about her and during the day, at the company, there's a fucking siege in the lobby."

"Free publicity," Zach said sarcastically.

"Go to hell, Zach." Jason tossed back his drink. "It's started here, too, at the house. It upsets Nicole and Shelly and . . . I feel like I did when London was kidnapped—all the reporters camped out at the gate."

Zach remembered the throng of newspeople that had pummeled the family with questions, called at all hours, crowded around the gates to the house; he'd heard from his crew still cleaning up at the hotel, that the press had been ever-present in the lobby. Even his office in Bend wasn't immune; Terry had phoned and told him that a few reporters had shown up looking for him ever since Adria's meeting with the press.

"It's worse than I'd imagined," Jason was saying as he reached for the bottle again. "Even the lawyers are beginning to worry. They want to talk to Ms. Nash, but I advised them to wait a while."

"Just let me handle her." He didn't want her hustled away by a herd of bloodsuckers like the attorneys for the Danvers family. Impatiently, he jammed one hand through his hair.

"Has she hired an attorney yet?"

Zach lifted a shoulder. "I don't think so. But she's with Mario Polidori tonight."

"Polidori?" Jason's face muscles flexed in disbelief and his nostrils flared in disgust. "Why?"

"Don't know. She didn't say."

"So, the vultures are already circling. Great, Zach, that's just great," he said sarcastically, then pointed a finger at his younger brother. "You can't let him get to her."

"It's none of my business."

"Like hell! Polidori, through a smoke screen of lawyers and holding companies and silent partners, has been trying to buy off chunks of Danvers International for years—waterfront property and the old hotel, downtown real estate, even a couple of sawmills. You name it, he wants it as long as it's got the Danvers logo attached. He has this thing about acquiring our castoffs—so far we've held him off."

"His money no good?"

"It's not the money, it's the idea that he wants it all," Jason said and Zach smiled at the irony of it all.

"Aren't you the guy who said 'it's always money'?"

"Not with the Polidoris. With them it's revenge," Jason said, staring morosely into his glass. Zach didn't argue; he'd grown up being told that the Polidoris were no-goods, out for blood, the worst of the worst. Zach had changed his mind over the course of the years, but he still didn't trust them, especially with Adria.

Before Jason could ask a lot of questions Zach didn't want to answer, he pushed himself away from the desk and left. Jason's case of nerves was getting to him.

He drove downtown and stopped at the Hotel Danvers, picked up some blueprints that had been left there for him, and grabbed a stack of messages, which he gave a quick once-over, then tossed into the trash. Reporters and more reporters. Jason was right on that score. Once they smelled the blood of scandal, the vultures kept circling until they finally swept in to pick the carcass.

He climbed into his Jeep and headed out of the city. Back to Adria. His foot pressed harder on the accelerator. The truth of the matter was that he was bothered that Adria was with Polidori and it had nothing to do with the feud or the family fortune. It didn't even have anything to do with London Danvers. The problem was more basic than that. It hit him at a gut level. Like it or not, Zach was jealous. He denied it to himself as he drove hell-bent-for-leather on the winding road to Estacada but when push came to shove and he was honest with himself, the truth of the matter was that he didn't like the thought of her with any other man.

"Idiot," he told himself and snapped on the radio. Squinting against oncoming headlights, he listened to a half-hour dedicated to Bruce Springsteen songs, but his mind drifted from the lyrics to Adria. Christ, what was he going to do with her? He knew what he wanted and it was either obscene or just plain stupid, or maybe a little bit of both, depending upon whom she turned out to be.

Adria glanced in her rearview mirror as she drove along the forested road to Estacada. Headlights bore down on her and she couldn't shake the feeling that she was being followed. During her dinner with Mario Polidori she'd been tense. Uneasy. Jumping at shadows, and when she'd left Portland, she'd felt hidden eyes upon her, watching her every move.

"You're as bad as the Danvers family," she muttered as the vehicle behind her, a huge pickup raised high off the ground, tore around her, spraying mist and dirt from the road onto her windshield. She flipped on the wipers and attempted to ignore the paranoia that threatened.

The truck, going over seventy on this winding road, disappeared around a corner and the beams of her own headlights splashed against the puddles, wet pavement, and mossy bark of the giant fir trees lining the country road.

She was exhausted, her mind running in crazy circles filled with images of Zachary and bloodied hotel rooms. She'd finally heard from Detective Stinson; the blood smeared on the broken mirror hadn't been human at all, but rat blood, probably drained from the rodent that had been left for her to find.

Her stomach curdled at the thought. Though she'd grown up on a farm and had dealt with the slaughter of animals each year or had helped butcher deer her father had killed on a hunting trip, or found the corpses of rats and birds caught by the barn cats, this was different. An animal killed, then drained of its blood to be used for the next act of terror.

She shivered and told herself to get over it. She'd known from the get-go that claiming to be London Danvers was sure to meet resistance; she just hadn't had any idea how much or how macabre.

A headache throbbed behind her eyes. Her meeting with Mario Polidori had turned out badly. His interest in her had changed from curiosity and mild interest to something deeper, something she didn't want to contemplate. She'd recognized a spark of challenge in his gaze as he'd stared at her, and she'd had the unlikely but unsettling insight that he'd wanted to sleep with her. At first she'd told herself she was imagining things, but as the evening had worn on and he had become bolder, his eyes darker, his smile just a little more wicked, she'd become certain that he wanted to seduce her. Not because he found her infinitely fascinating, but because she was associated with the Danvers family and because she was a challenge.

"Just try it," she muttered, turning on the wipers as the mist thickened.

What she didn't need was a man—any man—complicating things. Her emotions were twisted enough as it was with her attraction to Zachary. She cringed when she thought how close she'd come to making love to him. How much she'd wanted him.

She'd even told herself that she'd just been overreacting because of the stalker, but it was more than that. Much more, and dangerously unthinkable.

Her headache throbbed when she considered what might have happened, *would* have happened, if he hadn't come to his senses and broken off the embrace.

"Idiot," she muttered, and she didn't know if she was talking about him or herself. "Pull yourself together."

As she rounded a final corner just outside of the Estacada city limits, she saw the sign for the Fir Glen Motel flickering in green neon. Pink letters announced that there was a vacancy at the little motel.

Zach's Jeep wasn't parked in its usual spot and her heart dropped. Which was just plain stupid. Yes, it was reassuring that he was just next door, but more than that, she was starting to rely on him, to care about him, to think of him in terms that crossed all sorts of barriers. Sometimes she wished she wasn't London. That would solve some problems.

But it still wouldn't resolve whatever feelings he still harbored for Kat. Once in a while Adria would catch him staring at her and she was certain he didn't see her at all, but was caught up in memories of another woman, the woman she thought was her mother.

What a mess! She pulled into the bumpy lot and settled for

a parking spot not far from the front door of her sorry little unit. The drab motel was L-shaped, a single door and window for each unit facing the parking lot. Most of the windows were dark, only a few boasting slivers of light visible through the drawn shades.

She cut the engine and stepped outside, where the mountain air was damp and heavy against her skin as she locked her car and headed toward her motel room.

Home sweet home, she thought as the wind caught in her hair and a rattling truck rumbled past. Again she felt as if she were being observed, that someone was lurking in the shadows, unseen eyes ever vigilant. Her skin crawled and she turned quickly, half expecting someone to jump out of the darkness.

But no one appeared.

And aside from the occasional car on the road, the night was still, the mist thick.

"Get a grip," she muttered, but before she walked into her unit, she swept her gaze over the parking lot. Nothing was amiss. She recognized the owner's battered Chevy Suburban and saw the bluish glow of a television in the window of the office. The few other vehicles looked deserted for the night.

She took a step toward her door and heard no heavy breathing or footsteps scraping behind her. She was alone. Unnerved, but alone.

She thought about the package she'd received. The dead rat with her own locket wrapped around its throat.

She thought about the hotel room at the Orion with its mutilated picture of her and smeared blood.

She thought about the fact that the Polidoris, Zach, and the police knew where she was staying.

Slowly, her nerves tight as piano wires, she pushed her key into its lock and swung the door open. It creaked and banged against the far wall.

She stepped inside and reached for the light switch.
Click.

Nothing happened.

The room was still dark as night.

Every hair on her arms stood straight on end. "What the—?"

She heard it then, the sound of heavy breathing, laborious breathing. She turned, but it was too late. She saw a shadow, a dark figure raise its hand. She feinted right and something hard slammed down on her head.

Crack!

For a second the world went black. Pain blasted through her skull. Her knees wobbled and she fell against the door frame. She tried to scream but a hand was on her throat, cutting off her air, forcing her downward to slither down the wall. She kicked and clawed, gasping, trying to scream, attempting to fight.

"You never learn, do you, bitch?" her attacker growled as Adria swung hard with her fist, flailing in the direction of the sound, all the while trying to drag in air, her lungs on fire. She saw only a glimpse of a face, hidden by a mask, as her attacker struck again, pounding the side of her head. "Leave before it's too late," the voice—a voice she'd heard before, she thought weakly—warned before raising the heavy object again.

Adria saw the blow coming, lifted an arm, and as the attacker swung, the hand on her throat loosened. Adria screamed and rolled. The object slammed into the wall, crashing through the plaster, then glanced against the side of her head. The room spun and she nearly lost consciousness, but not before she let out another hoarse, painful scream. A gloved hand covered her mouth and a cloyingly sweet smell assailed her nostrils. Adria clamped down hard with her teeth.

Her assailant let out a hiss of pain and let go. Adria was ready. She moved quickly and screamed again for help. She was almost free! Kicking madly, inching toward the door, she yelled just as, from the corner of her eye, she saw it coming.

The same dark object aimed at her face. She recoiled, holding her arm over her head.

Smack!

Pain exploded through her skull and she thought she might pass out completely just as she heard the faint, faraway sound of a siren splitting the night.

Faintly, she heard a door open and a man's' voice yell, "Hey, what's going on?"

Her attacker froze. Adria clawed her way to a sitting position. "Help me!"

A kick landed in her chest. Painful and crushing, the blow made her wretch and curl into a protective ball.

"You goddamned bitch!" Breathing hard and limping, the intruder climbed off her and scrambled with an uneven gait through the door. Gasping, the metallic taste of blood in her throat, Adria struggled upright and crawled to the threshold. Just one look, that's all she needed, and she was sure she could identify the intruder. It was someone she'd met, she was certain of it, but the ache in her gut prevented her from thinking clearly and the edges of her vision blurred as if she might black out. She tried to concentrate, to hold on to consciousness as the attacker fled through the shadows of the huge trees surrounding the motel.

She took in deep breaths and held on to the door casing in a death grip as she squinted into the night. She saw the stars, and lights switching on in nearby units, but her attacker had disappeared. Damn it all, she thought as she spit blood onto the porch. She tried to yell again, but could make no sound.

A second door opened, just two doors down. Light spilled onto the small porch.

"Hey, you! Hey, are you all right?" A male voice. Unfamiliar. She drew in a long, painful breath.

Footsteps. Crunching on gravel. Running in her direction. Ready to kick her again. She cringed. A man loomed over her as the lights in the unit blazed on. Her stomach heaved suddenly and she retched.

"Oh, shit," he said, looking around the small room before bending on one knee. "Now, don't move, miss, you're hurt!" She squinted up at him, but couldn't make out his features as he turned toward the open door. "Marge!" he bellowed in a voice that pounded through her brain. "Marge, wake up the manager and call 911!"

"What?" a woman's voice screamed back as doors creaked open and banged closed, rattling the loose windows in their panes. The man knelt beside her again. "Now you just lay still, help's on its way."

Voices filtered in through the open door and pierced Adria's pain-racked brain.

"What the hell's going on?" a woman asked.

"Hey, shut up! People are trying to sleep over here!" A man this time.

"Holy shit, what's going on in unit thirteen?" A younger man. "Mary, come look at this, will ya?"

"Don't get involved." Mary wasn't too willing to help out.

Adria blinked and tried to stay conscious. There was something familiar about the attacker, familiar and horrible and . . . it teased the edge of her consciousness. What was it? Who was he?

"Hey, lady, I don't know what happened here, but it looks bad," the man who was tending to her said.

She lifted her hand to the back of her head and felt sticky blood matting her hair. Groaning, she pulled herself upright, her eyes squinting, trying to get used to the bright lights. As she did, her heart squeezed in fear. The room had been destroyed. Chairs turned over, the television set smashed, sheets torn and ripped from the bed, as if someone had been in a fury so wild—so blind, he'd needed to lash out at something, anything, to vent his rage. On the mirror over the bureau, scribbled in a grease pen's bold black letters, was a simple and horrifying message: DEATH TO THE BITCH.

Worse yet, tossed onto the bare mattress was a pair of black panties, the pair she'd had stolen; it was shredded, as if sliced over and over again by a razor.

"Oh, God." She felt suddenly sick again and the room seemed to spin around her. Her nose and mouth tasted foul, and she had to fight against the overwhelming sensation that evil still lurked beneath the bed or behind the curtains.

"What's going on here?" the man asked. "No—wait. You just lie still. Don't talk. Save it for the police."

Footsteps. Shouts. People closing in, some curious, some concerned. She hurt so badly she didn't care.

"Sumbitch, would you look at that!"

"Did someone call the frickin' ambulance?"

"Hell, yes, but Jesus H. Christ, it looks like a bear came in here and went on a rampage."

"Yeah, sure, and now bears cut up underpants."

"Hang on, miss. Marge—the manager—?"

Headlights flashed against the window and tires crushed the gravel in the lot.

"Adria!" She heard his voice, roaring through the crowd, a lifeline to reach out and cling to.

Zachary! Tears filled her eyes as she tried to scramble to her feet.

"You lie still!" she was ordered.

Zachary broke through the crowd beginning to collect at the door and gathered her into his arms.

"Adria, oh, God, Adria," he said, holding her as if he could protect her, as if the strength of his body could stave off the pain, the fear. Clinging to him, she fought the horrid sobs that suddenly clogged her throat as relief flooded through her. She was with Zachary and safe. So safe.

"Hey, you, I wouldn't touch her!" a man advised. "Leave her for the paramedics, they're on their way. She's bleedin', man, no tellin'—hey, are you her old man?"

"What the fuck happened here?" the manager yelled, only casting Adria a cursory glance. "Who did this? Holy Saint Peter, what a mess!"

"Did anyone call the police?" Zach demanded.

"Called 911, you get it all," the manager said. A short, balding man in boxer shorts and a nightshirt, he swore at the mess. "The insurance company will shit over this one."

"Don't worry about it." Zach kissed her forehead and wrapped her in his strong arms. "You'll be okay," he said, as if to convince himself. She shuddered and he pulled her tight against his chest. "You'll be okay."

She didn't believe it for a second.

She doubted he did, either.

Failed.

You failed!

You should have killed the bitch while you had the chance. Now she's alive, pretending to be London, bringing it all up again!

Adria's attacker eyed the haggard reflection staring back in the mirror mounted over the hotel sink. The plan had backfired. Because Adria Nash was stronger than expected. She didn't scare easily and now, it seemed, she wouldn't die easily, either!

Maybe she is London.

She'll prove it and the story will surface.

Now that she's been attacked, the police might be suspicious about Kat's death, the ruling of suicide reexamined.

Blood could be washed away but memories couldn't, and the memory of London Danvers just wouldn't die. It's as if over the years both she and her damned mother had been elevated to some kind of sainthood. At that thought, agony ripped through the brain of Katherine's killer, a pain so severe it cut more deeply than the physical wounds Adria Nash had inflicted.

Saints are usually canonized after they've died.

So see to it! Take care of Adria Nash.

Don't let her slip away again!

* * *

Every muscle in her body screamed and her head pounded despite the painkillers the doctor had prescribed. Adria stared out the passenger window of Zach's Jeep and tried to forget the last few hours. But scenes from the Emergency Room kept recurring while a litany of questions she'd been asked— first from the EMTs, then the nurses and finally the police—played through her mind. She was dead-tired, but figured she'd never fall asleep.

"Do you have any idea who would do this to you?"

"You're the woman claiming to be London Danvers, aren't you?"

"Are you allergic to any medications?"

"Did you get a look at the guy's face or see any identifying marks?"

"Do you have an insurance card?"

"You've got a report in with the Portland Police Department about a previous attack? What was the name of the detective involved?"

"Does this hurt?"

"Can you give me a time line? About what time did you leave the restaurant and when did you get back to the motel?"

"Is this your husband?"

Adria squeezed her eyes shut. The night had fled by in a whirl, and it seemed that the police agreed with her that someone from the Danvers family could be involved, although there had also been speculation that she'd collected her own special nutcase, someone who had been following the London Danvers story for years.

Adria had tried to answer all the questions that had been hurled at her. She'd even managed a weak smile at the detectives' jokes, but by the time the ER doctor had released her and Zach had tucked a blanket around her in the Jeep, she'd felt drained. Weary. And though no bones had been broken and she'd even managed to avoid a concussion, she was sore all over.

They'd spent most of the drive back to the motel in silence, both wrapped in their private thoughts, until Zach turned the final corner to the Fir Glen Motel and spied the media circus.

"Great," he muttered between clenched teeth.

"Guess I'm suddenly popular."

"Too popular."

Rather than stop and deal with the press, he cranked on the wheel and turned the Jeep around to head directly east. The road was steep, winding through the snow-dusted mountains that were already gilded with the first rays of the morning sun.

"Where are we going?" she asked, though she really didn't care as she pulled the blanket higher under her chin and tried to get comfortable. She wanted to stop running, to end this quest, to quiet the questions that raged through her mind.

"My place."

"Your place?" she repeated as she stared through the windshield. The Jeep was climbing steadily. Snowcapped peaks of the rugged Cascade Mountains loomed ahead. "I didn't know you had one."

He slid her a glance—hard and stubborn, yet laced with worry. "We're going to the ranch."

"In Bend?" she said, shaking her head before she sucked in her breath through her teeth and winced in pain from the movement. "I can't go there."

"Why not?"

"It's too far away. I've got people to see. Meetings in Portland. Interviews and appointments with attorneys and reporters."

"They'll wait," he predicted, his voice stern. He'd been silent through most of the interviews but as she'd explained what had happened, how she'd been with Polidori and come home to be attacked, he'd grown increasingly grim.

"No, Zach, really, I can't—"

"You were almost killed tonight," he shouted, clamping her

wrist with one strong hand. Steering with the other, he kept an eye on the road as it wound snakelike through the foothills. "Maybe you don't take that seriously, but I do. Whoever sent you those warnings has just gotten a little bolder and if he would have hit you a little harder, or in a little different place, we might not even be having this conversation right now."

Suddenly chilled, she tried to rub her arms, but his hand was digging into her muscles. "But I can't—"

"Of course you can. You've waited nearly twenty years to find out the truth—I think you can wait a few more days.

"Come on, Adria. Give yourself a little time to pull yourself together."

She wanted to argue, to tell him he couldn't run her life, but she couldn't find the words. And she was frightened. More frightened than she'd ever been in her life. "This is just temporary, right?"

A slow, wicked smile spread across his beard-darkened chin. "I'm not holding you hostage, if that's what you mean."

Nervously, she licked her lips. "That's what I mean," she said.

"You can come and go as you please."

"But my car—"

"I'll send for all your things. Including that bucket of bolts you call a car—after I have it checked by my mechanic."

"It's fine," she protested.

"It's on its last legs."

"Please, I need the car—"

"It'll get there. In a couple of days. In the meantime there are plenty of vehicles at the ranch—cars, trucks, hell, we've even got a tractor if you get desperate."

"Very funny."

"I thought so," he said, but the laughter faded from his eyes. "Come on, Adria. Give it a rest for a few days."

She was touched by his kindness and wondered fleetingly if his concern was genuine or if he was just doing his duty,

babysitting her and keeping her out of trouble. "You . . . .
uh . . . you don't have to do this, you know."

He let go of her wrist and grabbed the wheel. Lines of
worry etched across his forehead. "Of course I do." He didn't
add that he planned to stick to her like glue, that he was afraid
for her life, that he felt sick with guilt because he hadn't followed his gut instincts when he'd known, he'd *known,* that he
should never have let her out of his sight.

The sun, rising over the craggy, snow-covered mountains,
sent harsh rays through the valley. Zach switched on the radio
and glanced at the passenger side of the Jeep where Adria,
tucked in the blanket, was resting her head against the window and breathing steadily, as if she was soon to give in to
exhaustion and fall asleep.

Good. He tromped hard on the accelerator and the Jeep
leaped forward. His jaw was clenched so hard it felt like granite and he swore silently that if he ever found out who'd done
this to her, he'd kill the bastard with his bare hands.

21

"Idiot! What did you think you were doing?" Anthony Polidori wanted to rap his son over the head with his cane. He hadn't struck his son since the boy announced that he'd knocked up the Danvers girl years ago, but right now Mario deserved a swift, hard dose of reality—a swift kick wouldn't hurt either! Clamping his jaw shut, Anthony jabbed his cane in the soft grass of the backyard.

"I just wanted to feel her out—"

"I'll bet. That's the problem with you. Women. Any woman. For the love of God, stay away from her—you're only causing trouble!" Anthony wondered what he'd done to deserve such a stupid son. Stiffly he crossed the backyard and tried to rein in the anger that had kept him awake all night—ever since the phone call from his informant watching the Nash woman. He knew there would be trouble and he'd been proved right.

He paused by the tennis courts where he'd spent so many hours coaching his only boy. Now dandelions and long grass grew through the cracks in the cement courts. A climbing rosebush, untrimmed, sprawled up the tall fence, mistaking the mesh of chain links for a trellis. Dear God, where had the time gone? Had it all been spent feeding that hateful beast called "the feud?" Had he lost all sense of what was real? He remembered the years of hoping that his son would someday grow into a shrewd businessman, a leader capable of handling the considerable businesses that his own father had passed to him and he had hoped to hand down to his son—his only child, but Mario had never been much interested in business. He'd been an athlete, and even while he was in school his decided lack of brains—or at least of discipline—had been evident. That was the problem, the boy—well, man now—had enough gray matter if he only knew how to or wanted to apply it. But he never had. Aside from a little gambling business he'd run for a time, Mario hadn't worked a day in his life. Life had been too easy for him. Handsome by Hollywood standards, skilled on the tennis court or racing down the ski slopes, Mario had seen no reason to study and learn; his showing in school could only be described as poor, but he'd developed a way with girls. All girls. Including Trisha Danvers.

When Trisha had gotten pregnant—which was probably part of the slut's scheme to trap Mario and make life miserable for her father—Anthony had been furious with his son, but had blamed Mario's considerable lack of judgment on his youth. But this . . . this courtship of the Nash woman was asking—no, *begging*—for trouble, especially since the girl had been attacked last night. Mario was long past the time when Anthony could write off his stupid actions as part of the folly of adolescence.

With a heavy sigh, Anthony said, "The police have already been here asking questions and guess who I got a call from? Remember Jack Logan—the police captain, now retired? He was a detective sergeant at the time of the Danvers kidnapping. Apparently he's still working for the Danvers family and more than happy to start in on us again."

Mario seemed unruffled. He showed no outward signs of remorse. "How was I to know she'd be attacked? Jesus, Dad, I didn't have a clue! How could I?" His dark brows slammed together. "Don't tell me one of your men was behind it!"

"Of course not!" Anthony snapped and felt a quick pain under his breastbone, the same pain that shot through him whenever he was under a great deal of stress. He took a deep, calming breath and ignored the irritating little jab. "We're in negotiations with her, aren't we?"

Mario's lower lip protruded thoughtfully and he shook his head. "Apparently not. She claims she's not interested."

"But she will be, if we make it worth her while." Anthony was sure of himself. He'd played this game before. Many times. And he always won. "But we must be careful," he said, gesturing futilely with his hands. "We must use a little decorum, be patient and cautious so as not to tip our hand."

"What's the point? She already knows what we want. You told her yourself that you were interested in the old hotel. I wasn't tipping anything."

"No?" They walked along the kick path leading through the rose garden to the back of the house. Mario held the door of the breakfast room open for his father and Anthony, able to breathe now that his heartbeat was regular again, climbed up the stairs. He sat in his usual chair, spooned some sugar into his coffee cup, and tossed the morning edition of the *Oregonian* onto Mario's plate. The paper landed squarely over Mario's neatly sliced grapefruit.

"What the—" Mario stopped when he saw the picture of a cheap motel and below it a smaller photograph of Adria. Even in grainy black-and-white she was beautiful; the smooth lines of her face and her wide eyes reminded him that he wanted her.

"Read it," Anthony advised as he snapped his napkin across his lap, then waited impatiently while the maid brought juice and coffee. "You'll find your name in paragraph three, I think. A Detective Stinson is coming by to take your statement this morning. She's with the Portland Police Bureau and she's handling her end of the case because Ms. Nash seems to be the target of some rather nasty letters." He stirred his coffee, rattling the cup with his spoon.

Mario's mouth flattened into a thin line of disapproval as he read the article and realized that he had been the last person to see Adria before she was assaulted.

"This is only an educated guess," Anthony said, dropping

his spoon and lifting his cup to his lips. "But I think you've probably made the early morning news broadcasts as well."

The maid silently deposited a basket of muffins onto the table, then slipped quietly back to the kitchen. "From now on, son," Anthony suggested as he reached for a bran muffin, "let me know when you plan to see Ms. Nash." He broke the muffin in half and spread a sparing amount of butter on it. "I just might be able to save you and the family a lot of embarrassment."

Zach paced from one end of the den to the other, stretching the telephone cord to its limit. He muttered curses under his breath and nearly slammed the receiver down.

"If I could just set up an interview with Ms. Nash at her convenience—" Ellen Rigley wheedled. She was pushy, a reporter who didn't seem to understand the word *no*. Zach glanced out the windows to the acres of ranch land that spread as far as the eye could see. It wasn't enough land. There wasn't enough to hide Adria.

"I'm sure she wants her side of the story told—"

Zach held firm and stared down at the front page of the local newspaper that lay open on the desk. Adria's picture was on page one, along with an old photograph of Witt, Kat, and London. The headlines were thick and black and seemed to scream—WOMAN CLAIMING TO BE DANVERS HEIRESS ATTACKED.

It hadn't taken the press long to react. They'd only been at the ranch two days and it was already a madhouse.

Zach felt as if he were trying to plow through quicksand. The faster he went, the farther he tried to get, the deeper and deeper he sank until he felt as if he were choking and there was no way out. No way to save Adria.

Great, he thought sarcastically. Being this close to Adria and keeping his hands off her was hell; trying to keep her from getting herself killed was proving to be nearly impossible. The woman was already talking about returning to

Portland, for crying out loud, when the bump on her head was still fresh, her stitches not yet healed.

The all-business female voice hadn't given up. "—so I could fly out this afternoon or tomorrow morning, meet her at the ranch and—"

"I told you Ms. Nash has no comment." Zach had enough.

"I need to talk to her, Mr. Danvers." She was obviously trying to bully him. "Adria Nash showed up claiming she was London Danvers, then was attacked in a tiny motel way out of the city by an unknown assailant. The *Post* wants to have an interview with her so she can tell her side of the story—"

Zach slammed down the receiver and pressed a button for the answering machine to pick up. He was tired of reporters and police and the whole mess. The phone jangled instantly and Zach, ignoring the impatient ring, threw his keys onto the counter.

He'd just returned to the ranch house after spending three fruitless hours at the office. A bevy of reporters had kept Terry busy on the phone or shown up and made themselves at home, swilling and complaining about his coffee, waiting for a quote from Zach. He'd given one, largely unprintable, and most of them had taken the hint and slunk out the door with their tails between their legs. But a couple of tough, salty types had lingered, hoping that he'd crack and give them some bit of news that would make their copy different from the others that were being written into word processors around the nation.

Zach had given up trying to get any work done, told Terry to close up shop for the rest of the week, stuffed some papers into his briefcase and tucked a couple of blueprints under his arm. He'd locked the press out of his office, climbed in his Cherokee and driven like a madman back to the ranch, to the eye of the storm. He would have turned off the phones to the house except that he wanted to stay in contact with the sheriff's department in Clackamas County, and the police in Portland. Then there was Sweeny's report. Zach's stomach clenched at the thought of it. Two days had passed since he'd talked to the slimy private investigator and, according to Jason, there was still no word.

The sleaze-ball detective was probably holding out on him. Or Jason was.

Ever since the attack on Adria, Zach trusted no one.

Yanking his jacket from a hook near the pantry, he stormed down the hall and out the back door. A blast of icy air greeted him and though the snow had melted at the lower elevations, a fine layer of white powder was visible in the foothills. The sky was clear, the sun high but without any warmth, and only a few clouds clustered around the highest peaks of the surrounding mountains. On any other day, he'd be glad for the bracing air and cool promise of winter. But not today.

The ranch wasn't impregnable, and before he'd thrown out the reporters and photographers who had insisted upon hanging around the front porch, he hadn't been able to hear himself think.

Fortunately, Manny had decided to take matters into his own Native-American hands. Wearing his well-practiced, stern-Indian expression, he'd wrapped a thick, horsehair blanket over his shoulders and positioned himself in his pickup at the front gate. A no-nonsense rifle was propped against his dashboard and a NO TRESPASSING sign had been posted on one of the weathered fence posts, in full view of the road.

No one suspected the .22 wasn't loaded or that Manny Clearwater was the self-proclaimed worst shot in the county and one of the easiest-going guys Zach had ever met. His severe countenance, shaded by a black felt hat decorated with silver and feathers, was enough to keep even the most ambitious reporters off the property.

For now.

Zach had envisioned bringing Adria here until she'd healed and hoped that the news about her attack would die a quick but quiet death. But his plan had blown up in his face and it seemed as if the entire world knew where she was.

Including the man who wanted her hurt. The muscles in the back of his neck drew together and his jaw clenched so hard it ached. Since she'd declined police protection, Zach had made it his personal responsibility to keep her safe. And alive. But it seemed as if the world, and Adria herself, were against him.

The bottom line was that she wasn't safe here. And that bothered him. It bothered the hell out of him.

He found Adria by the stables, the sunlight catching in her blue-black hair. Forearms bridged over the top fence rail, she watched a herd of mares and half-grown foals picking at the sun-bleached stubble of the field.

A whirlwind, laden with thick dust, danced across the dry paddock, picking up a few dead leaves and spinning them across the ground while the horses moved lazily from one tuft of dry grass to the next. Their hides were dusty and uneven, already beginning to change to the thick, longer coats of winter.

Unaware that he was behind her, she shifted, leaning on her opposite leg, her face turning in profile. His gut clenched at the sight of her and he told himself to forget that she was a woman. "You're a popular lady. The phone's been ringing off the hook."

"Why do you think I escaped out here?" She ran a finger along the dusty edge of the top rail and her cheeks had turned a deep shade of pink with the cold. "At first I talked to them, but the questions got too heavy, so I decided to take a break."

"Manny's keeping them at bay down at the gate—the answering machine should catch anything we need to know about." He propped a foot on the bottom slat and stood next to her. Pretending interest in the ridge of mountains on the horizon, he asked, "How're you feeling?"

"Kind of like an eighteen-wheeler drove up my back." Smiling a little, she showed off the hint of a dimple that he found incredibly sexy. "But I'll live and I'm afraid that's going to disappoint a lot of people."

"Don't even say it."

But she wasn't finished. "You know, Zach," she continued, turning to face him as the breeze teased soft, curling strands out of the band that held her hair away from her face, "I can't stay here forever."

"It's only been a couple of days."

"I have my life."

"You mean London's life." He cocked a dark brow and scowled at a few white clouds as a wavering flock of geese, trying and failing to maintain a "V," honked into the wind and flew steadily southward, as if making up for lost time.

With one hand she shaded her eyes against the lowering sun. "It's time I settled this."

"How?"

"I think I need to hire an attorney and a private investigator. Get things moving along."

She was staring at him so intently, her gaze shifting from his eyes to his mouth, that desire swept through him like a hot prairie wind that no man could tame, no mortal could control. He remembered kissing her, nearly making love to her by the river, and it was all he could do to slide his hands into his pockets to hide the swelling that was beginning to warm his groin. He wanted to reach out and grab her, press his lips over hers and kiss her until neither one of them could breathe. He imagined bending her backward till her hair swept the ground.

Hell, this was getting him nowhere!

She was still talking about hiring a detective. ". . . best for all of us."

"Jason's already retained a guy—a creep named Oswald Sweeny. He'll get the job done."

"For Jason. And for you."

The corners of his mouth tightened involuntarily. "You said you wanted to know the truth."

"I still do," she said, squinting against the sunlight. "Correct me if I'm wrong, okay? Sweeny's working for the family, right? He's digging around, trying to prove that I'm a fraud. So he might not tell me—or the family might not feel the need to inform me—if he found proof positive that I'm London. Only if I'm not." She dusted her hands on her jeans. "So I think I'd better start looking for a few guys on my team. Good guys in white hats."

He dug in the dirt with the toe of his boot. "From what I hear, you can't afford much."

She'd been expecting that, but not from Zach. From the others, of course, but not Zach, and she couldn't stop the little stab of pain that reminded her that he'd found out things about her and hadn't confided in her—that he'd shared them only with the inner circle of the Danvers family. The chosen few. Her throat caught. She'd always considered him an outsider, but, as painful as it was, the truth of the matter was that she, and she alone, was the outsider. Obviously there were secrets Zach kept from her and she wondered how much he and the rest of his family discussed her behind her back. Had he told them the secrets she'd confided to him about her home in Montana, had he laughed when he'd discovered she was flat broke, had his eyes lighted with an evil little fire when he'd hinted that she'd nearly made love with him?

Being around Zachary Danvers was like walking a fraying tightrope strung taut across a steep canyon. One false step in either direction and she would pitch down the sharp emotional cliffs. Too much tension and the rope would give way. She wasn't fool enough to believe that he'd be there to catch her. "What is it you want from me?"

He hesitated, his eyes searching hers, and she felt as if he could stare straight into her soul. "I just want to keep you safe."

"So that your family can prove me to be a liar." She felt the air shift between them. "You can't keep me here, not against my will."

"Is that what I'm doing?"

She licked her lips. "I think so. Yes."

His eyes were the color of flint, his brows pulled together in frustration, though she didn't know if his vexation was with her, himself, his family, or the world in general. They were close enough to touch yet he moved closer, advancing upon her, his expression turned hard and suddenly cruel. As his shadow fell across her face, his fingers curled in the lapels of her old leather jacket. "Do you remember that someone tried to kill you?" he demanded in a harsh whisper. "Less than forty-eight hours ago?"

"I can't run scared." But her breathing was shallow and fast. The scents of coffee and leather and musky male cologne swirled around her.

He gave her a little shake and his eyes sparked with anger. "Can you recall what it felt like to nearly have your brains bashed in?"

She blanched. "Of course."

"Who do you think did it?"

"I—I don't know."

"Neither do I, but he's still out there, darlin', and my guess is that he doesn't give up easily."

"I don't, either."

"Okay," he said, pressing his face close enough that she saw the striations of green in his gray eyes. "Let's talk about the sheets—the ones on your bed in the motel. Did you get a good look at them?"

She swallowed with difficulty but refused to give in to the urge to step backward.

His fingers clenched more tightly. "They'd been ripped to ribbons, as if some enraged animal with six-inch teeth as sharp as razors had worked himself up to a maniacal frenzy and started shredding and just couldn't stop."

He yanked her closer, lifting her off her feet, drawing her nose-to-broken-nose. "While we're at it, did you happen to see the message on the mirror, the one meant for you? What did it say?"

"It doesn't mat—"

"What did it say?" he repeated more loudly.

"Something about—"

"Not *something about*—it said *Death to the bitch*. Fairly specific, I'd say. In fact, crystal fucking clear. Do you know what kind of psychotic it takes to do something like that and let's not forget your shredded panties. What if your attacker had used that razor on you instead?"

"I—I really don't want to think about it."

"Well neither do I, but I force myself because it's not over yet."

She managed to notch up her chin and stare into eyes that glittered with determination. "I just can't run away from this, Zachary. I started it and I've got to finish it."

"Or wait until it finishes you," he snarled and looked at her mouth in a way that made her insides turn to jelly. As quickly as he'd grabbed her, he let go and she nearly fell as her heels hit the ground again.

Disappointment settled in her heart when he stepped away from her.

"The way I see it, you've got no choice but to lay low for a while, wait until the police nail this guy or until the story dies down. Right now you're a target, not only for the psychopath who attacked you, but for any other copy-cat prankster looking for a way to get his jollies and his name in the press. These aren't nice people you're dealing with, Adria. So just stay put." He glared at her for a few silent, tense seconds, then swore loudly and stalked to the stables.

Heart thudding, she ran, catching up to him and following on his heels. She tamped down the fear that he'd managed to bring right to the surface of her mind and told herself to ignore the erotic message that had seemed to radiate from his eyes. "I'm not going to let anyone—not you and certainly not someone who runs around ripping bedsheets—intimidate me," she insisted.

"Then you're not as smart as I gave you credit for." He opened the door and strode inside. The door would've banged shut behind him, but she caught it and, clenching her fists in determination, followed him into the musty interior.

Several horses nickered. His boots rang on the old floorboards and the scents of horseflesh and dung, oil and leather, hay and dust mingled and assailed her nostrils, reminding her of the farm she'd left behind to follow this quest here, this damned quest! She touched a rough fir post supporting the hayloft where an old kerosene lantern, tarnished, rusted, and covered with cobwebs, still hung neglected.

Zach strode the length of the building and shouldered open a door at the far end. Old hinges creaked as he disappeared inside. She considered following him, but thought better of it and stayed near the horses, petting each curious, velvet-soft nose that was thrust in her direction, feeling the hot jets of breath against her palm.

What was she doing here? What was she trying to prove? She should go back to the house and leave Zach and his lousy mood. Better yet, she should steal his damned truck and return to Portland where the answers to her life lay hidden.

Still she lingered, using the excuse of her injuries as reason to stay out here, away from civilization, alone with the one man who had touched her heart. For years she'd sheltered herself and her emotions, but with Zachary she'd let down her guard, willingly come to care for . . . oh, God . . .

His footsteps echoed through the old building and she glanced up sharply. With only a cursory look in her direction, he hauled out a saddle, bridle, and blanket and kicked open the gate of the first stall, where a rangy buckskin gelding was tethered. The horse snorted and tossed his great head, but Zach managed to slip the bit between the buckskin's teeth and strap the bridle on. His will was iron-clad and he won the battle between man and beast.

Adria suspected he was used to winning—a man who discovered what he wanted in life and ruthlessly went after it. Not unlike Witt Danvers. His father. *Her* father.

Zach spread a blanket over the gelding's back, slid the saddle into place, and pulled the cinch tight. He was intent on his work, as if he'd forgotten her. The silence, aside from the restlessness of the horses in their stalls, was deafening.

"You're going for a ride?"

"What's it look like?" he said.

"Where?" The question fell off her lips. He glanced over his shoulder and their gazes caught in the dim light of the stables. His eyes were dark and still glinted with a silent, pulsing fury. For several breathless seconds he held her stare and she found it hard to breathe.

"Why?"

She lifted a shoulder, then didn't move. He was staring at her so intently she could barely breathe and she felt as if, with that harsh gaze, he was mentally stripping her—one piece of clothing at a time. She couldn't swallow and her heart was drumming wildly.

His eyes lowered to the base of her throat where her pulse was throbbing erratically. When his gaze touched hers again it was pure seduction. "Do you want to come?" he drawled in a voice so low it could barely be heard over the shifting of the horses' hooves and rustle of straw.

Oh, God! Barely able to breathe, she fingered a rope that had been left wound around a post. Her heart thundered. She stared into his intense, hot eyes and felt her joints go slack.

"Pardon?"

"Do you want to come?" he repeated slowly, the double entendre hanging heavy in the air between them.

She couldn't breathe, couldn't think.

"Well?" he demanded. "Are you up for it? Or still too sore from the attack?"

No attacker was going to stop her from what she wanted to do. She nodded, staring into his smokey eyes. He was staring at her so hard, she could barely breathe. She licked her suddenly dry lips and heard the rush of wind whistle through the old rafters. "I think so." Her voice was so breathless she hardly recognized it as her own.

"You're sure?" One dark brow cocked dubiously and he hooked a thumb in his belt loop, his fingers riding low against his fly. "Could be a rough ride."

Her knees suddenly felt as if they were made of rubber and she leaned her hips against the stall for support. "I know."

"Could be dangerous."

She swallowed with difficulty and felt a tiny spot of sweat bead between her breasts. "I'm not afraid," she said, as though to convince herself. Her heart was racing, her mind spinning into wildly erotic images.

"Then you are a fool, Adria," he said and swore beneath his breath. Clucking his tongue, he led the gelding out of his stall and through the back door of the stables.

Adria, feeling as if she'd had the wind knocked out of her, stalked after him. He'd been playing with her, was only teasing her, and she felt a new, white-hot rage sear through her blood. "Wait a minute!" she cried as he swung into the saddle.

He ignored her and kicked his horse hard in the flanks. The buckskin took off, breaking into a gallop.

"Wait! Zach, please—" she screamed at the top of her lungs.

He yanked back on the reins. The horse reared and whirled. Zach's eyes flashed like lightning sizzling through a night-dark sky and his lips thinned in anger. A rugged cowboy, determined to have his way. "You don't want this," he said, his nostrils flaring, his face set in stone.

"You don't know what I want!"

"Sure I do. All you want—all you've ever wanted was a way to get your hands on the family's money. Well, it won't happen through me."

The wind was beginning to rise, to whip her hair in front of her face and brush her cheeks. "That's not what this is all about, and you know it. Why don't you tell me what you're afraid of?"

"Afraid of?"

"That's right, Zach. You're running scared and it has nothing to do with what happened in the motel the other night."

His mouth curved into a self-deprecating smile. "What I'm afraid of. Isn't it obvious?" His gaze held hers in a stare that stripped her soul bare. With a whistle, he turned the buckskin again and leaned forward in the saddle. The horse took off, galloping rapidly across the dry grass, sending up a cloud of red dust, leaving her alone.

Adria sagged against the exterior wall of the stables. Closing her eyes, she leaned her head back and felt the rough-cut cedar walls press into her shoulders. Her fists curled in frustration and slivers jabbed at her bare knuckles. "Don't be afraid, Zach," she said, her eyes burning with unshed tears. "Please, don't be afraid." The man was so damned maddening and yet . . . Oh, God, and yet . . . she thought she was falling in love with him.

You can't!

But I can't stop myself.

He was in love with Kat!

That was a long time ago.

He's your brother!

I don't know that. Not for sure.

But you can't afford to gamble! Not now! Not when everything you've worked for is at stake!

Like hell!

"He's right," she said, furious with herself. "You *are* a fool." Pushing herself upright, she headed toward the house. She was intent on forgetting him, on finding a way to escape, on putting as much distance between his body and hers as she could. She could take his Jeep or a truck or call someone to come get her . . .

Or she could go after him.

In the distance a coyote howled and the sun slid behind a cloud. Her footsteps hesitated for just a second before she realized that she couldn't let it lie. Rolling over and playing dead wasn't in her nature and she'd come too far and suffered through too many emotional struggles to just curl up and die and let the whole thing go.

Turning back toward the stables, she decided to tempt fate. She flung the door open. Her legs moved of their own accord, her boots ringing as she ran along the smooth floor to the tack room. She found a bridle and hurried back to the row of stalls. A black mare poked her nose over the door and Adria didn't miss a beat. She slipped the bridle over the mare's head, then, running, ignored her lingering pain and led the trotting horse outside. Zach was nearly out of sight, only a speck on the horizon, but Adria wasn't going to let him get away. She climbed on the mare's bare back, leaned forward, and clucked her tongue. "Let's go!" She dug her heels into the black's flanks.

With a surge of power, the horse moved beneath her, muscles bunching and stretching, the cold, hard ground flashing beneath steel-shod hooves. Adria's back and arms ached but she held on. The wind screamed through her hair and brought tears to her eyes as the eager little mare ate up the distance, racing over the vast acres of grassland where the dry pastures rolled upward into foothills green with old-growth timber. In the distance craggy, snow-covered mountains cut jagged ridges against the darkening sky.

She urged the horse faster and faster, afraid that if she slowed down for even a second she would see the folly in this dangerous chase, yank back on the reins, and force herself to return to the ranch—to safety—away from the one man who could save her or destroy her.

Zach's horse galloped through the low-growing timber and Adria followed. "Come on, come on," Adria cried, the breath being torn from her lungs, fear of facing her destiny shadowing her mind. But still she plunged on, chasing a man and her dream, moving closer.

Finally he drew back on the reins and his horse slowed at the banks of a wide river that sliced through the hills and fell in a wild, silver torrent down the face of a cliff. Then, as if suddenly sensing that she was chasing him, he twisted in the saddle.

Her heart nearly stopped as she stared at his profile, all tough angles and planes, like the sheer mountains that rose behind him, wild as the river that slashed furiously through the canyon and cut a raging swath through the forest. His jaw hardened and his eyes narrowed in silent rebuke, but she didn't pay any attention. Instead, she kicked her horse faster. There was no trace of amusement in his face.

Zach's eyes followed her every move as she pulled back on the reins. When she was close enough to hear, he said, "You should go back."

"Back to Montana?"

"Back to the house."

"Not yet." She slid to the ground and Zach followed suit. Eyebrows drawn downward, his mouth pulled into a furious frown, he strode up to her, looking as if he'd like to strangle her . . . or worse, that he wanted to kiss her and never stop.

"For Christ's sake—"

"No. For mine. For yours," she said, breathing hard. She stared up at him stubbornly, squaring her shoulders and meeting his furious gaze with her own.

"You never listen, do you?"

"Not when it's something I don't want to hear." She felt the spray of the waterfall, cool against her neck, and heard the roar of the water tumbling fifty feet to the rocky bottom of the canyon. She stood toe-to-toe with him, refusing to back down, silently challenging him with her eyes.

"You have no idea what you're asking," he said hoarsely.

"Tell me."

He stared at her long and hard, his eyes narrowing in the lowering sunlight, his breath fogging in the cool mountain air. "You never give up," he said and his voice sounded tortured, as if he was battling with himself and losing the war. Reluctantly he pushed an errant black curl from her face.

"No reason to."

"There are lots of reasons, Adria."

"None that I want to hear." She held her head high, angling her chin, daring him to argue, feeling the breeze tangle in her hair.

His gaze fastened to hers and held, causing her heart to trip in anticipation. Raw, unbridled passion glowed dark in his eyes as he looked down at her. Adria's chest was suddenly tight, as if bound by steel cords, and she wondered fleetingly if he was right, if chasing him into the forest was so clever after all. She wanted him, yes, probably loved him, but being with him was treacherous and deadly, for she never seemed to get enough.

As if reading her thoughts, he struck, quickly wrapping his strong fingers around the back of her neck and pulling her roughly to him, kissing her until she couldn't catch her breath. His free arm circled her waist, dragging her willing body closer still, so that she could feel the thunderous beat of his heart, the thick evidence of his desire straining at his fly. He smelled of leather and sweat and tasted of coffee laced with liquor. A slow-burning heat from deep inside her spread throughout her body.

His hands splayed across her back, possessively, angrily crushing her breasts against the hard wall of his chest.

Winding her arms around his neck, she gave herself to him, refusing to listen to any lingering doubts in her mind. She opened her mouth to him as she would willingly open her body.

She clung to him as he dragged her to the ground, pulling her with him, dropping to the bed of dry grass and leaves scattered over the forest floor. He spread kisses along her neck and over her eyes and twisted her hair in his fists. "You're sure?" he asked, his voice breathless and dry as the wind racing through the trees.

"I want this, Zach," she said, staring deep into his eyes. "I want you."

He hesitated but she pressed her lips to his and all his defenses tumbled down. She knew why he was reticent—he still believed they were half-brother and -sister, but she was certain there was a mistake. Surely they couldn't be related. She wouldn't believe it; she wouldn't fall in love with her own half-brother. Most people thought he'd been fathered by Anthony Polidori and he looked so much more like the Italian than Witt. This was right! So right! He nuzzled her neck and she lolled her head back, offering him more.

His fingers found the buttons to her blouse and the clasp of her bra and soon she was stripped to the waist, her breasts bare, her dark nipples puckering in the cool air, her body heated by the inner fire that swept through her blood.

His hands were rough but magical as he reached around her and traced the valley of her spine. Pleasure rippled through her body and she held onto his shoulders as if for life.

Love me, Zachary, she silently cried.

His fingers dipped beneath the waistband of her jeans, stripping her of the unwanted denim and leaving her in a scant pair of panties. She moaned as he took her breast between his lips and her own hands moved to the front of his shirt, tearing at the buttons, feeling the springy, dark hair of his chest as her fingers grazed the strident muscles of his shoulders, the flat buttons of his nipples.

He moaned loudly—a primeval sound that made her quiver.

"Adria," he whispered hoarsely as he gazed down at her.

She held a finger to his lips. "Don't," she whispered and a coil of warmth whirled in her midsection when he drew her finger between his teeth and sucked. Wet. Hungry. Hot.

Heat coiled at her center, pulsing and liquid, as he continued to stare at her.

Her throat was tight and the moist darkness between her legs began to throb with desire. She wanted him, all of him, regardless of the consequences. Gaze fastened to hers, he slipped his hands lower, along the rift of her buttocks until she was squirming, her body silently pleading for more.

"You're sure?" he asked and his pupils had nearly obscured the gray of his eyes. Above him, clouds scudded across the sky.

"Yes!"

"This could be wrong." Doubts shadowed his eyes and his fingers dug deeper into her flesh.

"Never," she whispered, guiding his head back to hers until his breath fanned her face. "Love me, Zach," she whispered, casting caution to the wind and closing her ears to the demons that screamed in her mind. "Love me and forget about everything else."

His throat worked and then the wind seemed to shift. Kissing her, he ran his fingers along her body, and beneath the silk of her panties. Lowering his head, he nibbled at her skin and lowered himself. His tongue slid around the circle of her navel and she bucked upward, wanting more, wanting him—all of him.

He slid lower still and she thought she would die when he stripped her of her panties and breathed hot and damp against the curls at the apex of her legs. Squirming, writhing, she felt him touch her, slowly at first and then more quickly, causing her to melt inside.

"Zachary," she whispered hoarsely.

"Not yet," he whispered and guided one of her hands to his fly. With a hiss, it lowered, and she slowly pushed his jeans over his slim hips. With anxious fingers she caressed his buttocks, and felt the muscles of his legs flex at her touch. She ran her fingers up the flatness of his abdomen and felt him suck in his breath.

Heat flowed from his body to hers.

"You're sure about this," he said again when they were naked and breathing hard, their bodies slick with sweat, nerves strung tight in anticipation.

In answer she kissed him and he moved atop her, his strong hands holding her arms over her head, his eyes burning with a pulsing desire that seared into her soul.

He kissed her again and then roughly, as if he were fighting and losing an inner struggle, he prodded her legs apart. She lifted her hips off the ground as he drove into her and she felt his manhood, heavy and thick, break through the barriers of their lives and delve deep into the core of her soul.

She closed her eyes, but he kissed her cheek. "Watch me," he said hoarsely. "We can't forget that this is happening. We can't ever forget." His words were like the prophecy of doom, but she stared up at him and moved with his sweet, hungry rhythm. There was no pause, no minute to catch her breath. He pushed into her harder and harder, faster and faster, until the colors behind her eyes began to blend and whirl.

She was moist and warm, like thick, hot honey, and she felt him gather steam just as something erupted within her.

"Adria, oh, sweet, sweet Adria!" His voice, a raspy whisper, bounced off the walls of the canyons and the chambers of her heart. Lights exploded behind her eyes and her body convulsed around him, holding him tight within her as if she was afraid to lose the precious link they'd found, the ecstasy of loving each other. Her throat worked.

Love me, she silently cried, wrapping her arms around him as he fell against her, his sweating body melding perfectly to hers. *Love me, Zachary Danvers, and don't ever stop.*

Tears touched the back of her eyes—from joy or relief, she didn't know—but she refused to give in to the persistent drops and wouldn't think about tomorrow.

It would come soon enough.

22

"Tell me about my mother." Adria, shivering as the after-glow faded, stared up at the swaying, long-needled branches of the pines to the blue sky beyond. A few filmy clouds moved slowly through the heavens but didn't spoil the day.

Beside her, Zach tensed. "I didn't know your mother." He reached for his faded Levi's and slid into them. "She lived in Montana with you."

"My other mother," she clarified, refusing to let him vex her, but she wasn't going to let him put her off as he had in the past. They were lovers now—they could share everything. "Katherine." The ground was cold and goose bumps rose on her flesh as she found her jeans and sweater.

After making hot, furious love to her, Zachary had held her against his naked body. She'd seen the scar on his shoulder, been reminded of the night that London had disappeared and had convinced herself that she couldn't be related to him. Either he was Polidori's son or she wasn't London Danvers. Now, as her mind cleared, she wasn't so certain.

He seemed more remote than ever, as if the shock of what they'd done had been a slap of reality—cold water in his face.

"Katherine wasn't your mother," he said with conviction.

"You don't know that."

That much was true, Zach thought as he yanked on his boots. He had to get away, far away. Being with her was like being trapped in a seductive spider's web, sticky and warm and exciting but infinitely dangerous. Whether she'd decided to make love to him because she suddenly didn't believe they could be related, or because she thought he would let down his defenses and give her more information about the family, or because she wanted to blackmail him later, or, God forbid, because her motives were pure and she was falling for him, he knew it just couldn't happen. He should have been stronger. Ever since Kat, he'd been in control and had never let a woman seduce him. He'd always been the predator. His will where sensual women were concerned had been strong. Until now. With Adria. He ground his teeth together in disgust and stood, swiping at the dust covering his jeans.

He'd been unable to resist her—the defiance in her blue eyes, the challenging tilt of her chin, her soft, sensual lips, and the provocative invitation that touched him in a deep, roughly animal place, where his body took over and his mind shut down. He'd wanted sex. With her. Lusty, hot, get-your-rocks-off sex, and he'd ended up with more. Too much. An emotional whirlpool that threatened to drag him under.

Just like Kat!

He slammed his eyes shut and told himself it was just a matter of time. If he could maintain some distance from that body of hers, he could stay in control. At least until he had all this figured out.

Like hell, Danvers. How're you going to stay away from her? Now that you've had a taste, a teasing nibble of her, how are you going to fight the craving that even this minute is tearing you up inside?

The muscles in his back drew so tight they hurt. Angrily, he threw on his jacket. "We've got to get back. It's cold."

He stiffened as her fingers touched his shoulder. "You don't have to feel guilty," she said over the roar of the river as it dived from the cliffs to the gully far below.

"I don't."

"Then why—"

"Look, Adria, we can't do this. Not anymore. Not until we

find out for sure." He placed firm hands on her shoulders and held her at arm's length. "It just can't happen."

"So you're starting to believe me."

"For Christ's sake, do you know what we're talking about here?" he said, nearly screaming. "Incest!" The word hung between them, seeming to haunt the forest, standing still in the chill afternoon light.

"It's not—"

"How do you know? If you're so damned sure that you're London, then how do you know?"

He watched her swallow with difficulty. "Because," she said, tossing her hair away from her face, "I believe that you're not Witt's son."

"Christ!" His face turned ashen. "Is that your rationalization?" He grabbed her arms so hard that she felt his fingers digging deep into her flesh through her jacket. "Now listen to me, *sister,* I'm *not* Polidori's son."

"How do you know?" she threw back at him, tossing the very words in his face that he'd spit at her.

"Don't you think that when Eunice and Witt split up, when she was stripped bare of everything she claimed she wanted, don't you think she would have turned around and laughed in his face, told him that his second son had been fathered by his enemy, insisted that I stay with her?"

"Not if she wanted her reputation to stay intact. Her reputation, as I understand it, was as important to her as you children, so she would never say anything to tarnish it."

"As we children? What a laugh. We were never important to her."

"I think—"

"You don't know. As for her reputation, it was already black as tar."

He made a disgusted sound in the back of his throat.

"I don't believe she intended to hurt you."

Eunice's words, uttered at his bed in the hospital, whispered through his head. *I hate to admit it, Lord knows a mother shouldn't, but you've always been my favorite. Of all my children, you were the one closest to my heart.* As if he was different. As if he *wasn't* Witt's son. Oh, God, no! All the spit dried in his mouth and he stared at Adria as if he were looking into the window of his future. "You couldn't have done this"—he motioned to the bed of pine needles under the tree—"on the outside chance that I wasn't a Danvers."

"I did it for the same reasons you did, Zach. Because I wanted to. Because I couldn't stop myself. Because from the first time I saw you, I knew it would happen. Because . . . because, damn it, I think I love you."

She lifted up on her toes then and kissed him hard on the lips. He told himself to back off, that they were playing with fire, that no matter what happened, there could be no good ending to this, they would both be burned and yet he couldn't stop himself. His arms fastened around her slim waist and he wouldn't let go. He kissed her and held her and stripped her of her clothes, looking in fascination at the beauty of her breasts, white, with a fine webbing of blue veins hidden deep beneath the firm flesh, her nipples perfectly round and hard as he touched them and kissed them and buried his face between the two warm mounds.

He kissed the skin of her abdomen, drawing lazy circles around her navel before he slid lower and she writhed in pleasured torment beneath him. She tasted of woman and earth and all things primeval.

While the wind teased her hair, her fingers and hands worked their own sweet magic on him, shedding him of his clothes, tracing intimate circles along his spine and chest, dipping low beneath his jeans to push the tight denim over his butt.

Her eyes shone as she kissed him and tasted his hard-button nipples and skimmed her tongue down his breastbone and along the dark hairs that formed a line beneath his navel.

He fought the urge to close his eyes and stared at her, this woman who was forbidden, this woman whom he believed

"You really believe that?" he demanded, shock giving way to anger.

"It only makes sense."

"That's garbage, darlin', and you know it!" He rolled over and grabbed her arm, forcing her to drop her top. His fingers coiled possessively over her wrist and he shoved his face to within inches of hers. Their noses nearly touched and he witnessed the shades of blue shift in her eyes. "From the get-go, you practically threw yourself at me," he pointed out. "You chased me down." With his free hand he motioned to the horses trying to graze on the grass that grew in patches between the trees. "In fact, you nearly ran me off the edge of the damned cliff."

"But—"

"So enough of this Kat stuff, okay? Sure, you remind me of her and that's more of a problem than you know. I'd rather forget her forever, but I'm not going to lie to you just to make you feel good. Yes, you look like her. Near enough to be her damned twin. But the resemblance is only on the outside. Believe me, you are nothing—no-damned-thing—like her! Got it?"

She didn't answer and he shook her wrist.

"Got it, Adria?"

"I guess." But she didn't sound convinced.

"You *know*. What happened here—between us—isn't about Kat. Never was. Never will be."

"All right, all right," she said, and pulled her arm from his grasp. "You've made your point, Danvers."

"But you don't believe me."

"I don't know what I believe anymore," she admitted. "I don't even know what I want to believe. You and me . . . what's happening?"

"I know." He glanced up at the heavens. How in the world had he let it go this far? And now that it had, could he ever break it off? When it came to this woman, he couldn't think straight and he had the unsettling feeling that he would never get enough of her. Maybe she was more like Kat than he'd admitted. Christ, what a mess. When he glanced back at her, she was smiling, as if finding the vexation that had to be evident on his features amusing.

"Funny, is it?" He shook his head.

"More like impossible."

"I'll buy that."

"Of all the things I thought would happen when I came to Portland, I never considered that I'd get involved with one of the Danvers family. I mean, I knew there would be resentment and distrust and a lot of pressure for me to back off, but this . . . what's happening between us . . . believe me, it never crossed my mind until I saw you."

"And then?"

"Yeah . . . and then." She nodded and let out a long breath. Zach felt a smile crack his lips as he let go of her.

"Yeah, and what is funny, or maybe *egocentric* is the better word, is that you're accusing me of chasing *you* down. Seems just the opposite."

"Me?"

"Mmm." She nodded, her dark hair moving against her skin. "I might have chased you but it was, after all, those long, smoky stares you sent my way. After all the times you nearly kissed me, but didn't. After you drove me up to the Clackamas River with the intention of seducing me, then backed out, I think, just to make me want you more." She picked up a blade of grass and twirled it in her fingers. "Now I'm the bad guy?" She winked at him and he felt his blood stir again. "I don't think so."

"You're missing the point."

"Which is?"

He took both her hands in his and regret softened the harsh planes of his face. "That this has gotten way out of control. *Way* out of control. We both know it."

"And how're we going to get back in control, hmm?" she asked as, once again, he reached for his jeans. "By acting like this . . . attraction doesn't exist?"

"Maybe."

"It won't work"

"Then we'll find whatever it is that does," he said gruffly. He started to dress, quickly. He didn't have time for this. He needed answers and he needed them fast. When he turned, he was surprised that she, too, had thrown on her clothes, though her hair was mussed with pine needles and her face had the glow of a woman satisfied after weeks of deprivation.

She swung lithely onto the back of her little mare, sent a dazzling smile his way, and said, "Race ya," as he was still yanking on his boots. With a holler that resounded through the trees, she kicked the black and galloped away, her laughter trailing after her. As if she didn't have a care in the world. As if she wasn't nursing wounds from an attack. As if no maniac was stalking her. As if she wasn't involved with a man who could be her half-brother.

"Damn that woman," he muttered, but he was up for the dare and hoisted himself onto the back of his buckskin. Within seconds he was chasing her, the trees and river flashing by in his peripheral vision, his objective, a woman with streaming black hair, in his sights.

Right or wrong, he was going to catch her, and when he did, he was damned sure the earth would move again.

The last thing Adria expected was for Zach to change his mind, and so quickly. But after she'd talked for hours with reporters and they were virtually assured that her face and story would be in the news yet again, he grew restless and told her that they'd leave and head back to Portland as she'd wanted. First thing in the morning.

Her feelings were ambivalent. She'd love to close off the rest of the world, to stay here with Zach and pretend that nothing else mattered, but she couldn't. She wasn't about to give up now.

While Zach was outside, cutting firewood, Adria poured

herself a glass of wine and strolled into the den. Cedar walls
and a river-rock fireplace surrounded a room filled with worn
furniture, baskets of old magazines, and Indian blankets used
as throws. Watercolors of horses and cattle and peaceful
ranching scenes adorned the rough-cut walls. It was a cozy,
well-used room that smelled faintly of ashes and burnt wood.
She imagined Zachary spending his evenings here, his boots
kicked off, the bottoms of his stockinged feet propped on
the timeworn ottoman. A cozy vision, a warm thought, something she could envision herself being a part of. But that was
crazy. Just because they'd made love, she was already fantasizing that they had a future together.

Stupid.

She ran her fingers along the spines of the books in the
bookcase and found, tucked in a corner of one shelf, an old
album with pictures of the family.

"I didn't know I still had that," Zach said, glaring at the
album as he entered the room with an armload of firewood.
The wind swept in with him and she smelled the scents of
pine and musk mingling with the smoke as he struck a match
on the stone hearth and lit the dry kindling. Flames crackled
and sparked and she curled in a corner of the couch.

"I poured you a glass," she said, nodding toward her wine.
"In the kitchen."

He returned with a bottle of beer as well as the glass of
wine and set the stemmed glass on the coffee table for her.
Then he lowered himself into a chair opposite her, twisted off
the cap of his beer, and watched her as she sipped her
chardonnay and slowly turned page after page.

"You won't find much in there." He drank slowly, and she
felt his eyes upon her. Restless eyes.

"Is that right?" She didn't stop gazing at the flat images.
The pictures in the album were old and a little faded, some of
the color washed out. Though there were none of Eunice,
some spaces pointedly blank, a page yellowed around an
empty spot where a snapshot had been removed, there were a

few of Zachary, never smiling, always sullen, glaring at the camera as if it were his enemy.

There were shots of Katherine, too, playful poses where she smiled and flirted with the lens, a natural tease in front of the camera. Adria bit her lip as she studied the pictures and her heart twisted at a photograph of Katherine carrying a dark-haired toddler on her hip.

Zach took a long pull on his bottle, then bent over the fire again, tossing in two chunks of mossy maple.

"You never really told me about her," Adria said, as Zach dusted his hands and stared at the hungry yellow flames licking the new wood. "You just dance around the issue."

"I thought we already had this discussion."

"As I said, 'danced around' the issue."

"There wasn't much to tell. She accused me of helping kidnap London and then later, when I tried to console her, one thing led to another and we ended up in the sack. Witt found out and threw me out. End of story."

"Except that you fell in love with her."

He snorted. "Don't try to put any romantic spin on it, okay? I was a horny kid and she was a desperate woman who was hurting. I should never have . . . oh, hell, what does it matter? It was years ago. And she's dead." A muscle worked in his jaw and he took a long swallow from his beer.

"And you blame yourself?"

"No? Yes? Oh, who knows. She committed suicide because she never got over London's disappearance, I guess." He gazed at the fire. "Maybe I played a part in it. Who knows?" He glanced back at her. "But it was odd—the suicide. Katherine . . . well, she was one of those people who took a big bite out of life, and sure, she was destroyed when her baby disappeared and I guess she was despondent, but she never struck me as the type of person who would actually take her own life." He shook his head and took a long pull from his bottle. "It always bothered me."

"Because you loved her."

"Stop it, Adria. I didn't love her. Ever. It was just a physical thing that happened." He turned and glared at her. "If you want to know if it would have continued if Witt hadn't caught us, who knows? Maybe. Depended on a lot of things. I didn't want to start something with her, I knew it was trouble, but I was young, randy, and the opportunity presented itself. Every day I wish I'd been a whole lot smarter about it, but, considering what happened today, it looks like I'm still not."

She gritted her teeth. "Low blow, Danvers."

"It's been a day for 'em. And don't go into this holier-than-thou routine, okay? 'Cuz it just won't wash. You're sitting there half condemning me for being with my stepmother and yet you could be my half-sister and it didn't stop you, did it?"

The album dropped to the floor. "I don't think we should go there."

"Not a pretty picture, is it?" He took a swig from his bottle and gnashed his teeth.

Adria felt as if she'd been slapped. She struggled to her feet and backed away from him. "I'm not—"

He moved swiftly, pushing her back onto the couch, placing his hand on either side of her, imprisoning her in the old cushions. His head was so close to hers she could see the pores on his face, smell the beer on his breath. "Isn't that why you're here, *London?* Isn't that all part of the plan? To prove that you're my baby sister and—"

"No!" she cried, unwilling to believe what he insisted was the truth. She sprang from the couch and he caught her in arms as strong as steel bands.

"I warned you—"

"You made vague insinuations. But not this. Never this! You could have told me that you . . . you—"

"That I what?" he said, holding her gaze with his. "That I made love to the woman who could be your mother?"

"That you fell in love with her!" The words cracked through the room like the sharp unleashing of a whip.

"I was not 'in love' with her. I already told you. "She was

hot, Adria. And I was a horny kid. I don't have any excuses.
It was wrong."

"So that's why Witt cut you out of his will."

His smile was hard. "One of the reasons."

"Oh, God. How did you ever look him in the eye again?"
she asked.

"When she began sleeping with Jason, the old man kind of
forgave me. It took a while, but we struck a deal. I got the
ranch and he got his old hotel restored like he wanted it." His
fingers cut into her flesh. "You asked why Kat killed herself,"
he said. "Because of me. Because of Jason. Because of London and Witt. Because of the curse of being a Danvers—the
curse you're so ready to embrace!"

She shoved away from him, dragging in ragged gulps of
air, her eyes as dark as midnight. "Don't make this any worse
than it already is," she spat and watched as a muscle worked
in his jaw. For a minute she thought he might kiss her again
and a part of her still wanted to hold him, to kiss him, to make
love to him . . .

"I don't think it could be," he said and stormed out of the
room and decided to get drunk. No, not just drunk, but stink-
ing, shit-faced, falling-down drunk. He grabbed his coat and
strode outside. The temperature had dropped and a few light
flakes of snow were beginning to fall. He'd find a woman. A
woman without any strings attached. A woman looking for a
one-night stand. A woman who wouldn't even ask him his
name.

He slammed the door behind him, rattling the windows.

Manny, despite the cold, was seated in a rocking chair on
the porch of a small cabin at one end of the parking lot. A cigarette hung from the corner of his mouth and he was whittling
as he listened to the transistor radio in the window. He looked
up as Zach passed him on the way to his Jeep. "You leaving?"

"Yeah."

"Looks like you could spit nails."

"For starters."

"When you comin' back?"

"Don't know." He cocked his head toward the main house. "Watch her, will ya?"

"I'm a Paiute, Danvers, not a friggin' jailer."

"Just make sure she stays put, and no one shows up here and tries to get to her. I won't be gone long."

"Woman trouble," Manny said, his expression unchanging. He drew on the cigarette and smoke shot from his nostrils. "The worst kind."

"Amen." Climbing into his Jeep, Zach stabbed the key into the ignition, fired the engine and roared away from the ranch house. What the hell was it with him? First Kat, now a woman who looked so much like her it was eerie—damned eerie.

Somehow, some way, he had to get away from her and break free of this circle of sin that kept spinning around him, trapping him in its dangerous, life-crushing, but oh-so-erotic coils.

They left the ranch the next evening and didn't say a word on the way back to Portland. That suited Zach just fine. His head was pounding from his intimate relationship with Jack Daniel's the night before, his only relationship. He'd never gotten past a brief nod of his head toward the blonde who'd shown him so much interest last night. Her easy smile and freckles had been cute, her full breasts obviously restrained by a tight yellow T-shirt, but he couldn't drown memories of Adria with any amount of liquor. He'd turned down the blonde and she'd found another, more willing cowboy. Zach had nearly drowned himself in whiskey. Manny had sent a ranch hand to town to collect him.

And today he was paying. Shit, was he paying.

He slid a pair of sunglasses onto the bridge of his nose to break the glare of sunlight off the road, but truth to tell, the sun was hidden behind a heavy bank of clouds and his eyes ached from too much whiskey, the sting of smoke, and lack of sleep.

He flipped on the radio, listened to the tinny sound of country music and wished he knew what the hell he was going to do with Adria when he got to Portland. He'd called the police but so far there were no significant leads, at least none they would confide to him. Or Adria.

Adria.

So far she hadn't told him her plans but he suspected she intended to ditch him. Hell, he couldn't blame her—he'd been cruel to her last night, but it was the only way he could get away from her, and he had to get away. For both of them. And yet he had to protect her from whoever it was who was stalking her.

As they drove into the city, he said, "I booked a room for you."

"Let me guess—it's not at the Orion," she said sarcastically. She didn't even glance in his direction.

"You'll be safe at the hotel."

Turning hostile eyes in his direction, she silently accused him "Safe? Are you crazy? Safe from whom?" A dark, skeptical eyebrow rose imperiously over her eyes. "The Danvers family? The person who attacked me? *You?* I don't think so." She saw the vexation in his eyes and told herself she didn't care. "Isn't staying at the Hotel Danvers like taking a suite in a lion's den?"

"Not when I have control of the situation."

"Oh great, *you* have control," she mocked.

"All right. You name it then."

"I don't know. Just take me to my car and I'll—"

"Your car isn't fixed yet."

"Not fixed? But it was running just fine—"

He snorted. The mechanic had called this morning. "I don't know what you call *fine* in Podunk, Montana, but according to a man who knows his way around a Chevy, you need new brakes, shocks, spark plugs, fan belt, the list goes on and on—"

"Fabulous! Don't tell me. You authorized him to do it!" She couldn't begin to imagine how she could afford to get the little Nova out of hock.

"Don't worry about it. I'll get you a car. One that's dependable."

"I don't want your help, Zach—"

"But—"

"Or your pity."

"You need a car."

"Or your stubborn streak. Okay? Just take me to the airport. I'll rent one there," she said crisply. Everything was spinning out of control and she had to get a grip on her life, find out the truth, and then decide what she was going to do.

He shot her a glance. "You should stay with me."

"Oh, where it's safe?" she threw back, unable and unwilling to hide her sarcasm.

"Yes."

"Forget it."

He sliced her a look, then drove on, past the turnoff to the airport and headed straight into the heart of the city. He didn't stop the Jeep until he was in the parking lot of the Hotel Danvers.

So furious she could barely see straight, she said, "I'll just call a cab," as he hauled her bag out of the back.

"Fine."

"Being here is a big waste of time."

"Whatever you say." He punched the button for the elevator with his elbow and waited, holding her suitcase in one big hand, the toe of his boot tapping in irritation. The car arrived, he waited for her to step in, and they sped upward to the lobby. At the front desk, he pulled the manager aside. Gray stare drilling into the shorter man's eyes, he ordered, "Ms. Nash needs a private suite with only one key. No one, save

Ms. Nash, is to have access to the room. And that includes any of the staff, or any of my family—is that understood?"

"Absolutely." The man's Adam's apple bobbed.

"And I want round-the-clock security by her door, a man posted—"

"No. Zach, this is ridiculous," she interjected.

"—twenty-four hours a day. When she's in the room and when she isn't, a guard will be there. Got it?"

"Of course, Mr. Danvers."

"She'll take phone calls, and guests can wait in the lobby after she screens them, but no one, not even Jason, is to rescind this order. If anyone tries, I want to be notified immediately. I'll be in my usual rooms. And she doesn't need to register. She's my guest."

"Yes, Mr. Danvers," the manager said crisply. He slid the key across the desk to Adria and she, grinding her teeth together in frustration, accepted it. For the time being. Just until she could rent a car and relocate.

Zachary wasn't finished. "I'll take her bag up myself and as far as you know, the person who's in the rooms is a VIP and no one, I mean *no one,* is to know that she's here."

Adria started to protest, but held her tongue. Let him do this. It would take only a few more minutes and then she would be totally independent. Or would she? A contrary part of her heart begged to differ as she watched him, all quiet authority and rugged good looks. Telling herself that she could force herself to be immune to him, she followed Zach into the elevator, where his presence all but dominated the little car, and up to the sixth floor to a corner suite with several rooms, fireplace, private veranda, and Jacuzzi. He tossed her bag onto the couch and locked the door behind him. It clicked so loudly she nearly jumped.

"I'd feel better if I stayed with you," he said, cocking his head at the floral couch where her bag rested.

"I think, under the circumstances, that would be a big mistake," she said, but already, her pulse was jumping. The thought of being alone with him caused a warm, wanton sensation deep in the pit of her stomach.

"I can't protect you if I'm not with you," he said. The distance between them was only a few feet and she could barely stand it.

"And I can't protect myself if I am with you." She rested her rear against the ledge of the window. "This has gone too far, Zachary, and I'm not blaming you. It happened between us and it was a mistake . . . I can see that now, but I don't know, I'm just not sure that I can trust myself if you're here with me." She spoke from the heart and she felt as if she were shredding inside because a part of her longed to be held by him, to kiss him, to feel his hands upon the crook of her waist. She bit her lip before she said something that she shouldn't.

"This is your call, Adria," he said, his voice low and soft, almost a caress.

Her heart shattered. She remembered the feel of his hands on her, the taste of his skin, the way he sighed against her ear. "Then it's the way it has to be."

Zach's shoulders stiffened and the brackets around the corners of his mouth grooved deep. "I'm in 714."

Her throat closed in on itself at the mention of the suite from which London had been stolen all those years ago.

"Call me if you need me."

I need you. I need you now! Her fingers curled over the window ledge and she held back the urge to run to him.

Back ramrod-stiff, he walked out of the room and closed the door behind him.

Swearing under his breath, Zach pulled into the parking lot of the headquarters of Danvers International. The lot was closed, but he used a special card and the gates opened as if for royalty. Danvers royalty.

He hadn't been happy about leaving the hotel, knowing that Adria would probably bolt, but he'd talked to Detective

Stinson to advise her and knew that Adria was keeping in touch with the police. Right now, Zach had to find answers and any he'd gotten from Jason on the telephone had been evasive and vague. He'd called, tracked his brother to the offices, and decided that if he had to, he'd knock Jason senseless, because it was time to find out the truth.

Before he fouled up Adria's life forever.

Spoiling for a fight, he parked in a spot reserved for a vice president and took the elevator to the floor housing the suite of executive offices. During the day the building was crawling with people; at night it seemed like a tomb.

He walked down the short hallway lit only by security lamps, past the empty reception area, and through the carved wooden doors to the president's office.

Jason, dressed in a crisp suit and tie, was sprawled on the leather couch angled in front of the television in the corner. He must've had one helluva day, because his hair was slightly mussed and his tie was loosened. Propping one heel on a glass coffee table, he sipped from a glass of amber liquid.

Zach let the door bang shut behind him and studied the room where all the important decisions of the company were made. The two exterior walls were glass, offering a panoramic view of blazing city lights and two bridges spanning the Willamette River.

Inside, trophies and plaques were hung on a wall of rough cedar, a tribute to the forests that had been the source of so much of the Danvers fortune.

"You're angry," Jason guessed as he stood and tucked his shirt into the waistband of his slacks.

The understatement of the year. "A little."

"Adria?" Jason clicked off the television and reached for his drink.

"She's got a mind of her own."

"Thought you liked that in a woman."

"Not in this one."

Jason lifted a skeptical brow.

"Heard she was attacked. Is she okay?"

"She'll be fine."

"Do the police have any suspects?"

"Probably."

"What does your friend Len Barry have to say?" Jason asked, feigning disinterest.

"Nothing."

"Isn't that odd?"

"Of course not. The police will get in contact with Adria when they have something."

"And she'll tell you?"

Zach shrugged. "Why don't you ask her yourself?"

"Hey, I didn't mean to pry."

"Like hell."

"Help yourself to the bar."

"Not tonight." Propping his hip on the corner of Jason's wide desk, he said, "I just came here because I want to get in contact with Sweeny."

"He called earlier." Jason polished off his drink. "Big news."

Zach's blood seemed to freeze.

"He called to crow, really," Jason continued as he walked to the bar and added more Scotch to his melting ice cubes. "Seems he's found Bobby Slade, the one who we hoped would turn out to be Adria's real father. Robert E. Lee Slade. He's Ginny Watson's ex-husband, all right, and he's living' in Lexington, Kentucky—has himself some kind of auto repair shop or something." Jason made a dismissive gesture with his hands, as if whatever it was that kept Bobby Slade employed didn't really matter. "According to Sweeny, Slade doesn't know where his ex-wife is, hasn't kept up with her since he heard from her two years ago when she'd taken some kind of nanny job in San Francisco."

Zach's hands began to sweat and he remembered Ginny Slade as a plain woman in dowdy suits and heavy shoes who looked ancient compared to Kat. But somehow the birdlike woman had managed to steal her precious charge right out from under Witt's nose.

"What else does the guy have to say?"

"Plenty. Bobby claims his wife was a nutcase. Totally bonkers. She lost any grip on reality she had when their toddler daughter was killed in a drowning accident. She blamed him, he blamed her, and their marriage fell apart. Sweeny says Slade was glad to be rid of her."

"So what about London?"

"Here comes the clincher," Jason said, looking up at the ceiling. "Slade says that years ago—the mid-70s, he thinks, just before he moved to Kentucky—she showed up in Memphis out of the blue. Ginny had a kid in tow, a dark-haired girl of about four. He thought it was strange at the time, but just assumed that the kid was hers as she claimed. She'd always had a thing about babies, even before losing her own." Jason looked straight at his brother and the hidden anger in his eyes bordered on hatred. "The odd thing about the situation was, and it kind of gave Slade the creeps, that she named the kid Adria, the same name she'd given their little girl who'd died."

"Jesus Christ," Zach whispered.

"My sentiments exactly. I hate to admit it, but it looks like Adria might just be London."

Zach gripped the edge of the desk. This was all wrong. It had to be. Adria couldn't be his half-sister. No way! She wasn't related to him! He thought of her being battered, nearly killed by an attacker. Someone who thought of her as a fraud. His insides grew cold. If the would-be killer discovered the truth . . . Jesus! And there was another more personal issue. One he wanted to forget. But he couldn't. He remembered her lying beneath him, her body shiny with sweat, her voice moaning in gentle rhythm to his thrusts . . . for the love of God . . .

"Nelson's fit to be tied. He's on his way over here."

"What about Trisha?" Zach asked, though he could barely keep his mind on the conversation.

"Couldn't get hold of her," Jason admitted. "She's probably out prowling again."

"Let me talk to Sweeny. He's probably lying—"

"Shit, Zach, get a grip."

"I need to talk to him!"

"Why?"

"I just need to ask him some questions," Zach said, and Jason favored him with a smug little smile that said he could read his brother like the proverbial book.

"The number's on the desk, Zach, but it won't do any good. The facts, as they say, are the facts. Adria Nash is probably our sister. The good news is that she doesn't know it."

"Yet," Zach said, with a sinking sensation.

"Ever." Jason's jaw hardened and he suddenly looked so much like their father, Zach winced. "As far as I'm concerned," Jason said with deadly calm, "she'll never know."

23

"We finally caught ourselves a break," Sweeny said, his voice self-satisfied and oily as it sang through the wires.

Every muscle in Zach's body contracted an inch and he could barely breathe. "You have an address where Ginny Slade can be found?"

"Nope, but I've got one where she worked a couple of years ago. Pacific Palisades in San Francisco."

"Let's have it."

The detective hesitated only a second, then gave Zach the name and number of Virginia Watson's last employer of record. It wasn't much, but it was all Zach needed. He hung up just as Nelson shouldered through the double doors of Jason's office, took one look around, and paused, his face blanching slightly. "What the hell's going on?"

"Sweeny found Ginny Slade," Jason said. "Well, nearly. He thinks she's in San Francisco."

"Then it's true—?" Nelson was speechless as he plopped down in one of the side chairs and rubbed his temples with his fingers. It was obvious that he thought his life was unraveling. "I can't believe it. She's really London?"

"Looks that way," Zach said tightly.

"We don't have to believe it!" Jason was adamant. "We don't have to buy into it—we just have to keep our mouths shut."

"No way. She deserves to know," Zach said, though it twisted his guts and a vile taste rose in the back of his throat when he realized that he still wanted her. Despite the nearly certain truth that she was his long-lost half-sister, he couldn't stop thinking of her as a woman.

Nelson pinched the bridge of his nose as if trying to forestall a headache. "First Mother, then this . . ."

"Eunice?" Zach's head snapped up.

"She slipped and fell chasing after that damned cat of hers," Nelson said. "She's all right, just banged around a little. A few scratches. Nothing serious, thank God. But this London business. It's unbelievable." He glanced up at Zach and his mouth twisted into a shadow of his former smile. "You know, a long time ago, you were my hero. Getting beat up, having yourself a prostitute . . ." His voice faltered and his gaze shifted to the floor. He sighed loudly, a tortured soul who'd been cast adrift years before. "I guess that's all gone now."

Zach couldn't think about the might-have-beens. Nelson had always been out of step—no reason that having London resurface would change anything. He clamped a hand on his youngest brother's shoulder, then let go. With renewed conviction, he crossed the room and thrust open the doors.

"Hey—where're you going?" Jason's voice followed him into the hallway. "Wait a minute. Zach! Oh, shit, what's he going to do now?"

"Who cares?" Nelson said. "It's over, Jase."

"Not yet—"

The rest of whatever he was saying was cut off when the doors closed. Zach pounded on the elevator call button with his fist. Though he was sick inside at the thought of Adria being London, he told himself it had been inevitable and was probably for the best. Deep in his gut he didn't believe it. The good news was that they were closer to the truth and the pall that had been shrouding the family for years might finally be lifted. The bad news was that he'd never be able to touch her again.

* * *

Trisha was pissed.

She climbed into her Alpha and took off, putting the little sports car through its considerable paces, and driving through the night without knowing where she was going. She'd hoped to meet Mario, but her plans had fallen through. Again. Her fingers tightened over the steering wheel and she took a corner a little too fast, the tires screeching, the car skidding into the oncoming lane. Headlights bore down on her. The driver of the other car swerved, nearly taking out a tree, and laid on his horn as Trisha maneuvered her car back into the right-hand lane. "And fuck you, too," she muttered under her breath, then glanced at the rearview mirror to make sure the jerk didn't turn around and chase after her. Well, let him. She'd show him what a real car could do. She was in one bitch of a mood.

Because of Mario. And Adria.

Mario claimed he couldn't meet her, that some kind of business had come up, but Trisha wasn't fool enough to believe him. Though he'd apologized over and over again, she hadn't heard the slightest hint of any true regret in his voice. She knew the reason—he had a new woman, someone more exciting, someone who presented him more of a challenge. She didn't have to be a brain surgeon to figure out that he planned the newest notch on his bedpost would be Adria Nash.

Ever since he'd been with Adria the other night, Mario had avoided Trisha, begging off with one flimsy excuse after another. But Trisha knew the score. Whenever he was involved with a new woman he became distracted and unapproachable but eventually—sometimes only days, other times excruciating months—he came back, not the least bit contrite, resuming their affair with a renewed passion and vigor, claiming to love her.

The sex was always worth the wait.

The emotional strain was not.

So now he was interested in Adria and that bothered her—more than any of the others.

"Bitch!" Trisha hissed, thinking of the pistol locked in her

glove compartment. She didn't know whom to shoot first.
Mario or Adria. Maybe the two of them together. She'd
bought the gun for protection and never had to use it, but
tonight, her fantasies were running wild and if she caught
Mario—her Mario—with that two-bit hustler from Montana,
she was sure she would blow them both away.

Adria, who looked so much like Kat! Trisha's insides
twisted when she remembered her stepmother, the bitch who
had convinced her to get an abortion to save Mario from
Witt's wrath and the threat of prosecution for statutory rape.

Well, Kat ended up getting hers, hadn't she? *What goes
around, comes around.*

And that bastard no-good Mario. How many times would
she let him break her heart?

Trisha's fingers were sweaty as she shifted down for another curve. The thought of murder was appealing, very
appealing. Disgusted with herself, she pushed the cigarette
lighter in and considered making a buy. A little coke would
lift the old spirits and maybe give her enough guts to go
through with her murderous plans. She shook out a Salem
Light and placed it between her lips.

The cellular phone jangled and she smiled to herself.
Mario had changed his mind. Steering with one hand, she
picked up the phone. "Yes?" she said breathlessly and was
disappointed when Nelson's voice crackled in the receiver.

"I thought you should know," he said, his voice heavy with
despair. "It looks like Adria might be London."

"Shit, no—"

The cigarette lighter clicked and Trisha wedged the phone
between her shoulder and head while she stuck the burner to the
end of her cigarette and pulled in a deep breath. Her eyes never
left the road. Smoke puffed from the corner of her mouth.

"I don't believe it, either, but Sweeny seems to think he's
got proof positive."

"That little prick wouldn't know his own dick if it weren't

attached to his balls." She shoved the lighter back into the dash and took in another lungful.

"Do you always have to be so crude?"

"Has the press found out?"

"Not yet. But they will. Zach's running wild—"

"Zach?" she said, frowning as she blew out a stream of smoke that temporarily fogged the windshield.

"Yeah, he's back in town."

"With the bitch?"

"I think so." Trisha's blood ran cold as her suspicions proved true. No wonder Mario was busy tonight. "Jason's trying to keep the story quiet. He doesn't want anyone outside the immediate family to know—least of all, Adria—but Zach rushed out of here like a madman and I think he's going to tell her."

"Shit." Trisha's world began crumbling at a faster rate. First Mario, now everything that went with being a Danvers—her whole life, her future—falling into little pieces. Because of Adria.

"My feelings exactly."

"Where is she?"

"Get this," Nelson said, his voice tinged with irony, "Zachary's got her hidden in the damned hotel. Jason already checked, though that little creep of a manager, Rich, wouldn't tell him which room. Jason warned the guy that he'd fire him, but he still held his tongue."

"Zach must've threatened him with bodily harm." She braked for a red light.

"Probably. Sounds like our brother," Nelson said morosely.

"This just gets better and better," Trisha said, her mind already spinning ahead.

"Or worse and worse," Nelson complained.

"Why does Zach care if Adria knows?"

"You tell me, Trisha. You're always so good at reading everyone's emotions."

It all suddenly clicked into place. Her suspicions crystallized and she smiled wickedly to herself as she jammed the

Alpha into first just as the light changed. The tires chirped as she stepped on the accelerator. "I bet our stoic, love-'em-and-leave-'em brother has fallen in love with her," Trisha said, disgusted at the thought of it. "I can't stand it. She's his . . . our . . . oh, hell, this is fucking unbelievable." She cruised through another yellow light. "You know, this could work to our advantage."

"I don't see how."

"You will," Trisha promised as she hung up the phone and turned toward the river. She flipped on the radio and began to sing along to an old Tina Turner song that blasted over the speakers. Finally she was certain she could deal with Adria Nash.

After Zach left, Adria went right to work. She called the police and talked to Detective Stinson, though she learned nothing new. When she phoned a rental car agency and reserved a car, before dialing Zach's mechanic and leaving a message that she wanted her vehicle back as soon as possible. Her next move would be to find a way to hire a good lawyer, something she'd been avoiding.

She'd been approached several times since the press release and she had over a dozen business cards of smooth-talking men in expensive wool suits who had offered to look over the facts of her case. A few had hinted that they would work for her on contingency, with no money up front, but they all had seemed so slick . . . too smart for their own good, and she hadn't been ready to hire anyone yet.

Now, things had changed.

And for the worse.

She flopped back on the bed and draped her forearm over her eyes.

Forget him!

If only she could, but everywhere she went, she thought of Zach, remembered the craggy angles of his face, felt again the tingling sensations of his lips touching hers, turned liquid inside with the want of him.

Fool! Do you think he's moping over you? You were probably just a quick distraction to him . . . and yet . . .

The phone rang and she nearly jumped out of her skin. Zach. It had to be Zach. No one else knew she was here. She picked up the receiver and forced her voice to remain calm. "Hello?"

"Adria," a female voice cooed. "So you are here."

Her heart somersaulted as she recognized Trisha's voice.

"Zach wouldn't tell anyone where you were, but I took a stab in the dark and though the desk is downright rude about letting me know your room number, they did deign to put me through." She sounded irritated.

"What do you want?" she asked, wondering if she really could be related to this woman.

"I need to talk to you."

"Now?"

"You have better plans?" Without waiting for an answer, Trisha said, "I'm in the parking garage now. I could meet you in the bar in five minutes, or . . . if you'd rather go somewhere else. . . ."

"The bar's fine," Adria said. "I'll see you there." So much for being safe, she thought, but really didn't care who knew where she was. She was tired of looking over her shoulder and jumping at shadows. Maybe it was time to flush out the culprit who had jumped her and in so doing, find out exactly what happened nearly twenty years ago. She ran a brush through her hair, slipped a jacket over her jeans and blouse, and locked the door behind her.

She nearly stumbled over the security guard, a beefy, red-haired man with a pockmarked face, posted in the hallway. "Mr. Danvers requested that I stay here," he said, almost apologetically. "You going out?"

"Just for a little while."

"Where to?"

"Just downstairs," she said, disliking the man for intruding into her privacy, though she knew he was only doing his job. She had only to recall her recent attack to remind herself to be on her guard. Trisha, who seemed harmless, might be more dangerous than she appeared. Adria hurried into the elevator, tapped her fingernails nervously on the rail as the car descended, and bolted through the doors as they opened silently.

Zach was waiting for her.

Lounging against a post, propped up by one denim-covered shoulder, arms crossed over his chest, he stood, staring at the elevator, like a cougar waiting to pounce on unsuspecting prey. "Goin' somewhere?" he drawled and a slow, sexy smile curved across his jaw.

A nest of butterflies erupted in her stomach.

"No, I—" she stammered, then held her tongue. "Have you been down here the whole time, waiting for me to try and escape?"

The smile disappeared. His eyes flashed angrily. "You're giving yourself too much credit. Way too much."

"Then don't get in my way," she warned, trying to brush past him.

"Where do you think you're going?"

"To the bar."

"Thirsty?"

"Is there any particular reason you're being a jerk, or is it just your nature?"

"Ouch."

"You asked for it. Now, not that it's any of your business, but I'm meeting your sister."

"Trisha's here?" he asked, throwing a dark look toward the glass doors of the bar.

"Waiting. So if you'll excuse me."

He didn't. Instead he strode ahead of her. He threw open the door and scanned the room with eyes set into a hard-as-nails expression. His dark gaze landed squarely on his sister, who was sitting in a corner booth, holding a stemmed glass of clear liquid in one hand and a burning cigarette in the other. With Adria at his heels, he crossed the patterned carpet. "What the hell's going on here?" he demanded, his lips barely moving.

"Just thought I'd have a drink with my . . . *our* sister." Trisha tapped the ash from her cigarette. "Join us?"

Adria's breath seemed to stop.

"Oh, God, don't tell me I ruined the surprise," Trisha said, pretending dismay, her fingers fluttering over her chest in mock surprise. "Didn't he tell you?" She threw her brother a look of shocked dismay and clucked her tongue. "Honestly, Zach, she deserves to know, don't you think?" She switched her gaze back to Adria. "They, meaning my brothers and their detectives, have nearly located Ginny Slade and it looks very much like you're going to end up the winner in all this. Oh, Zach, don't pretend to be so stricken. I know you knew all about it."

"No one's talked to Ginny yet," he said.

"Only a matter of time."

"Yet?" Adria whispered, hardly believing that after all these months, all the effort, she might be proved to be . . . Her gaze flew to Zachary's and she felt a wrenching deep in her soul. If she were London, then, unless Zach wasn't Witt's son . . . She knew her face drained of color and her knees felt wobbly for a second, though she'd known all along this could happen. Wasn't it what she'd wanted?

"This isn't a bad time to let the cat out of the bag, is it?" Trisha asked as Zachary slid into the booth opposite her, yanked on Adria's arm, and pulled her onto the soft leather bench beside him.

"Why didn't you tell me?" Adria asked, turning bewildered eyes on Zach. Zach, who had protected her. Zach, who had stolen her away. Zach, who had made love to her. She could barely breathe.

"I just found out."

Trisha's gaze moved from her brother to Adria. "This makes things complicated, doesn't it?"

Zach glared at his sister. "It's always been complicated."

"I know, but I mean for you two."

The waiter came by with a refill for Trisha. Zach ordered a beer. Adria, swallowing hard, asked for chardonnay and noticed the curl of Trisha's lip. "White wine, the drink of choice in—was it—Elk Hollow, Montana?"

"Stop it, Trisha," Zach warned.

"Oh, little brother, you've got it bad, don't you? And for your half-sister. That's a real pisser." She picked up her first drink and finished it off. "A real pisser."

The waiter dropped off fresh glasses and Adria picked up the stem of her wineglass with trembling fingers. Her nerves were strung tight, but seemed jangled. Too much was happening too fast—she couldn't absorb everything. "Why did you want to meet me?" she asked.

Trisha's smile was brittle. "To tell you to stay away from Mario Polidori." At the lift of Adria's eyebrows, Trisha explained. "We go back a long time."

"I'm not seeing him."

"Oh?" Trisha obviously didn't believe her.

"Not the way you mean. I met him for drinks. We talked business."

"He held your hand, laughed at your jokes." Trisha took another drag and squashed her cigarette in the tray. "Look, don't play games with me, okay? Mario's off limits."

"Who do you think you are?" Adria asked, her temper, already frayed, finally splitting apart. "Both of you. You," she turned on Zach, "trying to keep me a virtual prisoner, and you, Trisha, telling me whom I can or cannot see. Give me a break. I'm outta here—" She started to leave, but Zach caught her arm and held her firmly against him.

"Just a second," he said, then turned his blazing eyes on his sister. "Is that it?"

"Not quite." Trisha shook her head. "Just in case you're not quite sure about a few things, I think you should know that if you two are involved, it's a big problem."

"Back off, Trisha," Zach growled.

"If you're London, Adria, and it's starting to look like you are, then you'd better accept the fact that Zach's your half-brother. I've heard all the rumors and so has Zach for all of his life, and I'll bet you both are banking on the fact that he's supposed to be Anthony Polidori's son. He's not."

Zach's jaw clenched so tight the bone showed beneath the skin of his chin. "I'm warning you—"

"That's right. Mom checked it out years ago. Remember, Zach, when you accused me of listening at cracks and peeking through keyholes? Well, I did. Every chance I got. It was the only way I could survive, the only way I knew what was going on. And I learned a helluva lot. I remember the day Mom, through rather discreet methods, found out Anthony Polidori's blood type. She was devastated because it proved beyond a shadow of a doubt that there was no way he could be your father. You, her favorite, the son she hoped didn't belong to Witt."

Adria felt sick inside.

"So, if you two have been screwing around, just remember that you're closer than you ever thought possible."

"Shut up, Trisha."

"It's sick, Zach. Just plain sick."

"Let's go—" He pushed Adria toward the end of the seat.

"Wouldn't the press love to hear this new little twist," Trisha asked. "I wonder what they'd say about all this . . . well, incest is such an ugly word. It could get tricky," she added, before plucking another cigarette from the open pack sitting on the table.

"Do anything of the sort and I'll wring your neck," Zach warned.

"Sure, you will. Christ, Zach, give up the melodrama. It doesn't suit you."

"Try me," he warned. "I wouldn't push it, if I were you."

Adria couldn't stand it another minute. She had to get away, to think clearly, to breathe fresh air, to put some distance between her and all the horrid, tangled emotions. Barely able to find her feet, she scrambled from the booth. She started running, across the carpet, through the doors, past the lobby, and outside to the night. Rain was pouring from the sky, peppering the street and gurgling through the gutters. People on the sidewalk huddled under umbrellas, their collars turned to the wind as they rushed from street corner to street corner, under the shimmering glow of street lamps.

Adria kept running, around the block, darting through traffic, ignoring the blast of horns, feeling the cold, wet drops catch in her hair and slide beneath the collar of her jacket. Her body ached, her heart felt battered, and she was certain she'd never been so alone, so alienated in her life. Oh God, how had she trusted him, touched him, fallen in love with him? The city was cloying, the truth about the Danvers family as dark as the night.

"Adria!" Zach's voice boomed from somewhere behind her and she nearly stumbled over a man sitting in an alcove, his legs sticking out.

"Spare change?" he begged as she raced onward, blindly, running to an unknown destination and away from all the pain, the rage, the fatal mistake of loving the wrong man. Tears mingled with the rain and she gasped. Why had she come to Portland? Why? What did she care if she did turn out to be London?

"Stop! Adria!" He was getting closer—she could hear the soles of his boots slapping the wet pavement and she willed her legs to move faster. *Run! Run! Run!* Get away. Go back to being Adria Nash. Give up this dream of being London Danvers! Leave Zachary forever!

At the crosswalk, she stepped off the curb, against the light. A car sped past her, nearly clipping her leg and throwing up a sheet of water that drenched the lower half of her body.

Zach's arms clamped around her and she screamed, "No!"

thing about the kidnapping. I was only a child when it happened and I lived in New York City . . . Ah, well, I've rambled on, haven't I? I'll call Virginia down and you can speak with her in here. Please, please, have a seat. I'll have Martha bring you drinks—tea, lemonade, something stronger—?"

"We're fine," Zach assured her.

"Yes, well, I'm sure there's something. Now, if it does turn out that she's this Slade woman . . . oh, dear, well, she can't be looking after Chloe now, can she?" Still fluttering on, she left them alone in a room decorated in soft taupe shades.

Adria sat on the edge of a love seat and Zach stood near the window, staring out across the bay.

While Mrs. Bassett was away, a maid slipped into the room and left a silver tea service on a glass-topped coffee table.

Footsteps echoed in the hallway and Adria braced herself. Would she recognize the woman who may have stolen her away from her natural parents, the woman who had changed the course of her life forever?

"—but I'm not expecting anyone," a reed-thin voice protested.

"I know, but they say they're friends of yours, long-lost acquaintances."

"Really, Mrs. Bassett, I don't know anyone—"

The voice, like the scent of a sachet locked for years in a forgotten drawer, drifted into the room and caused Adria's heart to skip a beat. The floor seemed to fall away from her feet as a woman stepped into the room. She was small, birdlike, with graying dark hair and plain features, but when her gaze landed on Adria, she stopped stock-still. "No," she mouthed, but emitted no sound. What little bit of color had been in her face drained quickly away. "Oh, dear God," she whispered faintly. Recovering slightly, she asked, "Who— who are you?" She forced a detached smile, but her lower lip trembled slightly.

"Take a guess," Zach suggested.

"I don't know—"

"Sure you do, Ginny. This is London."

Virginia's eyes darted from one to the other. "London?"

"London Danvers, the girl you took to Montana to live with Victor and Sharon Nash, the girl you pawned off as your daughter though your own child had been dead for years."

"No!" she said, but she licked her lips nervously. "Mrs. Bassett, I don't know what kind of lies these people have been telling you, but—"

"The police have been called, Virginia," Velma said calmly. "If they're lying—"

"Oh, Mother Mary!" Her hand flew to her chest, covering heart. "You didn't—"

"Why don't you explain everything," Zach said, motioning to a chair. "There's a chance we can work something out."

"Oh, my Lord—" she protested, but dropped onto the sofa and gazed out the window to the clouds rolling over the green waters of the bay. Tears collected in the corners of her eyes and ran slowly down her cheeks as her gritty determination gave way to acceptance of what had to be. "I'm so sorry. So, so sorry."

"Tell us, Ginny," Zach said, relentless while Adria's heart went out to the woman who seemed to have aged twenty years since stepping into the room.

Velma Bassett stood near the doorway, bracing herself on the painted woodwork as she stared at the nanny she had trusted with her child for over eighteen months.

"I—I didn't want to do it," Ginny said, reaching into her pocket and finding a handkerchief to dab at her face. "But it was so much money."

"What was?"

"I was promised fifty thousand dollars if I would take London away."

Adria's heart twisted painfully.

"I knew it was wrong, but I couldn't resist. All I had to do was disappear with the girl."

"But why? And who?" Zach demanded.

"I don't know."

Adria could hold her tongue no longer. "But someone paid you, met with you—"

"It was all arranged over the telephone. At first I thought it was a joke. Then I got a package. Ten thousand dollars. More money than I'd ever seen in my life, and I was called again, offered another forty thousand dollars. All I had to do was leave town. Five thousand dollars more was sent to a private post offfice, and the rest when I got to Denver. From there I was to head anywhere, to put as much distance between myself and Portland as I could. It was supposed to happen earlier, but London wouldn't go to bed and we almost didn't make it. I was so scared, but so desperate. Oh, God, what am I going to do now?"

"Well, you're sure as hell not going to take care of my daughter any longer," Mrs. Bassett said. "I'll pay you severance pay, whatever it takes, but, believe you me, you'll not be spending another night in this house!" So enraged she was shaking, she hurried out of the room and the soles of her prim red pumps clacked loudly on the steps as she hurried upstairs. "Chloe? Where are you?"

Ginny shoved a strand of hair from her face and her fingers quivered. "How did you find me?"

"It took some time," Zach admitted.

Adria leaned closer. "But surely you know who paid you?"

She shook her head and turned guilt-riddled eyes on Adria. "I don't have any idea."

"Man? Woman?"

"Really. I don't know. I never met with anyone and the money was all in cash—small bills."

She looked so miserable—her cheeks hollow, her eyes vacant as she dabbed at them—that Adria believed her.

"Someone paid you off."

"Yes."

"Someone with a lot of money."

She nodded, but Adria got the impression she wasn't listening, that she was remembering the past and how she'd escaped with someone else's daughter.

"You'll have to talk to the police," Zach said.

"I know."

"It may not be easy."

She turned haunted eyes up at Zach. "It never has been," she admitted. "For twenty years I've looked over my shoulder, expecting this day to come. I knew you were back in Portland, you know," she added, staring at Adria. "I heard it on the news. Saw your face, listened to your story, knew that you'd be reunited with your family."

"You could have run," Adria said.

Ginny gave a self-deprecating little snort. "Where to? I really didn't think you'd find me." She pushed herself upright. "You look just like her, you know. It's . . . well, it's scary."

"So I've heard."

"Why didn't you come forward for the reward?" Zach asked.

She just stared for a minute. "Because Witt Danvers would have killed me for taking his little girl." She cleared her throat. "Would you give me a few minutes to get my things?" she asked with a weak smile. "Then I'll go with you to talk to the police."

"Fine," Adria said.

"I don't think we should let her out of our sight," Zach cut in.

"Don't worry, Mr. Danvers," Ginny said, studying Zachary as if for the first time, trying to picture him as the man who'd grown up from the rebellious son of the richest man in Portland—the hellion who had given his father fits. "It's time for this to end."

She left and walked to a door at the foot of the stairs.

So, it had come to this, Ginny thought, slowly descending the stairs. Somehow, deep in her heart, she had always known there would be a reckoning, a time when she'd have to admit her complicity in little London's disappearance. And the money she'd imagined would set her up for life had slowly disappeared.

She walked into her tiny room and felt weary. She'd hoped to be free of rich people and catering to their whims, looking after children they should have cared for themselves, but as her finances had dwindled, she'd had to return to the only way she knew how to make a living. Even the money she'd received from the Nashes hadn't saved her. Now, she'd spent most of her adult life being little more than an indentured servant. She surveyed her tiny room with its cheery curtains hung over impossibly small windows and nearly laughed at her own naivety. Fifty thousand. She should have asked for double that or triple. Even then, it might not have been enough. Money had always run through her fingers like water.

On the floor was a braided rug, a cast-off from her employers. The quilt she'd made herself but it had faded. Like she had.

She closed her eyes and sank onto the mattress wondering if she should just end it all. To face the police. The press. The Danvers family.

Unthinkable.

And yet she knew she didn't have the heart to take her own life. Not like Katherine Danvers . . . which seemed impossible. Witt's second wife was the last woman Ginny would have thought would have committed suicide. She was so full of life, so vibrant.

But she'd lost her child. Because of you, and you know how that feels, how morose one can get, how depressed.

Tears burned the back of her eyelids.

She heard the creak of a footstep and thought it was coming from upstairs. They were waiting. Probably impatient. She should really get her things together, even though she knew she'd end up in jail and her meager belongings would be confiscated.

She sniffed, a tear sliding from the corner of her eye.

Again she heard a footstep and it sounded closer . . . in the hallway?

She decided to pull herself together before Zachary found her down here blubbering like a baby.

Angry at herself, she ran a hand over her eyes as she opened them. She pulled her suitcase from the top shelf of the closet and opened the bureau drawers. Her stomach felt as tight as a clenched fist as she haphazardly tossed in some of her clothes.

Prison.

She shuddered, couldn't imagine herself there. She blinked again, crying softly, holding back her sobs as she walked into her small bathroom for a tissue. As she dabbed at her eyes, she thought she saw a movement in the reflection of the mirror over the medicine cabinet, as if the shower curtain were fluttering.

All of the sudden she felt cold and realized the window was open.

Had she left it that way?

No . . .

Oh, God.

Through the haze of tears she glimpsed a dark figure just before the curtain was thrown back and her attacker leapt over the edge of the tub.

She gasped.

Before she could scream a gloved hand covered her mouth.

Oh God!

Her vision cleared.

She was staring into eyes she recognized.

Her heart froze.

Surely this was the person who had paid her off, had warned her never to tell the truth.

She struggled wildly, adrenaline pumping through her bloodstream. She kicked and scratched and fought but it was too late. She was too weak. She was forced back against the wall, a towel bar gouging her shoulders.

And then she saw the knife.

Small.

Deadly.

Wicked.

It gleamed in the dimly lit room.

No! She fought harder, but she was no match for her attacker, who had a small pillow and shoved it over her face. She tried to drag in air, to scream, to save herself, but it was too late. Her attacker was too strong. Too determined. Her vain efforts at kicking and hitting pitifully feeble.

Her lungs were on fire.

Pain blinded her and she struggled frantically.

But it was no use.

With a sickening realization, Ginny Slade knew she was about to die.

"So what do I call you now?" Zach asked as he paced to the window. "Adria? Or London?"

"Adria," she said, her throat thick, her eyes misting. This was the first of their good-byes. "I hope to you, I'll always be Adria."

The minutes, recorded by the grandfather clock in the hall, ticked by; outside, the ever-present traffic moved sluggishly up the hill.

Adria wondered how much longer she had with Zach, how few minutes. Her heart felt as if it were breaking into a thousand pieces as she stared at him. His broad shoulders were rigid, tense with strain; one thumb was hooked through a belt loop and his fingers hung near the faded denim of his fly. His jaw was dark with a beard shadow and his eyes, beneath heavy black brows, were narrowed suspiciously. He shifted from one foot to the other, pretending interest in the view from the bay window before glancing back to the stairwell.

"Shit, what could be taking so long?"

"She's packing her things . . ." Adria said, but even she was conscious of the time.

Mrs. Bassett, with a golden-haired child of about seven in tow, clomped down the stairs and hurried back into the room. "I don't know how I can ever thank you enough," Mrs. Bassett said, her eyes shifting quickly to the stairwell and back again. "To think that I trusted her with my precious Chloe. Oh, God, it just makes me shudder. I called Harry and he wants to press charges against her for false representation or whatever you call it. He's phoning our lawyer right now. Oh, dear." Kissing her child's crown, she said, "Why don't you go practice your piano, baby."

"Don't want to," the girl said churlishly, though her mother was shepherding her toward the upright near the fireplace. Chloe crossed her chubby arms stubbornly in front of her chest.

"Well . . ." Wringing her hands, Mrs. Bassett spied the basket of cakes near the tea service. "Here, then, how about a sweet?" She placed the platter in front of the girl. "Oh, my, I've completely forgotten my manners. Could I please offer you a cup of tea? The least I could do, you know."

"Thanks," Adria said, but Zachary only shook his head and glowered at the stairwell as if he were afraid Ginny might disappear again.

Mrs. Bassett frowned suddenly. "I thought you called the police."

"We did. They should be here any minute—" Adria said.

"Is there another way out of the basement?" Zach asked suddenly.

"Oh, no . . . well, there's a coal chute, but it's been closed for years, and some old cellar stairs, but they're boarded over. If there were a fire, the windows are large enough—"

"Christ!" Moving with the speed of a cheetah, he raced out of the parlor, across the foyer, and down the stairs with lightning speed.

How could he have been so stupid? Vaulting over the rail

e stairs, he landed loudly on the cement floor and felt the
l rush of fresh air before he saw the curtains fluttering
selessly in the breeze.

The basement was dark and he walked unerringly to a
mall, cozy room in a back corner where the bedroom light
lowed warmly. "Ginny?" he called, feeling an eerie breeze,
the premonition of doom scurrying up the back of his neck.

Muscles rigid, Zach stepped into the room. A suitcase,
lying open, had been thrown on the bed. Clothes dangled
from hangers in the open closet. One drawer in a tiny bureau
was askew, underwear and nightgowns falling onto the floor.
"Ginny?" he called again, but there was still no answer.

The hairs on the back of his neck raised as he crossed the
room and threw open the door to a tiny bathroom. Red
splashes were everywhere. Blood stained the walls and splattered the sink and toilet. Ginny Slade was lying on the
cracked linoleum. Her tongue hung limply from her mouth,
her eyes stared blankly at the ceiling, and her wrists were
slashed, blood still oozing from the open wounds. A sharp
knife was clenched in her right fist.

Zach stepped back, recoiling from the room splattered in
blood and the sightless eyes that stared up at him. "Call 911!"
he yelled up the stairs. "Adria, call the police! We need an
ambulance."

He heard the thunder of footsteps and turned to find Adria
on the landing. "Don't come down here and for God's sake
keep the kid upstairs!" he ordered.

"What—" She stared past him to the blood creeping from
the bathroom and onto the bedroom carpet. "Oh, God."

"It's Ginny—call 911!"

"Mrs. Bassett already has."

But Zach wasn't listening. He forced himself to return to
search for a pulse, to find some sign of life, but he knew that
it was useless. Ginny Slade, the only witness to what had happened to London Danvers all those years ago, was dead.

24

"You're saying she didn't kill herself?" Adria asked after giving her statement to the police. She was seated in an interrogation room, her chair on one side of an old Formica-topped table, Zach leaning on wainscoting near the door. The room was bare save for the ever-present smell of smoke, an overflowing ashtray, and a trash can half filled with empty plastic coffee cups.

The man in charge was John Fullmer, an investigator who wore thick glasses and whose one vanity seemed to be to disguise his baldness by combing long, sandy-colored strands of hair from the back of his head forward.

Fullmer was full of nervous energy. He smoked and chewed gum at the same time, alternately popping his stick of Wrigley's spearmint and taking a drag from his Camel.

It had been hours since Zach had discovered Ginny's body and Adria had believed that Ginny, knowing that she would be exposed as a kidnapper, had decided to end her own life. Fullmer had other ideas.

Warming her hands around a strong cup of coffee, Adria asked, "But how would someone have known where to find her?"

"We're not sure yet, and we don't like to give out the kind of information that only the killer would know, but there are clues. The window had been forced, so it looks like someone was in the house, waiting for her." He took off his glasses and polished them with the hem of his shirt. His gum snapped loudly.

Zach stared at Adria. "It's because she's left-handed," he said flatly. "The knife was in her right hand and she was left-handed. The slashes were angled wrong."

The detective's head snapped up and he stared at Zach, long and hard. "You know that?"

"I remember." Zach's gaze traveled to the center of the room but Adria guessed he was miles away, lost in a time when he was only a boy.

"How?" Adria asked.

"Because once . . . a long time ago when London was still living with us, Ginny had a pair of scissors—used them for mending, I think. She left them out once and I picked them up. I had to open some package and couldn't find my knife. I tried to use her damned scissors, but they didn't work. I couldn't figure it out for a minute, then I discovered they were left-handed. Unique at the time. Ginny caught me and had a fit, told me to leave her things alone." He shrugged. "We didn't get along all that well." His gaze focused on Adria again. "But that's no surprise."

The detective drew on his cigarette, then crushed it in the full tray. "I don't have an official report on cause of death. We'll have to wait for the M.E. for that, but there were signs of a struggle—footprints in the blood and the splatter pattern—that suggests she was killed. It looks like someone subdued her, took the knife, wrapped the fingers of her right hand around it and opened her veins. End of story."

Adria shuddered and rubbed her arms.

The detective dumped the ashtray into the trash, before lighting up again.

They talked for a while more, then were allowed to leave. "Look, we know you two didn't do old Ginny in," the detective said, handing them each a card, "but we might have a few more questions . . ."

Zach's eyes met Adria's. "You can find us through Danvers

International, or the Hotel Danvers in Portland," he said, scribbling the numbers on the back of a business card for his construction company in Bend.

They left the station and Adria felt drained, her entire life turned inside out.

So she was London Danvers.

So she would inherit millions of dollars.

So what?

"Come on, I'll buy you dinner," Zach offered, though he looked as tired as she. Beneath the shadow of his beard his tanned skin seemed paler, his eyes haunted. The strain was telling on them both and she wondered how long they could keep up this charade, pretending that the attraction they felt for each other didn't exist. "I know a great place in Chinatown. We'll stay in town tonight, then go home and break the news."

Home. Would she ever think of Portland as home?

She shuddered to think how quickly Ginny's life had ended. "Who do you think could have done it?"

"I wish I knew," he said, frowning as they stepped outside where darkness had fallen. The wind blowing in off the ocean was cold, cutting in icy gusts that climbed the steep hills of the city; it swept through her jacket and cut her to the bone.

Zach took her hand in his. She tried to pull away, but his fingers tightened over hers as they walked the three blocks to the space where he'd parked the rental car.

Once inside the Ford, he checked the mirror, then melded with traffic. "Watch in your side-view," he said, moving from one lane to the other.

"You think someone is following us."

"Good guess, don't you think?"

"Here in San Francisco?" she asked, but she'd leaped to the same conclusions as he, the same one drawn by the police.

"You think that we led the murderer . . ." Her voice trailed off and she stared hard in the mirror, watching other cars switch lanes, seeing nothing out of the ordinary.

"Obviously there was a conspiracy of some kind years

ago," Zach said, his brows drawing together. "And it didn't involve your mother or . . . or Witt. So we have to assume that whoever wanted you out of the picture then, was willing to kill Ginny to keep his secret." His fingers tapped upon the steering wheel. "It makes me wonder about Kat. Was it suicide or murder."

"Oh God." Adria shivered. "You think the two deaths, Ginny's and Kat's, were linked."

"Not just linked but committed by the same killer."

"But who?" she whispered.

"Could be anyone."

"Someone in the family." Her stomach knotted. Someone she was related to.

"Maybe."

"Or someone from the Polidori family," she said, though the list of suspects was shrinking. True, Anthony Polidori could have been behind the kidnapping and she was certain that he was having her followed, but the Danvers heirs as well could have been a part of the kidnapping. Jason was power-hungry, Trisha, a wounded animal wanting to hurt her father as much as she was hurt by him. Nelson would have been too young, only about fourteen at the time, and Zach, he had been a kid, too.

Satisfied that they weren't being tailed, Zachary drove to Chinatown and parked in an alley. The restaurant was small, noisy, dimly lit, and packed nearly to capacity. Dishes rattled, people spoke in sharp foreign phrases, and grease sizzled through the open window to the kitchen. They were offered a table for two near the kitchen and Adria didn't object, though she could barely understand the waitress or any of the patrons who all seemed to speak rapid-fire Chinese.

Still, she was grateful for the crowd. It made things easier. Being alone with Zachary was the difficult part. They ate hot-and-sour soup, spicy chicken, and some shrimp dish that was so hot her nose ran, and washed it all down with Chinese beer. But the food seemed tasteless and she couldn't forget

Ginny Slade's ashen face, her unseeing eyes, and all the blood in the small bathroom.

After the meal, she drank a thin tea with a flowery aroma that filtered up her nose and brought back a memory—harsh and ugly. The night of the attack, she'd smelled something sweet as this blend—the underlying scent of jasmine. Her fingers slipped. The cup slid to the table and rolled, spilling tea across the varnished surface. Hot tea dripped from the table to her thighs.

"Adria?" Zach asked.

She knew the instant the smell of jasmine reached her nostrils who had attacked her.

"What is it?" Zach demanded, staring at her with harsh gray eyes.

"Everything." She started wiping up the tea, refusing to look at him, telling herself over and over again she had to be wrong. But she knew. She *knew.* He grabbed her hand, squeezing it, refusing to let her keep mopping the spill with her napkin.

"What?"

"I think I know who attacked me in the motel," she said unevenly, wishing she didn't know the truth.

"What?"

"The person who sent me the nasty notes."

"How?"

"This tea." She motioned to the cups on the table. "It's jasmine, the same scent that was on the person who attacked me."

A knot formed at the hinge of his jaw and he sniffed the brew. Denial seemed about to fall from his tongue before he shoved the cup of tea away, sloshing hot tea onto the table. "Eunice," he bit out, his eyes mere slits.

Adria nodded mutely, unable to form the words that hovered between them—that Zachary's mother had killed Ginny Slade.

* * *

"I need to speak with you. Alone." Eunice left the message on Zach's cell phone. "There's something important I need to tell you and the only way you'll ever learn the truth is to talk to me. Please, Zach, I know you think awful things about me, but they're just not true. Let me explain what really happened. You're the only one I can trust." She slid the receiver into the cradle of the wall phone in her kitchen and didn't doubt for a minute that Zach would show up.

Soon.

As she sat at the kitchen table and read the newspaper article about Ginny Slade's murder, Eunice knew that it was only a matter of hours before Zach would come and accuse her of killing Ginny.

He wouldn't believe her when she denied it.

Frowning, she glanced through the paned windows to the greenish waters of Lake Oswego, as if in looking at the murky water she could figure out what to do. Few times in life had Eunice given up and she wasn't about to start now.

But who had killed the wimpy little nursemaid? Surely someone associated with the family; perhaps even a family member.

One of her own children?

Someone clever enough to know that Zach, and probably the police would accuse her. Someone, perhaps, who knew that Kat's death hadn't been a suicide, that Eunice had played a vital role in the second Mrs. Witt Danvers's demise.

"Bloody hell," she muttered, angry that her plans had gone awry. Why hadn't that little money-grubbing bitch left town? Why hadn't she backed off from her claims to be London, Witt's most precious baby?

It made her sick. Even now her stomach roiled and filled the back of her throat with a horrid taste and the rage she felt, the white-hot fury, pumped through her blood. She'd borne Witt four fine children. *Four!* And he'd turned away from them when that gold digger had batted her fake eyelashes at him.

Foolish, foolish old man.

He'd gotten what he deserved by losing his special child and finding his arm-candy wife in bed with his son. Her knees buckled at the thought of Zach and Kat. Sick, that's what it had been. Dirty. Incestuous; and now . . . now he was taking up with that horrid woman's child.

It was unthinkable.

Eunice had no doubt that Adria was London; the girl's resemblance to Kat was eerie. It made Eunice's skin crawl. If only Zach had been sired by Anthony Polidori, everything would have been better. So much easier. Cleaner.

As it was . . .

Eunice shivered and rubbed her arm where a huge bruise had formed when she'd tackled Adria in that horrid dive of a motel. She was sore and still limped because of the attack that hadn't quite worked. She'd been so angry, so worked up, so frenzied. She remembered lying in the dark, waiting, knowing that Adria, like Kat, was with Zach.

Jesus, why didn't he learn? Why was he drawn to his own stepmother and her daughter? His half-sister? Eunice thought she might throw up at the thought and she began to shake violently.

Calm down . . . you must remain calm. That's the only way. You need to deal with Zach. Soon. And possibly London! God, why hadn't Ginny Slade kept her end of the damned bargain. No doubt Zach knew all about the kidnapping and he would have deduced his own mother's part in the crime.

For a second, she considered running. There might still be time to get to Canada or even Mexico.

And then what?

Katherine will win.

London will win.

"No!" she ground out, her fists clenching so hard her fingernails dug deep into her palms.

She had to finish what she'd started.

The next step was facing Zach.

She knew her children well and understood Zach better than the others. By now, he would have figured out that she was behind the attacks against his precious Adria and he'd want a face-off.

Well, he'd get one. She walked from the kitchen to the master bathroom and opened the medicine chest. An array of vials and bottles were lined up on the slim glass shelves, the result of her complaints of nagging aches and pains that no one doctor could pinpoint. Because there had been no pain. Despite her claims to the medical profession, she felt as fit and able as she had at thirty-five, perhaps even stronger, but she'd managed to collect samples and prescriptions from nearly a dozen doctors and combined with her own basic knowledge of chemistry, anatomy and medicine, she was able to create her own little "cocktails."

She remembered slipping a mixture of Valium and sleeping pills into Kat's vodka in her hotel room on the night of her death. While Kat had been out, Eunice had slipped into the room, compliments of a key she'd lifted from Kat's purse while Kat had been in the hotel bar. She'd entered the room while Kat was still ordering drinks. It had been so easy to doctor the bottle in the room, then wait on the balcony while Kat poured herself another drink and eventually ended up in the shower.

Kat had been weak.

Losing London had nearly killed the bitch. But not quite. She'd needed another push. Literally.

And Eunice had only been too glad to give it to her. It had been too easy to entice the pathetic woman onto the veranda.

"Mama," Eunice said now, in the same little girl's voice she'd used to lure her nemesis onto the balcony. "Mama." Kat had been so disoriented, she'd never realized the trap until it was too late and then her eyes had widened in terror and surprise just before Eunice sprang and pushed her over the edge.

Eunice had thought she'd gotten away with murder.

Kat's death had been written off as suicide due to depression and an unfortunate overdose.

But someone had known the truth, Eunice deduced as she picked up the vials and hypodermic needle she wanted and closed the cabinet door. The mirror slammed into place and she was suddenly staring into her own haunted eyes.

Yes, she'd wanted Kat dead.

But she'd had to live with the guilt.

And now, she suspected, someone else had known she was a murderer and was hoping she'd take the fall for Ginny Slade.

Who?

If not one of her own children, which she couldn't accept, what about Anthony or someone from the Polidori clan? Maybe this was payback for Ginny letting them take the heat for London's disappearance . . . no . . .

She frowned, deep creases showing between her eyebrows and around her lips. There was no time for speculation. She still had to deal with Adria—the one woman standing between Witt's fortune and her children. If she wouldn't scare away, then she had to die.

Even though Zach would try to intervene.

Too bad.

Eunice wasn't afraid of dying herself, but, by God, her children were going to get the legacy and inheritance that was rightfully theirs.

Even if Eunice had to commit murder again.

Even if she wouldn't get away with it this time.

Even if Zach tried to stop her.

One way or another, London Danvers was going to die.

It wasn't easy, but Adria and Zach managed to avoid and outrun the press even though the news was out: Adria Nash was London Danvers. The newspapers, radio and television stations had already aired the story all along the West Coast and by the time Zach and Adria arrived in Portland, the media had laid siege to the airport, the Hotel Danvers, Jason's house and even the ranch outside of Bend..

Zach had been cool, taken her hand and pulled her through the throng or reporters and cameramen at Portland International. She'd ducked into his Jeep and managed to avoid making a statement of any kind. If any reporter had followed them into the city, Zach had managed to lose them.

Sooner or later she would be forced to face them, Adria thought as the Jeep rocketed down I-84, headed into the heart of the city.

"You'd think they'd give me a minute to breathe," she grumbled, glancing in the side-view mirror and checking out the traffic trailing behind them.

"Oh, yeah, right." He slid her a glance as he merged into a lane for the freeway heading south. "You asked for it with that press conference."

"I suppose."

"You'd better get used to this," Zach advised. "You are major news, darlin' and until someone comes along who's more newsworthy, you're going to get more attention than a single mouse in a nest of snakes."

"Good analogy."

"I thought so." He managed to slide her a hint of a smile. "Face it. For the next couple of weeks you're going to be way more popular than anyone should be."

"Great," she muttered, but told herself this is what she'd wanted, to be accepted as London Danvers, to finally know the truth about her past.

He picked up his cell phone and listened to messages as he eased the Jeep onto I-5. His smile faded.

"What?" she asked when he hung up.

"There's a change of plan. Something I have to do. Alone. I'll need to drop you off at a police station."

"Who called you?"

He didn't answer, as he cut across traffic toward an exit that she knew led to Macadam Avenue.

"Zach, who called and what did he say?"

"Just be patient." He dialed a number, swore, then left a brief message. "Len, it's Zach Danvers. I'll need police protection for Adria. Call me back ASAP."

"Wait a minute," she insisted as he pulled into the lot of a restaurant near the Willamette River. "What's going on, Zach? You can't just dump me off and leave me. Who the hell called you." His lips tightened at the corners and he avoided her gaze. "Oh, God," she whispered and knew in an instant. "Eunice."

"We'll wait until I hear back from Len."

"Why? What did she want?" Fear caused the back of her throat to go dry. "Oh, God. She wants to meet with you, doesn't she?"

"Just stay here, inside, where you'll be safe. I'll be back soon."

"Are you crazy? I'm not sitting around here waiting while you go and face her.

"She's my mother," he said without any emotion.

"And a killer."

"We think."

"We know, Zach!" Adria grabbed his arm. "You're not going alone. I'll come with you."

"No."

"This is all because of me."

"And if we're right and she's behind this, then you'll be in danger, but I won't. Stay here. I'll call Len and tell him where you are. The police will come by or I'll be back and you'll be safe."

"Oh, yeah, right," she threw back at him as raindrops drizzled down the windshield. "Aren't you the one who said I needed a bodyguard, round-the-clock protection? What if someone followed us here? What if Eunice or whoever is banking on us splitting up? What if she's in collusion with a partner and used the phone call to lure you away?"

"Hell." Obviously the same thoughts had crossed his mind. "Isn't there anyone you can trust?"

"So that you can dump me off? I don't think so! Who would it be? Someone from your family? Trisha? Jason? Or the Polidoris?"

"Okay, okay! I get it." Impatiently he drummed his fingers on the steering wheel as the Jeep idled.

"I think it's better if we stick together."

Instead of arguing, he reached under the seat and pulled out a handgun in a holster.

"You have a gun?" she asked, shocked.

"Yeah. I've been on some jobs where I thought I might need protection. Never used it. But I have a permit for a concealed weapon. Do you know how to use it?"

"I grew up in Montana," she said as he handed her the weapon.

"Could you shoot it if you had to?"

"Yes." But she wasn't certain. Of course if someone threatened her life or Zach's . . . Just the thought of this caused fear to jet through her blood.

"Good."

"Wouldn't it be better if you kept it?" The pistol felt cold and heavy in her hands.

His jaw slid to the side as he shoved his rig into reverse, then wheeled out of the parking lot. "I was thinking if something unforeseen happens and we get split up . . . or . . . something happens to me . . . you'll have the weapon."

"What do you mean 'something happens to me.'"

He pulled out of the lot and drove south along the river. "I don't know. That's the problem. There's no telling what Eunice might do now that she's cornered. She begged me to come alone and speak with her privately, but I don't trust her."

"Why not call the police?"

"I will. When we get there. I don't want them bursting in ahead of time. Just in case she really does have something to say to me alone. . . or with you."

"Fair enough." Her heart pounding, her fingers clenched around the cold weapon, Adria barely noticed the forested cliffs on one side of the road, nor the steely gray waters on the other. Expensive homes peeked through the thick branches and lush shrubbery.

Zach's knuckles showed white as he guided his Jeep through the commercial area of the town, then turned along a narrow, twisting road that rimmed the lake. Splashes of green water were visible through the tall trees and homes perched along the shoreline.

Adria steeled herself and tucked the pistol into her jacket pocket. He glowered through the windshield, his jaw set, his lips a razor-thin line. "What's the plan?"

"I knock on her door and demand answers."

"With me."

"You stay in the Jeep. I'll park a few houses away." He glanced in the rearview mirror. "No one's followed us, so you'll be safe. As long as you keep the pistol."

"I said I'm coming with you. Eunice is probably expecting that you'll do just what you said."

"Listen, Adria, I don't like this—"

"Neither do I, but I'd rather be with you than off waiting somewhere, not knowing what's going on."

"Fine." A muscle worked in his jaw.

"Besides, I think I'm safer with you."

"Let's hope you're right," he growled under his breath as he pulled into the short drive of a two-storied cottage with white siding, dormers and black shutters. Though it was early afternoon, the day was gray and damp and warm interior lights blazed through paned windows. "Cozy, isn't it?" Zach mocked as he reached for his phone, dialed a number and quickly explained the situation to Len Barry of the Portland police, then hung up. "Okay, that should give us just enough time," he said and climbed out of the car.

Adria's palms were sweating , her heart jack-hammering as she and Zach walked up the stone path to a small covered

porch. Flowers bloomed brilliantly in boxes and the shrubbery flanking the house was clipped and neat, a perfect little
home in a prestigious community.

The home of a killer.

Zach didn't wait, but knocked loudly, his fist pounding on
the door. Adria felt the gun, heavy in her pocket, as her heart
pounded in dread.

Would she face the woman who had tried to kill her?

Ginny Slade's murderer?

The door opened and Eunice Danvers Smythe, dressed in
a black velour jogging suit, stood in the empty hallway. Sweat
beaded her forehead and flushed cheeks as if she'd been
working out. "Zach!" she said before her gaze traveled to
Adria. "Oh . . . I wondered if you'd drag her along." She
forced a smile as frigid as the bottom of the Columbia River.
"Come in. Both of you."

"What's this all about, Eunice?" he asked, not moving.

"I think it's time to explain a few things."

"Such as."

"I was going to start with Kat."

Adria's muscles tightened at the mention of her mother and
Zach's harsh expression turned even more severe. "Why not
Ginny?" he asked.

"Because it's best, don't you think, to begin at the beginning."

"We don't have a lot of time."

"Don't tell me. You've called the police." She was walking
down a hallway, her tennis shoes silent on the polished hardwood floors, her gait a little off, the scent of jasmine wafting
after her. "Oh, Zach, you're so predictable. I wish you would
have talked to me first." She glanced over her shoulder, her
gaze landing on Adria again. "Maybe it's better that you're
here after all. Close the door, would you?"

Adria, feeling as if she was truly walking into a lion's den,
complied. Zach waited for her and by the time they walked
into the kitchen, Eunice was already dipping a tea bag into a

cup of hot water. Two cups stood waiting, water already steaming from their porcelain depths. "Would you like some?" she asked, dipping a tea bag into the cup.

Zach shook his head.

"You?" she asked, glancing at Adria and there was a light in her eyes that gave Adria pause.

Something wasn't right here. The smell of jasmine from the tea seeped into the room and a chill as cold as all of December settled in Adria's bones. "I'm fine." What was with the tea?

"What is it you wanted to say, Eunice?" Zach, standing near the kitchen table, didn't take his suspicious gaze from his mother as she busied herself with her tea cup.

To Adria, the entire situation was surreal. She stood next to Zach, waiting to hear the worst, watching a woman who was probably a killer calmly fiddle with her cup.

"Sit down, Zach, and drink a cup of tea or coffee with me," she said, waving him into a chair. "It might be the last one we'll be able to share for a long, long time."

"I'll pass."

"Zach—"

"Get on with it, Eunice." He checked his watch. "The police should be here within a few minutes. You'd better tell me what it was you wanted to say before you have to tell it to a detective."

"You think I killed Ginny," Eunice said.

"You're way ahead of me."

"I didn't do it." She looked up, set the empty bag on the table.

"Right."

"I mean it. I said I should start with Kat . . . or more precisely, London. I did kidnap her and I paid Ginny to make certain she never surfaced again. But she failed." Her lips flattened as she glanced at Adria.

"So you decided to get rid of Ginny."

"No . . . there's someone who's one step ahead of me and trying to blame me for everything that's happening."

"Let's get through the bullshit," Zach said, stepping away from the wall, closing the gap between himself and the woman who had borne him. "I came here for answers, not smoke screens or excuses or lies."

"But it's true," she insisted, her eyes pleading as he stood, looming over the table, a big man with wide shoulders and sleek muscles and a fury so intense his lips had flattened against his teeth.

"Let it go, Eunice. There isn't much time. As I said, the police are on their way."

"I'm telling you the truth, Zach," she swore, almost desperate, her teacup trembling in her hands. She took a long sip and smiled as if at a private joke. "I didn't kill Ginny."

Adria didn't buy it, knew how evil this woman was.

Zach's eyes narrowed. "No?"

"No." Another drink of the hot brew.

"Then what about Kat?"

"Kat?" Eunice whispered, stunned. Every muscle in her body stiffened before she forced them to relax. Her eyes flickered with uncertainty. "She committed suicide. That's what the police decided." Again she swallowed and there was something that didn't quite fit . . .

"I'm not so sure," he said, his gaze skewering his mother's. "In light of what's been happening around here, I've asked them to reopen the investigation surrounding her death. I've come to believe that she was killed. Someone made certain she was high on pills and booze and helped her off the verandah of the hotel room. Seems to me you're the most likely candidate."

"For the love of God, Zach, are you nuts?" Eunice whispered, but couldn't help licking her lips nervously.

"Not me."

"So now you're accusing me of being crazy?"

"Psychotic."

She nearly dropped her cup. All of her composure evaporated. "You're accusing me?" Rage pulsed through her face. "This is insane."

"Exactly."

She was shaking, unraveling before Adria's eyes. "So now you've decided to become detective, judge and jury. And you don't even have your facts straight. I thought better of you, Zach."

"All you have to do is prove that you didn't overdose Kat with pills and then push her over the balcony wall."

"You just can't let it go, can you? First you were involved with that slut and now this . . . this woman who's your own half-sister."

Adria cringed inside.

"Do you know how disgusting that is? How sick? How perverted?" Eunice ranted, her composure evaporating, her eyes dilating.

"Let's talk about her. Adria. London," he said, not backing off an inch. "While you're trying to prove that you didn't kill Kat and Ginny, you can make a case about not terrorizing Adria, too."

"I don't know what you're talking about," she snapped, her nostrils flaring slightly.

"Cut the crap, okay. Let's see your hand."

"What?"

"Your hand, the one Adria bit when you tried to kill her up at the motel in Estacada."

All the blood drained from Eunice's face. "This is ridiculous."

Far in the distance the sound of sirens cut through the air.

Eunice's eyes closed for a second and when she reopened them, Adria noticed a new, steely determination in their clear depths. "You're turning your own mother in, is that it, Zach? All because of something she"—Eunice motioned dismissively toward Adria—"contrived."

"I didn't 'contrive' anything."

"It turns out she is London, Eunice. And you tried to kill her. Only you didn't get away with it, not like you did with Ginny."

"For the last time, Zach. I did *not* kill Ginny." She pointed toward the nearest chair and said in a voice that was barely above a whisper, "Now, please, sit down."

"No, thanks."

"Sit down and drink a cup of tea with me," she said, lifting her chin proudly. The sirens screamed louder. Closer. Eunice swallowed hard. She was scared, yes, but there was something else in her gaze. Triumph?

Why?

She stared at the woman and was met with Eunice's chilling stare.

She's going to beat this . . . somehow. Adria knew it in an instant. But how? Fear crept through her blood though Zach seemed unintimidated by this woman who was his mother, this monster who had tried to murder her. "You tried to kill me," she pointed out.

"You were in the way."

Adria felt it then, the cold hatred whispering through the air. Eunice's angry gaze slid to her. "Of what?"

"My children's rights, of course. Their claim to their father's estate."

"So it all boils down to money," Adria charged.

"Money is only part of it. Prestige. Birthright. It all goes hand in hand." No longer did she bother to mask her loathing. "If you would have left things alone, none of this would have happened. None. The children, *my* children would have gotten what they deserved from their father's estate, but you couldn't stay away, could you? Oh, no." Her lips flattened against her teeth. "I've done a lot of things I'm not proud of. A lot."

"Including the kidnapping," Zach pressed.

Eunice hesitated.

"You did it, didn't you and let me take the rap!"

"That wasn't part of the plan."

"Well, it's what happened, Eunice."

"Oh, Zach."

"Jesus, you're unbelievable. You did it, didn't you? You kidnapped a child!"

"Not a child! An interloper!" She shot to her feet and seemed a bit unsteady.

"And later you killed Kat!"

"No, I—" She braced herself on the counter as if her legs would suddenly not hold her steady.

"You always hated her. Hated London." He pressed his face to within a hair's breadth of hers. "I've thought about it a long time and decided that Kat didn't kill herself. No way. She was too into self-preservation, self-promotion. No matter how desperate she was, she wouldn't commit suicide. So either she had an accident, which is damned unlikely, or someone helped her off that balcony." His lips were bloodless, his eyes dark and knowing. "You're the only person who hated her enough to do it. Probably all for the sake of your children and their inheritance, the same reason you kidnapped London."

"No," Eunice said weakly.

"Come on, *Mother*, you wanted me here to hear your confession, so let's hear it."

"But I didn't—"

Bam! His fist slammed against the table. The teacup jumped. Adria started. Far in the distance sirens shrieked.

"Oh, God," Eunice whispered, seeming pathetic. "I didn't mean to hurt anyone."

"Bull! You killed her!"

"Yes, okay, yes, yes, yes!" Eunice's eyes were filled with tears and she blinked rapidly.

Adria, though she'd expected the news, was stunned—to actually hear a confession to murder. "You pushed her?"

"Of course I did!" Some of Eunice's starch returned. "As pathetic as she was after she lost her daughter, she wasn't suicidal. Not Kat. God, she was a disgusting creature." She turned her gaze on Zach. "That surprises you? That your own mother could kill?"

A muscle worked in Zach's jaw and he'd paled.

"It was easy, really. To slip into her room, to doctor her drink, to lure her onto the balcony . . ." Eunice's voice turned to the barest of whispers. "All I had to do was pretend . . . put on a little girl's voice . . ." She did then, sounding suddenly like a child. "Mama . . . Mama . . ." Eunice's eyes glazed for a second, her thoughts turning inward, as she replayed the horrid scene. "She was disoriented, believed that I was London and I hid near the railing . . ."

"You murdering bitch," Adria said, shaking all over.

Eunice snapped back to the present. "And I'd do it again. For my children."

Adria's blood turned to ice. So it wasn't over.

"Save it, Eunice. No one's buying the altruistic act," Zach stated.

"I don't expect you to, Zach, but believe this," she insisted. "I didn't kill Ginny."

Zach's fists curled. "After that last confession, you expect me to trust you?"

The sound of sirens wailing was closer but Eunice didn't seem to notice. "I didn't even know where she was."

"But you admitted to having her kidnap London. Paid her off." Zach grabbed Adria's purse from her arm and poured the contents on the table. Lipstick, brush, wallet, keys and letters fell out—duplicates of the notes she'd given to the police. Stabbing a finger at one of the ugly notes, Zach said," You sent these."

Eunice stared at the items and a tic developed under her eye as Zach, furious, added, "You also dropped off a dead rat at her hotel room."

The twitch quickened. Eunice twisted her hands together. Her eyes seemed to glaze.

"And you tore up Adria's bedsheets and her panties."

"No . . . Kat's bedsheets . . . Kat's panties . . ."

"Not Kat. Adria. London."

"The same thing," she said, nostrils flaring as if she'd suddenly noticed a bad smell. "Kat . . . London . . ."

"Not at all."

She held out her hands in supplication and to Adria she seemed suddenly pathetic, an older woman, but not weak. One strong enough to have pinned her to the ground and tried to kill her, a twisted person who could kill a rat and drain its blood, a maniac who could destroy a room, shred clothing, smear a mirror with blood.

"I couldn't stand the thought of you two together, Zach. Not with Kat. Not Kat . . ." Her voice cracked and she blinked . . . as if clearing her head. She wrapped her arms around her middle and started to rock. "I mean, not with London . . . not with Kat . . . I couldn't let that happen . . . I had no choice."

"No choice?" Adria repeated, suddenly repulsed. "No choice but to try and kill me?" Who was this woman? A mother. A socialite. A murderer. She took a step away as Zach zeroed in on the woman who had borne him.

"Everyone has a choice, Eunice." He turned away from her.

"It's not that easy." She sniffed, stuffing her hands into the pockets of her velour jacket.

"Sure it is. You made it hard. By trying to kill Adria and when you got hurt, you told Nelson you got hurt by falling when you were chasing the cat. Christ, you're something. And you expect me to believe you didn't follow us to San Francisco and kill Ginny?"

She hesitated. "I have an alibi."

"Convenient. Who?"

She let out her breath and her shoulder's slumped slightly. She dabbed at her nose with a tissue she'd found in her pocket. "Nelson. On the night Ginny was killed he was here with me."

"For crying out loud, don't you think I know he'd lie for you?"

"Possibly, but he doesn't have to. I was here, Zach, in Lake Oswego when Ginny was murdered."

"I don't trust Nelson."

"Then trust his friend." She lifted her chin and met Zach's condemning stare. "Nelson was with someone the night he was here. They didn't stay all night, of course, because I'm not supposed to know that Tom is Nelson's lover, but they stopped by for a few hours—just old pals, you know—and we had dinner and played cards. If you don't believe me or your brother, ask Tom."

The sirens sounded so close, they screamed through the house.

"You'll have to tell the police and maybe they'll buy it, but I don't."

"It doesn't matter anymore."

"Of course it does," he said, then seemed to notice the weird smile playing at the edges of her lips. "Wait a minute . . ."

"It's over, Zach."

"What do you mean? Over?" His gaze shot to the teacup. "What have you done?"

"What I had to, Zach," she said. "I always do what I have to. You don't believe me, but everything I've done is because I love you."

"Shit, Eunice," he swore, "what the hell have you done."

As sirens blasted outside, Zach's gaze swept the counter and into the partially open cupboard. "Oh, no . . ." He threw open the cupboard door and picked up several vials. "You didn't," he whispered, looking at her teacup as the sound of tires crunching and voices filtered through the walls. Zach swept the teacup from the table and it crashed into a thousand pieces. "You didn't have to do this, Mom."

"Of course I did. This is for you, Zach." At that moment she lunged at Adria, and the hand that had been hidden in her pocket shot out. In her closed fist was a small knife. Its wicked blade gleamed deadly in the light.

Adria's heart leapt to her throat.

"No!" Zach yelled.

Eunice stabbed wildly. "You can't do this, Kat! I won't let you!"

Adria feinted and twisted, kicking upward at Eunice's hand. The knife swung downward, ripping Adria's shirt.

"Adria!" Zach tackled his mother and she landed hard on the tiled floor. And then she looked up at her son as he reached for the blade.

Deftly, she wiggled away and as her eyes met those of Zach, she twisted her hand around and turned the blade on herself. "You know, Zachary," she said as she plunged the knife into her abdomen. "You always were the smart one. My best and brightest."

"No!"

Zach wrestled the knife free and blood smeared his hands, pooling red through Eunice's jogging suit.

"Oh, God, why?" he cried as the door burst open and thundering footsteps pounded through the house. "Police!" one hoarse voice cried. "Drop your weapons!"

Usually, Anthony Polidori didn't like to be awakened from sleep, but when the informant called and told him that Eunice Danvers Smythe had been taken to the hospital and was charged with the kidnapping of London Danvers, Anthony thanked the man for his information. Too bad Eunice had been the culprit.

He felt more than a little sense of guilt thinking of her, for he knew that she'd fallen in love with him thirty-five years before. He'd cared for her, yes, but he hadn't loved her with the same passion she'd felt for him, and, in truth, he'd only bedded her to get back at Witt. Eunice had guessed his reasons. They'd been kindred spirits in that sense, enjoying each other at Witt's expense.

The bastard.

So Eunice had decided to destroy Witt's life. Although for

years his family had been blamed for the deed, Anthony respected her gall. Maybe he shouldn't have been so hasty to drop her once Witt had discovered their affair.

He climbed out of his bed and found a striped robe that was worn in the sleeves and tattered at the hem. His wife had bought it for him nearly half a century before and though it was now a rag, he had never had the heart to get rid of it.

He wondered if Mario was home or if he was with some woman—not that it mattered. Shuffling down the tiled hallway, he thought back over his life and was surprised that the deep-seated hatred he'd felt for the Danvers family had seemed to dim over the years.

He rapped on the door and waited. Nothing. Knocking harder, he scowled, then tried the knob. It was locked. "Mario, son, open up."

He heard a groggy response.

"Come, open the door."

"Jesus Christ." Growling and kicking things in his way, Mario finally appeared, his hair wild, his beard dark "Wha—?"

"We need to talk?"

"Are you out of your mind? It's four in the morning!"

"Get up and come downstairs."

Mario rubbed a hand over his face and yawned. As he stretched, his back popped. "Let me get my cigarettes and slippers," he said, then turning, tripped over something else and swore under his breath.

The boy would never grow up.

Anthony made his way downstairs and had uncorked a bottle of champagne by the time his only son stumbled into the kitchen. "What the hell's going on?" Mario said. He rubbed his teeth with his tongue and shuddered.

"We're celebrating."

"Shit, couldn't it have waited until a decent hour—you know, six or seven in the morning?"

"No. And this is no time for sarcasm."

"Whatever you say, Pop." Mario clicked a lighter to the end of his cigarette. "Okay, I'm dyin' to know. What's up?"

"Several things. Come, come." Anthony patted the arm of his chair and indicated that Mario should sit on it as he had when he was a boy. Spewing smoke from the corner of his mouth, he obliged the old man. "Good. Here—" Anthony held a glass to his son; then, after Mario had taken the crystal goblet, touched the rim of his to his son's. "To the future."

"Yeah. Right. The future." Mario, thinking the old man had really lost it and was one step away from the loony bin, began to drink, but his father's hand stayed him. "And to the end of the feud."

"Christ!"

"All right. To God as well," Anthony said magnanimously.

"What're you talking about? The fucking feud is over? How can that be? You crack out the best champagne and just make some sort of statement that it's over and all the shit that's gone on for nearly a hundred years is forgotten? Just like that?" Mario snapped his fingers loudly. Then he rubbed his eyes. "I'm dreaming. That's what this is—some kind of nightmare."

"There's one more thing we're celebrating."

"Oh, great. What's that?"

"Your marriage."

"Now I know I'm dreaming."

"No, Mario. It's time. You need a wife. I need grandchildren. We have to think of the future and not the past. You'll be married and have children and we will all be happy."

"Oh, sure, right. What happened tonight, eh?" Mario asked. "When I went to bed everything was the same and now you're dragging me out of bed, talking like a fortune-teller. Did you get knocked over the head or what?"

Anthony ignored his son's ravings and clicked his glass yet again to the rim of Mario's. There were many possibilities for a wife for his son and he hadn't ruled out Adria Nash—Lon-

anvers—as a potential candidate. She was beautiful and
and smart. Who could ask for anything more from a
ghter-in-law? Of course there was the chance she
dn't want him. Well, there were other eligible young
men. Fertile women, beautiful, but not necessarily as smart
this London.

"There's only one woman I've ever wanted to marry,"
Mario said, suddenly sober, and Anthony had to tamp down
is old feelings of disgust. "Trisha."

Gritting his teeth, the old man swallowed his last bit of false
ride. "I won't stand in your way." Then, he took a sip of his
hampagne, stared up at his son's disbelieving face and laughed,
ong and hearty, as he hadn't laughed in years. He patted Mario
n the knee with a fondness that he'd forgotten—a fondness
e'd once felt when his wife was still alive, and Mario was four
r five and hardly any trouble at all. "Drink up. Enjoy. And let
e tell you what happened tonight. . . ."

Zach was grim as they walked out of the hospital near
owntown Portland. He'd watched without a word as the po-
ce, Eunice's lawyer, and Nelson had arrived, all arguing and
houting. Jason had shown up and his mood had been sour.
risha, when she'd deigned to appear—in a full-length er-
ine coat, no less—had breezed past Adria and said to Zach,
Now look what you've done."

A crowd of reporters was clustered near the door. Voices
houted over one another, trying to capture her attention.

"Ms. Nash? Is it true that you've finally proven yourself to
e London Danvers?"

"It looks that way, yes."

"How does it feel to finally know your natural family?"

"I haven't sorted it all out yet." She felt odd about it all.
hough Eunice was expected to live, she was still in the hos-
ital under police guard.

"You're inheriting a great deal of money, aren't you? What are your plans?"

"I don't have any yet."

Zach looked about to step in, but Adria placed a hand on his arm. "Look," she said, speaking into the microphone thrust in her direction. "I'm very tired right now. Of course I'm glad to know that I'm London," she said, refusing to meet Zach's eyes, refusing to listen to the pain in her heart, knowing that he was her half-brother, "and I've no immediate plans for the future."

"Will you move to Portland permanently?"

"I don't know."

"What about the charges pending against Eunice Smythe?"

"I can't comment on them."

"Is it true she attacked you in that motel in Estacada?"

"I have nothing more to say at this time."

"But now that you're one of the wealthiest women in the state, surely you—"

"Excuse me."

She shouldered her way through the crowd and Zach was with her every step of the way. She couldn't meet his eyes, didn't want to think about her future. For nearly a year she'd thought that if she could prove that she was London, if she could find her real family, her life would change for the better. She could make a difference. She'd fantasized about the money, of course, and seen herself as a shrewd business woman who would sit on the boards of charities as well as handle the affairs of Danvers International. Witt Danvers's little lost princess. The treasure he'd loved above all else, including his other children.

She'd been a fool. A silly fool with girlish dreams.

And she hadn't planned on falling in love with Zachary.

They climbed into his Jeep and Zachary nosed the Cherokee into the street. Half a dozen cars followed his lead. "Great," he muttered, eyeing the rearview mirror. "Just great." He glanced at Adria. She was dead-tired, leaning against the

indow, staring at him with eyes that seemed to see straight
to his soul. "They'll be at the hotel," he said, turning abruptly
and watching the headlights follow him.

He drove crazily, changing lanes at the last minute and
turning corners abruptly. She sensed the change in direction,
saw the towering lights of downtown fade behind them.

"Where are we going?"

"Someplace private."

"Just the two of us?"

He hesitated, his fingers curling over the steering wheel until
his knuckles showed white, then nodded curtly. Something inside her—something she'd rather not acknowledge—began to
awaken. "Just the two of us."

Jack Logan was too old to be driving like a wild man, chasing a lunatic in a Jeep. He was tired and grumpy and if it
wasn't for the bottle of Irish whiskey that kept him going, he
would have called Jason Danvers and told him to follow his
own damned family. But he'd been paid and paid well and he
figured that later he could sleep all day if he wanted to.

Retirement hadn't settled well with him; he missed the
action and excitement of the department. True, his arthritis
was bad enough to make him limp and he wasn't as quick as
he used to be, but his mind was sharp and he could spend
only so much time gardening or fiddling at the workbench his
daughter, Risa, had insisted was so therapeutic. No, he missed
the sport of it all, the feeling alive, and hated the notion that
just because he'd reached a certain age, he'd been put out to
pasture.

So he kept taking Danvers's money, not so much to sup-
plement his social security and pension, but to keep his blood
pumping, to make him feel alive again. He followed the Jeep,
hanging back, turning off at different streets, nearly losing the
rig several times, but always finding it again.

He had an uncanny sense about these things and he

guessed where the rig was heading in its crazy, zigzaggin course that always led north, toward the interstate bridge, t ward the huge body of water separating the souther boundary of Washington from Oregon: the Columbia Riv and the marina where the Danvers yacht was berthed.

The Jeep turned off the interstate and Logan continued o driving, across the bridge, barely noticing the wide blac abyss that was the Columbia. On the far side of the river, i Vancouver, just over the Washington border, he turned his ca around and headed back to the freeway, this time headin south. To celebrate, he took a little nip from his bottle an drove unerringly back to the marina. Flashing his outdate badge at the guard manning the gate, he drove quietly into th parking lot and saw Zachary's Jeep tucked in a darkene space.

Bingo.

"You still got it, Logan," he told himself, and uncapped hi bottle yet again before taking a long swallow that warmed th pit of his stomach and spread through his blood. He didn' have a cell phone, but he knew there was a Safeway stor nearby with a couple of phone booths near the front doors He'd let Jason sweat awhile, have himself a couple of drink at a topless bar not all that far away, then call the bastard While he was at it, he might just ask for a raise. Hell, he de served it.

25

The smell of the river rose off the water and tickled Adria's nostrils as she walked along the wooden pier that rimmed the dark water. Her footsteps echoed loudly over the rush of the river and the wind that raced down the gorge from the east. Expensive boats, moored at the marina, lay empty, their masts spindly, their sails furled, their engines silent as they undulated with the ever-shifting water.

She let Zachary help her onto the Danvers yacht, a gleaming vessel that, she supposed, was now partially hers. It was all such a waste, she thought, considering Eunice and her hatred of Katherine. Adria didn't doubt that Eunice had not only terrorized her, but killed Kat and Ginny Slade, despite Nelson's vehement claims otherwise.

She glanced at Zachary. Tall. Rugged. Troubled. The kind of brooding, dark man she should run from. She was alone with him for what was to be the last time in her life. It just had to be.

The wind tugged at her hair and she told herself this was the price she had to pay for the truth. She'd gotten everything she wanted, and more than she'd bargained for. A heavy weight had settled deep in her heart and she thought about her future—so bright to the outside world, so barren and bleak without Zach's love.

Don't even go there. Get over it, for crying out loud. It's not life-or-death. Just heartache. You'll live.

"Drink?" he asked, once they climbed down a short staircase and entered the main salon, a long room decorated in gleaming teak and brass.

"Why not?" She dropped onto a navy blue sofa that was attached to the wall. What would one drink hurt? It had been a long couple of weeks and she was dead tired, but too wound up to fall asleep. She watched him sort through the bottles and felt a pain slice through her heart.

He's forbidden.

Off limits. Way off limits.

"What do you want?"

How could he act like nothing was wrong? "That's the problem," she admitted. "I have no idea what I want."

"How about a glass of brandy?"

"I wasn't talking about the drink."

"I know, but I thought we should keep the conversation light."

"Impossible, considering." She leaned back against the cushions.

"Listen, the way I see it, you've got it all, London—"

"Don't call me that!"

"It's your name. The one you worked hard to have pinned to you. You'd better get used to it."

"I know." She flung herself to her feet and scowled. "But not from you, okay? Just . . . not from you."

He paused, poured the drinks, and shook his head.

"It just doesn't feel right."

He walked across the salon and stopped so close to her she could feel his heat. Tall. Rugged. Unshaven. His jeans riding low on his hips. Like a damned cowboy.

He handed her a glass and their fingers brushed for a split second, but Adria felt it. That same electricity that seemed to sizzle whenever her skin touched his.

Damning the fates, she sipped, scowled as the liquor hit the back of her throat, then tossed back the whole damned drink. Maybe the alcohol would dull her senses so that when she looked at him she wouldn't feel this painful agony ripping through her heart, she'd forget the erotic feel of his hands on her, wouldn't get lost in his gaze.

She held up her glass for a refill and he cocked an interested eyebrow. But his gaze was unreadable. "Getting drunk?"

"Maybe.

"Not a good idea."

"Definitely not."

"But you're not going to reconsider."

"No."

"Adria, I don't think—"

"Don't lecture me, okay? I don't need it from you or anyone else." She marched to the bar and poured herself another stiff shot. Already she felt the mellow warmth of alcohol running through her blood and as she swirled another couple of shots in her glass, she felt bolder. "So what're you gonna do now, Zach? You know, now that you know I'm your half-sister."

"Run like hell."

She laughed, but felt a secret longing, deep and forbidden, begin to uncoil and stretch within her. "You're still here," she observed.

"Because I'm not certain that there isn't a murderer still on the loose."

"I thought you believed your mother is the culprit."

"I do . . . but there's something that doesn't ring true to all of it."

"So now you're buying her story."

"Just part of it."

She decided to play devil's advocate. "So because of this other threat—another killer—you're going to what? Stick around me until he's behind bars. Be my personal bodyguard?" She sipped a little more brandy.

"That's the plan."

"Maybe I don't want a bodyguard," she said, giving in to the impulse to say exactly what was on her mind. "Maybe I want a lover."

"Then you'll have to find yourself one, won't you?" He downed his drink and ignored the urge to pour himself another. Getting shit-faced wouldn't help the already volatile situation. Adria—*no, London. Remember, she's London. Keep that in mind!*—was already losing control, not that he blamed her. They'd both been wound tight as watch springs.

But he wasn't convinced the danger had passed. Something just didn't seem right.

Or is that just an excuse to be with her? To be close to her? To hope that you'll forget who she is long enough to make love to her?

His gut tightened as she regarded the bottom of her glass sullenly, then pinned him with her erotic blue eyes. "But I want you, Zach. *Just you.*"

He closed his eyes and swore under his breath. "You can't. You know it's impossible."

"Is it?"

Finishing her drink in a flourish, she took a bold step toward him and shook her head. Black hair feathered around her face. "You want me, too."

"Christ, Adria, don't do this," he said, his voice strained.

She didn't stop until she reached him then stood on her tiptoes, ran her fingers up his chest, and pressed her full, anxious lips to his. "We've done it before."

"Not when we knew—oh, God."

She nuzzled his neck, then touched the seam of his lips with her tongue. His bones threatened to melt and with all the willpower he could gather, he grabbed her quickly by both wrists.

"Don't, Adria!"

"Zach, please, 1 love you—"

"For God's sake, you can't! I can't!" His brain argued with him. *Why not? It's not as though you haven't stepped over this threshold before. One last time and then good-bye, adios, forever. Take her, take her now!* Desire thundered like stampeding cattle racing through his blood and pounding at his temples. The pressure in his crotch was already hot and urgent against his zipper. He closed his eyes to block out the anxious, loving look shining in her eyes. "We'll regret this," he ground out, feeling like a powder keg ready to explode.

"Never," and the pain in her voice broke through his hard shell.

Shoving her up against the wall, he kissed her, brutally, angrily. He pinned her hands above her head as his lips and tongue assaulted her. Her breasts were heaving, rising and falling beneath her jacket and he cupped one in his hands. "Is this what you want, London?" he said, forcing the furious words over his tongue as he wedged his pelvis between the "V" of her thighs, pressing hard against her mound.

Her eyes widened in horror. "I'm not—"

"You are! And you'd better face it!"

Inside he was shaking with desire, ready to throw caution to the wind and take her willing body. The barrier of their clothing was thin, easily destroyed, and then they would be naked. Alone. Man and woman.

Brother and half-sister.

No! If they didn't stop this dangerous game, he would give in to the urges running rampant through his body and take her. Hell, if she didn't stop looking at him like that— He kissed her again and this time the kiss wasn't punishing, and he let go of her hands, dragging her body against him and losing himself in the wonder of her. He wound his fingers in the thick tangles of her black hair and felt her mouth open to him. His tongue explored, sleekly darting in and out, and she moaned so softly he barely heard it.

He reached for her breast, delving into her bra, feeling the tense little nipple, hearing the sound of want deep in her throat.

"I . . . I can't," she whispered, tears streaming down her cheeks.

"I know." He swallowed back his lust just as he heard it—

the sound that was out of place—of leather against boards. His galloping heart stopped for a second.

They weren't alone.

Hell!

Slowly lifting his head, he placed his hand over her mouth and motioned for her to be quiet. Over his callused fingers he saw her eyebrows draw together for a second, then shoot upward. She got the message. "Stay here," he whispered against her ear.

"No—" she said against his hand, but he shot her a look that brooked no argument, motioned for her to go back into the cabin, and slowly, quietly, mounted the stairs.

Her heart pounding, she watched in mind-numbing fear. What if the person on deck was the murderer that he insisted still existed? What if Eunice wasn't the killer? Who else could it be? Her heart pounded. She couldn't let Zachary fight him alone. Quickly, she searched the salon for a weapon, found nothing, and took the stairs silently to the deck.

"—so it doesn't matter if she's your sister or not, you still want to fuck her."

Jason Danvers's voice whispered over the rush of the wind.

Adria's skin crawled. What was he doing here? Had he followed them?

She eased up the stairs and spied Jason standing on the main deck, his back braced on the boom, the night wind causing his jacket to flap around his hips. Rain was beginning to fall heavily and yet he stood, bareheaded, his eyes trained on his younger brother.

Adria felt as if she were in the presence of pure evil. Was there a phone on board? Could she slide back down the stairwell unnoticed and make the call? Or would it be on the bridge? A radio of some kind?

"Christ, Zach, you never learn, do you? First Kat and now her daughter."

Adria froze. "You were with Kat," Zach said calmly, his back to the stairwell as he squared off with his brother.

"But I didn't move on to London."

"Probably because you were too busy killing Ginny Slade."

"So you figured that out, little brother. Jesus, if you try a little harder you might just get some kind of Agatha Christie award or something. You and Adria—no, London—have become quite the detectives."

"You didn't need to kill her."

"Didn't want her to go shooting her mouth off. I knew about Mom. Knew that she was the one behind the kidnapping." He grinned, his leer wickedly cruel in the darkness. "I figured I'd use Mom's plans to get what I wanted. Just go a little bit further. I even knew that she'd killed Kat. I'm just surprised the police never figured it out."

"They will now."

"Too late. I'm just lucky Sweeny finally located Ginny. I've been looking for her for years."

"To what end?"

"To ensure that our little half-sister never showed up."

Adria tried to slink back down the stairs.

"Don't go anywhere, London," Jason said, and she froze. "Didn't think I'd seen you?" He clucked his tongue. "Come on up and join the party."

"This is no party. Leave her be."

"Can't do that." He waved Adria up the stairs and she saw the gun, steely and cold, glistening in his hand. So this was it. The final standoff. Unless she and Zach could stop him. "Tell me," Jason said, "how does it feel to be the wealthiest woman in Portland? Better enjoy the feeling, because it's not gonna last long."

"What are you doing here?" she demanded, climbing the stairs and feeling icy raindrops pelt from the sky.

"Just having a chat with my brother. You're part of the family now, so you can join in."

"How'd you find us?"

"Oh, well, that was real tough," Jason mocked as the wind kicked up. "I knew you'd be together somewhere. It was just a matter of figuring out where you'd want to spend your time together. It had to be somewhere close by but private. Jesus, Zach, I know you like to think of yourself as some kind of irreverent rebel, but screwing your own sister?"

"You miserable son of a bitch!" Zach lunged, hurling himself at Jason, but Jason did a quick side step and grinned so evilly, Adria's heart froze.

"No!" she cried, expecting the sharp report of a gun.

Instead Jason pushed hard on the wooden boom, and the huge beam came around, catching Zach in his midsection and propelling him against the rail.

"Oh, God!" Adria threw herself at Jason, but it was too late. Jason tackled his brother and hit him squarely in the back of his head with the butt of his gun.

Adria screamed.

Zach's legs buckled.

"You bastard!" Adria lunged, grabbing at Jason's arm, and he flung her off to slam against the railing. *Crack!* Pain splintered through her brain. Her head bounced against the hardwood and she staggered, her feet slipping on the slick deck, her gaze fastened on the brothers.

Zach reeled forward and kicked upward, catching Jason in the groin.

With a roar of sheer agony, Jason doubled over.

Staggering, Zach tried to kick his brother again.

Jason was quick. He caught Zach's boot in his hands and jammed Zach back against the rail.

No! Oh, no! Adria staggered forward as Jason twisted Zach's ankle. Zach roared in pain and Adria propelled herself forward, her feet slipping as she launched herself onto Jason's back.

He still held the gun in one hand, but she didn't care as she tore into him, kicking and clawing, fighting with every ounce

f strength in her body as the boat rocked and the rain came
own in sheets.

Jason wrenched Zach's ankle again and Zach howled at the
ickening sound of tendons ripping from bone. Adria felt all
e muscles in Jason's back bunch as he shoved hard, hurtling
is brother into the frigid inky waters of the Columbia.

"Oh, God, no! No!" Adria cried, kicking harder. She
ouldn't lose Zach this way. Wouldn't!

Jason flung her off. "You're been a pain in the ass from the
econd you showed up in town." His gun was aimed right at
er heart, but she didn't care, not when Zach was drowning.

"And you're a murdering bastard," she said, fury surging
rough her veins. "Rot in hell!" She ran to the railing and
aulted over, certain she would hear the sound of a pistol
racking as it was fired.

But there was only silence as she plunged downward into
e icy water and she prayed that she'd be able to find Zach.
efore it was too late.

Jason watched her fling herself into the river and he low-
red his weapon. She wouldn't last two minutes in the river.
he water temperature was near freezing and if the current
ot to her, it would carry her downstream in a torrent. He
ouldn't have to take the rap for either of their deaths and
ith the right seeds planted, the press and police would prob-
bly believe they had a suicide pact, that they were doomed
vers who had found out they were brother and sister and had
ecided to end it all.

Yeah, that would work, he thought, shivering and wet. He
ought of Zach and felt nothing but disgust. Years ago, on the
ight of the kidnapping, Jason had set Zach up, killing two
irds with one stone. He'd known Polidori's toughs would
ome looking for him at the Orion. Sophia, the hooker, had
een bait and Zach had been an innocent. That he'd taken
e fall for London's kidnapping had been a stroke of luck. At

least for Eunice. The police had bought her alibi and Zach'
was so paper-thin, he'd become the number one suspec.
Jason considered his mother, lying in the hospital. Possibl
dying. Was there a way he could somehow blame her for thi
mess with Zach and Adria? Of course not. She was being
watched around the clock by the police. Even Jack Loga.
couldn't get near her.

Wiping the rain from his face, Jason scanned the stygia.
waters of the Columbia for any sign of life.

There was none.

Maybe they were dead already. Which would make thing
easier. When Adria had shown up in Portland, Jason had pan
icked. Sweeny's news that she was really London had been :
hard blow, but he'd known instinctively what had to be done
Surprisingly, he'd found it easier to kill than he'd firs
thought. Once he'd paid for an alibi, he'd beat Adria and Zacł
to San Francisco, hoping to kill Ginny before they'd called the
police or spoken with her. That, of course, hadn't happened
But he'd managed to sneak out of the house before getting
caught.

He'd learned well from his mother.

Eunice would never realize what she'd taught him. He'c
watched her over the years and recently seen what she'd beer
capable of. He'd always thought his ability to do anything
necessary to preserve the Danvers name and fortune hac
come from his father. Of course, he'd been wrong. Eunice
was the strong one in the family.

He checked his watch and scanned the waters one last time
It had been nearly half an hour since Zach and London hac
gone overboard. Long enough for the river to do its job.

It was show time.

"Help!" he yelled, cupping his hands in the direction of the
gatehouse. "Man overboard! Can anyone hear me? For God's
sake, I need some help down here! Slip eighteen! Help!" He
raced downstairs, found the phone, and punched out 911. He
gave himself time until the first person on a neighboring boat

ppeared and the sound of sirens screamed in the distance.
Then he kicked off his shoes, tossed off his jacket, and dove
into the water to wait. By the time the police arrived, the current would have swept the remains of the newly found London
Danvers and her lover—her half-brother—out to sea. The police might suspect him, but it would never be proven . . . two
more lives claimed by the power of the river.

Zach coughed and drew in water, then coughed again. God,
he was cold. So damned cold. His head felt as if it had been
hit by a two-by-four. Instinctively, he struggled upward, feeling the current pull him downstream. He surfaced, gasped
deep lungfuls of air, and was swept under again.

All of his muscles were sluggish and one leg barely moved,
but he forced himself to the surface and drew in another deep
breath. Something was wrong—horribly wrong, but he
couldn't remember what. He breathed in air and water and
saw lights, not that far away. With effort he began to swim,
still coughing, dragging his body through the water, feeling
the icy fingers of the river try to pull him under yet again.

Slowly his memory returned. As he stroked laboriously,
pieces of the night came together. He pushed himself harder,
plowing through the water, wishing the dead weight in his
right leg would fall off, fighting the current.

Adria! She was with Jason on the yacht. Oh, God, if she
wasn't already dead. Adrenaline surged through his blood and
he swam faster, ignoring the frigid cold, refusing to give in to
the cramping in his muscles and driving himself through the
water. He only hoped it wasn't too late. *God! Please, let me
get to her!*

He was nearly a quarter of a mile downstream when he
finally grabbed hold of a piling, and coughing and shivering, dragged himself out of the water, threw himself on the
rocky shore and retched, spewing water, feeling as if he
would die. He'd lost a boot during the ordeal and he kicked

off the other. Pain screamed up his leg. Gritting his teeth
he scrambled up the bank as best he could. Hopping on one
leg, he pulled himself forward, over a concrete embank
ment, fell onto the puddle-strewn pavement of an all-night
service station. Hobbling, he made his way past the island
to the small office.

Under flickering fluorescent lights, an attendant with a butt
of a cigarette burning on his lips took one look at Zach and
reached under the counter for his gun. "Jesus H. Christ
would you look at that?" he said to the empty room.

"Call the police," Zach ordered, bracing himself on the
door frame.

"No shit, I'll call the police . . ." With the gun aimed at
Zach's midsection, the attendant reached for the phone and
dialed with trembling fingers. "Hey, this is Louie at the Tex
aco just off Marine Drive. We got ourselves a little problem
here . . ."

". . . I told you I don't know what happened. I was down
stairs in the salon and all of a sudden I heard something go
overboard. I ran upstairs and both Adria Nash and Zach were
nowhere to be seen. That's when I called for help and jumped
into the water," Jason said convincingly. His teeth were chat
tering, his body shaking, his clothes wet and dripping as they
clung to his body.

The police had arrived and a patrol boat was on the river
while other officers were in the yacht, questioning him and
searching the boat. Divers had already jumped into the near
freezing water and broad searchlights skimmed the river's
dark, murky surface.

Another squad car, lights flashing, arrived. More cops
Jason steeled himself for another barrage of questions, only
to watch as the cruiser parked near the others and two offi
cers emerged. But they weren't alone. They took the time to
help a third man from the backseat.

He squinted into the darkness and as the officers and their passenger walked under the security lights, he thought he might be sick. The third man was Zach. Very much alive. Hobbling on his bad leg and angry enough to spit nails. Dread, hot as acid, burned its way through Jason's stomach. Somehow he had to turn this around.

Zach knew too much.

There had to be a way to stop him from spilling his guts. But he wasn't the kind of man who could be bought off. Money wouldn't do it. No, his weakness was women, and the one woman who could persuade him to keep quiet was gone, her body no doubt floating out to sea.

For the first time in his life, staring at the furious face of his brother, Jason Danvers knew fear. Real, bone-chilling fear.

Using crutches, a slicker tossed over his shoulders, Zach hitched his way up the gangway and onto the yacht. He was pale, wet, bedraggled, and mad as hell. His chin jutted at a merciless angle and his gray eyes were murderous as they focused on his older brother.

"Zachary!" Jason forced himself to sound relieved when he thought he might piss himself. "Jesus, I was afraid you'd been lost when you fell over—"

"Where's Adria?" Zach demanded.

"Not here. She dived in after you, I think."

"You think? You *think*? Where the hell is she, you lying piece of shit?" Zach lunged at Jason, dropping his crutches and nearly falling as his ankle gave out. His fists closed around his brother's wet shirt and he rammed his face up to Jason's. "If anything's happened to her, I swear to God, you'll pay."

"Hey! That's enough! Take it easy," one cop yelled, hurrying forward.

Zach didn't listen. He swung hard, a fist crashing into Jason's nose.

Crunch!

Cartilage shattered. Blood sprayed.

Pain burst through Jason's face.

He tried to protect himself, to throw a punch, but it was too late.

Frenzied with fear, Zach landed a jab to Jason's ribs that nearly doubled him over.

"You bastard. You goddamned murdering bastard," Zach yelled as a cop peeled him off his brother. "You killed her."

"Whoa, slow down," one of the cops advised, but Zach found his crutch and swung it hard.

Jason ducked and the bigger cop grabbed Zach. "Mr. Danvers reported that the two of you fell or jumped into the river—"

"Fell? Jumped? No way. He goddamned pushed me in." Zach whirled on his brother. "So where the hell is she? In the river? Oh, God, you'd better pray that she's all right!"

"Zach," Jason said, his voice full of reproach. "I'm sorry—"

"The hell you are. You're hoping I'll cover for you, aren't you? Well, no way. No damned way! You tried to kill me," he said through gritted teeth. "For all I know, you tried to kill her, too."

"We'll sort this out downtown," one of the officers said.

"No! You've got to find her!" Zach insisted, trying to reach the rail. Desperately, he searched the black waters. "You've got to!"

"It's been over half an hour, Mr. Danvers—"

Zach flung himself to the rail, his eyes squinting against the darkness. He started to climb over but felt one hand being yanked behind his back, then the second wrenched behind him as handcuffs clicked into place.

"You can't—"

"Come on, Mr. Danvers."

He tried to struggle but his ankle gave out, sending pain jarring up his leg. The officers shoved him into a waiting car and Zach was certain he'd never see her again. Never be able to admit that he loved her, never for the rest of his life feel the way he did when he was with her. No doubt Adria Nash or London Danvers, whatever she wanted to be called, was gone forever.

Zach hadn't slept in days. One twenty-four-hour period seemed to bleed into the next and he had no idea of the time, or the date, just lived with the sickening knowledge that Jason was behind bars and his mother, once she recovered from her wounds and was released from the hospital, would face prosecution. Jason's accomplice, a burly man on parole, had been shooting his mouth off in a bar near Fisherman's Wharf and a police informant had nailed him. It hadn't taken much persuasion to get him to talk and Jason's name had come up.

Nicole, already having packed Shelly off to Santa Fe, was clamoring for a divorce and Kim had made a quick disappearance. No one had seen her, though many suspected it had been she who first told the press about Adria being London Danvers. As far as Zach was concerned, his older brother and his mistress deserved everything they got and more.

Trisha had sworn off Mario Polidori for good, telling him bluntly to get out of her life when he'd asked her to marry him. Zach didn't believe it would last. Trisha was and always had been a fool where Mario was concerned.

As for Nelson, he finally seemed to get some backbone and was actually trying to help Eunice. For years he'd been a lost soul, trying to balance who he was with who he thought he should be, still trying to please his father.

Most people thought that Adria was dead.

Pain cut through his heart and spread through his body.

The police and volunteers had searched the river, dredged where they could, but the news reporters and the police speculated that her body had been washed out to sea, claimed by the giant Pacific. He closed his eyes and felt the hot pressure of tears against his eyelids. He hadn't cried for years and yet now he felt reduced to bawling like a baby.

In his mind's eye he saw her, a little wicked, a little innocent, her eyes round and blue and filled with desire as she'd lain beneath him, begging him to love her. She'd sacrificed herself for him, flinging her body into that ugly river when it should have been the other way around. He should have been the one trying to save her. He should be dead and she should be alive and vibrant and starting life as London Danvers.

"Son of a bitch," he growled as he uncapped his friendly bottle of Scotch again and poured a long stream into his empty glass—one that he'd picked up in the bathroom of this—his albatross—the Hotel Danvers. He wondered if his father could see him now. "Hope you're laughing your ass off!" He glared at the ceiling, then thought better of it, because if there was an afterlife, Witt Danvers wouldn't be wandering around on the other side of the pearly gates, no sirree, he'd be down in hell, trying to cut a deal with the devil.

Zach's teeth ground together in silent fury.

The press had enjoyed a field day with even more scandal, compliments of the infamous Danvers family, and still they were camped outside the hotel, the yacht, the ranch, the sawmills, logging operations, and the damned company headquarters. Zach tossed back three fingers of Scotch and checked the clock. It was barely ten. Christ, he was a mess. His mouth tasted like crap and his guts burned. The phone rang near the bed and he picked it up, silently hoping to hear her voice, knowing that he never would again. "Yeah?"

"You in charge now?"

"Who's this?" he asked.

"Don't tell me you don't recognize me?"

"Sweeny," Zach said with a sinking sensation.

"That brother of yours, the one in jail, he owes me."

"I'm sure he does."

"Thought you might like to do the honors."

Zach found the half-empty bottle and took a long pull. "I don't think so."

"Got new information."

"Screw you."

"It's about London."

Every muscle in his body clenched. *Don't fall for this.* He wanted to slam down the phone, but he didn't. Just held his breath and waited.

"You gotta pay me first."

"Fine. I'm in room 714."

"I'll be there."

Click. Zach eyed the bottle and wondered if he could finish it before he had to deal with the likes of Oswald Sweeny.

Ignoring his crutches, he climbed off the bed, looked in the mirror, and winced. His face was still discolored and what he'd thought was a two-day growth of beard looked like it was really about six. "Shit," he muttered as he stripped off his clothes and sat in the shower, trying not to get his damned cast wet, hoping the hot jets of water would sink into his flesh and flush away all thoughts of her. But the steamy spray did little to quiet the images that seemed to be with him always.

He shaved, looked at his reflection, and glowered. He still looked like hell.

Sweeny arrived to find him dipping into the bottle again. Balanced on the crutches, the bottle swinging from one hand, he opened the door. Without preamble, he asked, "How much do we owe you?"

Oswald hesitated as he walked into the room.

"I'll check it out when I see Jason," Zachary said, knowing the man was going to bluff him out of a few extra bucks. He hobbled to the desk and rested a hip on the corner. "Want a drink?"

Sweeny smiled, showing off his little teeth, but something in Zachary's gaze, probably the hard, dead edge, convinced him to decline. "I got a bill right here."

He handed it to Zach, but he didn't bother opening it. "Tell me what else you know."

"Not before I get paid."

Zach didn't move a muscle, just stared at Sweeny, glaring at him like the cockroach he was.

"The papers will pay plenty for what I know."

"The tabloids?" Zach snorted. "Don't cut off your balls to spite your face."

"All right, all right." He held up his fleshy palms. "Look, I couldn't just give it up. The whole London thing was too intriguing. I thought, hey, I might just write myself a book, one of those tell-all exposés."

The look Zach sent him stopped him short.

"Anyway, I kept digging and guess what I found out? Your old man was impotent." He let that sink in for a minute, but Witt's limp dick wasn't big news. Not to Zach. What was Sweeny getting at?

"That's right," Sweeny said when Zach's eyes narrowed over the rim of his glass. "Witt Danvers couldn't get it up, at least not very often. Not often enough to ensure him siring another child—fathering London. I checked, and it took a while, but I found out that your stepmother, while she was supposed to be visiting friends in Victoria, really ended up at a clinic in Seattle where she got herself artificially inseminated by a private donor."

Zach's head snapped up. "What are you saying?"

Sweeny grinned that evil, little smug grin as if glad that he'd finally got Zach's attention. "I'm telling you that Adria Nash is London Danvers, but she's not Witt Danvers's kid, not technically—or biologically—speaking."

The glass fell from Zach's hand and Scotch splashed on the floor and the bottoms of his jeans. His head pounded.

"If she were alive, she'd still inherit it all, I suppose. It would take a team of lawyers to figure it out, but since she was the kid Witt was so crazy about, she'd still be his princess—heiress to it all, and since half your family is dead or behind bars, she'd get it. No doubt?"

"If she were alive," Zach ground out, his lips barely moving.

"Yeah, well . . . nothin' I can do about that."

"You can substantiate this, I assume."

"Of course. Records could be pulled—court-ordered, you know—and I found a nurse who's willing to talk. It's just a shame that London's dead."

Zach carried his bags down to the hotel lobby. He'd stayed in Portland longer than he'd planned. It had been over a week since he'd talked with Sweeny and the media was no longer laying siege to anything with the Danvers name. He was still wearing a cast, but he could walk and he wanted to get the hell out of town. He doubted that he'd ever come back.

It was time to move on.

On impulse, he left his bags by the lobby desk, then mounted the stairs to the ballroom, to the first place he'd seen her. He opened the doors, half expecting her to appear, but as he snapped on the lights, he found the room empty and cold and without a breath of life.

He was left only with memories, a bad ankle, and the sober realization that he'd never be the same.

"Fool," he ground out, walking inside the huge room and letting the door swing shut behind him. He remembered London on the night she was kidnapped, how impish she'd been, how precocious. Well, she'd grown into one helluva woman. Adria in the black coat or the shimmery white gown, her eyes blue, her lips teasing—a little naughty and a little nice.

He felt dead inside.

But, he was a practical man. At least he always had been. Whether he liked it or not, he'd have to face the fact that she was gone, that he'd loved her, and that he'd never love again. It was probably all for the best. He wasn't cut out for emotional entanglements. Again the hot tears stung his eyes and he swore at himself. He didn't believe in grieving. It didn't solve a thing.

Angry with himself, he switched off the lights and left the

room. He would drive to Bend and then get so drunk Manny would have to drive him home, but he wouldn't go looking for a woman. Not for a long, long time.

He had parked on the street and as he carried his bags outside he felt the pale heat of the winter sun filtering between the towering office complexes and past the leafless trees that had been planted in front of the hotel. Sunlight danced on the wet streets and he slipped a pair of shaded aviator glasses onto the bridge of his nose before he rounded the corner and stepped toward the Jeep, only to stop dead in his tracks.

She was there, one jean-clad hip propped against a fender, her eyes as blue as the sky, her witch-wild hair catching in the breeze. A vision.

"What the—"

"You gonna stand there all day with your mouth hanging open, or are you gonna take me home?" she said and her voice cut a slice right out of his heart.

"Adria—"

It couldn't be!

His heart kicked into double time, but he wouldn't believe the image. He couldn't.

"Well, cowboy?"

His throat worked. He dropped his bags and took a step forward. With a laugh, she ran to him and threw herself into his arms. Telling himself that she was real, he held her as close as he could, letting the warmth of her body seep into his, ignoring the pain in his bad ankle. "But you're—what happened?"

She kissed him with a passion that burned through his skin.

"I couldn't stay away," she said, her voice husky. "I tried." Her face was serious now. "I dragged myself out of the river and told myself that the best thing for you was to think I was dead. I had enough money in my pockets to rent a cheap room and I even managed to buy a few clean clothes. I waited, trying to figure out how to get my car, my ID, and go back to Montana without you ever finding out."

His jaw grew rock-hard. "You would let me think—"

"Shh." She pressed a finger to his lips. "I still thought we were brother and sister and . . . well, then the story came out about Katherine and the fact that I wasn't Witt's biological daughter and I thought . . ." She smiled up at him, love glistening in her eyes. "Well, I thought we could do something about that."

His voice was hoarse. "Why didn't you come sooner—?"

"I wanted to be sure. And I didn't want to come back as London Danvers," she said, tossing her hair out of her face. "I found out that I like being Adria Nash, that I don't need a birthright, nor any of the Danvers money." Her throat worked and she lifted her chin, daring him to argue with her. "I'm back here because I love you, Zachary," she said bravely. "I want to be with you. No strings attached."

He regarded her for a heart-stopping moment and his lips slowly curved. "Well, how about that?" he said. "I've loved you from the first time I saw you and I've gone through hell and back for you. Believe me, there'll be strings, lady, and plenty of 'em." Grinning he lifted her from her feet, and, hobbling a bit, carried her into the hotel. She laughed that throaty laugh that made him tingle inside and her black hair nearly swept the ground. People turned and watched, eyebrows raised; women gasped as he shouldered open the front door of the Hotel Danvers and climbed the stairs to the ballroom. Zach hardly noticed.

Once inside the dark room, he dropped her to her feet and locked the door behind them. Taking her into his arms, he kissed her on the neck, brushing his lips over her soft skin. She wound her arms around his neck. "Now, Ms. Nash . . . let's start over," he suggested as he toyed with the top button of her blouse.

Adria smiled at the man she loved. She wound her arms around his neck and knew that she'd come searching for her past . . . a life of luxury and wealth, only to discover that love was the richest treasure of all. "And let's not stop," she suggested.

"Good idea." He winked at her as her blouse parted. "This time, darlin', we're gonna take it real slow and do it right. Trust me."

"I do, cowboy," she swore. "I do!"

Dear Reader,

I hope you enjoyed SEE HOW SHE DIES. Rewriting TREASURES into SEE HOW SHE DIES turned out to be a big task, but I think revisiting Adria and Zach was worth the effort! The storyline for it has always been one of my favorites. I hope you agree!

My next new novel for Zebra Books is DEEP FREEZE. If you like mystery/thrillers and romance, then you're sure to love this one. DEEP FREEZE is the story of Jenna Hughes, a harried single mother of two, who senses that someone is stalking her. It's the coldest winter in fifty years in Oregon and with the first snowfall comes a cold certainty that someone is watching and waiting. Jenna fears for the lives of her two teenage daughters as well as for herself as a serial killer who calls himself The Ice Man begins to prowl and kill. As the days pass and the nights lengthen Jenna can trust no one, including Sheriff Shane Carter, a handsome but reclusive lawman. The Ice Man has his sights set on Jenna and her family as the frigid winter becomes her enemy.

DEEP FREEZE will certainly make your blood run cold. For an excerpt of the story, just turn the page!

Meanwhile, be certain to visit *www.lisajackson.com* and *www.themysterymansion.com*. I've updated the web sites and they've got cool contests, games and polls that I think you'll have a lot of fun with. Write me and let me know what you think of the books, vote for your favorite character, play games, visit the lairs of the villains or take part in a quest.

Of course, there's an excerpt of DEEP FREEZE on the web site, too . . . so check it out!

Keep reading!

Lisa Jackson

Please turn the page for an exciting
sneak peek of Lisa Jackson's
newest romantic suspense thriller
DEEP FREEZE
now available!

She was there.

Inside.

Somewhere in the rambling log home.

No doubt Jenna Hughes felt secure. Innocently safe.

But she was wrong.

Dead wrong.

As the first flakes of winter snow drifted from the gray sky
nd the wind screamed down the gorge, he watched from his
iding spot, a blind he'd built high in the branches of an old-
rowth Douglas fir that towered from this high ridge. Her
anch stretched out below in frozen acres that abutted the Co-
mbia River.

The rustic old house was the core of what he considered
er compound. Graying logs and siding rising two stories to
eaked gables and dormers. From lights behind the ice-glazed
indows, cozy patches of light glowed against the frozen
round, reminding him of his own past, of how often he'd
een on the outside, in the freezing weather, teeth chattering
s he stared at the smoke rising from the chimney of his
other's warm, forbidden house.

But that was long ago.

Now, focusing the military glasses on the panes, he caught
glimpse of her moving through her house. But just a teaser,
ot much, not enough to focus on her. Her image disappeared
s she turned down a hallway.

He refocused, caught a bit of movement in the den, but it

was only the old dog, a broken-down German shepherd wh
slept most of the day.

Where was she?

Where the hell had she gone?

Be patient, his inner voice advised, trying to soothe him.
Soon you'll be able to do what you want.

The snowflakes increased, powdering the branches, cover
ing the ground far below and he glanced down at the whit
frost. In his mind's eye he saw drops of blood in the icy crys
tals, warm as it hit the ground, giving off a puff of steam the
freezing slowly in splotches of red.

A thrill tingled up his spine just as a stiff breeze, cold a
Lucifer's piss, screamed down the gorge, stinging the bit c
skin above his ski mask. The branches above and around hir
danced wildly and beneath the mask, he smiled. He embrace
the cold, felt it was a sign. An omen.

The snow was now falling in earnest. Icy crystals fallin
from the sky.

Now was the time.

He'd waited so long.

Too long.

A light flashed on in the master bedroom and he caught an
other glimpse of her long hair braided into a rope that hun
down her back, baggy sweatshirt covering her curves, n
makeup enhancing an already beautiful face. His pulse ac
celerated as she walked past a bank of windows then into
closet. His throat went dry. He refocused the glasses, zoome
in closer on the closet door. Maybe he'd catch a glimpse c
her naked, her perfectly honed body, an athlete's body wit
large breasts and a nipped-in waist and muscles that wer
both feminine and strong. His crotch tightened.

He waited.

Ignored a light being snapped on in another part of th
house. Knew it was probably one of her kids.

Come on, come on, he thought impatiently. His mout
turned dry as sand and lust burned through his chilled blooc

he master bedroom with its yellowed-pine walls and softly
urning fire remained empty. What the hell was taking her so
ong?

God, he wanted her. He had for a long, long time.

He licked his lips against the cold as she reappeared, wear-
ng a black bra and low-slung black jeans. God, she was
eautiful. Nearly perfect in those tight pants. "Strip 'em,
enna," he muttered under breath that fogged through his in-
ulated mask. Her breasts nearly fell from the sexy black
ndergarment. But she headed into her bathroom and he read-
usted the lens as she leaned over a sink and applied lipstick
nd mascara. He saw her backside, that sweet, sweet ass
training against the black denim as she leaned closer to the
nirror and within that smooth glass surface, he stared at her
vide eyes, silvery green and rimmed in thick black lashes.
or a second she seemed to catch his eye, to look right at him
nd she hesitated, mascara wand in hand. Little lines ap-
eared between her arched eyebrows, a hint of worry. As if
he knew. Her eyes narrowed and his heart pounded hard
gainst his ribs.

Turning quickly, she stared out the window, to the gathering darkness and the snow now falling steadily. Was it fear he
saw in her hazel eyes? Premonition?

"Just you wait," he whispered, his voice lost in the shriek
of the wind, the snow becoming thick enough that her image
was blurred, his erection suddenly rock-hard as he imagined
what he would do to her.

But that instant of fear was gone and her lips pulled into a
half smile, as if she'd been foolish. She flipped off the bathroom light, then headed back to her bedroom. She yanked a
sweater from her bed and pulled it over her head. For a few
seconds he felt ecstasy, watching as her arms uplifted and for
a heartbeat she was blindfolded and trapped in the garment,
but then her head poked through a wide cowl neck and her
arms slid through the sweater's sleeves. She pulled her rope

of hair from the neckline and walked quickly out of view, snapping the lights off as she entered the hallway.

Hot desire zinged through his blood at the thought of her.

Beautiful.

Arrogant.

Proud.

And soon, very soon, to be brought to her knees.

By Best-selling Author

Fern Michaels

_About Face	0-8217-7020-9	$7.99US/$10.99CAN
_Kentucky Sunrise	0-8217-7462-X	$7.99US/$10.99CAN
_Kentucky Rich	0-8217-7234-1	$7.99US/$10.99CAN
_Kentucky Heat	0-8217-7368-2	$7.99US/$10.99CAN
_Plain Jane	0-8217-6927-8	$7.99US/$10.99CAN
_Wish List	0-8217-7363-1	$7.50US/$10.50CAN
_Yesterday	0-8217-6785-2	$7.50US/$10.50CAN
_The Guest List	0-8217-6657-0	$7.50US/$10.50CAN
_Finders Keepers	0-8217-7364-X	$7.50US/$10.50CAN
_Annie's Rainbow	0-8217-7366-6	$7.50US/$10.50CAN
_Dear Emily	0-8217-7316-X	$7.50US/$10.50CAN
_Sara's Song	0-8217-7480-8	$7.50US/$10.50CAN
_Celebration	0-8217-7434-4	$7.50US/$10.50CAN
_Vegas Heat	0-8217-7207-4	$7.50US/$10.50CAN
_Vegas Rich	0-8217-7206-6	$7.50US/$10.50CAN
_Vegas Sunrise	0-8217-7208-2	$7.50US/$10.50CAN
_What You Wish For	0-8217-6828-X	$7.99US/$10.99CAN
_Charming Lily	0-8217-7019-5	$7.99US/$10.99CAN

Available Wherever Books Are Sold!

Visit our website at **www.kensingtonbooks.com.**